In Good Company

WORKING HEARTS SERIES
BOOK ONE

JOANNE ALMONTE MASON

HEATHLINE PRESS

First edition, 2026

ISBN: 979-8-9950993-0-7

Cover design by Juan Rafael Almonte

Published by Heartline Press

For those who believe love isn't always neat or perfectly timed...sometimes it begins with two imperfect people finding their way to each other.

Playlist

Before you dive in, here's a piece of the heart behind In Good Company. This playlist carried me through late nights, rewrites, and moments of doubt, shaping Alma and Callum's tension, longing, and everything they couldn't say out loud. Some songs sparked scenes, others got me through slumps, and a few felt so much like them I had to keep them on repeat.

As you listen, I hope you feel the ache, the heat, and the push and pull of their story, and maybe experience it the way I did while writing it.

Playlist

- "So It Goes..." - Taylor Swift
- "Got Me Started" - Troye Sivan
- "Bad Intentions" - Niykee Heaton
- "Skin" - Rihanna
- "Shameless" - Camila Cabello
- "Figure It Out" - VOILA
- "I Wanna Be Yours" - Arctic Monkeys
- "Confidence" - Justin Bieber feat. Chance the Rapper
- "Stealin' Love" - Leigh-Anne
- "I Feel Like I'm Drowning" - Two Feet
- "Dangerous Woman" - Ariana Grande
- "Heaven" - Julia Michaels
- "Collide" - Justine Skye feat. Tyga
- "Sexual" - NEIKED feat. Dyo
- "Fetish" - Selena Gomez feat. Gucci Mane
- "Iris (Acoustic)" - The Goo Goo Dolls
- "The Heart Wants What It Wants" - Selena Gomez
- "Please Me" - Abigail Barlow
- "Sex With Me" - Rihanna
- "Call Out My Name" - The Weeknd

- "Please Don't Fall In Love With Me" - Khalid
- "Tonight (Best You Ever Had)" - John Legend feat. Ludacris
- "GOOD GIRL" - SLOWBURN
- "Cornelia Street" - Taylor Swift
- "Once In A Lifetime" - John Michael Howel

Chapter One

ALMA

"I got the job," I announced, deadpanned, stabbing a piece of overcooked brunch potato like it personally wronged me. "Confetti, applause, someone cue a slow clap. This is the part where I'm supposed to be excited, right?"

My best friend, India, blinked at me from across the table, her braids swinging over one shoulder as she leaned in like I've just confessed to a crime. "Okay, pause. Rewind. You got the job, the one you've been spiraling about for weeks, and you're acting like someone just told you oat milk is discontinued. What's happening?"

"I know, I know," I groaned, dropping my fork with a dramatic clatter. "I should be excited. I should be casually mentioning it to strangers in line at Starbucks..."

"You would be that person," India cut in, unimpressed.

"...but instead I feel like I just signed up for something I can't unsubscribe from. Like one of those free trials that asks for your credit card upfront."

India narrowed her eyes at me, clearly not buying my existential crisis. "Alma. You practically built a shrine to this job. There were color-coded notes. There was a vision board. You lit a candle."

"It was a vibe candle," I defended, pointing at her. "And it worked, clearly, because here we are."

"Here we are," she repeated slowly, then leaned back in her chair, crossing her arms. "So what's the actual problem? And don't say 'I don't know,' because that's not an answer, that's a cop-out."

I sighed, dragging a hand down my face. "I think I liked wanting it more than I like having it."

Studying me for a second, she snorted. "Wow. That is deeply annoying of you."

"Thank you," I said, raising my glass in a half-hearted toast. "I strive for that."

Sunlight streamed through the large windows of Nesto's, the trendy café nestled in the heart of Franklin, where the city's charm and constant motion came together. The colorful array of drag performers twirled and sashayed between tables. Their sequined outfits and the infectious energy of the brunch contrasted sharply with the weight of my realization. *I am not excited for this next chapter of my life.*

We were nestled at a corner table, surrounded by the electric energy of the place, our plates piled high with pancakes, eggs, and bacon. Laughter, clinking glasses, and the vibrant hum of conversation filled the air, and yet here I was numb to everything except the dread of what was to come.

"It just feels weird," I said, dragging the word out like it personally victimized me. "We graduated months ago, and now I'm expected to swan dive into adulthood like I didn't just spend the last of my student loan money on takeout and questionable online purchases." I shook my head, exhaling. "Like, poof, suddenly I have an adult job. On purpose. Against my will." I took a sip of my drink, frowning slightly. "I'm not emotionally prepared. I still consider cereal a balanced dinner and 'checking my bank account' a horror movie."

India nodded, surprisingly sympathetic for someone who definitely had her life more together than I did. "Okay, fair. It is a big shift. But also, this is what you wanted. You were basically drafting your LinkedIn announcement during the graduation ceremony."

"I was manifesting," I corrected, pointing at her. "There's a difference."

"You were refreshing your email every five minutes in a white dress and heels."

"Again," I said, as I lifted my mimosa, "manifesting."

She gave me a look. The kind that said I love you, but you're being ridiculous.

I sighed, pushing my eggs around my plate like I was hoping they'd form a life plan. "And the job...the job is in sales. Tech sales nonetheless." I paused for effect, like I just revealed I'd been cast in a low-budget horror film. "That couldn't be farther from Public Relations if it tried. I mean, I hate pushy salespeople. If a car salesman so much as breathes in my direction, I'm already halfway out the door."

India huffed out a laugh. "You once pretended to get a phone call to avoid a skincare kiosk."

"It was aggressive," I protested. "She lunged at me with moisturizer."

"And now you're worried you're going to become her?"

"Yes," I said plainly. "What if I wake up one day and I'm chasing strangers through the mall like, 'Excuse me, have you considered upgrading your software package?' I can't live like that, India. I won't."

She shook her head, smiling despite herself. "You're being dramatic."

"I'm being realistic," I insisted, even though I knew I was toeing the line. "But also, this job market is a nightmare. It's like The Hunger Games, but instead of fighting to the death, we're fighting over entry-level positions that require three years of experience and a personality that sparkles on command. I had to take the first thing that said yes."

That part hung heavier between us.

Because the truth was, this wasn't just about passion or career paths or whether I accidentally morph into a human pop-up ad. It was about home.

I picked at my food again, my appetite officially gone, my chest tightening in that familiar, quiet way I tried not to think about too much. I didn't say it out loud. I couldn't. Because if I did, it made it too real and too heavy for a table covered in syrup and powdered sugar and drag queens lip-syncing to Britney in the background.

But it was there anyway. Mami. Papi. Bills that didn't care about my degree or my dreams or whether I felt "fulfilled." I was the one who stayed and got the degree, i.e., the one who was supposed to make it mean something. So no, this wasn't my dream job, but it was a paycheck. And right now? That has to be enough. I did not want this job, but I needed it, for them. They were counting on me.

India watched me for a second, her expression softening like she could read at least part of what I'm wasn't saying. "Hey," she said gently, nudging my foot under the table. "You're not signing your life away, you know. It's just a first job. Not a life sentence."

I let out a small laugh, even though it came out a little weaker than I intended. "Tell that to my anxiety. She's already picking out office outfits and planning my emotional breakdown schedule."

India grinned. "Okay, but if you're going to spiral, at least do it in a cute blazer."

"Obviously," I said, lifting my glass again. "If I'm going to suffer, I'm going to be well-dressed while doing it."

"Honestly? It's normal to want to cling to college a little longer," India said, shrugging as she speared a piece of fruit. "And from what I can tell, adulthood is just doing a job you don't care about so you can afford rent and iced coffee."

"Wow. Sell it to me harder. Really, make me excited for my future." I continued. "It's not even that I want to cling to college either," I said. "It's that we had to graduate during a recession. Of course we did. Because why wouldn't the universe have perfect comedic timing?"

"Of course." India nodded solemnly.

"Jobs in PR? Practically nonexistent. The ones that do exist want 'entry-level candidates with five years of experience, three internships, and a personality that could host the Oscars.'" I leaned forward, lowering my voice like I was about to deliver the punchline of a conspiracy theory. "How am I supposed to get experience without experience? Riddle me this."

India pressed her lips together, trying not to laugh.

"And meanwhile," I continued, pointing at her, "you just casually land a job in advertising like it's no big deal. Like you tripped and fell into a career."

"What can I say? I blacked out and suddenly had benefits."

"I hate you," I said but there was no heat behind it.

"Please." She waved me off. "Who even wants to adult all the time? It's wildly overrated. I tried to build an IKEA shelf last week and nearly had a full identity crisis. There were extra screws, Alma. EXTRA. What does that mean?"

"It means you did it wrong," I said immediately.

"Rude," she shot back. "I chose to see it as creative freedom."

I laughed, shaking my head, but the knot in my chest didn't fully go away.

"And get this," I added, frowning. "I start on a Tuesday."

India blinked. "Okay...?"

"Tuesday," I repeated. "Not Monday. Not a clean, fresh start to the week. A Tuesday. That's weird, right? Why can't I just start on a Monday like a normal person? It feels suspicious."

She raised an eyebrow. "Maybe they just don't like Mondays either."

"Or," I said, leaning in again because clearly I've chosen paranoia as my personality trait today, "they're firing someone and bringing me in to replace them."

India snorted. "Oh my God."

"No, think about it," I insisted, fully committed now. "What if I walk in and everyone's like, 'Oh, that's the girl who took Janet's job. Janet, who we loved. Janet, who brought in donuts on Fridays.' I can't compete with a Donut Janet, Indi. I simply can't."

"You are spiraling," she said, but she was laughing.

"I have too many thoughts!" I groaned, dropping my head into my hands. "None of them are helpful, all of them are loud."

She nudged my arm. "Okay, relax. Worst case scenario? You bring better snacks than Janet."

I peeked up at her. "You think muffins could carry me through social exile?"

"Absolutely," she said without hesitation. "Muffins are universally respected."

I considered that for a moment, then nodded. "Okay. So my career plan is now: survive, sell tech, and weaponize baked goods."

India lifted her glass. "Now that sounds like a strategy."

I clinked mine against hers. "God, I hope HR agrees."

"Remind me again what your new job actually does?"

I blinked. "Johnson & Paul are an IT solutions provider."

She squinted. "I don't know what that means."

"Yeah, me neither, but they hired me, so I'm choosing to trust the process."

We were still laughing, like full, mascara-threatening giggling, when India suddenly tilted her head, eyes narrowing in that I'm about to ask something intrusive but with love.

"Sooo," she said, dragging it out just enough to make me nervous, "what's the deal with you and Owen? Graduation was, what, months ago? And I know you two aren't together together, but..." She lifted a brow. "I did see him swing by the house last week. Care to explain to the class?"

My smile faltered, fingers tightening slightly around my glass. "Oh, it's official. Officially over," I said, aiming for casual and landing somewhere closer to fragile. "We are broken up broken up."

India blinked. "Like official official?"

I stared down at the condensation ring forming under my drink. "Yep. No take-backs, no 'let's circle back,' no 'right person, wrong time' speech. Just done."

She softened immediately, all teasing gone. "Alma..."

I let out a small laugh, but it didn't have any real humor in it. "And before you ask, no, seeing him last week didn't magically make it easier. Time did not do its job. I would like to file a complaint."

"What was he doing there?" she asked gently.

"Dropping off my stuff," I said, shrugging like it wasn't big deal, even though it absolutely was. "Apparently, I had been slowly migrating into his apartment like I paid rent there. He found a sweater, a book, my favorite mug..." I paused. "Rude, honestly. I liked that mug."

India winced. "That's very breakup-core."

"Very," I agreed, swallowing past the tight feeling in my throat. "It felt like one of those montage scenes where the girl stands in the doorway holding a box while sad music plays, except there was no music, and I was in sweatpants, and I definitely did not look cute crying."

She studied me for a second, then shook her head slightly. "I'm not gonna lie, I'm surprised he broke it off. You guys seemed really happy."

I nodded slowly. "We were." My voice dipped, quieter now. "We were talking about moving in together once our lease was up." I let out a breath that felt heavier than it should. "Which is obviously not happening now."

India's expression softened even more, if that was possible. "God, Alma..."

I shrugged again, because apparently that was my coping mechanism now. "Plot twist of the year, honestly."

She leaned forward, resting her chin in her hand. "What happened, though? Every time I tried to ask you this summer, you basically barricaded yourself in your room like a Victorian widow."

I let out a quiet laugh. "Accurate. I was one fainting couch away from full commitment."

"I'm serious," she said, nudging my arm. "You wouldn't talk about it. You barely left your room. I was considering sliding food under the door."

"You should have," I mumbled. "I might've emerged sooner."

Her gaze softened. "I was worried about you."

I picked at a nonexistent crumb on the table, my chest tightening again, but this time it was warmer, laced with something like gratitude. "I know. And I'm sorry. I just...I couldn't do it. Talking about it made it feel too real, and I was already drowning in it."

India nodded thoughtfully, like she got it, even the parts I wasn't saying out loud.

"But," she added, a small smile tugging at her lips, "the last month? You've been better. Like, actually leaving the house, making jokes, wearing real outfits. I am starting to think I got my best friend back."

I glanced up at her, offering a small, genuine smile. "Yeah. I think I did too." It's not the whole truth. Not even close, but it's something, and right now, something feels like a win.

* * *

Sitting in my dimly lit bedroom later that evening, I waited for the video call with my parents to connect. When their faces filled the screen, their familiar smiles softened the knot of tension I didn't realize I'd been carrying all day. My mami wore her favorite floral house dress, her salt and pepper hair pulled back in a neat bun, while my papi sat beside her in his usual white guayabera, his reading glasses perched low on his nose. The sight of them, sitting in a small but cozy living room back in the DR, filled me with a bittersweet longing.

"Mi hija!" Mami's warm voice wrapped around me like a hug. "You look tired. Are you eating enough?"

"Sí, Mami," I assured her with a small laugh, the sound more forced than I wanted it to be. "Life has been busy, but I'm fine."

"We're so proud of you," Papi chimed in, his voice steady. "Your new job sounds like a great opportunity."

I nodded, the weight of their pride settling on my chest like a heavy blanket. "It's going to go well, I'll work hard and learn a lot." I didn't add that the pressure to excel felt like an ever-tightening vise, or that I was already scanning job boards late at night, hoping to find something in PR, something that aligned with the degree I'd worked so hard for.

The conversation shifted to their week, updates on neighbors, a small gathering at church, and my father's follow-up appointment for his heart. Just as I was about to ask another question, Mami cut me off. "It was just a checkup," she said quickly, anticipating my concern. "Everything is stable, gracias a Dios."

I swallowed the lump in my throat. Stable for now wasn't exactly comforting, but I let it go. "I can send more money next week," I offered, my voice quieter than before.

Mami's brow furrowed. "You don't need to do that, Alma. You have your own expenses to worry about."

But I could see it in her eyes, the relief she tried to hide behind her words. They needed the help, and I was the one who stayed. The one who chose the United States and the opportunities it promised. It felt like my duty, my way of showing gratitude for the sacrifices they had made for me.

I still remembered that call from Mami, two months ago, the way her voice sounded thinner than usual. Papi was diagnosed with cardiac arrhythmia, and doctors had to place a pacemaker to regulate his heartbeat. He was alive, gracias a Dios, but recovery would take time, and time was something they didn't have. It meant stepping away from the bodega on the corner, the one he'd opened every morning for as long as I could remember, the one that kept their little casita paid for.

Without that income, things would get tight fast. Tighter than they already were, so I made a plan to be able to send money home. Helping my parents wasn't a favor or a burden. It was just the way things worked. Family showed up. Even if it meant putting everything else on hold.

"I'll figure it out," I said firmly, more for myself than for them. "You just let me know if anything changes."

As the call ended, I lingered in the quiet of the townhouse. Their smiles stayed with me, but so did the unspoken expectations. I loved them fiercely, but the weight of being their safety net was exhausting. I needed to succeed, not just for me, but for them. There was no room for failure, no room for mistakes.

Chapter Two

ALMA

On Tuesday morning, I stood in line at my usual coffee shop, brick exterior softened by creeping ivy and a chalkboard sign out front advertising oat milk lattes and lavender honey cold brew in looping handwriting. Inside, it smelled like roasted beans, warm sugar, and something buttery that reminded me of mornings in Mami's kitchen, pan dulce and coffee steaming in mismatched mugs. The air hummed with low conversation, the hiss of the espresso machine, the rhythmic clink of ceramic against saucers. Indie music played softly overhead, the kind of song that made everything feel slower, gentler.

I stepped forward as the line moved, the menu board glowing softly above the counter. "Lavender honey latte," I said when it was my turn. "With oat milk, please."

The barista nodded, already turning to the espresso machine. It hissed and steamed as she worked, the sound sharp and familiar. I paid, slid my card back into my wallet, and waited while the drink came together, breathing in the smell of coffee and sugar.

She set the cup down a moment later, sleeve already on. "Careful, it's hot."

"Thanks." I wrapped my fingers around it, then moved to the small counter off to the side where sugar packets and creamer were laid out in neat rows. I popped the lid, added a little more oat milk out of habit, snapped it back on, and slung my bag over my shoulder as I turned.

Straight into someone.

"Oh!" The collision was small but perfectly timed. My coffee tipped just enough for a warm splash to arc out, landing on his khaki pants and spotting the front of my blouse in the process.

We both froze.

"Shit," I said at the same time he said, "Ah, wow."

I looked down first. The damage was minimal, two faint drops darkening the fabric over my chest, already cooling, but my heart was pounding like I'd committed a felony.

"I'm so sorry. I wasn't looking." I reached for napkins from the nearby counter.

He glanced down at his pants, then back at me. Tall. Broad shoulders. Leather jacket. Annoyingly sharp blue eyes.

"It's fine," he said, though his mouth twitched like he was fighting a smile. "I'll survive."

I reached out and dabbed at his leg before my brain could catch up with my body and immediately realized, way too late, that his crotch was mere inches away.

I yanked my hand back like I had just been personally betrayed by my own reflexes, my face heating so fast I was pretty sure I could fry an egg on it. "Sorry," I blurted, cringing. "That was instinct. Clearly not a good one."

He laughed under his breath. "You always spill coffee on strangers, or am I special?"

He leaned back slightly, one hand tucked into his pocket like he was posing for a "Corporate Men Who Think They're Charming" calendar, head tilted just enough to make it clear he already knew his own answer.

God. "You walked into me," I shot back, crossing my arms like that was going to salvage any of this.

His brow lifted, unimpressed. "I was standing still."

I stared at him. "No, you weren't."

"I was," he said, way too calm for someone currently wearing my coffee. "You just weren't paying attention."

"Oh, I'm sorry," I snapped, gesturing between us. "Was I supposed to anticipate you looming over me like some kind of human roadblock?"

His mouth twitched, like he was enjoying this entirely too much. "If that's what it takes for you to stop assaulting people with caffeine, then yeah. Probably."

I narrowed my eyes at him, already deciding I do not like this man. Not even a little.

"You're unbelievable." I let out a sharp laugh.

He smiled like that entertained him, which irked me. "Strong opinions for someone holding a very aggressive latte."

"It's lavender honey," I corrected.

"That explains the hostility."

"Excuse me?"

"I'm kidding," he said. "Mostly."

I straightened, napkins clenched in my hand. "If you're going to insult my coffee, you could at least apologize."

"I did."

"You said 'wow.'"

"Tone matters."

I stared at him. He stared back, nonchalantly, clearly enjoying this.

"Well," I said, stepping around him, "try not to loiter near the condiment station. It's dangerous."

"Duly noted," he replied. "I'll wear darker pants next time."

I paused despite myself. "Next time?"

He shrugged. "Something tells me we're not done annoying each other."

I scoffed and started toward the door. "You're very confident for a man who almost got taken out by oat milk."

"Confidence is a survival skill," he called after me.

I didn't look back, already annoyed, even though the spill on my blouse was minimal at best. I probably overreacted. Still, for my first day, it felt like enough to throw me completely off.

* * *

Fifteen minutes later, and thankfully still early, I stood at the entrance of the sleek, modern office building in downtown Franklin, feeling my nerves fluttering through me. The glass facade reflected the early sunlight and the steady stream of professionals going about their day.

My phone buzzed, and I glanced down to see a WhatsApp message from Mami:

"Buena suerte en tu primer día, mi amor. Estamos tan orgullosos de ti."

My heart clenched. I could practically hear her voice in the words, warm and full of love, wishing me good luck on my first day. It was the kind of message that made me feel both stronger and heavier at the same time, like the weight of their hopes and dreams rested squarely on my shoulders.

I tugged at the hem of my blouse, uncomfortable in my office attire. The fitted navy blazer and pencil skirt felt a far cry from my usual jeans and T-shirts. My sensible black heels clicked sharply on the polished marble floor as I entered the building and made my way to the front desk.

Inside, the lobby was bright and open, with minimalist decor and potted plants adding a touch of green. A familiar man approached me with a warm smile.

"Hi there, Alma," he said, extending his hand. "Not sure if you remember from the countless interviews, I'm Chris, your manager. Welcome to Johnson & Paul, or as we all call it, J&P."

I met his outstretched hand with a firm shake. "Yes, of course I remember. Nice to see you again, Chris."

He gestured for me to follow him. "Let me show you around before we dive into your first day."

"We're not heading upstairs?" I asked as we kept walking straight through the first floor, my heels clicking like I was in a low-budget corporate montage.

Chris glanced over at me, already shaking his head. "No, upstairs is where the executive offices are. That's where we do interviews. You know, for privacy and intimidation."

"Love that for me," I muttered under my breath.

He gestured around us. "This floor is where our department is, along with a few others."

I nodded, trying to look like I belonged here and not like I was two seconds away from asking where the nearest exit was.

We walked through the lobby and into a wide corridor lined with glass-walled conference rooms. Each room buzzed with teams engaged in animated discussions. The clacking of keyboards and the ringing of phones grew louder as we approached the main office area.

The office was a vast, open space filled with cubicles. Each one was personalized with photos, plants, and various knick-knacks, reflecting the personalities of their occupants. Some were pristine and organized, while others were cluttered with papers and coffee cups.

"Welcome to the heart of our operation," Chris said, sweeping his hand across the sea of cubicles. "This is where the magic happens."

I nodded, absorbing everything around me. Chris guided me through the maze, pointing out different departments and introducing me to a few coworkers as we walked.

Everyone seemed friendly, but I couldn't shake the feeling of being overwhelmed by the sheer size of the office.

We finally reached the back of the floor, where a cluster of cubicles created a cozy nook that Chris dubbed the "cubicle cul-de-sac."

"All right, everyone, gather around!" Chris called out, his voice echoing across the area.

People started emerging from their seats, their curious eyes focused on me. An immediate wave of nerves hit me as I became the center of attention.

"This is Alma, our new team member," Chris announced with a welcoming tone. "She's joining us in renewals, so let's give her a warm welcome."

A chorus of greetings and a few polite claps followed. I managed a smile, feeling slightly more at ease.

As Chris introduced me to the team gathered in the cubicle cul-de-sac, he turned to me. "Why don't you tell us a bit about yourself, Alma?"

I took a deep breath, trying to steady my nerves with the weight of my new colleagues' gaze. "I'm Alma Ruiz," I started, "I've lived in Franklin all my life and just graduated from Belgrave with a degree in Public Relations."

A familiar tall guy with a skeptical look muttered under his breath, "Does that place even count as a college?"

It took half a second too long for it to click, and then it did. Coffee shop guy, or shall I say, Mr. Rude. The leather jacket. The irritating confidence. The one I'd nearly baptized in oat milk less than an hour ago. Of course it was him.

I caught his comment, my brows furrowed. "Excuse me?" I retorted, my voice carrying a hint of challenge.

He turned fully toward me, piercing blue eyes, almost sapphire, locking onto mine, and something like recognition flickered there, too. He shrugged nonchalantly. "I mean, it's not like it even has a football team or anything. How serious can it be?"

Was this dude for real, or was this his idea of hazing? I narrowed my eyes and played along. "Just because we don't have a football team doesn't mean it's not a real college. We focus on academics, not sports drama."

He chuckled, leaning back against the cubicle wall. "Sure, sure. But come on, Ruiz. Real colleges have school spirit and a mascot. What's your school mascot? The Franklin City Commuter Cats?"

I crossed my arms, a grin tugging at my lips. "Okay, maybe we don't have a mascot, but we have community spirit and a commitment to education. That's what counts."

Mr. Rude raised an eyebrow. "Community spirit and education? Sounds like you're describing a library, not a college."

"Well, it's a real college, my friend. I'm sorry you didn't get in," I said, tilting my head to the side. I couldn't help but notice the stifled laughs from the surrounding cubicles. The spirited debate between Mr. Rude and me had clearly caught the attention of my new colleagues, drawing quite an audience to our little corner of the office.

"Okay, okay," Chris chuckled. "I think it's about time everyone gets back to work."

Clearing my throat, I turned to Chris with a sheepish grin. "Sorry, Chris. I think we got a bit carried away."

"No worries. Callum has that effect on people. It's good to see some friendly banter around here." He laughed. "Just don't quit on me. That wasn't the best first impression of the team."

"Of course not. All playful sparring," I reassured him.

"That's what I like to hear. Okay, let me show you to your desk," Chris said as he led me to a row of cubicles where a woman was just taking her seat. "Alma, meet Tamara. She'll be your cubicle neighbor."

Tamara, sporting brightly colored hair and an array of quirky desk ornaments, waved enthusiastically. "Hey, Alma! Welcome to the madhouse."

As Chris disappeared, probably off to do important manager things like send emails and intimidate people, I was left standing there, pretending I totally knew where to put my hands.

Tamara leaned over immediately, eyes sparkling like she's been waiting her whole life for this moment. "Okay," she said, dropping her voice like we're about to discuss state secrets. "Your run in with Callum? Iconic. Truly. If you haven't figured it out yet, that man is a problem."

I let out a small laugh, sliding into my chair. "Callum," I repeated, like I was testing it out. "Good to know he has a name. I've just been calling him Mr. Rude in my head." I glanced at her. "He's a lot."

"That's a generous assessment," Tamara said dryly.

I leaned in a little. "So what's his deal? Is he always like that, or did I just catch him on a particularly charming day?"

Tamara snorted. "Oh no, that was him being charming." She paused, then added, "He's one of the junior managers under Chris. Training to be a supervisor."

I blinked. "You're kidding."

"I wish," she said, shaking her head. "Which means, unfortunately for all of us, he's not going anywhere."

"Great," I complained. "So I've already made an enemy in upper management-adjacent territory. Love that for me."

Tamara grinned. "Honestly? Standing up to him on your first day? Bold. Impressive. Slightly unhinged, in a good way, of course."

"I'll take it." I shrugged. "Someone has to keep him in check."

She laughed. "Oh, people have tried. He's like one of those guys who always has a comeback locked and loaded. It's exhausting."

"Good," I said, a smile tugging at my lips. "I love a challenge. Keeps things interesting."

Tamara studied me for a second, then nodded approvingly. "I like you. You're either going to thrive here or absolutely combust. Either way, I'm invested."

"Those are my two speeds," I said easily.

She patted my shoulder. "Well, I've got your back. Welcome to the team." She paused, then added with a smirk, "Population: people who have beef with Callum."

I raised my brows. "Wow. Honored to be part of such an elite group." I looked around the expansive first floor and find what I was looking for. "I'm going to head to the bathroom really quickly. Be right back."

As I navigated through the maze of desks, I took in the bustling atmosphere of the office. People were deeply engrossed in their tasks, some engaged in animated discussions, while others multitasked on phone calls. The environment was both energizing and a bit overwhelming.

When I returned to my desk, I noticed Callum standing in the cubicle directly in front of mine. I was suddenly thankful for the tall, beige dividers that shielded me from his view when I was seated.

He was deep in conversation on the phone, a hint of intensity in his expression, and I couldn't help but observe him.

Callum's dark, shaggy hair fell messily over his forehead. His piercing blue eyes flickered with a mischievous spark, framed by a stubbled jawline that hinted at a laid-back demeanor. Despite the corporate setting, the edge of a tattoo peeked out from under his rolled-up sleeves, adding a rebellious touch to his otherwise professional attire.

I sat down and leaned back in my chair, idly tapping my pen against my notebook, pretending to know what I was doing. That was when I noticed the tiny horizontal slits in the cubicle wall. Through it, I could see a glimpse of Callum on the other side, sitting back down and typing away at his keyboard.

His gestures were confident, his voice smooth as he discussed product features and benefits with what seemed like a potential customer. There was a charm to his manner that I begrudgingly acknowledged, despite our earlier squabble.

I couldn't deny that Callum had a certain charisma, even in the middle of a busy office. As I watched him navigate the call with such ease, I wondered how someone so laid back managed to maintain a reputation as the office's resident D-bag.

Deciding to keep my interactions with him strictly professional, I refocused on my own tasks. I was determined to make a positive impression in my new role, even if it meant occasionally dealing with Mr. Rude and his quirks.

Pulling on my headphones, I braced myself for the obligatory training video that awaited me. The screen flickered to life with animated corporate logos and a voiceover that was far too enthusiastic about company policies.

About an hour into nodding along to compliance rules like a bobblehead with anxiety, I was dangerously close to merging with my chair. I had taken exactly three notes, none of which I understood, and I was pretty sure the training video just used the word "protocol" five times in one sentence. So when I felt a tap on my shoulder, I nearly jumped out of my chair. I turned, pulling one headphone off, and found Tamara standing there like a caffeinated angel of mercy.

"You look like you're one slide away from a breakdown. Want to come grab coffee in the kitchen?"

I blinked at her. "Is that even a question? Yes. Immediately. Right now."

She laughed as I yanked off my headphones like I was escaping captivity. Honestly, if this video had gone on five more minutes, I might've started a rebellion.

We sauntered on over to the kitchen, which wasn't very far from our department's cubicles, and instantly the smell of coffee hits me like salvation. I grab a mug with the urgency of someone who hasn't known peace in hours.

"This is the best thing that's happened to me today," I said, pouring coffee like it was a personality trait.

Tamara leaned against the counter, stirring hers. "Give it time. The day's still young. Plenty of chaos ahead."

"Can't wait," I said, taking a sip and immediately feeling like a functioning human again.

We fell into easy conversation, office gossip naturally, because what is a workplace if not a live-action reality show? She filled me in on who was dating who, who microwaved fish (criminal behavior), and which team had just landed some huge win that apparently everyone was still talking about.

I nodded along like I totally knew these people, mentally taking notes like: Avoid Fish Person. Identify Power Players. Stay Alive.

Then Tamara glanced at me over her mug, a mischievous little smile forming. "You know, you actually got hired at the perfect time."

I narrowed my eyes. "That sounds ominous. Should I be concerned?"

"Oh no," she said quickly, clearly enjoying this. "You should be excited."

I crossed my arms. "I don't like surprises. This feels like a surprise."

She leaned in slightly, lowering her voice like we were about to plan a heist. "The annual company trip is coming up in a few months."

I perked up despite myself. "Okay, I'm listening."

"And this year," she added, pausing for dramatic effect, because apparently everyone in this office was committed to theatrics, "we're going to Jamaica."

I blinked. "Shut up."

"I'm serious."

"Shut. Up."

She laughed. "I'm not kidding."

"Jamaica?" I repeated, fully abandoning all chill. "That's...are you... what? That's amazing!" I shook my head, trying to process. "Chris mentioned a company retreat, but he was all vague and mysterious about it."

Tamara rolled her eyes fondly. "Oh, he loves the mystery. Thinks he's building suspense."

"Well, congratulations to him," I said, taking another sip of coffee. "Because it worked. I'm intrigued. I'm invested. I would now like to fast-forward my life."

She grinned. "Same. Trust me, it's the highlight of the year."

I leaned against the counter, already picturing it: sun, beach, not a single compliance video in sight.

"Okay, maybe adulthood isn't completely terrible."

Tamara raised her mug. "Give it time."

I clinked mine against hers. "Let me have this moment."

Tamara grinned, clearly enjoying the effect this was having on me. "And when I say trip," she said, lifting a finger for emphasis, "I mean the whole nine yards. Flights, resort, food, drinks, everything's covered. All-inclusive. You literally just show up."

I blinked at her. "I'm sorry, are you pitching me a job or a fantasy?"

"Dead serious," she said. "You don't even have to pretend to be financially responsible. It's actually encouraged that you're not."

I clutched my mug a little tighter. "Oh my God. A company that supports my poor decision-making? I've never felt more seen."

Tamara laughed. "It's one of the perks of working somewhere that actually wants to keep its employees."

I raised a brow. "Okay, what's the catch? There's always a catch. Do we have to, like, do trust falls on the beach? Is there a mandatory bonding exercise where I have to share my deepest fears in front of coworkers?"

She winced. "Okay, there might be one awkward team building thing. But you can usually fake a stomach ache and escape."

"Noted," I said seriously. "Always have an exit strategy."

Taking a sip from her coffee, Tamara shrugged. "I mean, it doesn't pay insanely well. You're not going to be rolling in luxury apartments anytime soon. But the perks? Solid. Health insurance, trips like this..."

I nodded slowly. "Ah, so it's like college."

She pointed at me. "Exactly."

"College," I repeated, thinking it through. "But with a paycheck, more uncomfortable outfits, and significantly more email anxiety."

"And just as much chaos," Tamara added with a knowing look. "Messy dating scenes, office gossip, people making questionable decisions after two drinks."

I groaned. "So a corporate frat house."

"Basically," she said, completely unfazed.

I stared into my coffee for a second, then looked back up. "Okay, I have one very important question."

She raised a brow. "Hit me."

"On a scale of one to deeply regrettable," I asked, "how bad are the drunken karaoke situations?"

Tamara grinned. "Oh, Alma."

My stomach dropped. "That bad?"

She just took another sip of her coffee, still smiling.

"Cool," I muttered. "Love that for my future reputation."

And then, because the universe clearly had a twisted sense of humor, Owen, my Owen, just casually strolled into the kitchen like he didn't single-handedly ruin my emotional stability at graduation.

I froze. Like, full-on romcom froze. Internal record scratch. Someone should have been yelling "cut!" because there was no way this was real life. I subtly pinched myself. Nope. Still here.

"Cool," I thought. *"Not a dream. Possibly a nightmare."*

He looked exactly the same, of course he did. Blond hair, perfectly tousled like he just walked out of a cologne ad, warm brown eyes that I used to know better than my own reflection. And now those same eyes locked onto mine as he stopped dead in his tracks.

"What are you doing here?" he asked.

I just stared at him because my brain? Gone. Evacuated. Left the building.

This was the guy who broke my heart. The guy I dated for the entire second half of college. The guy I very casually thought I might marry one day. And now he was standing in my office kitchen. On my first day. Amazing. Incredible. Love that plot twist.

He frowned slightly. "Alma," he said again, a little sharper this time, "what are you doing here?"

"Um…" I blinked, words finally buffering back in. "I work here?" I said, except it came out like a question, which felt correct because I, too, would like confirmation at this point.

He rolled his eyes. "Since when?"

"Since today. It's my first day."

Narrowing his eyes he asked, "Did you know I worked here?"

And just like that, something in me clicked back into place. Because excuse me? Who does he think he is? I straightened slightly, crossing my arms. Because the audacity of him standing there like I showed up to personally haunt his workplace, as if.

Before I could say anything else, Tamara cleared her throat from beside me, and I completely forgot she was even there, which, honestly, felt like a crime.

"It seems like there's some history here," she said, glancing between us like she just walked into a live episode of daytime drama.

"Just a bit," I muttered.

Tamara gave me a look that said you owe me details later, then gestured vaguely toward the door. "I'm gonna let you two talk."

And just like that, she slipped out of the kitchen, abandoning me to whatever this was. Traitor.

CALLUM

It had taken me a beat longer than it should have. Something familiar had tugged at the back of my mind while she kept talking. Then it clicked, sharp and inconvenient.

Coffee shop.

Lavender honey latte. The woman who'd splashed coffee on my pants, insulted my spatial awareness, and walked out like she hadn't just hijacked my morning. I'd thought about her more than once since the coffee shop incident this morning, which annoyed the hell out of me. How her apology hadn't sounded like one. How she'd looked at me like I was a problem she hadn't decided whether to tolerate or eliminate.

And now for the biggest curveball thrown at me, she was standing in the office kitchen, deep in conversation with Owen.

She looked more polished under the office lights, but the edge was the same, chin tipped up like she was always braced for a challenge, mouth clearly built for arguments she had no intention of losing. I should've recognized it sooner.

I leaned back in my chair and glanced toward the kitchen; the usual office noise faded into the background. I couldn't help but notice how Ruiz's dark curly hair bounced with every movement, wild and untamed in a way that oddly drew me in. Those large almond-shaped eyes of hers, almost hazel when the light hit just right, made it hard for me to look away, which was low-key frustrating.

That familiar heaviness began to settle in my chest. It had been creeping up on me for a while now, this dull, persistent weight that made everything seem just a little bit harder, a little bit darker. Seeing her with him was a reminder of something I didn't like to admit to myself. A reminder of the emptiness that lingered just beneath the surface, the void that no amount of flirting, work, or casual flings could ever really fill.

As the heaviness pressed in, I knew I had to act before it swallowed me whole. I'd been through this enough times to recognize the signs, the suffocating numbness, the way everything lost its color, its meaning. It was necessary to start implementing my coping skills when the depression reared its ugly head, pushing me toward that dark place I knew too well. I glanced around and grabbed my sketchbook, my lifeline in moments like this. Sketching always calmed me, brought a kind of clarity that helped me get out of my head, if only for a while. The lines began to form on the page, the tension in my chest eased slightly, and for a moment, I could breathe again. Support group later that afternoon would be necessary to decompress and talk things through.

I looked back up to see Ruiz still in deep conversation with Owen. Why was that bugging me so much? I just met this girl. She was different, though, no doubt about that. It was unsettling, this quiet pull she had on me. But it also made me aware of how tired I was. Tired of the routine, tired of the superficial connections, tired of pretending like I had it all together when, in reality, I felt like I was barely holding on.

The days had started to blur together, one indistinguishable from the next, marked only by the rising and setting of the sun, each one more colorless than the last. I'd wake up, drag myself through the motions, and end the day with nothing to show for it except the gnawing emptiness in my gut. I'd lost the drive, the spark that used to keep me going. Now, everything just felt...muted.

And then suddenly there was Ruiz. I was drawn to her and how she made me feel alive, challenged, even if just for a moment. She had brought with her this spark of something I hadn't felt in a long time, which may have be more than I could handle. I should keep my distance and not let myself get caught up in it and this dangerous game with all the baggage I didn't want to admit I carried and didn't have the strength to unpack. Beneath the spark Ruiz brought, something darker existed, something that reminded me of all the things I'd buried. Like the breakup with Soledad.

I leaned back in my chair again and watched her from a distance, a strange attraction simmering beneath the surface while a familiar darkness whispered in the back of my mind. It reminded me that no matter what I did, it was always there, waiting for me to slip.

Owen said something, and instead of laughing, Ruiz rolled her eyes, quick, automatic, like she'd done it a hundred times before. I caught it, that little flicker of something tense. Or maybe I was reading into it. Maybe I just wanted there to be something there.

I shook my head, dragging my focus back to my sketchbook like it suddenly mattered. It didn't because somehow, I was still thinking about her. I looked back up to watch her for a beat too long, irritation curling into something else entirely. Interest? Maybe. Trouble? Definitely.

Chapter Three

ALMA

A few weeks had passed since I first stepped into the bustling office, and I managed to settle into my new role with surprising ease. The initial jitters and sense of being out of place had gradually faded, thanks to the warm camaraderie of my coworkers and the everyday challenges that came with starting a new job.

The first few days had been a whirlwind of shadowing Tamara, learning the ins and outs of client relations, and figuring out the intricacies of the company's sales processes. Her support had been invaluable, and I found myself genuinely enjoying our afternoon coffee breaks.

Tuesday morning, exactly four weeks after my first day and right when I was growing accustomed to my new role, Chris delivered surprising plans for my development during our weekly catch-up.

"Alma, starting tomorrow, you'll be shadowing Callum for the rest of the week," Chris said, his tone matter-of-fact and unyielding.

My heart sank a little at the announcement. During my first week, Tamara warned me that Callum was not the easiest person to work with. His sharp wit and sometimes brusque manner had earned him a reputation for getting results but also for ruffling a few feathers along the way.

I replayed the argument from the other week in my head, the way Callum had been so insistent that his way of handling the renewal process was the right one. I'd asked him for help since Tamara was stuck in meetings, and I knew he was capable, but it still grated on me how stubborn he could be. I was taught a different method, and I tried to explain that, but he kept pushing, confident in his approach. It wasn't a huge fight, just a mild clash of perspectives, but it left me frustrated. His certainty always made me second guess myself, even when I knew I was right, which I loathed.

"Sure, Chris. I'm ready for the challenge," I replied, trying to mask my reluctance with a forced smile. I didn't want to let on how apprehensive I felt about working with Callum.

Chris nodded, clearly satisfied with my response. "Good. Callum will give you deeper insight into our client interactions and negotiation strategies. It'll be a valuable experience for you. I also wanted to share that there may be an opportunity for you to take part in a potential PR campaign opportunity for one of our clients that may be expanding their business with us. Given your major, I think you might be a good candidate to be a part of the team."

"Oh wow, that would be great! Thank you for thinking of me."

As I left Chris's office, a twinge of annoyance lingered from my assignment to shadow Callum. I had been looking forward to continuing working Tamara, who had been an incredibly supportive mentor. The idea of spending extended hours with Callum, deciphering his methods, and trying to keep up with his pace, felt daunting.

But the potential opportunity to both gather experience for what I actually wanted to do with my career and become an integral part of the company excited me. I wondered if the added responsibility would come with a pay raise. I could really use the extra money to send to my family back in the DR.

Freelance PR gigs had been my lifeline. I'd taken to them out of necessity at first, writing press releases, crafting media kits, and drafting pitches for small companies that couldn't afford full-scale agencies but needed someone to make them look polished. It was a hustle, piecing together one-off projects late into the night after my day job.

Still, the extra money made a difference. Every time I wired a little more to Mami, knowing it might cover a week's worth of groceries or Papi's medication, it felt worth it. Sure, it meant fewer nights out, no big splurges, and hardly any time for myself, but how could I complain when it helped my family?

* * *

The next morning, I braced myself for my first full day shadowing Callum. As I approached his cubicle, I took in the organized chaos of papers and gadgets scattered across his desk. Callum looked up from his computer, his piercing blue eyes locking onto mine.

"Morning, Ruiz," he said, his voice dripping with casual confidence. "Ready for a crash course in the art of the deal?"

I forced a smile, determined to keep things professional. "Morning, Callum. Let's do this."

We quickly settled into a rhythm. Callum took me through the ins and outs of tech sales, explaining the subtleties of client interactions and the importance of closing deals with precision. Despite my initial apprehensions, I found myself absorbing a lot from his seasoned experience.

During a lull in our work, Callum leaned back in his chair with a mischievous grin. "So, Ruiz, tell me more about your college. What was it again? Commuter Cats U?"

I rolled my eyes, a smile tugging at my lips. "It's actually called Belgrave. You know, the one that didn't accept you. And no, we don't have a football team, but we do have a strong academic program, in case you forgot."

Callum smirked, clearly enjoying the banter. "Sounds riveting. I went to Crescent Valley University, you know. Home of the wildest parties this side of the Mississippi."

I raised an eyebrow, unable to resist a playful jab. "Oh, a party school? Impressive. I'm sure you majored in beer pong and minored in keg stands."

Callum laughed, shaking his head. "Hey, there's more to it than that. We actually had a football team, you know."

I couldn't help but chuckle. "Ah yes, because nothing says quality education like tailgating and frat parties."

He leaned in, his eyes sparkling. "Don't knock it till you've tried it. Besides, there's a certain charm to the chaos of a big state school."

I met his gaze, my tone light but firm. "I'll take my commuter college's dedication to academics over endless parties any day."

"Fair enough. Different strokes for different folks, I guess."

"So let me guess," I said, leaning back in my chair. "You were one of those guys who peaked during intramurals and still brings it up at parties."

Callum's mouth twitched, like he was trying not to smile. "Bold assumption. But no, I saved my peak for emotionally devastating office banter."

I snorted before I could stop myself. "That tracks."

"What about you?" he asked. "Please tell me you weren't a campus legend."

"Hardly," I said. "I went to class, worked two jobs, and tried not to lose my mind. Very glamorous."

"Ah," he said, nodding seriously. "A woman of mystery."

"Don't get used to it," I shot back.

We continued our conversation, and I found myself begrudgingly appreciating Callum's quick wit and confident demeanor, even if he did have a knack for getting under my skin.

As the day went on, shadowing Callum wasn't as daunting as I'd feared. His approach to sales was direct and effective, and despite our occasional clashes, I could see the value in learning from someone with his level of experience.

By the end of the day, I felt a sense of accomplishment. I had navigated my first full day with Callum without losing my cool, and I'd even picked up a few valuable insights. As I packed up my things, Callum glanced over with a sly grin.

"Not bad for a Commuter Cat," he remarked.

I smirked, grabbing my bag. "Not bad for a party school alum either. See you tomorrow, Callum."

CALLUM

The next day dawned and Ruiz brought apprehension with her when she stepped into my cubicle. I could sense it, and barely looked up from my computer screen to acknowledge her presence. My mind was elsewhere, tangled up in the mess of work. I could see the unease in her eyes, but I couldn't bring myself to engage, couldn't let myself get distracted, not today.

"Morning, Callum," Ruiz ventured cautiously.

I glanced up briefly. "Morning," I snapped, my attention back to the spreadsheet in front of me, irritation bubbling just beneath the surface.

She, undeterred, took a deep breath and tried to engage. "So, what's on the agenda for today? Any new leads or follow-ups?"

I sighed, frustration clear in my voice. "Look, Ruiz, I need you to pick this up faster. We don't have time for me to explain everything twice."

The truth was, my chest had been tight as soon as I woke up, that familiar restless pressure I pretended not to notice. Sleep had been a joke again, too many half-formed thoughts, not enough quiet. By the time I'd gotten to the office, I already felt behind, like I was sprinting just to stay in place. When that happened, I got sharp. I looked for something solid to push against, someone to absorb the edge so I didn't have to sit with it myself. Ruiz happened to be there, and instead of envying that ease, I let it irritate me. It was easier to be annoyed at her than to admit I was unraveling a little.

I couldn't shake this irritation thinking back to how chipper she had been yesterday, like she didn't have a care in the world. Ruiz had done a fairly decent job keeping up with the tasks, but compared to my current mood, her upbeat attitude grated on me, especially as I tried to fight the chaos in my mind. Sure, she got the work done, but that energy...it was exhausting at a time when I just couldn't.

And despite all that, I didn't want to admit that I enjoyed being around her. The way she looked at me, the easy laughter between us, the banter that felt too close for comfort. Yesterday had been a nice day. Too nice. The kind of day that made you start questioning things. But that wasn't what I signed up for. Those types of feelings complicated things, made you vulnerable, and I wasn't up for that. The last thing I wanted was to lose control, to let someone in just to get hurt later. Like Soledad.

The thought of Soledad brought a familiar ache that I tried to bury every day. She had come into my life like a whirlwind, full of energy, passion, and everything I thought I wanted. I was so in love with her that it blinded me to the signs, the small cracks in our relationship that slowly widened until they became impossible to ignore.

Soledad ended things as abruptly as she had started them. One day, she was the center of my universe, and the next, she was gone, leaving nothing but a hastily written note and a shattered heart in her wake. I was completely destroyed. The worst part wasn't just that she left; it was how easily she walked away, like I was just a chapter she had finished reading and was ready to close.

That breakup didn't just hurt; it fundamentally changed me. It taught me that love was dangerous, that letting someone in was an open invitation for pain. So, I built walls. I focused on my work, on the thrill of the chase, on keeping things light and unattached. Relationships weren't worth the risk anymore. Not after Soledad.

And now, with Ruiz, I could feel those same dangerous emotions creeping in, threatening to pull me back into a place I'd sworn I'd never return to. And that was after one day of working directly with her. How was that possible? I couldn't afford to get hurt again. Not when I knew how devastating it could be.

Maybe that was why I was so short with Ruiz. Pushing her away before she could get any closer, before I could start wanting something I knew I shouldn't. I could only imagine the feel of her delicate throat under the pressure of my hand, the soft feel of her lips. I blinked twice to shake the thought out of my head.

Defensiveness flashed in her eyes when she finally responded to my criticism, and it hit me harder than I expected. "I'm doing my best here, Callum. If there's something specific you need me to focus on, just let me know." Her words were edged with frustration, and I knew I was pushing her too hard. But I couldn't help it, this whole situation, my internal battle, was getting under my skin.

Our interactions felt like a tightrope walk, every word a careful step to avoid a fall. I tried to keep it together, but my patience was thinning with every question she asked. I knew I was being harsh, but the tension between us made it hard to think straight. Each time she sought clarification, my irritation built, a pressure cooker waiting to blow.

As we clashed over client proposals and negotiation tactics, I could see Ruiz growing more tense with each passing minute. My sharp remarks and clipped responses weren't doing either of us any favors, but I couldn't seem to stop. The more we butted heads, the more irritated I became, and I could see her shoulders tense.

By midday, she was gripping her pen like it personally betrayed her, and I was pretending I didn't notice.

"Okay," I said, tapping the desk lightly. "Walk me through it again."

She exhaled, sharp and controlled. Not calm. Definitely not calm. "I just did."

"Right," I nodded. "And I'm just saying, you skipped a step."

Her head snapped up. "I didn't skip a step."

"You did," I said, leaning back in my chair like I had all the patience in the world. I didn't. "Right after the client objection, you pivot too fast."

"I pivot because you said," she cut herself off, pressing her lips together. "You literally said to keep it concise."

"Concise doesn't mean confusing," I shot back.

Her eyes narrowed. "I'm not being confusing."

"You kind of are."

She let out a quiet, disbelieving laugh, like she was deciding whether or not I was worth the energy. "You know what? Fine. Next time I'll just hand you the script and you can do it yourself."

"Not helpful," I muttered.

"Neither is that," she snapped, gesturing vaguely at me, my tone, my face, my entire existence, probably. Touché.

There was a second where neither of us said anything. Just silence. Thick. Annoying. Then she pushed back from her chair. "I'm getting coffee."

"Great," I said, too quickly. "Maybe it'll help."

She paused, turning just enough to level me with a look. "Maybe it'll help you."

And then she was gone. I watched her walk out, jaw tightening, fingers tapping once against the desk before I still them. Yeah, that could've gone better.

I spun my pen between my fingers, the office humming around me: keyboards, quiet chatter, someone laughed two rows over. I glanced toward the hallway she disappeared down, then quickly looked away like I wasn't just checking. She said coffee, not a cross-country move. Still, it had been a minute.

I tapped the pen against my desk, once, twice, then stopped because it was starting to feel a little too much like waiting. Which I wasn't doing. I dragged a hand over my jaw, eyes flicking, again, toward the hallway. It was ridiculous. She'd been gone, what, three minutes? Four? Not enough time for me to be sitting there wondering if she'd be coming back with that annoyed little crease between her brows.

As Ruiz returned to my cubicle, she looked calmer, more centered than before. I had to give her credit for that; she wasn't the type to back down, even when things got tough. That made my dick twitch. But there was a wall between us, and I hated that I was the one putting it there.

The rest of the afternoon dragged on. I kept my focus on the work in front of me, but every now and then, I'd catch a glimpse of Ruiz out of the corner of my eye, her head bent over her tasks, determination etched into her features. Despite my being a total ass, she was still trying to learn, still absorbing whatever she could. It was admirable, really, but it only made me feel more conflicted about how I'd handled things today.

By the time the end of the day rolled around, the office had quieted down. The usual buzz of activity was fading, and people were starting to pack up and head out. I glanced at the clock, the weight of the day's tension finally beginning to lift. Ruiz finished what she was doing and turned to me, waiting for some acknowledgment, but I was still buried in my screen, pretending to be more engrossed than I actually was.

I hoped she'd just leave, but finally, she spoke, her voice careful. "Callum, is there anything else you need me to do before we wrap up for the day?"

I looked up, and for the first time all day, the tight grip of irritation loosened. The frustration that had been simmering all day started to ebb, and I couldn't help but soften a little. I'd been too hard on her, she didn't deserve the brunt of what I was feeling.

"No, Ruiz, that's all for today," I replied, the edge in my voice replaced by something closer to regret. "You did okay. Just keep at it."

She offered a small smile, a flicker of relief passing over her face. "Thanks. I'll keep working on it."

Before I could say anything more, Owen strolled over, except his usual shit-eating grin, the one that made him look too chipper for my comfort, was gone. Flat, serious, off-kilter. "Hey. We need to talk," he said.

Alma straightened a little, eyes lit up just enough to make me notice. She smiled, quick and careful, like she was trying not to give away that she was actually thrilled to see him. "Sure," she said, voice breezy, too breezy, "we can talk."

I watched them, and my brain clocked the shift in her demeanor. The way Owen wasn't his usual annoyingly happy-go-lucky self. Something was up. History. There was history there.

He glanced at her, nodded once, then added, "I'll text you this weekend." Then walked off.

I cleared my throat, trying to act casual, though I knew I was failing. "So...you and Owen, huh?" I said, because apparently my mouth didn't understand subtlety. "Office relationships can be interesting."

Alma tensed ever so slightly. "It's nothing," she said.

"It's something," I replied before I could stop myself, the corner of my mouth twitching. "And man, that little exchange? So awkward. I feel like I should've handed out popcorn."

"There was history. But not anymore."

I raised an eyebrow. "That's not how history works," I said, smirking, though inside something hit like a punch to the gut.

Watching her, seeing that flicker of attention she just gave him, it hit me. A wave of jealousy curled through my chest like I didn't see it coming. And of course, I have to asked myself again, *why the hell am I jealous?*

"Anyways," she said, a little too quick, already stepping back like she was hitting the emergency exit on this conversation, "I should go. Have a good weekend, Callum."

I leaned back in my chair, watching her like I had all the time in the world. "Oh, I will," I said easily. "Try not to miss me too much."

She snorted. "That won't be an issue."

"Cold," I pressing a hand to my chest. "After everything we've been through today?"

"Everything?" she echoed, raising a brow. "You mean you criticizing me for eight straight hours?"

"It was constructive," I corrected.

"It was exhausting."

I grinned. "You're welcome."

She shook her head, but there was a hint of a smile there. "Survive the weekend without terrorizing anyone else, okay?"

"No promises," I said. "But I'll put in good effort."

She paused for a second, like she was about to say something else, then didn't. Just gave me one last look before turning to go.

"Hey," I called after her.

She glanced back.

"Try not to spill anything on anyone else."

Her eyes narrowed. "Try not to stand in people's way like a human traffic cone."

"No promises."

She rolled her eyes and walked off, and yeah, there it was again. That feeling. Inconvenient.

Chapter Four

ALMA

"The fact that you have to work with your ex is like punishment from the divine gods above," India said, sprawled across the couch, margarita in hand. "What kind of karma is that?"

"You're telling me," I groaned, sinking deeper into the cushions, the TV was playing something mindless in the background. "And he had the audacity to say he'd 'text me.'" I literally did air quotes. "What the hell is that?"

India snorted. "That's man code for 'I want to keep you on standby.'"

"Rude," I muttered, my brain already sprinting because what if he did want to get back together? Like, what if that was his grand realization moment? His *I made a terrible mistake* era? What if we fixed things and everything went back to how it was supposed to be?

Oh my God.

Oh. My. God.

"Alma," India said slowly, like she could hear my thoughts getting out of control, "where did you just go?"

"Nowhere," I said quickly, taking a sip of my margarita like that was going to ground me. It didn't.

We were mid-spiral, okay, I was mid-spiral, when my phone buzzed on the coffee table. I froze.

India's eyes snapped to me. "Well, don't just sit there. Check it."

I grabbed my phone, my stomach doing that annoying little flip. I glanced at the screen and, yep.

"Speak of the devil," I said.

India leaned over immediately. "What did that gremlin say?"

I shot her a look. "Hey. Don't call him that."

"He broke your heart," she said without missing a beat. "I'm allowed to not like him. Girl code."

I tried not to smile. I failed slightly. Then I looked back at my phone.

Owen: *Can you meet tonight?*

I sat up straighter. "He wants to meet. Tonight."

India watched me carefully. "Of course he does."

"I mean..." I tried for casual and landed somewhere around visibly excited. "That's normal. Right? Totally normal."

"Alma," she said, setting her drink down, "you're going to do what you want. You're a big girl." She paused. "But be careful. You don't need to go through heartbreak from the same man all over again."

I nodded, even though my brain was already ten steps ahead, was planning outfits and conversations and alternate timelines where everything worked out.

"Are you going to be home tonight?" I asked.

India hesitated. "No, actually. I'm going out."

Of course she was.

"Great," I said, already typing.

Me: *Sure, you can come over.*

He replied almost instantly.

Owen: *Does 9 work?*

"Wow," I muttered. "Eager."

Me: *yep*

I looked up at India, grinning like I had completely lost my mind, and then I chugged the rest of my margarita in one go.

"I have to get ready."

India squinted at me. "Get ready for what? It's not a date. Do not get any ideas, Alma."

But I was already standing, already halfway down the hall, already with all the ideas.

* * *

By the time Owen knocked on my door, I was prepared. Like, shaved, exfoliated, moisturized within an inch of my life. My curls? Perfect. Effortless but also clearly not effortless. If this was a bad decision, and it probably was, I was at least going to look incredible making it.

I took a breath, smoothed down my top like that was going to calm the absolute chaos happening in my chest, and opened the door.

And, of course, he looked good. Annoyingly good and that same cologne hit me instantly and made something in my chest ache. Home or what used to feel like it.

"Hey," he said, softer than I expected.

"Hey," I echoed, stepping aside to let him in like it was normal. Like he hadn't just walked back into my life and completely wrecked my equilibrium. "So," I said, closing the door behind him, "small world, or are you just everywhere I go now?"

He let out a quiet huff of a laugh. "Didn't know you worked there."

"Yeah," I said, a little tighter than I had meant to. "I didn't know you did either."

Which made sense, considering I stopped keeping up with his life the second he made it clear I wasn't part of it anymore.

"Different departments," he added.

"Right." I nodded. "Completely different worlds."

Cool. This was going great. Super chill. No emotional baggage anywhere.

He rubbed the back of his neck, glancing around my apartment before looking back at me. "Look, if we're going to be working in the same building, I figured we should at least try to be civil."

I blinked. "I thought we were being civil."

He tilted his head slightly. "Were we?"

I narrowed my eyes. "I didn't throw anything at you in the kitchen. That feels like growth."

That earned a real smile. "Fair."

There was something softer in his expression now. Familiar. Dangerous.

He took a little step closer.

"And besides," he added, voice dipping just enough to make my stomach flip, "we never really got our hate sex out of our system."

"I don't hate you."

"Could've fooled me earlier," he said lightly, eyes flicking over me. Then, quieter, "You look good, Alma."

And there it was. That stupid, unfair, heart-tugging thing he did. I should have rolled my eyes. I should have made a joke. I should not let that land.

But I did. Of course I did.

"Thanks."

He was closer now. Close enough that I could see the tiny shift in his expression, the way his gaze dropped to my lips like it used to. And I didn't move, which was probably my first mistake.

His hand brushed lightly against my arm, and that was it, that's all it took before the space between us disappeared, and suddenly we were kissing, and yeah. Second mistake.

His hand drifted to the waistband of my pajama shorts, slow and deliberate, like he was giving me time to stop him. I didn't.

They were just soft, elastic shorts, purely coincidental, obviously. Completely innocent. Not at all chosen with that exact scenario in mind. Nope.

His fingers dipped just beneath the fabric, and the touch alone sent a shiver racing up my spine, my breath catching as I felt the warmth of his hand against my skin. Everything suddenly felt sharper: his touch, the air, the way my pulse was absolutely betraying me.

There was a quiet pause, like he was checking in without words, and then he slid the fabric down, taking his time, leaving my skin buzzing in his wake. My breath stuttered, my hands found his shirt, and gripped it like I needed something to hold onto.

Our breathing turned uneven, tangled together, and he pulled back just long enough to tug my tank over my head. I lifted my arms without thinking, letting it go, feeling the cool air against my skin.

For a second, neither of us moved.

Then he stepped back just enough to step out of his shoes, his shirt following, and I couldn't help the way my eyes traced over him, familiar, but somehow not. Like I was seeing him for the first time and remembering him all at once.

He took his time, like there was no rush, like that moment was something to be felt, not hurried through.

Owen's eyes roamed over my body, appreciating every curve. The desire in his gaze sent a slow heat through me. I took in his body too, noting the definition of his muscles and the strength in his build, each detail etched into my mind.

My heart pounded in my chest. Owen reached out, pulling me gently toward him, and started kissing me. Our hands explored each other, tracing lines and contours, savoring the sensation of skin against skin. Owen's touch was gentle yet insistent as he moved his hands over my breasts, my stomach, my hips. I responded in kind, my fingers trailing down his back, feeling the strength of his muscles.

He kissed me deeply, our tongues dancing together, and I felt a heat spreading through my body.

He trailed kisses lower, moving to my neck, collarbone, and then my breasts. My breath hitched as he took one of my nipples into his mouth, his tongue swirling around it. I moaned softly, my hands tangling in his hair, urging him on.

He found my lips again, like he couldn't stay away for long, and I let myself melt into it as we started moving backward, slow, a little unsteady, like neither of us was fully thinking this through.

My legs hit the edge of the couch first, and the next second we were falling onto it together, a soft, breathless kind of landing, still tangled up in each other.

Owen positioned himself between my legs, and as he hovered over me, he looked down, his eyes dark with desire. "You still on the pill?" he asked softly.

"Yes," I whispered, my voice filled with need.

Owen entered me slowly, and I gasped at the feeling. He moved with a steady, gentle rhythm, his eyes locked on mine. I wrapped my legs around his waist, pulling him closer, deepening the connection between us.

We moved together, our bodies fitting perfectly, our breaths and moans intertwining. The experience was sweet and tender, filled with affection and care. Though a small part of me still yearned for something more intense and passionate.

I couldn't quite put my finger on it, but it was as if there was an itch I had yet to scratch, something that pushed boundaries in a way I had never fully explored before with any of my two other sexual partners. It wasn't that I didn't appreciate the tenderness; I just couldn't shake the feeling that there was something more out there, something that would awaken a part of me I hadn't yet discovered.

As we continued, Owen's movements grew more urgent, and I responded by gripping his shoulders. The pleasure built and built, and I approached the edge.

With a final, deep thrust, Owen brought us both over the edge, and I cried out, my body trembling with the intensity of my climax. Owen followed, his own release taking over.

Oh my God. What did I just do? The thought hit me all at once, like a bucket of cold water dumped straight over my head, as reality came rushing back in.

I stared up at the ceiling, my chest still rising and falling too fast, my heart completely out of sync with the situation I had just thrown myself into. What did this mean? Because it had to mean something, right?

I turned my head toward him, searching his face for anything, something familiar, something grounding, something that told me this wasn't just that.

But he was already sitting up. Already pulling away.

"Hey," he said, like he could feel the shift too. He ran a hand through his hair, not quite looking at me. "Don't think too much into it, okay?"

My stomach dropped.

I pushed myself up slowly, and wrapped my arms around my middle like that might hold me together. "Don't think too much into it?" I repeated.

He exhaled, like this was the reasonable thing to say. "Yeah. We just needed to get it out of our system."

Out of our system. The words landed heavy and final.

"Oh," I said, nodding even though it felt like something just cracked straight down the middle of me. "Right. Of course."

Because of course that was what that was to him, just something to check off. A loose end to tie up. Meanwhile, I was sitting there trying to piece together why it felt like more.

He stood, already reaching for his clothes, like that was routine. I watched him, something tight settling in my chest.

"Was that all it was for you?" I asked before I could stop myself.

He paused for half a second, then shrugged into his shirt. "Alma..."

"No, it's fine," I cut in quickly, even though it was clearly not. "I just wanted to make sure we were on the same page."

He sighed. "We can't go back to what it was."

I swallowed. "I didn't say we could."

But I thought we both knew I wanted something closer to that.

He finished getting dressed, glanced at me once like he wanted to say something else, but didn't.

"Take care, okay?" he said instead.

I nodded, because what else was I supposed to do?

"Yeah," I replied, forcing a small smile that didn't quite reach my eyes. "You too."

And then he was gone. Just like that. The door clicked shut behind him, and the townhouse felt way too quiet.

I sat there for a second, stared at nothing, replayed everything, and hated how quickly it all unraveled.

"Cool," I whispered to myself, letting out a hollow laugh. "Really nailed that one, Alma."

Chapter Five

CALLUM

I stepped into the bar, the warm glow of the ambient lights casting a relaxed yet vibrant atmosphere. It was one of those places that seemed to buzz with energy, the clinking of glasses and low hum of conversation creating a backdrop that always felt inviting. I'd had a long week and was ready to unwind.

The bar itself was a polished mahogany, and the shelves behind it were lined with an impressive array of bottles. I made my way to a spot near the end, ordered a whisky, and settled in, scanning the room for anything or anyone that might catch my eye.

After I'd gotten my drink, I swirled the amber liquid in my glass, letting the scent of the whisky fill my senses before taking a small sip. It was rich and smoky, just the way I liked it. But tonight, I knew I had to take it easy. The temptation to let the burn of the alcohol numb the edges of my mind was strong, but I couldn't afford to lose control. Not with the meds I'd just taken.

The doctor had warned me, no heavy drinking. The medication was supposed to keep me steady, keep the dark thoughts at bay, but it also meant I had to be careful. A couple of drinks, sure. But the days of drowning my sorrows in a bottle were long behind me. Or at least, they were supposed to be.

I took another measured sip, and the warmth spread through my chest. It was enough to take the edge off, but not enough to tip me over. I couldn't afford to spiral tonight. Not when I was already feeling the weight of everything pressing down on me. The last thing I needed was to wake up with more regrets than I already had.

That's when I saw her. She was seated a few stools away, and even in the dim lighting, her auburn hair was like a beacon. It cascaded in soft waves over her shoulders, catching the light with every movement. She wore a deep blue blouse that accentuated her features perfectly, her breasts perky and inviting.

I decided to make my move and slid off my stool to approach her, drink in hand. "Hey there," I said with a casual grin. "Mind if I join you?"

She looked up, her green eyes meeting mine with a hint of surprise, followed by a playful smile. "Not at all," she replied, her voice smooth and engaging. "I'm Emily."

"Callum," I introduced myself, taking a seat beside her. "So, Emily, what brings you out tonight?"

Emily took a sip of her drink and shrugged slightly. "Just looking for a little break from the usual routine. How about you?"

"Same here," I said. "It's been one of those weeks. Thought I'd come out and see what's happening."

We talked about nothing in particular, just enough to pass the time. She told me she was an elementary school teacher, and I nodded, asking a few questions out of politeness. I mentioned work, kept it vague, and we moved on to harmless things, where she liked to grab dinner, a show she'd been half watching lately, the kind of music she put on in the car. It was an easy, forgettable conversation, filling the time without asking for anything more.

"Want to continue this somewhere quieter?" I asked after a while.

Emily raised an eyebrow, a playful smile tugging at her lips. "Lead the way."

We left the bar together, and I guided her to my apartment, a short walk away. I was already imagining the things I'd do to her, my cock ready to plunge into her.

Inside my apartment, we settled on the couch, talking and laughing. The conversation eventually slowed, and Emily leaned in closer. Our lips collided in a rough, urgent kiss.

I led her to the bedroom. Once inside, there was no hesitation, just the two of us, stripping away the last layers that separated us. I slid on a condom as I mapped out every curve, every inch that I had longed to touch since she caught my eye.

The room filled with the sounds of our bodies colliding, the heat of the moment pushing us further, faster. But as I found my rhythm, an unexpected image of Ruiz flashed through my mind. Her dark curls and those striking hazel eyes seemed to intrude on my thoughts. I quickly tried to push the image away, focusing instead on Emily as I pushed inside her.

Despite my best efforts, Emily's presence underneath me did little to quiet the persistent thoughts of Ruiz that kept intruding. As I took Emily to the edge, trying to stay in the moment and the rushed rise and fall of Emily's breathing, Ruiz's image stubbornly lingered in the corners of my mind.

Her eyes seemed to dance in the shadows behind my eyelids. Every time I tried to push the thoughts away, they came rushing back, more vivid and insistent. Her laugh, her intense gaze, it was as if her presence was imprinted on my mind, refusing to fade into the background.

The thought of her urged me to push harder into Emily, faster, deeper. In my mind's eye, it was Ruiz under me, letting me claim her. As Emily came undone around me, I gave one last thrust, imagining Ruiz call my name. I shifted off Emily, trying to remind myself of the evening's pleasant distractions. But the more I tried to concentrate on the woman in my bed, the more Ruiz's image seemed to intrude. It was a nagging, unsettling feeling, like a melody stuck on repeat that I couldn't shake.

The night stretched on, and no matter how hard I tried, I couldn't escape the thoughts of her and find sleep, even with Emily in my bed asleep. The image of Ruiz lingered, a persistent echo in my mind, making it difficult to fully relax or find the peace I was seeking.

<h1 style="text-align:center">Chapter Six</h1>

ALMA

It was Sunday, which apparently meant I had chosen to punish myself twice, once emotionally and once physically, because I was on an elliptical next to India, pretending I had my life together while my legs felt like they might actually fall off.

"I'm stupid," I said, gripping the handles like they personally offended me. "Like, clinically. There should be a study."

India didn't even look surprised; she just kept her pace steady, sipping from her water bottle like she'd been waiting for this. "This about Owen?"

I let out a dramatic groan. "Of course it's about Owen. Who else is out here ruining my life on a Sunday morning?"

She glanced over at me. "You slept with him, didn't you?"

I stared straight ahead. "I hate that you know me so well."

"Oh my God, Alma."

"I know," I said quickly. "I know. You warned me. You literally said, 'don't go through heartbreak from the same man twice,' and what did I do?" I gestured vaguely. "Exactly that."

India shook her head, but there was no real judgment there. Just a little *I tried to tell you* energy.

I sighed and slowed my pace as the weight of it all settled back in. "And the worst part?" I added. "Of course he just wanted to..." I lowered my voice, even though no one here cared. "...fuck. Like, wham, bam, thank you ma'am, have a nice life."

India winced. "Oof."

"Yeah. Oof," I repeated. "Meanwhile, I'm over here like, 'maybe this means something, maybe this is our second chance, maybe we get our lives back on track.'" I cut myself off, shaking my head. "Delusional. Absolutely delusional."

She finally slowed her machine a bit, turning to look at me fully. "You're not delusional. You just wanted him back."

I pressed my lips together, blinking a little faster than usual. "Yeah," I admitted quietly. "I did."

Then India bumped her elbow lightly against mine. "Okay, well. Step one: we don't text him. Step two: we sweat this out. Step three: we remember you're too hot and too smart to be anyone's emotional rebound situation."

I huffed out a small laugh. "Bold of you to assume I won't break step one in approximately two hours."

She pointed at me. "Don't you dare."

"No promises," I muttered, picking up my pace again like I could outrun my own bad decisions.

India sighed. "I'm taking your phone away when we get home."

"Rude."

"Necessary."

I shook my head, but a small smile slipped through anyway because if I was going to spiral, at least I had someone there to drag me out of it.

CALLUM

I was heading toward the sauna, towel slung over my shoulder, already half-thinking about zoning out for ten minutes, when I saw her.

And I actually stopped. Because there was no way.

My brain did that thing where it tried to rationalize, *you're tired, you're hallucinating, this is what happens when you skip breakfast,* but no. There she was. Ruiz. Very real. Very...Ruiz.

She was on the elliptical, talking to a tall, stunning Black girl with long braids and a matching hot pink set that could probably be seen from space. Meanwhile, Ruiz was in biker shorts and a cropped Mickey Mouse tee, like she got dressed in the dark and somehow still made it work.

Her hair was thrown up in a messy bun, strands falling out, curls framing her face, and there was a line of sweat along her forehead, one drop tracing down her temple.

And I...Yeah. Girls didn't realize that was hot, but it was.

I watched for a second too long, catching the way she laughed, the way her whole face shifted, and something in my chest did that annoying, tight thing I chose to ignore.

Then I pushed off the wall and headed over, because standing there staring like a creep was not the move.

"Ah," I said, slipping into an easy smirk as I approached, "if it isn't double trouble."

Ruiz's friend glanced over first, grinning like she was already entertained. She grabbed her water bottle mid-stride and gave me a mock salute. "Guilty as charged. And you are?"

I nodded once, like I had been waiting for this introduction my whole life. "Resident mischief-maker," I said smoothly, "and the mysterious and charming Callum." My gaze flicked to Ruiz. "Has our dear Ruiz not spoken of me?"

Ruiz rolled her eyes so dramatically I was surprised she didn't pull a muscle. "Oh, I've mentioned you," she said, breathing slightly uneven, leaning casually against the machine like she hadn't just been working out. "Usually in passing. Like a footnote in a very boring novel."

I huffed out a laugh, shaking my head. "A footnote? That's rough."

"Accurate," she shot back.

"Well," I said, taking a step a little closer, "I'm here to steal the spotlight, whether you like it or not."

She smirked, wiping her forehead with the back of her hand. "Good luck with that. The spotlight's fickle. One minute it's on you, the next it's off finding someone more interesting."

I raised a brow. "Lucky for me, I thrive in the shadows too."

"Yeah, I can tell," she said immediately. "What, were you watching us from afar? That your thing now?"

"Don't flatter yourself."

"Mmhm," she hummed, unconvinced.

"I just joined," I added, nodding toward the gym floor. "Closer to J&P. Figured I'd make one responsible life decision this month."

Ruiz snorted. "Let me know how that goes for you."

I grinned. "Oh, I will. I've already run into you twice outside the office. Feels promising." I leaned against the machine next to hers like I had nowhere else to be, even though I definitely did. "So," I said, glancing at her, "did your dear *'we don't have history'* Owen get in touch with you this weekend?"

She made a face. "Ew. Getting in my business now?"

Before I could fire back, her friend cut in, not missing a beat. "In fact, he did. And trust me, he's history if I have anything to say about it."

I let out a low laugh, looking between them. "Ah. So the smart, beautiful friend is not on board with dear Owen making a comeback." I nodded slowly. "Now the plot thickens."

Ruiz shot me a look. "Callum, go find someone else to annoy. We're not on the clock. I don't have to endure you."

Her friend hopped off the elliptical, grabbing her water. "I'm gonna hit the bathroom," she said, pointing at Ruiz. "Locker room in a minute?"

"Yeah," Ruiz nodded.

The friend gave me one last *I'm watching you* look before heading off, leaving the two of us in that charged, slightly too-quiet space.

I tilted my head, watching Ruiz. "Of course," I said smoothly. "Wouldn't want to keep you from your Sunday reset routine. Very important." I paused, then added, just a little sharper, "Besides, I'd hate to interrupt whatever cookie-cutter love-making reunion you and Owen had planned."

There it is, that flicker. A flush creeped up her cheeks, and I knew I hit something real.

"You don't know what you're talking about," she shot back, arms crossed like armor. "And you really don't know when to stop, do you?"

I pushed off the machine, stepping a little closer, not too close, but just enough. "Oh, I think I do," I murmured, voice low, easy. "But hey, if playing it vanilla is your thing, who am I to judge?"

She glared at me, but I could see it, the way it got under her skin, the way she was trying not to react. And yeah, I shouldn't have enjoy that as much as I did. But I did.

Chapter Seven

ALMA

It was the next day and Callum's parting shot still lingered in my mind. His teasing was clearly a facade for something deeper, but I refused to let his jabs get to me. Despite his obnoxious demeanor, his words had touched a nerve, and I felt a twinge of irritation.

As I settled into my cubicle and started reviewing the client lists, I shoved those thoughts aside. Today was about proving myself in this new role, and I wasn't going to let Callum's remarks, or any lingering doubts, distract me from that goal. I focused on the tasks at hand, determined to make the most of this opportunity.

Just then, my phone buzzed with a message from Mami:

Mami: *hola mi amor. I wanted to confirm I received the money wire yesterday. Thank you for sending it over, but there's no need to send so much. You deserve extra money for yourself, to stay on top of your expenses.*

I stared at the message, my chest tightening. Of course I sent too much. I couldn't help it. I needed to. Making sure my family was taken care of was something I could control, unlike everything else in my life. That weight was on me, and this job, no matter how much I hated the idea of it, was part of how I was going to carry it.

The day flew by in a blur of emails, phone calls, and data entry. I found myself settling into the rhythm of the work, feeling productive and capable. Whenever I hit a snag, Tamara was there to offer guidance and encouragement. Surprisingly, Callum proved to be helpful too, despite maintaining that hint of arrogance from yesterday's gym exchange. His assistance came with a casual confidence that occasionally irked me, but I had to admit his knowledge of the systems and clients was useful. His insights were on point, even if he couldn't resist throwing in a teasing remark here and there.

By the time the workday finally wound down, I felt like I had lived seventeen different lives and at least five of them involved me questioning my career choices.

I found Tamara in the kitchen, both of us hovering near the coffee machine like it was a safe space, and I let out a small breath, soaking in the first moment of peace all day.

"You survived," she said, smiling like a proud coach.

"I did more than survive," I said, grabbing a cup. "I only cried internally twice. Personal record."

She laughed, then nudged me lightly. "No, seriously, you rocked it today. I could see you're getting the hang of everything. It's actually kind of impressive. Like you've been doing this forever."

I felt my cheeks warm, ducking my head a little. "Okay, let's not get carried away," I said, smiling. "But...thank you. I just had a really good teacher."

She gave me a look like she was about to say obviously, but then her expression shifted, eyes narrowing slightly, a mischievous little smirk forming.

Uh oh.

"So, Alma," she said, leaning in like we were about to exchange classified information, "word on the grapevine is there's some very juicy gossip about you and Owen."

I nearly choked on my coffee.

"I'm sorry, what grapevine?" I coughed.

She crossed her arms. "The one that's offended you didn't personally brief me. As your work wife, I expect transparency."

I groaned. "Oh my God."

"Spill," she insisted.

I sighed leaning back against the counter. "Fine. But you're not allowed to judge me."

"No promises."

"Great," I muttered. "Love that." I took a breath. "We dated in college. For almost two years."

Her brows shot up. "Oh, that's not casual."

"No," I said, shaking my head. "Very much not casual. Like meet-the-friends, talk-about-the-future, maybe-move-in-together kind of not casual."

"And then?"

"And then he broke up with me. On graduation day."

Tamara's jaw dropped. "You're joking."

"I wish," I said. "Spent the entire summer trying to get over him, only to find out, surprise! We now work in the same building."

She winced. "That is criminal."

"Right?" I said. "Thankfully we're in different departments, so it's not like I have to see him all the time, but we've already had a few run-ins and honestly? One was already too many."

Tamara shook her head slowly. "Men are trash."

"Correct," I said immediately. I glanced at the clock, then back at her. "I've had enough of this week."

"It's Monday," she pointed out.

"Exactly," I said. "That's how you know it's bad. Which is why," I continued, straightening slightly, "you should come out with me tonight. I want you to meet my roommate, India. We're grabbing cocktails downtown."

Tamara didn't even hesitate. "Oh, I'm in."

"Perfect," I said, already feeling a little lighter. "I'll text details, but just know, strong drinks and questionable decisions are highly encouraged."

She grinned. "Say less."

* * *

Downtown Franklin was alive in that chaotic, glittery, main-character kind of way, and somehow India and I ended up exactly where we were supposed to be, inside Rhythm & Spirits, which looked like a Pinterest board and a fever dream had a baby.

The walls were covered in quirky art and vintage signs, neon lights casting everything in this flirty, electric glow, and the music? Loud enough that you could feel it in your chest. A DJ spun something with a beat that made it physically impossible to stand still.

"I love it already," India shouted over the music.

"I knew you would." I grinned, scanning the crowd. Tamara texted that she was here already, and sure enough, I spotted her at a high-top near the dance floor, waving like she was flagging down a helicopter.

"Hey, girl!" I called, weaving us through the crowd.

Tamara practically launched at me, wrapping me in a hug. "There you are! I was about to send a search party."

"Please," I laughed. "I always find my way to cocktails." I turned, gesturing between them. "India, this is Tamara. Tamara, India, aka, best friend meets work wife."

They grinned at each other instantly, and just like that, the vibes? Immaculate.

We ordered a round of colorful, borderline suspiciously bright cocktails, and within minutes we were laughing like we had known each other for years. India was telling a story, Tamara was fully invested, and for a second, I forgot everything else. Until we headed back to the bar for round two.

I casually pulled out my phone, opening my banking app like I wasn't about to emotionally spiral in public. The number loaded and, okay. Okay, I was fine. Barely fine. Like two drinks and a tip if I behaved fine.

I quickly locked my phone, slipped it back into my bag like nothing happened, mentally doing math I absolutely should have paid more attention to in high school.

"Next round's on me, ladies!" Tamara announced, already flagging down the bartender like the hero she was.

Relief flooded through me so fast I almost laughed. "I love you," I told her sincerely.

"I know," she grinned.

A few songs later, we were on the dance floor, and India was, unsurprisingly, the star of the show. She had these wild, carefree moves that pulled people in, and Tamara jumped right in with her, no hesitation. I followed, laughing, letting myself get lost in it.

At some point, Tamara leaned in, yelling over the music, "I thought this was supposed to be a chill, two-cocktails-and-done night!"

I laughed, tossing my head back. "I never said that!"

"I see how you roll, Ruiz!" she shouted, grinning.

My last name snapped me to attention. The same way he said it. My stomach flipped.

Out of nowhere, Callum flashed through my mind, those stupidly piercing blue eyes, that perfectly undone hair, the faint shadow along his jaw that I...I blink, shaking my head hard. Okay. What the hell was that? Absolutely not.

I grabbed my drink, taking a sip like I could drown the thought before it got any louder, forcing myself back into the music, the lights, the moment. Yeah, we are not unpacking that tonight.

Chapter Eight

CALLUM

Tuesday evening hit like a brick after a long day, and by the time I pushed open the door to the group room, I was already running on fumes. The space was big, a little too bright, folding chairs were set up in a circle that felt both comforting and exposing at the same time. I passed the table on the way in, National Alliance on Mental Illness (NAMI) printed across the front, a box of donuts sitting there like a quiet peace offering. I didn't know where I would be without these nights, without this place that let me just show up and exist for a minute.

I slouched in my chair, the familiar creak of metal legs against linoleum filling the room as others settled in. The circle of faces around me was a mix of new and old, some who had been attending for as long as I had, others who were still learning the rhythm of opening up. My fingers absently traced the edge of my worn leather jacket, something of a comfort object now. The smell of weak coffee lingered in the air, a staple of the meeting space, though no one ever really drank it.

Dan, the group leader, cleared his throat and leaned forward in his chair, his clipboard resting casually on his knee. "Welcome back, everyone. I'm glad to see you all again," he began, his voice calm and steady, like a seasoned anchor. "Today's focus is progress. Where are we with the things we've been working on? What's going well, and what's still hard?" He looked around the circle, making eye contact with each person before his gaze landed on me.

"Callum," Dan said gently, "how about you? How've things been since we last saw you?"

I straightened a little, my jaw tightening before I exhaled. The room felt small, and my chest was heavy, but I knew this was the space to let it out. I'd been coming here long enough to trust the process. My eyes flicked to a few of the regulars, an encouraging nod from Anna, a steady gaze from Pete, and then back to Dan.

"It's been...up and down," I began, my voice rougher than I intended. "You know, like it always is." A few quiet nods met my words. They got it.

I took another breath, running a hand through my hair. "But I've been trying to focus on what my therapist suggested. Art...creating. She said it might help channel some of what I'm feeling." I shrugged, unsure if it was helping yet but trying to convince myself it could.

Dan leaned forward, his eyes focused but soft. "How's that been working for you? What kind of things have you been creating?"

I shifted in my seat. I wasn't used to talking about my art in a personal way, at least not outside the creative space I kept to myself. "It's mixed media, I guess," I said slowly. "I've been working with clay, some watercolors, and I've even gotten into chalk and coal. It's messy, but that's kind of the point."

Dan offered a small, knowing smile. "Messy can be good. Messy means you're working through something."

I huffed a small laugh, though it wasn't exactly amused. "Yeah, well, there's a lot to work through. It's been a while since I've felt like I was moving forward. The art, though, it helps keep my hands busy, at least. Stops the spiraling sometimes."

Dan nodded thoughtfully, keeping his voice calm but encouraging. "That sounds like progress to me, Callum. You're finding ways to manage the hard moments, even if it's just for a little while."

I swallowed, feeling a flicker of something, maybe hope, maybe just relief. "Yeah, maybe. But it's hard when it feels like there's always something pulling me back down, you know? Even when I'm working on something, there's this part of me that wonders if it's just temporary. Like I'll fall back into the same hole."

Dan's expression softened, and a few others in the circle shifted, some nodding in quiet agreement. "That's real," Dan said. "And you're not alone in feeling that way. The setbacks, the fear of slipping, it's part of the journey. But what matters is that you're here, and you're working on it. You're showing up for yourself."

My gaze dropped to my hands, my fingers idly tracing the lines of my knuckles. I knew Dan was right, but it didn't always make it easier to swallow. Still, the weight in my chest lightened just a little, enough to feel like I wasn't completely stuck.

"I guess," I murmured, "I just need to remember that it's not about getting it perfect every time. My therapist said that, too. It's about trying. Just trying, even when it feels pointless."

Dan's smile widened, and he leaned back slightly, giving me space to absorb the moment. "Exactly. Trying is what counts. And each time you pick up that brush, that lump of clay, you're reminding yourself that you have control over something, your own hands, your own process."

There was a quiet stillness in the room as his words hung in the air. I glanced around the circle at the different faces, some tired, some hopeful, all of them understanding in their own way. It was comforting, in a way, to be in a room full of people who didn't need him to explain everything. They just got it.

"I guess I'll keep trying," I finally said, my voice softer but more sure. "One day at a time, right?"

Dan gave me a nod, his eyes warm. "One day at a time."

Chapter Nine

ALMA

The week flew by in a blur of coffee, confusion, and me pretending I knew what I was doing. And somehow, miraculously, it was already Friday.

I was shutting down my computer, stretching like I had just survived a marathon instead of a corporate job, when Tamara popped up like she'd been waiting for this exact moment.

"Okay," she said, leaning against the divider, "what are you doing tonight?"

"Sleeping," I answered immediately. "Emotionally and physically recovering."

She rolled her eyes. "Boring. There's a party. Someone from accounting, Marcus? It's his birthday."

Before I could respond, Chris appeared out of nowhere, like he had been summoned by the word party.

"Oh yeah," he said, nodding. "Marcus is having something tonight. I'll see you both there?"

And then he just walked away. Like it was completely normal to casually RSVP to a party with your employees in the middle of the office.

I blinked after him. "Is it weird to party with your supervisor?"

Tamara didn't even hesitate. "Nope."

"Not even a little?"

She grinned. "Alma, what did I tell you? This place is a frat house with a paycheck."

"Right," I muttered. "How could I forget."

I glanced up and that was when I saw him.

Across the floor, Chris had stopped, now talking to Callum. He was leaning casually against a desk, one arm braced behind him, head tilted as he listened, like he didn't have a care in the world. I didn't mean to look. I really didn't. But somehow, I ended up watching him like a full-on creep.

It was just that he looked different there. Relaxed. Confident in that effortless way that was equal parts annoying and, unfortunately, very effective. His sleeves were pushed up slightly, hair a little tousled like he'd run his hands through it one too many times, and there was this ease to him that made it hard to look away. Which was ridiculous because I had barely spoken to him all week. On purpose. Clearly, distance equals sanity.

And yet, my stomach did that stupid little flip anyway.

"Okay," Tamara said slowly, following my line of sight. "Why are you staring at Callum like you're in a music video?"

I immediately looked away. "I'm not."

"You are."

"I was observing."

She snorted. "Mhmm. Very scientific of you."

"Shut up," I muttered, grabbing my bag. "Are we going to this party or not?"

"Oh, we're going," she said, looping her arm through mine. "You need to loosen up. And I need entertainment."

"I am not your entertainment."

"You absolutely are."

We made our way out, still bickering, when Tamara suddenly veered off. "Crap, I forgot something at my desk, meet you outside?"

"Yeah," I nodded.

And just like that, I was on my own.

I slung my bag over my shoulder, heading toward the exit, and of course, because the universe hated me, I passed right by Callum.

He glanced up mid-conversation, eyes catching mine immediately, like he'd been aware of me this whole time.

"Ruiz," he said, that familiar hint of amusement already there.

"Callum," I replied, keeping my tone neutral. Cool. Totally unaffected.

"Leaving already?" he asked, straightening slightly.

"Some of us don't linger for dramatic effect," I shot back.

He smirked. "Shame. I was just getting used to the view."

I rolled my eyes, but I could feel the heat creeping up anyway. "I'm sure you'll find something else to stare at."

"Oh, I'm not worried," he said easily. "I tend to get what I'm looking for."

I paused, just for a second, meeting his gaze. "Is that so?"

"Usually." He shrugged.

I tilted my head, a small smile slipping through despite myself. "Good luck with that."

His eyes flickered, like he was about to say something else, but I didn't give him the chance.

I turned and kept walking. And I could feel it. That pull. Annoying. Persistent. And very much still there.

Chapter Ten

CALLUM

That night, I was actually looking forward to the party, hoping it might offer a break from the routine and a chance to clear my head. The living room at Marcus' place was buzzing with the familiar faces from the office, and the atmosphere was lively with the excitement of the celebration.

As I mingled, half-listening to a story I couldn't care less about, trying to shake off the week, the door opened, and there she was. Ruiz walking in with her gym friend like she owned the place. It hit like a splash of cold water. God, she looked good tonight.

She was in jeans and a fitted top that shouldn't be legal, something that hugged in all the right places without trying too hard. Her curls were down, wild and soft around her shoulders, catching the light every time she moved. There was this glow to her, maybe the lighting, maybe the confidence, maybe just her.

And I swore, every guy in the room noticed. Which, for some reason, immediately irritated me. I dragged a hand over my jaw, exhaling slowly, trying to play it off like I didn't just lose my train of thought entirely.

As I leaned against the kitchen counter, taking in the lively scene of the party, Ruiz and her friends wandered in to grab some drinks. The clinking of glasses and the buzz of conversation created a vibrant backdrop, but I fixed my attention on them as they approached.

I raised my plastic red cup with a smirk. "The dynamic duo, together again."

"Ah yes, Callum, was it?" Ruiz's friend said, sizing me up with a grin.

"You never introduced me to your mysterious friend, Ruiz. You're horrible at introductions."

Ruiz rolled her eyes. "There was no need. You're no one important."

"Oh, burn," I muttered under my breath, but she heard me and shot a look that was half amused, half warning.

"I'm India," she said, voice serious but playful, raising an eyebrow. "The protective roommate."

"Well, you know my name," I said, tilting my cup toward her, "but my title? Master of mild chaos and occasional charm." Alma snorted at that, her eyes sparkling, and I couldn't resist. "See? Already improving the vibe. I'd say I'm a team player."

"You mean a troublemaker with a cup," she fired back, mock glaring, but the smile tugging at her lips betrayed her.

"Ah, touché," I said, leaning just a little closer. "But I'd argue the kind of trouble that's fun, not terrifying. You'd admit it if you tried it."

"I'm not sure I'd survive that kind of fun," she said, pretending to consider it. "You're way too confident."

"Confidence is my cardio," I replied with a wink. "Keeps the heart racing and the smiles coming."

She shook her head, laughing softly. "You're ridiculous."

"And you love it," I teased, smirking at the way her cheeks tinted just a little.

ALMA

As India twirled, her braids moving with the music, she leaned in close to me, trying to make herself heard over the music and the chatter of the crowd. "You know, there's some serious electric chemistry between you and that guy, Callum," she said, a mischievous glint in her eye.

My steps faltered, and I looked at her in shock. "What are you talking about?" I asked, taken aback.

"Oh, come on, Alma. Don't tell me you haven't noticed how he looks at you. And that gruff exterior of his is pretty hot."

I shook my head, my confusion clear. "You're crazy. Callum and I? We would kill each other. That's never going to happen."

India rolled her eyes playfully. "Seriously, you two would make a hot couple. There's definitely something there, even if you don't see it. I bet sparks fly whenever you two are in the same room. It's kind of undeniable."

I laughed, a hint of disbelief in my voice. "You have seriously lost it. And sparks fly? That's corny as hell! Callum and I are just friends, if you can even call it that. He may irk me too much to be considered friends. There's nothing more to it."

We kept dancing, letting the music and the carefree atmosphere wash over us. As I twirled and swayed, my mind kept drifting back to my friend's comments, trying to push them aside.

Then, out of the corner of my eye, I saw Owen across the room. My breath caught in my throat. He leaned casually against the dining room table and chatted animatedly with a tall blond. The sight sent a jolt through me, emotions swirling in my chest.

India noticed my sudden change in demeanor and followed my gaze. "Isn't that Owen?" she asked, raising an eyebrow.

I nodded, my voice carrying a hint of bitterness and hurt. "Yeah, that's him."

"Ignore him. He's probably just trying to make you jealous."

A wave of realization hit me hard, catching me off guard. I knew Owen was friendly and well-liked but seeing him with someone else stirred up emotions I'd been trying so hard to keep under control. The warmth drained from my cheeks as I turned away, the dance floor closing in around me.

I hurried out of the living room, each step feeling heavier than the last. My heart pounded painfully in my chest. As I neared the corridor leading to the bathroom, my vision blurred with unshed tears, and I struggled to keep my composure. Panic threatened to overwhelm me.

Just as I reached the bathroom door, I collided with someone solid. Looking up through tear-filled eyes, I saw Callum. "What, gah, you?" The words tumbled out sharp and uneven as I swiped at my face. "Why are you always in my way?" My voice cracked despite my best effort. I tried to push past him, my hands pressing uselessly against his wide chest, but my eyes betrayed me, burning with tears I hadn't managed to outrun.

His expression shifted from surprise to concern immediately. "Ruiz, hey, are you okay?" His voice was calm, grounding me amidst my emotional storm.

Callum gently guided me into the bathroom, where inside he offered me a tissue. His touch was comforting as he brushed a stray tear from my cheek.

"Is it Owen?" Callum asked softly, his brows furrowing with concern. I nodded, unable to put into words the ache in my chest. "Do you want me to go kick his ass?" he offered with a half-smile, trying to lighten the mood.

I managed a weak laugh through my tears. "No, it's okay," I whispered, grateful for Callum's attempt to make me smile. "Thank you, though."

Just as I was beginning to calm down, I immediately began to ramble anxiously, my words tumbling out in a flurry. Callum gently placed a hand on my shoulder and guided me to take slow, deep breaths. "Come on, Ruiz," he murmured, his voice a soothing anchor. "Inhale slowly with me." We synchronized our breaths, and the rhythm started to calm the rapid beats of my heart. With each exhale, a measure of peace settled over me, the tension in my shoulders easing under Callum's reassuring touch. In that quiet moment, amidst the echoes of distant laughter and music, his simple act spoke volumes, grounding me in a shared calmness.

"I swear," I muttered, my voice edged with exasperation, "working with your ex is like signing up for a never-ending soap opera."

Callum smirked, leaning casually against the wall. "Ah, the drama of office romances," he replied with a feigned dramatic sigh. "Mixing business with pleasure is a recipe for disaster."

I rolled my eyes. "Yeah, yeah, Mr. Relationship Guru," I shot back, my tone laced with sarcasm. "So, what's your sage advice now? Find someone to play my fake boyfriend?"

Callum's eyes glinted with mischief. "Well, isn't the saying 'fake it till you make it?'" he quipped, folding his arms across his chest. "There are plenty of guys in the vicinity." His eyes flicked past me, then back again. "Minimal effort, maximum damage."

I briefly considered it. Callum to be my fake boyfriend? But the thought was as ridiculous as it was fleeting. There was no way that would work. We annoyed the hell out of each other on a regular basis. Sure, we had chemistry, but we'd probably kill each other before the charade was over. The idea of putting up with his smug grin and cocky attitude for longer than necessary made my skin crawl. Nope, that was a disaster waiting to happen. I shook the thought from my mind and shot him a smirk.

"Please," I said. "A fake boyfriend? That'd be pathetic, and definitely a last resort."

Through with Callum's ludicrous suggestion, I exited the bathroom and caught a glimpse of Owen across the room, leaning in close to whisper something into a blond's ear. His smile was playful, flirtatious, the same way he used to look at me, and it made my stomach drop. My chest tightened, and before I could stop myself, I stepped back quickly, retreating. In my haste, I bumped into something, no, someone, again. Callum's hard body pressed against mine, steady and unmoving. I turned, heart racing, meeting his eyes for only a moment before grabbing his arm and pulling him back into the bathroom with me, away from everything. Away from Owen.

"Shit, shit, shit, shit, shit!" I yelled as I retreated, Callum in tow. I paused, considering his earlier words with a thoughtful frown. "So I may be desperate after all. You know what, Callum?" I said, my voice brightening. "You might be onto something with that fake boyfriend charade."

Callum raised an eyebrow, his smirk widening. "Oh, really? Planning to put on a show for our dear Owen, are we?"

"Why not?" I replied with a shrug, a smirk mirroring his. "I mean, we both know you'd make a terrible real boyfriend. Might as well put you to good use."

Callum feigned offense, placing a hand over his heart in mock hurt. "Ouch. You wound me," he replied dramatically. "But what makes you think I want to play your pretend boyfriend? What's in it for me?"

I raised an eyebrow, considering Callum's playful challenge. "How about this," I proposed with a smirk, "if this fake boyfriend thing works and Owen wants to get back together, I'll owe you a night out at an awful karaoke bar as a thank you. Or better yet, I'll play your wing woman on a night out. And if the fake boyfriend play doesn't work, no harm, no foul."

Callum thought for a moment. "Karaoke? When have I *ever* declared a love for karaoke? And a wing woman? That's weak."

I tilted my chin and crossed my arms. "Fine. What do you propose then?"

"Ah, the plot thickens," he teased, his tone shifting as his piercing blue eyes locked onto mine with an intensity I hadn't seen before. His voice dropped to a low, serious murmur. "You. For one night, I want you."

My breath caught in my throat, the weight of his words hanging heavily in the air. A thrill, unexpected and electrifying, ran down my spine, sending a shiver through my entire body.

Callum's expression was a complex blend of raw lust and something deeper, something that made my heart race. My thoughts spun in a chaotic whirl of excitement, fear, and curiosity.

He stepped closer, his presence almost overwhelming in the small space between us. "Ruiz," he murmured, his voice softer but no less intense. "No strings, no complications. Just sex."

My pulse quickened, and my mouth went dry as I struggled to find the right words. All our interactions flashed through my mind, those stolen glances, the flirtatious jabs. I realized, in that moment, that I had always felt a spark between us, something I had been reluctant to admit to myself.

I looked up at Callum, meeting his gaze head on. His eyes locked onto mine, filled with an undeniable hunger. The thrill of his proposition clashed with the uncertainty and risk of what it could mean for us.

"Callum," I whispered, my voice did that slightly traitorous thing where it wobbled just enough to betray me. "I don't know if that's a good idea." I shook my head, trying to piece together a single rational thought. "And how does that even work? If this whole plan works, Owen's going to think he's my boyfriend again. What, am I supposed to cheat on him five seconds in?"

Callum just leaned there against the sink, one shoulder propped up, that infuriatingly calm, cocky smirk playing on his lips like he was already ten steps ahead of me.

"Well," he said, voice low, almost amused, "if you want me to play the part of your fake boyfriend..." His eyes flicked over me. "You've got to agree to my terms."

Of course he had terms.

I hesitated, my stomach flipping in that *this is a terrible idea* kind of way. Because this was Callum. Complicated, arrogant, impossible Callum.

"And your terms?" I asked, narrowing my eyes like I was not already halfway pulled into whatever this was.

His grin deepened, like he had been waiting for that. "You have to trust me. Completely."

Before I could even process that, what that meant, why it felt like more than just fake dating, his hand was suddenly at the back of my neck. Warm and firm.

My breath caught as he guided me back a step, the cool tile of the bathroom wall pressed against my shoulders. The contrast sent a shiver straight down my spine.

"I've seen the way you look at me," he murmured, close enough that his voice felt like it settled under my skin. "Don't tell me there's nothing there."

My heart was pounding. Loud. Obvious.

"This?" he added, his gaze locking onto mine, steady and sure. "It's not one-sided."

I should argue. I should push him away. I should definitely not be standing here, completely frozen, hanging on every word like this was a scene I had somehow lost control of.

Instead, my voice came out soft. Breathless. "Deal."

His mouth curved slightly, like he knew I'd say that all along. He leaned in just enough that I could feel the hotness of his breath, that almost-there distance that made everything feel sharper.

"Good," he murmured, that smirk still lingering. "Fake boyfriend at your service."

Chapter Eleven

CALLUM

I released my grip on the back of her neck, my touch shifting to a gentle hold on her hand. The power of the moment hung in the air as I led her toward the door without saying a word.

"Wait, what are you doing?" Ruiz asked, her voice edged with urgency. She clearly didn't want anyone at the party to get suspicious about what had happened in the bathroom.

I turned to her, maintaining that same intense look. I squeezed her hand reassuringly and let a cocky smile curve my lips. "Don't worry, Ruiz. Just follow my lead."

Her trust in me was both reassuring and exciting. I opened the bathroom door and stepped out, my demeanor casual and relaxed, as if nothing unusual had happened.

Ruiz and I stepped back into the party like nothing just happened, like we didn't just rewrite the rules in a bathroom five minutes ago.

The noise hit immediately, laughter, music, someone yelling over a game in the corner, but my focus stayed on her. I kept my grip on her hand steady, not tight, just enough, guiding her through the crowd like it was second nature. She shifted beside me, shoulders a little too high, fingers cool in mine. Tense.

I glanced over, catching the way her eyes flicked around the room like she was bracing for impact.

"Hey," I murmured, leaning in just enough so she could hear me over the music. My thumb brushed lightly over her knuckles, slow, grounding. "Relax. You're with me, remember?"

She let out a small breath, like she didn't realize she was holding it.

"I'll make it look convincing," I said.

Her fingers tightened slightly around mine, and yeah, I felt that.

"Try to look like you don't hate me," I teased under my breath.

She huffed, but it was softer this time. "That's asking a lot."

I grinned. "Do your best."

From across the room, Tamara and Ruiz's friend, India, turned their heads in unison. Their eyes widened and their jaws dropped as they took in the sight of us, hand in hand, coming out of the bathroom. It was clear they'd stumbled upon something they hadn't anticipated.

The rest of the party carried on as usual, oblivious to what had just happened. I leaned in close to Ruiz, keeping my voice low and just for her. "See? Easy," I whispered, letting my breath brush against her ear.

I released her hand and made my way over to a group lounging on the couch, wanting to give her some time to adjust to the idea and not overwhelm her.

ALMA

The second Callum let go of my hand, it was like a signal went off because suddenly, boom, India and Tamara were there.

India crossed her arms immediately, a slow, knowing smirk spreading across her face. "Okay," she said, dragging the word out. "Spill. What was that?"

I blinked at her, going for casual and probably landing somewhere closer to visibly flustered. "What ever do you mean?" I asked, like I wasn't just hand-in-hand with the human embodiment of bad decisions.

Tamara nodded enthusiastically, eyes wide. "Yeah, no, we're gonna need a full explanation."

India pointed at me like she was presenting evidence in court. "Earlier tonight, you said there was nothing going on between you and Callum. So I'm just curious, what changed in the last, like, ten minutes?"

I sighed, tucking a curl behind my ear, buying myself a second. "Look, it's complicated."

"Oh, I love complicated," Tamara said immediately. "Go on."

"We're just"—I gestured vaguely, because words were failing me at an alarming rate,—"hanging out. That's it. No strings."

Both of them just stared at me.

"Just hanging out?" Tamara repeated slowly. "With Callum?"

India let out a short laugh. "Girl, please."

I shook my head, trying to hold my ground even though I could feel the heat creeping up my neck. "I'm serious. There's nothing more to it. Can we not make it a whole thing?"

Tamara squinted at me. "It is a whole thing."

"It's not," I insisted. "And also, where did you even come from?"

She lifted a shoulder. "I literally just got here."

"Convenient," I muttered.

"Don't try to change the subject," she shots back. "Look, we're here if you want to talk about it. For real."

India nodded, less teasing, more watchful.

I exhaled, offering them a small smile. "I know. Thanks. But for now? Can we just enjoy the party?"

India raised a brow but let it go. "Fine. Temporary ceasefire."

Tamara grinned. "But this conversation is not over."

"Great," I murmured. "Can't wait."

The music picked up, and we started dancing, letting the conversation fade into the background. Laughter and chatter filled the room, creating a warm and lively atmosphere.

As the night wore on, I found myself standing by the window, gazing out at the city lights. My friends were still dancing and chatting, but my mind was elsewhere, consumed by thoughts of Callum's proposition.

I could still feel where his hand was, like a phantom imprint at the back of my neck, warm, steady, a little too easy to remember. It was equal parts thrilling and completely confusing, and I hated how much my body seemed to recall it without asking me first.

I pressed my lips together, taking a slow sip of my drink, trying to ground myself as the party hummed around me, music, laughter, people moving like none of this is a big deal. But it was a big deal because now there was something. Something with Callum. And I didn't even know what that was, let alone what it meant.

I glanced across the room, catching a glimpse of him through the crowd, my stomach doing that annoying little flip again, and I quickly looked away like that was going to fix anything.

Exciting. Terrifying. Complicated.

I exhaled, shaking my head slightly because if this was how I felt after five minutes of fake boyfriend chaos with Callum, what did that say about everything I thought I still felt for Owen?

Chapter Twelve

ALMA

Saturday found me exactly where I needed to be, my favorite place to pretend the rest of my life wasn't mildly spiraling. The gallery. Free entry, no expectations, and just enough quiet to hear my own thoughts, which was sometimes a risk, but today? I'd take it.

My footsteps echoed softly against the hardwood floors as I wandered in, that familiar sound instantly calming me down. It was weirdly grounding, like the second I stepped in there, everything slowed just a little.

Paintings lined the walls, each one doing the absolute most, and I stopped in front of a giant abstract piece that looked like someone threw every emotion they'd ever had onto a canvas and said, deal with it. Swirls of color, bold, messy, dramatic. Relatable.

I tilted my head, studying it like I was going to uncover some deep, life-changing meaning, when really I was just letting myself breathe for the first time all week because a lot had shifted.

Work, for one, wasn't completely terrifying anymore. I wasn't saying I knew what I was doing, but I could fake it with significantly more confidence, which honestly felt like growth. Tasks that used to make me want to fake a power outage were starting to feel normal. I got the occasional approving nods, a "nice job," and suddenly I was like, wait, am I good at this? Who allowed that?

I smiled to myself, folding my arms loosely as I took a step back from the painting. For the first time since starting, I felt like I actually belonged there. Which was wild.

And outside of work? I had been sending money home. Not a ton, but enough to help. Enough to matter. Every time I did, there was this quiet little sense of pride that sneaked in, like, okay, you're doing something right. Mami and Papi don't say much about it, but I knew it helped. And that was enough for me.

Then there was the side PR gigs aka, my chaotic alter ego. Late nights, deadlines that came out of nowhere, me aggressively typing like I was in a movie montage, but I kind of loved it. It was starting to feel like something mine. Like maybe one day it wouldn't just be "extra work," it would be the thing. And yeah, the extra cash? Thank goodness for it.

I let out a small breath, looking back at the painting, the colors still loud and unapologetic. For the first time in a while, things felt steady. Not perfect and definitely not figured out, but steady. And honestly? I'd take that.

And now there was this whole situation with Callum. This ruse. I exhaled, shifting my weight as I stared at a painting I was definitely not processing anymore.

Was this actually going to work? Was I really about to fake date the most frustrating man I knew just to, what, win Owen back? Because that was the goal. That had to be the goal. Right?

I just wanted things to go back to the way they were. Back when my life felt semi-put together and I wasn't constantly guessing what came next. Back when I had a plan. Back when I had him.

College me really thought she had it all figured out. Degree, career, boyfriend who'd be there through it all...I let out a small, humorless laugh. Yeah, that worked out great.

I chewed on the inside of my cheek. Because the truth was, I didn't just lose a boyfriend. I lost the version of my life I thought was guaranteed. And now I was here, trying to, what? Recreate it? Force it back into place?

My gaze drifted, unfocused. And Callum. I didn't want anything from him. Just the plan. Just the fake boyfriend thing. That was it. Nothing else. Definitely not...I cut myself off immediately, shaking my head. Yeah. No. Absolutely not. Could you gaslight yourself? Because I felt like I was doing a pretty solid job.

I took a slow breath, finally letting the quiet of the gallery settle back in around me, the soft hum of the space, the stillness, the way everything felt just a little less chaotic in there. And for a moment, standing among all this color and chaos frozen into something beautiful, I felt calm. Not perfect, but steady. Like maybe I didn't have everything figured out, and maybe I didn't have to. Like maybe, for once, I could just stand here and be.

CALLUM

I was a little surprised Ruiz actually agreed to let me go over to her place. I'd thrown it out there mostly to get under her skin, maybe watch her roll her eyes on Monday. But no, she said yes. And yeah, my ego, my dick, and, let's be honest, the rest of me, was very on board with that decision.

I checked my phone again, just to make sure I had gotten the right townhouse, even though I had already double-checked twice. Then I rang the doorbell, and shoved my hands in my pockets like I was not at least a little curious how this was about to go.

The door swung open, and there was her friend India. She looked me up and down like she had already formed an opinion.

"Oh look who it is," she said, smirking. "The infamous Callum."

I nodded once, easy. "The one and only."

She stepped aside, letting me in. "Alma," she called over her shoulder, "Romeo is here."

I winced. "That's aggressive."

"Wish I could stay and play chaperone," she continued, grabbing her bag, "but I have a date." She paused at the door, turning back to me with a pointed look. "Please behave. You seem like a man whore."

I pressed a hand to my chest, feigning offense. "Me? I'm wounded."

She raised an eyebrow.

"Okay," I admitted, holding up my hands. "Former playboy. Reformed. I'm basically a Boy Scout now, especially since I've had the pleasure of meeting your gorgeous roommate."

That earned me a pause. She studied me for a second, like she was trying to decide if I was full of it.

"That was actually kind of cute," she said slowly. "You better have meant it."

"I did," I replied, a little more honest than I expected.

Her expression softened just a fraction. "Don't hurt my girl."

And then she was gone, the door clicking shut behind her, leaving me alone in Ruiz's space. I glanced around, taking it in.

It was her. Warm. Lived-in. Bookshelves lined with a mix of novels and random knick-knacks, framed photos tucked in between, friends, family, moments frozen mid-laugh.

I drifted closer, picking up one of the frames. Ruiz in a cap and gown, grinning like she owned the world. Yeah, that tracked.

"Sorry for making you wait."

I looked up. And there she was.

She was in sweats, low on her hips like she had just thrown them on without thinking, and an oversized, slightly worn college sweatshirt that was slipping off one shoulder in a way that felt dangerous for entirely different reasons. It wasn't even trying to be sexy, which somehow made it worse.

"So, recon?" she said, crossing her arms like she was bracing herself.

I dropped onto one end of the couch, stretching out like I belonged there, watching her as she reluctantly took the other side. Not far, just enough space to pretend this wasn't already charged.

"I've been doing some recon," I said, voice easy, a hint of a smirk pulling at my mouth.

"Okay?" she replied, cautious.

"On you," I continued, tilting my head. "I should know about my girlfriend's life now, shouldn't I?"

She shifted slightly. Uneasy. Good.

"And what did you discover?" she asked.

I leaned back, draping an arm over the couch. "Took a deep dive into your social media," I said casually. "You live a very safe life. Cozy nights in, brunches, the occasional beach trip. Very wholesome. Very predictable."

Her eyes narrowed. "So?"

"So"— I shrugged, eyes locked onto hers—"I think you need a little danger in your life."

"And you think you can provide that?" she asked.

I didn't even hesitate. "I know I can."

There was a beat and something shifted.

"Sometimes," I added, leaning forward just slightly, "you need to step out of that comfort zone of yours. A little thrill. A little risk. Makes things more interesting."

She was staring at me now. Really staring. Curious.

And that, yeah, that did something to me.

"Maybe you'll find that letting go a little is exactly what you've been missing," I said, voice lower, more deliberate.

Her breath caught, just barely, but I caught it.

"Relax," she said quickly, like she needed to reset the room. "You haven't won anything, Callum. The plan hasn't even started yet."

I grinned. "Your plan?"

"My plan," she repeated, sitting up straighter, like she was reclaiming control. "You said you wanted to help me, right? We make Owen jealous. But it has to be believable. Subtle. Like we actually like each other."

I huffed a quiet laugh. "That might be the hardest part."

She shot me a look. "You need to play your part. Perfectly."

I studied her for a second, the determination in her eyes, the way she was trying to take charge of something that was already slipping.

"All right," I said finally, nodding once. "I'll play your game. But remember, Ruiz," I added, voice edged with something real, "this goes both ways."

Her brows pulled together slightly.

"You get what you want," I continued, holding her gaze, "and I get what I want."

For the first time all night, I was not entirely sure she knew what that was.

Chapter Thirteen

ALMA

Monday morning, I was in the kitchen clutching my coffee like it was the only thing keeping me tethered to reality, when a neon-colored sign-up sheet practically screamed for my attention.

Company Basketball League

I leaned in, scanning the names, some familiar, some not, and of course Chris was already on there. Overachiever.

I was stirring my coffee like it was personally insulted me when Tamara walked in, all energy and zero regard for the fact that it was still morning.

"Hey, work wife," she sang. "How was your weekend?"

I took a slow sip, deadpan. "Emotionally questionable. Physically exhausting. Spiritually unclear."

She grinned. "Sounds productive."

"Thriving," I confirmed. I nodded toward the sign-up sheet. "Guess what? I was just thinking about signing up for the company basketball team."

Her eyebrows shot up. "Really? That actually sounds fun. I used to play a little when I was a kid. Let's do it."

I perked up instantly. "Yes! I practically grew up on the court. You're looking at a seasoned pro."

Tamara giggled, crossing her arms. "Oh, really? I'll believe it when I see it."

I leaned in, mock offense written all over my face. "You doubt me? Please. I've got moves even Michael Jordan would envy."

"Bold claim..."

"Dangerously accurate," I cut in.

"Did I just hear someone challenging MJ's legacy?"

I didn't even have to turn around. Callum.

He strolled in like he owned the place, leaning casually against the counter, that stupidly attractive smirk already in place.

I rolled my eyes. "Oh, spare me, Callum. You wouldn't last two minutes on the court with me."

He raised a brow. "Is that a promise or a threat?"

"Both," I shot back.

And then, like the universe really said *let's test her today,* Owen walked in. My stomach dropped so fast I was surprised it didn't hit the floor. I froze for half a second, brain short-circuiting, and before I could even decide how to act, Callum was suddenly right next to me.

Close. Too close. I felt him lean in, his breath brushing just near my ear as he murmured, low and amused, "Lights. Camera. Action."

I rested against the counter, trying to act casual, but my stomach was doing somersaults. Tamara chuckled, her eyes flicking between me and Callum like she could see the tiny war zone brewing.

"Looks like we've got some friendly competition brewing here," she said, all lighthearted amusement.

I shot Callum a sideways glance and caught that damn twinkle in his eye, the one Owen seemed blissfully oblivious to. My cheeks warmed, and I shifted, trying to steer the conversation somewhere safe, anywhere safe.

"Maybe you shouldn't sign up," Owen said casually, but the way he said it felt possessive, like he was already staking claim.

Callum tilted his head, smirk in full effect. "I think she's well within her rights to join the league. Isn't that right, Ruiz?"

"Oh, yeah," I agreed, trying not to make things awkward while also silently thanking him for having my back.

Owen huffed, crossing his arms. "I don't know why you're even involved in this, Callum. She doesn't need…"

Callum leaned casually against the counter. "Oh, I'm not involved, Owen. I'm just making sure she doesn't get bored while you struggle to keep up."

Owen snorted, leaning closer. "I'm pretty sure she's capable of seeing through your little theatrics."

"Oh, I'm not theatrics, buddy. I'm a feature presentation," Callum quipped, giving me a wink that made my stomach flip.

Owen groaned, running a hand through his hair. "You're impossible."

"And yet irresistible," Callum shot back with a sly grin, voice just loud enough for Owen to hear, making him visibly fume.

Callum sauntered over to the sign-up sheet like he owned it. Pen in hand, he scribbled his name and mine. He paused, pen hovering, then looked up at me.

"I hope to see you on the court," he said, low and teasing, that little spark in his tone making my chest flutter.

I raised an eyebrow, caught somewhere between amused and oh God, what was he doing to me?

Of course, Owen wasn't about to be outdone. He stalked over, grabbed a pen, and wrote his name, his jaw tight and eyes focused on me like I'd just declared myself the center of some war he hadn't signed up for.

Tamara was practically vibrating with mischief, her grin stretched from ear to ear as she watched Callum and Owen square off, her eyes flicking to me like *enjoy the chaos, kiddo*.

I thought the madness was over, that I might actually get a minute to breathe, when Callum tossed me a cheeky glance and said, "K, gotta get back to work. I'll talk to you later, babe."

My stomach did a backflip, my brain froze, and I swore I heard a record scratch somewhere.

Owen's head slowly turned toward me, eyes wide. "Babe? What the…fuck?"

Tamara, saint that she was, grabbed my hand with exaggerated urgency. "We're running late for a meeting!" she announced, dragging me toward the door with a flourish, ignoring the sound of Owen's jaw dropping behind us.

I caught one last look back, Owen standing there, red-faced and fuming, Callum already gone with a grin I knew would haunt me for the rest of the morning, and I had no idea how I'd gotten myself into this mess. But somehow, I was definitely not mad about it.

CALLUM

Later that night, we were back in Ruiz's apartment, this time at her invitation, which made the whole thing feel a little more intimate. I kicked off my shoes and leaned against the doorframe, drinking in the sight of her curled up on the couch in those soft sweats that somehow managed to hang lower on her hips, the kind of thing girls wear thinking it's just comfort but guys secretly find ridiculously cute.

"Why would you put me on the spot like that with Owen?" she asked, arms crossed, eyes narrowing at me like I'd orchestrated her public humiliation.

I smirked. "It was our grand introduction into his orbit as a couple."

"But then you left me to deal with the repercussions," she shot back, a playful edge to her voice.

"And how did that go?"

She rolled her eyes but smiled despite herself. "Well it didn't. Tamara saw me in distress and got me out of there so fast you'd think I'd pulled the fire alarm. She is my fairy godmother, that woman."

I moved closer, lowering my voice, teasing. "Well, Ruiz, he needs to know. That's the entire point of this ruse."

She leaned back, letting out a reluctant laugh. "Yeah, yeah, but I could've done it differently. Gracefully. With style. Instead of the chaos that unfolded."

"Ah," I said, my tone softening, "but that's the fun part. Chaos suits you." My gaze lingered on her face, taking in the way her curls tumbled messily around her shoulders, the little crease in her brow when she thought, the curl of her lip when she was both frustrated and amused. I could feel that familiar twist in my chest, the pull I'd been trying to ignore all week.

She shook her head, smiling at me like she knew exactly what I was thinking. "Fine. Let's think of ways to play up the relationship in front of Owen," she said, already reaching for a notebook.

I sat down beside her, letting our knees brush. "All right. Where does he usually hang out?"

She started jotting down notes, her pen moving quickly. "The coffee shop near our building, his favorite brunch spot..."

I chuckled, resting my elbow on the back of the couch, close enough to feel her warmth. "And the gym," I added, my voice low, teasing. "Chris is on the committee putting teams together for the company basketball league. I can make sure we all end up on the same team. You, me, and Owen."

Her eyes flicked up at me, a smirk playing on her lips. "Tamara has to be on the team too. She's my work wife."

I shrugged, mock-surrendering. "Fine. Fairy godmother included. You're building your dream team, after all."

She leaned closer, conspiratorial. "Other places he goes...there's that late-night diner he likes, claims it's the best pie in the city."

I cocked my head, letting my gaze linger on her. "You sure you know the guy?" I asked, my tone casual but my curiosity cutting sharper than I intended. "How long did you date?"

Alma's eyes flickered downward for a moment, a shadow of sadness passing through them. "Almost two years," she admitted softly.

Two years. I hadn't realized it had been that long. My chest tightened, and I caught myself thinking, half-joking, half-serious, that I was probably the last person in the world who deserved something like that. Soledad had made sure of that, carving out little pockets in my life where love just wasn't allowed to stick. And yet here was Alma, this beautiful, fiery, frustratingly captivating force in front of me, talking about her own history like it had nothing to do with me.

I shook the thought off and leaned forward slightly, lowering my voice. "And did it end badly? Or was it just one of those quietly dying things?"

She hesitated, tracing the rim of her coffee cup with her finger.

"Since when do you care, Callum?" She snapped out of whatever sadness trance she was in. "It ended. It was unexpected, basically the kind of thing where you think you're safe and then everything shifts."

I nodded slowly, letting the words settle between us. Something about the way she spoke made me want to protect her, to fix what I couldn't, and I felt that familiar pull, half frustration, half longing.

I let my gaze linger on her just long enough to make her shift in her seat. "There's something else I think needs to be addressed," I said, my tone casual, though I could feel the mischief coiling in my chest.

Alma tilted her head, curiosity lighting up her eyes. "Oh?"

"Do you have a roommate for the Jamaica trip?" I asked, careful to sound casual, though my heartbeat was definitely not.

"I assumed I was going to room with Tamara," she replied, shrugging, a faint smile tugging at her lips.

I shook my head, smirking. "Scratch that. I think we should room together." I let it hang there, letting the words settle in like a tiny, thrilling spark. "It would really sell the ruse. Enough so that, in combination with everything else, you might have dear Owen eating out of your hand by Valentine's Day. If not sooner."

Alma's brow furrowed slightly as she considered it. "Tamara's going to kill me," she muttered, half to herself.

"She'll survive," I said confidently, shrugging as if it were nothing. "Say the word, and I'll send the email to Chris and the Jamaica committee right now, before it's too late to switch things."

Her eyes widened. "And they wouldn't have a problem with it? I mean, you're a junior manager..."

"Exactly," I said, letting a sly grin creep onto my face. "Junior manager. Chris dated Brandy for months before officially telling HR, and he's still her manager. We'll be fine."

Alma chewed on her bottom lip, then nodded slowly. "Okay, as long as it's not an issue and I don't look bad."

I winked, letting the confidence slide off me like silk. "Relax. I've got this. So the plan is officially in motion. Time to watch the chaos unfold in style."

Chapter Fourteen

ALMA

A few days later, I was sliding out of my car when Owen appeared out of nowhere, like some broody romcom cliché that I wasn't exactly thrilled to live in.

"So, you and that asshole Callum," he said, voice dripping with sarcasm. "That was quick."

I straightened my shoulders, a flicker of defiance sparking through me. Where had the sweet, thoughtful guy I'd dated for almost two years gone? "First off, you broke up with me. Secondly, how is me moving on, months after you ended things, moving fast? And third, it's none of your business who I see in my free time."

His jaw tightened, and he stepped closer. "Convenient, don't you think? One minute you're heartbroken, the next you're cozying up to Callum."

I felt heat creeping up my neck. "Convenient or not, it's my life. Maybe you should wonder why you care so much if you were so eager to walk away."

Owen's eyes flickered, regret, jealousy, or maybe both, I couldn't tell. "I just don't want to see you get hurt."

"Funny," I said, biting back a laugh, "considering you're the one who hurt me."

He ran a hand through his hair, clearly frustrated. "Look, I just didn't expect you to move on so fast."

I took a deep breath, grounding myself. "I could say the same. And maybe I didn't expect it either. But here we are. You made your choice, Owen. Now it's my turn to make mine."

He opened his mouth like he was going to argue, then seemed to reconsider. With a final, frustrated glance, he turned and walked toward the office building, leaving me alone with my racing thoughts. Triumph and sadness tangled together, but underneath it all was a spark of determination.

I'd already been on edge before Owen decided to pop up and be a jackass. I'd just gotten off the phone with Mami, who casually mentioned that Papi had a little heart scare over the weekend. He was fine, she assured me, but of course my mind immediately went into overdrive. I made her promise to keep me updated, to let me know if they needed extra money to cover hospital bills.

The weight of responsibility pressed down hard. I wanted to make sure they were okay, even from a thousand miles away, even if it meant tightening my own budget, skipping a latte or two, and keeping my head on a constant swivel.

CALLUM

Another Jamaica committee meeting. By the time everyone shuffled into the cramped conference room, coffee in hand, half-awake, already over it, I knew exactly what we were here for. Chris had tipped me off earlier. Room assignments.

I was posted up near the end of the table, playing the role of "responsible junior manager shadowing leadership," which mostly meant I got a front-row seat to corporate debates disguised as casual conversations.

Chris stood at the head of the table, flipping through a printed spreadsheet. "All right," he said, clapping once. "Room assignments."

A collective groan rippled through the room.

Across from me, Mark Feldman from HR leaned back like he'd been waiting his whole life for this moment. "I knew this was coming."

"Of course you did," Nina Patel added, tapping her pen. "Every year it's the same drama."

Chris glanced at Mark. "You want to walk us through it?"

Mark shrugged, scanning the page. "We've got three couples requesting to room together."

Nina lifted a brow. "Only three? Wow. Growth."

"Lauren and Brandon. Meghan and Bryce..." He paused. Just for a second. "And Alma and Callum."

There it was.

I felt Nina and Mark's heads turn my way. I didn't move, just leaned back in my chair like this was the least surprising thing in the world.

"What?" I said, lifting a brow. "There's never been a rule against interoffice dating. As long as things stay professional, we're good, right?"

Nina smiled, amused. "Honestly? This is a pretty tame list."

Mark sighed. "The concern is optics. We are still a workplace."

"Sure," Chris said, taking a sip of his coffee, "but we're also not pretending people don't date here."

And that was the truth. This place wasn't a monastery. People worked long hours, traveled together, bonded over stress and late nights. Things happened. Sometimes they worked out. Sometimes they didn't, and then you still had to see that person at the coffee machine Monday morning.

"The issue," Mark continued, "is favoritism, discomfort, post-trip fallout."

"And the open bar," Nina added dryly. "Let's not forget the open bar."

Chris smirked. "We've handled this before. Clear expectations. No special treatment. And no PDA that makes everyone else question their life choices."

"Low bar," Mark grumbled. "Literally."

Chris leaned against the table, thinking. "The alternative is forcing couples to room separately and creating resentment."

"Which always goes great," Nina said flatly.

I let out a quiet huff of a laugh, then added, "I mean, if we trust everyone to manage million-dollar accounts, I think we can trust them to share a hotel room without burning the place down."

That got a few nods.

Mark exhaled. "All right. We approve the requests. Couples room together."

Chris lifted his coffee. "Democracy."

"And common sense," Nina added.

Chris jotted something down on the spreadsheet. "We'll send out a reminder. Expectations, conduct, adults behaving like adults."

The meeting wrapped, chairs scraping, people already mentally checked out.

I stayed seated for a second longer than I needed to, eyes drifting back to that list in my head.

Me and Alma. This trip was sure to be interesting.

Chapter Fifteen

CALLUM

Later that night, the gym buzzed with energy as employees from different departments gathered for the company's basketball practice. The sound of basketballs echoing off the hardwood, sneakers squeaking, voices overlapping in that chaotic, competitive hum that always came with pickup games. I scanned the room, spotting Ruiz among the crowd.

Across the court, lacing up her sneakers like she had something to prove. Tight workout shorts, fitted tank, curls piled up in a messy bun that was already starting to loosen. There was this focus about her, nervous energy wrapped in determination, and it pulled me in immediately.

Her eyes flicked up and caught mine. I gave her a slow wink. Game on.

As practice began, I found myself matched up against her on the court. I dribbled lazily at first, testing her. "Come on, Ruiz," I called, voice low, teasing. "That the best you've got?"

She dropped into position, quick on her feet, arms out, eyes locked on mine like she was already planning my downfall. "Don't underestimate me, Callum."

I stepped in closer.

She moved with me, and suddenly there wasn't much space left between us, her body brushing mine as she tried to cut me off, the heat of her skin, the faint sheen of sweat already starting to form. It was distracting. More than distracting.

I backed into her, shielding the ball, feeling her hands press lightly against my sides as she tried to reach around.

"Careful," I murmured over my shoulder. "You're getting a little handsy."

"Oh please," she shot back, breath just slightly uneven. "You wish."

I smirked and pivoted, but she stayed with me, tight defense, hips brushing mine again, her thigh pressing against my leg as she blocked my lane. For a second, it stopped being about the game.

It was just her. Focused. Determined. Way too close. I shook it off, spun past her, and sank the shot clean through the net.

"Still think you're MJ?" I called, backing up with a grin.

Her eyes flashed, cheeks flushed, not just from the game. "I'm just warming up," she said, already moving back into position. "Get ready to lose."

God, she had no idea what she was doing to me.

We kept going, back and forth, fast, competitive, but every time we matched up, it felt less like basketball and more like something else entirely. Bodies brushing, hands grazing, quick touches that lingered just a second too long.

I threw her a pass at one point, harder than necessary, and she caught it, shooting me a look.

"Trying to take me out now?" she asked.

"Just keeping things interesting," I replied, stepping in close again, lowering my voice. "Wouldn't want you getting bored."

She rolled her eyes, but there was a smile tugging at her lips.

The intensity of our one-on-one was undeniable, but soon the whole group was caught up in the game. Tamara was already on the court, making quick plays and adding to the energy. Chris, always up for a challenge, was running the court like he owned it. "Better keep up, Ruiz," I teased as I passed her the ball, grinning as I watched her focus shift into high gear. The court buzzed with our collective energy, the sound of sneakers on the hardwood and bursts of laughter turning practice into an all-out battle of skill and strategy.

During a break, she was catching her breath on the sideline, taking deep gulps of water. I swaggered over, my grin unapologetically cocky as I leaned against the bench next to her. "You're not bad out there," I teased.

Ruiz raised an eyebrow, her expression resolute as she met my gaze. "Thanks, I guess," she replied coolly.

"Keep it up," I said, my eyes locking with hers. "I'm enjoying this challenge."

A smirk played on her lips, her eyes lighting up with a spark of competitiveness. "Challenge accepted," she shot back, her tone laced with defiance.

Owen watched our exchange with a mix of frustration and jealousy, his focus constantly drifting toward Ruiz and me. At one point, he intercepted a pass meant for me, his jaw clenched with determination.

"Watch yourself, Callum," Owen grumbled, irritation clear in his tone.

I chuckled, letting my eyes briefly meet Ruiz's with a playful glint. "Always do, Owen," I replied smoothly, not letting my smirk fade.

By the end of practice, she and I had put on quite the show, leaving me with a rush of adrenaline. As we walked off the court together, I casually slung an arm around Ruiz's shoulders, my demeanor shifting to something more relaxed. Owen's bitterness was radiating off of him.

"Think he got the message?" I whispered in her ear.

"Definitely," she replied with a smirk.

"Let's grab a drink and blow off some steam," Tamara suggested as everyone started collecting their things. The idea was met with enthusiastic agreement from the group.

"Sounds good to me," I chimed in, my gaze flicking over to Ruiz. "Why don't you ride with me? It'll save you the trouble of driving."

She hesitated for a moment, her eyes darting toward Owen, but eventually nodded. "Sure, that sounds good."

As we walked towards the parking lot, I led the way to my sleek, black motorcycle. The polished surface gleamed under the parking lot lights, giving it an undeniable allure. I noticed her eyes widen.

"You've got to be kidding me," she murmured, eyeing the bike warily.

I sensed her hesitation. "Trust me, it's safer than it looks," I assured her, handing her a helmet.

"You always carry an extra helmet?" Ruiz asked with a raised eyebrow. "Let me guess, for the chance that one of your groupies might want to join you on a ride back to your place and make love?"

I smirked, not missing a beat. "First off, it's always smart to have an extra. Secondly, I'm not the make love type. I fuck."

She hesitated as she took the helmet from me, her fingers brushing against mine. She shot me a dubious glance, though her eyes betrayed a flicker of intrigue. "I don't know about this," she admitted.

I chuckled softly and tried to be reassuring. "I promise, you're in good hands," I said, sliding on my own helmet and swinging a leg over the bike. "Just hold on tight."

Ruiz took a deep breath, steeling herself as she settled behind me, her hands finding their place on my waist. Her arms shook slightly around me. The engine roared to life beneath us, its vibrations resonating through both of us as I maneuvered the motorcycle out of the parking lot and onto the street.

The cool night air rushed past us as we sped through the Franklin city streets, weaving through traffic with practiced ease. Her initial apprehension seemed to fade as the exhilaration of the ride took over. I could feel her grip on me tighten as we leaned into turns and accelerated down the straightaways.

I glanced back at her over my shoulder, a grin spreading across my face beneath the helmet. "Starting to like it, aren't you?" I shouted over the wind.

Her laughter rang out, carried away by the rush of air. Despite her earlier reservations, she was clearly enjoying the ride. The thrill of the speed and our close proximity seemed to be working its magic.

I leaned forward slightly. "Just imagine me between your legs," I called out. "It's the same sensation."

Her body stiffened behind me. The ride was having a powerful effect on her.

As we waited at a red light, the low hum of the motorcycle engine was the only sound breaking the quiet between us. Ruiz's hands gripped my waist and it felt good. I let my hand slide down to rest gently on her bare leg. The contact sent a jolt of electricity through me, and her skin responded with goosebumps popping up from the touch.

When the light changed to green, I reluctantly pulled my hand away and refocused on the road. She shifted slightly behind me, and I thought she might be disappointed at the loss of contact.

The city lights whizzed by us as we rode through the night, but her reaction to my touch was impossible to ignore. We arrived at the bar all too soon, and I parked the motorcycle with a smooth stop. Ruiz got off the bike, her legs a bit unsteady from the adrenaline. She took off her helmet, her hair a wild mess from the wind, but she had a bright smile on her face.

"Okay, maybe that wasn't so bad," Ruiz admitted, handing me back the helmet.

"Told you," I said, my voice full of triumph. "Ready for that drink now?"

We walked into the bar together, where Owen and Tamara were already gathered, drinks in hand. I gently took her hand, guiding her over to join them. As we approached, I leaned in close to her ear.

"What do you want to drink?" I whispered.

Ruiz looked at the selection, contemplating her options. "Any beer on tap is fine," she replied softly.

Owen glared directly at her, followed by a dramatic eye roll before he turned back to his conversation.

I released her hand and made my way to the bar to place our order.

I returned with the drinks to Ruiz taking a deep breath.

Chris arrived and took a seat next to me. I leaned against the bar, the post-practice adrenaline still buzzing in my veins. He nodded toward the rest of the team, who were scattered around, laughing and unwinding. "You know, Callum, I think this might be the best group we've had in years," he said, tapping his beer bottle against mine.

I took a sip, glancing over at the team. "Yeah, they're solid. Tamara's really stepped up her game lately. And Ruiz...well, she's full of surprises."

Chris chuckled, raising an eyebrow. "I've noticed you've been paying extra attention to her."

I smirked, playing it off. "Just making sure everyone's on their toes. Can't let them get too comfortable."

He grinned, shaking his head. "Right. Just keep telling yourself that. Also," Chris continued, a thoughtful look on his face. "We're looking at potential new client business, and it seems like we might be offering PR services now. Any thoughts on who you're considering for the team?"

I shrugged, trying to play it cool. "I've been thinking about Ruiz. She has a solid background in PR, doesn't she? And this would be a great chance for her to get her feet wet in something more challenging."

"Good call," Chris replied, nodding. "I was thinking we should bring in a couple of folks from marketing, too. We'll need a strong blend to really impress the client."

"Definitely," I said, already mentally drafting my Ruiz pitch. "I think having her on board would bring a fresh perspective, and she could really shine with the right guidance. But we can talk more about this at the office."

As the night wore on, I watched Ruiz enjoy herself, four beers in and clearly feeling tipsy. The bar was buzzing with energy, music playing, people chatting, and the room filled with the chatter of coworkers.

I wasn't trying to eavesdrop. I just happened to be sitting within perfect hearing distance. Totally different.

Tamara and Ruiz were off to the side, drinks in hand, and I caught Ruiz saying, "Thank you for not burning me at the stake and for understanding about the room assignments."

I had to bite back a grin.

Tamara waved her off immediately. "Please, you have nothing to thank me for. You would've been completely out of luck anyway, I already agreed to room with Terri from marketing."

Ruiz's head snapped toward her. "Oh, so you wouldn't have ditched Terry for me if the situation called for it?"

"Excuse you," Tamara shot back, laughing. "Terry already claimed me. It was legally binding."

"Unbelievable," Ruiz said, shaking her head, but she was smiling, really smiling. And I just sat there for a second, watching her, the sound of her laugh cutting through the noise of the bar, landing somewhere a little too deep in my chest.

As if on cue, Chris cleared his throat to get everyone's attention. "Just so you know, room assignments are going to be final by tomorrow," he announced. "So, if there's any last-minute changes or requests, now's the time to speak up."

I shot him a look, nodding in acknowledgment. "Ruiz and I are still good," I said, my gaze flicking back to Ruiz.

Chris gave me a half smile, clearly amused by the situation. "All right, then. Just making sure everyone's comfortable." He glanced around at the others, adding, "Should be a good trip. Let's keep things smooth, yeah?"

Just then, Owen's attention snapped to us, his expression darkening in a way that was almost immediate. He pushed back from his seat without a word and headed straight for the bathroom, jaw tight, like the news landed exactly where it was meant to.

I watched Ruiz's reaction, noting a mix of emotions as she glanced between me and Owen walking away. I took a sip of my beer, trying to act casual as the night's events took an unexpected turn.

Ruiz turned to Tamara and said, "I'm going outside for some air."

I had been keeping an eye on her, and without missing a beat, I stood up. "I'll join you," I said, not giving her a chance to refuse.

We stepped out into the crisp early winter night, the cool air a refreshing change from the bar's heat and noise. She leaned against the brick wall, shivering slightly as the chill set in. I took off my hoodie and draped it over her shoulders. She pulled it close, then visibly relaxed as the warmth from the fabric enveloped her.

"Thanks," she murmured, looking up at me with a grateful smile. The streetlights bathed us in a soft glow, casting a cocoon around us in the midst of the bustling night.

I stared at her for a moment, my gaze darkening, my heart racing. "Fuck it," I muttered, unable to hold back any longer. Before she could react, I pressed my body against hers and captured her lips in a searing kiss.

As our mouths moved together, the world seemed to blur and fade. The kiss was demanding and insistent, and she gasped against me. I took advantage of her reaction, deepening the kiss. My hand found hers and I pinned it above her head against the rough brick wall, holding it there with a firm, possessive grip.

My mind spun, but the thrill coursing through me was undeniable. Ruiz melted into the kiss, her body responding eagerly to mine. The cool night air, and my solid form pressing into her created a heady feeling that I knew would linger in my memory.

When we finally broke apart, we were both breathing heavily. My gaze locked with hers, filled with desire. "I've been wanting to do that all night," I admitted, my voice rough with emotion.

I eased my grip from her hands and throat, letting my touch linger for a moment before stepping back. Our breathing was still heavy, in sync with each other's.

"We should probably go inside," I whispered, reluctant.

Ruiz nodded, my skin still tingling from her touch. She straightened her clothes and took a deep breath, then followed me back into the bar. The noise enveloped us once more as we rejoined our friends.

Chris noticed our return and announced, "Okay, I'm going to head out." He glanced around and saw others nodding in agreement, signaling that it was time to call it a night.

Tamara glanced at Ruiz, concern etched on her face. "Alma, why don't you ride with me? You seem too drunk to drive and I'm sure you and Callum arrived on his death trap. You're definitely too drunk to hold on to him on his motorcycle. I can take you home."

A pang of disappointment hit me with the realization, but I nodded. "Yeah, that's a good idea."

Ruiz glanced between us, her expression reflecting gratitude and regret. "Thanks, Tamara," she said, offering me a small, apologetic smile.

She tugged my hoodie off her shoulders and held it out to me. I couldn't let her walk out in the cold like that. "It's cold out there, you should wear it," I said, pressing it back into her hands. She hesitated for a moment before pulling it on, and I felt a small sense of relief, knowing she was a bit warmer.

Tamara smiled reassuringly and put an arm around Ruiz's shoulders. "Let's get you home safe."

As we all moved toward the door, I trailed a few paces behind, my hands shoved into the pockets of my gym shorts. When we reached the parking lot, I stopped by my motorcycle and gave Ruiz a lingering look.

"Guess I'll see you tomorrow," I said, my voice low and carrying an undercurrent of unspoken words.

"Yeah, see you," she replied.

I watched as Tamara helped Ruiz into her car, my gaze lingering until they disappeared down the street. Seeing Ruiz walk away with my hoodie made me oddly happy, knowing that even in the smallest way, she carried a piece of me with her, but I shook that thought out of my head. The night air felt colder now, the rush of our earlier moment giving way to a lingering spark that I wouldn't easily forget.

Chapter Sixteen

ALMA

It was Wednesday night and my official first fake date with my fake boyfriend. What kind of sentence was that?

I was sitting in a corner booth at the diner Owen swore had the best pie in the city, the only place, according to him, that got cherry pie right. And if my memory served me correctly, Wednesdays were his favorite because that's when they ran the cherry pie special.

Which meant, yeah, I knew exactly what I was doing.

I smoothed my hands over the table, trying to ignore the tiny knot of nerves in my stomach when my phone buzzed. A WhatsApp message from Mami.

Mami: *Hi, mija! Just wanted to check in. Your papi needs some medication for his heart. Could you send a little extra to help out?*

My chest tightened instantly.

Me: *Of course, Mami. I'll send it right away.*

I wired the money without a second thought, even as my brain started doing that fun little spiral of numbers and budgets and okay, what can I cut this week. When it was done, I exhaled slowly, trying to shake it off. One thing at a time.

The bell above the diner door dinged.

I looked up, and of course, because the universe loves drama, Owen walked in. Wind-tousled blond hair, hands shoved in his jacket pockets like he just stepped out of a movie he didn't need to audition for. His eyes landed on me immediately.

He walked over, stopping at my booth. "Alma? What are you doing here?"

I lifted a shoulder, playing it casual. "Waiting for someone."

His brows pulled together. "Here?"

"Yes, Owen. Here."

He glanced around, already irritated. "You know this is my spot."

I blinked at him. "I'm sorry, is your name on the lease? Did I miss that plaque on the door?"

He sighed, running a hand through his hair. "You know what I mean."

"And you know you don't own public places, right?" I shot back, already feeling my patience thinning.

Before he could respond...ding. The door opened again. And there he was.

Callum.

Leather jacket, motorcycle helmet tucked under his arm. He took one look at the scene and strolled over, completely unbothered.

"Are you stalking my girl?" he asked Owen, like he was genuinely curious.

My girl.

My stomach did a tiny, traitorous flip.

Owen scoffed. "This is my spot."

Callum glanced around, unimpressed. "Didn't realize your name was on the lease."

I bit the inside of my cheek to keep from smiling.

Owen rolled his eyes, clearly over it. "Unbelievable. You two share a mind now, too?" He turned and headed to the counter, ordering his pie like this wasn't slowly killing him inside.

Callum slid into the booth across from me like he belonged there, setting his helmet down. "Is he still looking?" he asked casually.

I glanced past him. "Oh yeah. Front row seat."

"Good," he said.

And then, before I could even process it, he reached across the table and took my hands in his. Somehow warm, even though he'd just come in from the cold. My breath caught for half a second.

Out of the corner of my eye, I saw Owen stiffen, shake his head, and turn his back to us completely.

Callum squeezed my hands lightly. "You okay?" he asked.

I nodded, then let out a small laugh as Owen grabbed his pie, paid, and walked out without another glance.

The bell dinged again as the door shut behind him. I began to laughed uncontrollably. Because this? This was insane. And maybe...just a little bit perfect.

"Did you know we made the exact same joke?" I said, leaning forward, still laughing. "I nearly died when you asked him if his name was on the lease because I had literally just said that when he started whining about this place being his."

Callum blinked, then shook his head, a grin breaking across his face. "Who says that?" he scoffed. "Like, grow up, dude."

"Exactly!" I shot back.

And then, like we were both running on the same delayed brain signal, we froze. Because his hands were still wrapped around mine. I blinked down at them, then back up at him, and he was already looking at me.

We both moved at the exact same time, pulling back just a little too quickly, like we hadn't just been sitting there holding hands in the middle of a diner like it was completely normal.

"Right," I said, clearing my throat, tucking my hands back into my lap.

"Yeah," he grumbled, leaning back, dragging a hand through his hair.

Casual. Totally casual.

If you ignored the fact that my heart was suddenly doing jumping jacks and I was very aware of exactly where his hands had just been.

CALLUM

When I got home, the place felt too quiet. It always did. I tossed my keys onto the counter, shrugged off my jacket, and grabbed my sketchbook like it was some kind of lifeline. By the time I hit the couch, I was already flipping to a blank page, pencil in hand before I could even think about it. Because if I didn't draw, I thought and that was never a good idea.

My mind was loud tonight. Louder than usual. That low, familiar hum pressing in, like everything was just a little heavier than it should be. Like I was one wrong thought away from sinking into it.

So I sketched. Fast. Messy. Hard lines, rough edges, anything to keep my brain occupied. Anything but her. Ruiz. I exhaled sharply, dragging the pencil across the page like I could outrun it, but of course, I couldn't. She was there anyway. The way she laughed in the diner. The way her hands felt in mine, warm, soft, real. The way she looked at me like I wasn't...whatever the hell I usually was.

I pressed harder, the graphite digging into the paper. I hated it. I hated how she got under my skin without even trying. How she made things feel lighter for a second and then ten times heavier when I was alone again. That was the problem. That was always the problem.

I sketched faster, lines turning into shapes, shapes into something almost human before I scratched it out, frustrated. My jaw tightened as I dragged the pencil back and forth, trying to blur it into nothing. But she kept slipping through. In the curve of a line. In the tilt of a figure. In the space I couldn't quite erase. I gripped the pencil tighter, pushing until the page almost tore. Like if I pressed hard enough, I could get her out of my head. Out of my system, out of whatever the hell this was. But she didn't go. She never did.

* * *

A few nights later, I was sitting across from Chris in a late-night diner that smelled like burnt coffee and bad decisions. Not that diner. Different one. Neutral territory.

He was halfway through a stack of pancakes like it was a competitive sport, and I was stirring my coffee.

"You're not listening," Chris said, not even looking up.

"I am," I replied automatically.

"You're not," he repeated, finally glancing up, fork pointed at me like an accusation. "I just explained the entire Q3 pipeline strategy and you blinked at me like I spoke in ancient Greek."

I shrugged. "Maybe you did."

He squinted at me. "What's going on with you?"

"Nothing."

"Callum."

I sighed, leaning back in the booth. "I'm fine."

Chris set his fork down slowly, like he was preparing for battle. "You've been 'fine' for the last ten minutes while aggressively stirring an empty cup of coffee."

I glanced down. He wasn't wrong.

I moved the cup away. "Work's been busy."

"Sure."

"And the basketball thing."

"Sure."

"And..." I stopped myself.

Chris leaned forward slightly, eyes narrowing in interest. "And?"

I rubbed the back of my neck, exhaling. "Nothing. It's just Ruiz."

Chris's mouth twitched like he was trying not to smile. "Ah."

"Don't," I warned.

"I didn't say anything."

"You're about to."

He leaned back, folding his arms. "You said her name like it left a bad taste in your mouth."

I scoffed. "It did.."

"Sure it did.."

"She's just—" I paused, searching for the word. "A lot."

Chris nodded thoughtfully. "And yet you're here, not listening to me, thinking about her."

"I'm not thinking about her."

"You absolutely are."

I opened my mouth to argue, then stopped because damn it. I was.

Chris grinned now, fully entertained. "Wow. This is new."

"What is?"

"You," he said simply. "Like this."

"Like what?"

"Distracted. Annoyed. Slightly unhinged."

I rolled my eyes. "I'm always slightly unhinged."

"Yeah, but this is different. This has a name. And she wears slacks and talks back to you."

I huffed out a laugh despite myself. "It's not like that."

"It's exactly like that."

"It's not," I insisted, shaking my head. "It's just a thing. A situation."

"A 'situation,'" he repeated, amused. "Right. Because you usually sign up for shared hotel rooms for fun."

I froze for half a second. He clocked it immediately.

"Oh my god," Chris said, leaning forward. "You like her."

I shook my head, too quick. "No."

"You do."

"I don't."

"Callum."

I dragged a hand down my face. "It's not—" I exhaled sharply. "It's complicated."

Chris softened a little, the teasing fading just enough. "It always is."

I stared down at the table, jaw tight. "It's not a good idea."

"Why?"

I let out a dry laugh. "Take your pick."

He watched me for a second. "You know, you don't have to make everything harder than it needs to be."

I glanced up. "That's rich, coming from you."

He smirked. "I'm serious. It's okay to like someone, man."

I looked away, something in my chest tightening in a way I didn't love.

"You don't get it," I said, exasperated.

"Then help me," he said simply.

I hesitated because how did I explain that every time something good showed up, I was already waiting for it to go wrong? That it was easier to keep things surface-level, controlled, temporary? That letting someone in felt a lot like handing them a loaded weapon?

I shook my head. "It's just easier not to."

Chris studied me, then nodded slowly. "Yeah. Easier. But not better."

I didn't respond.

He leaned back again, picking up his fork like the conversation didn't just hit somewhere a little too close. "For what it's worth," he added casually, "she seems like she's worth the risk."

I huffed out a quiet laugh. "You don't even know her."

"I don't have to," he said. "I know you."

I shook my head, but there was no bite left in it.

And as much as I wanted to brush it off, to file it away under not happening, my mind drifted right back to her anyway. Like I had nowhere else to go.

Chapter Seventeen

ALMA

As I arrived at the gym for the first company basketball game with Tamara at the end of the week, nervousness settled over me. The gym buzzed with excitement, employees from various departments already warming up and chatting animatedly. Just as I was about to head towards the bleachers, Owen walked up to me, catching me by surprise.

"Hey, Alma," he said with a charming smile. "How's your week been?"

I blinked, a little flustered but pleased by Owen's attention. "Hey! It's been good, busy, but good. How about yours?"

Owen leaned in slightly, his tone flirtatious. "Same here, but seeing you makes it better."

A flush of happiness spread through me; maybe my plan was already working. Callum walked into the gym, his presence commanding attention as always. My heart skipped a beat when I noticed him narrow his eyes, his gaze locking onto me and Owen.

Was he reacting to me talking with Owen? A shiver of uncertainty ran down my spine. But Owen, completely oblivious to the tension, headed off to the bench to get ready for the game.

Callum strode over to me, his expression dark and unreadable. He stopped right in front of me, his eyes flicking briefly to where Owen had been standing before focusing back on me.

"Enjoying yourself?" Callum asked, his tone laced with irritation.

I crossed my arms, trying to appear unfazed. "Just catching up. Is there a problem with that?"

Callum's jaw tightened. "Funny, didn't seem like it was just catching up."

I raised an eyebrow, meeting his intense gaze. "What's it to you, Callum? This is part of the plan."

He took a step closer, his voice lowering to a growl. "You're right. Just don't forget our deal, Ruiz. I'm actually playing this game for you two to end up together. Then I get what I want, and you get what you want."

My heart pounded in my chest, a mix of fear and exhilaration at his proximity. "I haven't forgotten. But remember, we're supposed to be convincing everyone, including Owen."

Callum's eyes softened slightly, but I could still sense the jealousy simmering beneath the surface. "Just keep in mind who your 'boyfriend' is supposed to be."

Before I could respond, Tamara approached me, her cheerful voice cutting through the tension. "Hey, you two ready for the game?" she asked.

I forced a smile, nodding. "Yeah, let's do this."

The game started off intense, the gym filled with the sounds of squeaking sneakers, dribbling basketballs, and the constant cheers from the sidelines from others in the company. Callum and I moved together effortlessly across the court, like we'd been playing together for years. We called out plays, set each other up for shots, and our rhythm was on point. The scoreboard was proof of our efforts, our team was dominating.

Every time Callum passed me the ball, my confidence soared. I dribbled quickly, dodging defenders, and sank several baskets with precision. Callum was just as impressive, driving to the hoop with such power that he made difficult shots look easy. Our teamwork was undeniable.

But as the game progressed, I noticed something off. Callum was deliberately avoiding passing the ball to Owen, even when he was wide open. I could see the frustration building on Owen's face, but the adrenaline of the game kept me focused, pushing the thought aside as we continued to play.

By halftime, we were up by 12 points. As we gathered by the benches, Owen, his face flushed with anger, marched over to Callum. "What's your problem, Callum? I've been open the entire first half!"

Callum shrugged nonchalantly, taking a swig from his water bottle. "Does it matter? We're up by 12 points."

Owen stepped closer, his jaw clenched. "It matters to me. We're supposed to be a team."

The tension was thick as they squared off, and I could feel the unease in the air. I quickly stepped between them, arms outstretched to keep them apart. "Grow up, both of you! Act your age. This is a team effort, and we need to play like one."

Callum glared at Owen over my shoulder, but he stayed silent. Owen clenched his fists, taking a deep breath to calm down. The rest of the team exchanged uneasy glances, the celebratory mood of halftime dampened by the confrontation.

As the second half started, the tension could be cut with a knife. Callum kept playing with his usual power, but it was clear he hadn't changed his attitude towards Owen. He still refused to pass the ball to him, despite my earlier intervention.

The game picked up its high pace again, and Callum and I continued to dominate the court. I tried to compensate by passing to Owen whenever I could, but the strain on the team dynamics was obvious. Owen's frustration was clear in his increasingly aggressive play, and I couldn't help but worry about how this was going to end.

Despite the internal strife, we managed to maintain our lead. When the final buzzer sounded, we emerged victorious. The scoreboard flashed our win, the margin still comfortably in our favor.

As the team gathered to celebrate, the tension from earlier lingered. The conflict between Callum and Owen cast a shadow over what should've been a triumphant moment. I caught Callum's eye, silently pleading with him to make amends. He sighed, running a hand through his hair, but his expression stayed stubborn.

Owen, still simmering with anger, shook his head and headed towards the exit. I watched him go, relief and frustration swirling inside me. Sure, we'd won the game, but the cost of that victory left me feeling uneasy. As the team started to disperse, I could only hope that tonight's tension wouldn't carry over into the office by the time Monday rolled around.

* * *

The next day, I lounged lazily in bed, wrapped in my cozy blanket, flipping through the pages of a book. The morning light streamed through the window, casting a warm, golden glow on the words. My phone buzzed on the nightstand, and I reached over to check the message. It was from Owen.

Owen: *Hey, want to hang out today?*

My heart skipped a beat. I hadn't expected to hear from him, especially after last night's game. I quickly typed a reply.

Me: *Sure, sounds good. When and where?*

He responded almost immediately, suggesting we meet at the local park in an hour. I agreed, set my book aside, and reluctantly got out of bed. I brushed my teeth, dressed casually in jeans and a sweater, and pulled my hair into a loose ponytail.

I hesitated for a second, keys dangling in my hand like they were waiting for me to make a life-altering decision, which, okay, maybe dramatic, but still.

What would my fake boyfriend say about me going to meet my ex? I paused. He'd be proud, right? I mean, this was the whole point of the plan. Endgame: me and Owen, back together, riding off into the sunset like a perfectly stable, emotionally healthy couple who definitely didn't implode once already.

So Callum wouldn't care. He shouldn't care. Right?

I chewed on the inside of my cheek, overthinking it for a solid ten seconds before mentally shoving the actual answer, whatever that was, into a box labeled *Do Not Open.*

"Yep. This is fine," I muttered to myself. And with that, I headed out the door.

When I arrived at the park, I spotted Owen near a large oak tree, setting up a picnic. The sight of him made me smile. He looked up and waved.

"Hey," he greeted, his smile warm and genuine. "I brought a picnic."

"I can see that," I replied, feeling both excitement and nervousness. "This looks great."

We sat down on the blanket, the park buzzing with life around us. Birds chirped in the trees, children laughed and played on the nearby playground, and joggers passed by on the path, their footsteps rhythmic against the pavement. Owen had packed an impressive spread: sandwiches, fresh fruit, and a couple of thermoses filled with steaming coffee.

As we ate and talked, I relaxed into the moment. Owen was easy to be around, his charm and humor making the time fly by. It was nice, just being here with him, away from the chaos of work and the tangled mess of my thoughts. After a while, the conversation shifted to more personal topics.

"So," Owen began, his voice tinged with hesitance, "are you really dating Callum?"

I took a moment before answering, carefully choosing my words because, while I needed to convince Owen that Callum was my fake boyfriend, I also didn't want to hurt his feelings. "We're not officially dating. We're just spending time together."

Owen nodded slowly, looking thoughtful. I hesitated, but the question that had been nagging at me for weeks finally slipped out.

"Owen," I said, my voice softer than I intended, "why did you break up with me? You never really gave me an explanation."

He sighed, looking down at his hands like they held the answer, like maybe if he stared long enough the right words would magically appear. Then he looked back up at me.

"I was scared," he said. "I really loved you, and it all happened so fast. It freaked me out. I wasn't ready for how intense it felt."

"Fast?" I echoed, letting out a small, disbelieving laugh. "Owen, it was two years. That's not exactly a whirlwind romance. I wasn't out here pressuring you to put a ring on it." I crossed my arms. "Is that what you thought? That I was about to go full Bridezilla?"

He winced slightly. "Yes and no."

I raised an eyebrow. "Wow. Super clear. Love that for us."

He ran a hand through his hair, trying again. "I just, things were getting serious, and instead of leaning into it, I panicked. It wasn't you. It was me not knowing how to handle something that actually mattered that much."

"And now?" I asked, quieter this time, even though part of me wasn't sure I wanted to hear the answer.

Owen reached for my hand, his fingers wrapping around mine like they'd done a hundred times before.

"Now," he said, holding my gaze, "I want to keep seeing you. But slow. No pressure. I don't want to mess this up again."

My heart did that annoying little hopeful thing I thought I'd buried months ago.

We ended up talking for a while after that, lighter things, safer things. Old memories, inside jokes, the kind of laughter that feels like slipping back into something you already know by heart. The tension from earlier softened, easing into something almost comfortable.

And when we finally made it back to my car, Owen turned to me, that same familiar look in his eyes.

"I'll call you later?"

"Sure," I replied, wrapping my arms around him in a hug. "Thanks for today. It was really nice."

As we pulled away, Owen leaned in and kissed me goodbye. It was gentle and sweet, exactly how he was. But as soon as his lips left mine, my thoughts shifted back to Callum. His kiss was anything but gentle, heated, intense, full of a desire that left me breathless. My cheeks flushed at the memory of the kiss outside the bar, the way he made me feel like I was the only person in the world.

Owen smiled, watching as I got into my car and drove away. But as I headed home, my thoughts were consumed by Callum and the complicated feelings he stirred within me, making it impossible to shake him from my mind.

And just like that, I wasn't so sure where I stood anymore.

Chapter Eighteen

ALMA

The weeks flew by and as the end of the year approached, the company was in full swing, wrapping up sales numbers for the quarter. My days were packed with meetings, phone calls, and endless spreadsheets. I was determined to close out strong and hit my targets, pushing myself to the limit.

My hard work paid off. I not only met my goals but exceeded them, securing a significant end-of-year bonus. The recognition felt rewarding, and I took a moment to savor the accomplishment amidst the office's busy atmosphere. It was nice to feel proud of what I'd achieved as I joined my colleagues in celebrating the successful quarter.

Christmas arrived in a whirlwind of festive activities. India and I decorated our townhouse with twinkling lights and a small tree, creating a cozy holiday atmosphere. Exchanging gifts with friends, I enjoyed the simple pleasures of the season. It was a happy surprise to find out that the office was closed for the last week of the year, giving me a much-needed break.

During this downtime, I immersed myself in the comfort of home and I spent time with India, indulging in the nostalgic joy of baking cookies and watching movies. The laughter and sweet aroma of baking filled the air as we reminisced about old times and made new memories.

One late-December afternoon, as India and I lounged in my living room with a hot cocoa in hand, I received a text from Tamara.

Tamara: *Hey! I'm having a New Year's Eve party at my place. You and India should definitely come. It's going to be fun!*

Excitement bubbled up inside me. The thought of ringing in the new year surrounded by friends was exactly what I needed. I quickly responded with an enthusiastic yes.

"Tamara's throwing a New Year's Eve party, and we're invited!" I announced, unable to contain my excitement.

"Sounds perfect," India replied, her voice brightening. "I'm in!"

* * *

New Year's Eve arrived with a crisp chill in the air, the city streets glittering with festive lights. I spent the day preparing, slipping into a sparkly dress that shimmered under the light. I applied my makeup carefully, determined to look my best for the celebration. By evening, I was ready and eager to join my friends.

The car ride to Tamara's place was filled with laughter and music. India and I chatted excitedly as we made our way there. When we arrived, we were met with a warm, welcoming atmosphere. Tamara had truly outdone herself, decorating her apartment with streamers, balloons, and an array of delicious snacks and drinks.

As the night unfolded, the place buzzed with energy. People mingled and danced to the music. My friends and I took turns pouring champagne, toasting to the good times we'd shared and the new adventures ahead.

At one point, I stepped out onto the balcony, taking in the city lights twinkling against the night sky. The cool air was refreshing, and I wrapped my shawl tighter around my shoulders. Owen, who had arrived shortly after we had, joined me and handed me a glass of champagne.

"Hey," he said, leaning against the railing beside me. "Quite the view, huh?"

"It's beautiful," I replied, taking a sip of my drink.

We stood in comfortable silence for a moment, the party sounds muffled by the glass door behind us. The city below sparkled with life, a tapestry of stories unfolding beneath the night sky.

"I've been thinking," Owen said, his voice soft but steady. "I'd like to start the new year with someone special. Someone who means a lot to me."

I turned to look at him, my heart quickening. "Oh?"

He smiled, a touch of nervousness in his eyes. "Yeah. And I was hoping that your kiss would be the one I enter the new year with."

I felt my cheeks flush despite the cold air. "Owen, that's really sweet."

He moved a bit closer, his gaze fixed on mine. "I mean it, Alma. You know how much you mean to me, don't you?"

A swirl of emotions overtook me. I leaned against the balcony, putting the city behind me to face him, while my mind raced. I tried to calm my thoughts with what was happening inside when the front door swung open and Callum entered. His gaze locked onto mine immediately and sent a shiver through me.

I found myself drawn to him, unable to look away. Callum moved through the crowd with a deliberate ease, his eyes never leaving mine. The connection between us was electric, pulling me in despite the man wanting to kiss me at midnight right in front of me.

"Alma?" Owen's voice jolted me from my trance. "You okay?"

"Uh, yeah, I'm fine," I said, forcing a smile. "I just need to go inside for a moment. I have to go to the bathroom really quick."

CALLUM

I watched as Ruiz excused herself from Owen and slipped back into the apartment. The party was in full swing, but her focus was clearly elsewhere. She moved through the room with a subtle grace.

She was absolutely stunning tonight. Her sparkly dress clung to her curves in all the right places, highlighting her voluptuous figure. It shimmered under the lights, accentuating the way she moved with a natural elegance that was both captivating and magnetic.

As Ruiz made her way through the guests, I followed her discreetly, curious about what was on her mind. She ended up in a dimly lit room at the back of the apartment. I slipped in behind her and gently but firmly pushed the door closed.

The room was shrouded in shadows, casting an enigmatic glow over her features. The dim light accentuated her beauty even more, her dress reflecting the faint light and making her look like a vision from another world. Her breath caught as she turned to face me, her eyes wide with surprise.

"Callum," she whispered, her voice laden with tension.

I took a step closer, letting the intensity of my gaze convey my feelings. "Couldn't wait to see me, could you?"

She struggled to find her voice. "What are you doing here?" she asked.

A smirk curved my lips as I met her gaze. "I came to see you. And I think you've been waiting for me, too."

For the first time in a while, the weight that usually sat heavy on my chest felt lighter, almost manageable. There was a clarity in my thoughts, a steadiness in my mood that had been missing for so long. I could feel it, the subtle shift, like something inside me had clicked back into place. Maybe the new meds were finally doing their job, smoothing out the edges that had felt so rough for too long. It was a strange sensation, being this...okay. And with Ruiz standing so close, that okay felt even more solid, like I was starting to regain a part of myself I thought I'd lost.

She seemed caught between the need to push me away and the urge to pull me closer. The air between us crackled with tension, a magnetic pull that seemed to draw us together.

"You shouldn't be here," she said, though her voice wavered, betraying her resolve. "I wanted a moment to clear my head."

"But I am," I replied, stepping closer until there was barely any space left between us. "And you're glad I am. Admit it."

She looked up at me, the heat of the moment clearly overwhelming her. I could tell she wanted to deny it. Instead, she leaned into me, unable to resist the pull between us.

Just as I felt her giving in to the tension, the distant sound of the countdown to midnight began. The partygoers' voices surged, growing louder with each number, pulling us back into the reality of the cele-bration.

"Twenty...Nineteen...Eighteen..."

The countdown pulsed through the room, my mind racing. I had to pull away. "Gotta go," I grumbled, stepping back abruptly.

As much as I wanted to close the distance, to kiss her, to pull her into me like it was the most natural thing in the world, I didn't because my brain decided now was the perfect time to bring up Soledad.

New Year's. The last time that night actually meant something, it was with her. And the memory hit in that quiet, sneaky way, no warning, just suddenly there, sitting heavy in my chest like it owned the place.

I swallowed, jaw tightening. I couldn't explain it and I didn't want to. But I felt it. And the last thing I was about to do was mix that, what-ever the hell that was, with Ruiz. She deserved better than being tangled up in some leftover ghost I hadn't dealt with. So yeah, I wanted her. Badly. But I took a step back anyway.

Her confusion and hurt were evident. "What? Why?"

I paused at the door, struggling to mask the emotions beneath my cool facade. "I'm not exactly boyfriend material, remember?" I said, letting out a quiet breath, more to myself than to her. I shoved my hands in my pockets, rocking back slightly on my heels like that might somehow make it land lighter. "And New Year's kisses..." I glanced at her, then away again. "...those are kind of reserved for the real ones."

ALMA

"Fifteen...Fourteen...Thirteen..."

The countdown rang out, each number louder than the last. My heart was still racing, but I forced myself to push through the room and find the kitchen, needing a moment to regroup.

I moved through people, my steps heavy with the weight of what had just happened. I reached for a glass of champagne, but Owen was there, concern etched on his face.

"Ten...Nine...Eight..."

"Alma, you okay?" he asked softly, his voice filled with genuine worry.

I tried to smile, but it felt forced. "Yeah, I just needed a drink."

Owen handed me a glass, and our fingers brushed briefly. The touch was a small comfort, a grounding presence amidst the chaos of the night.

"Seven...Six...Five..."

The countdown echoed through the apartment, growing louder with each second. I stood there, feeling frozen, my heart aching from the unexpected turn of events. I took a deep breath, trying to gather myself before heading back to the party, seeking solace in the drink Owen had given me.

"Four...Three...Two..."

As the final seconds counted down, Owen stepped closer, his eyes searching mine. "Alma, can I...?"

"One...Happy New Year!"

Before Owen could finish his sentence, emotion surged through me. I leaned in, closing the distance between us, and pressed my lips to his. The kiss was warm and gentle, reflecting the kindness that Owen always showed. Outside, fireworks exploded, their colors painting the night sky, but for a fleeting moment, my mind flashed back to Callum. His touch, his kiss...they were so different from Owen's gentle affection.

When the kiss ended, Owen smiled down at me. "Happy New Year, Alma."

Owen leaned in. And for a second, just a second, I thought, this is it. This is what I planned. What I wanted. What I was supposed to help make happen. He was right there. Practically mine again. Mission accomplished.

So why did it feel like something in my chest was pulling in the opposite direction?

Because of him. Because of Callum. He hit me out of nowhere, like he always did, those stupid, piercing eyes. And suddenly, all I could think about was what it would feel like if he looked at me like that in a moment like this. If he chose me.

I tried to shake it off. Didn't matter, it didn't mean anything. I didn't want that. I didn't do that. Right? Except the thought stuck. Burrowed in. Made it hard to breathe for a second. Because here was the thing, he didn't want me. Apparently, he was not built for that. So what the hell was I doing, standing there thinking about him like he was something I could actually have?

I shifted, my hands coming up against Owen's chest as I leaned back, stopping him.

"Owen," I said, my voice steady, "we said we'd take it slow. You said you wanted to take it slow. So, that's what we're doing."

"Oh, okay. You're right," he replied.

The night kept moving, music, laughter, champagne popping somewhere in the background, but I wasn't really in it, not fully. Because no matter how much I tried to focus on anything else, my attention kept drifting back to him and I couldn't decide if that was a problem or something a whole lot worse.

Chapter Nineteen

CALLUM

A few days later, I sat on the familiar couch in Dr. Evans' office, the air thick with the scent of lavender. It was a cozy space, designed to put me at ease, but today I felt a little more restless than usual.

"How have things been going since we last spoke?" Dr. Evans asked, her voice calm.

I shrugged, fidgeting with the hem of my shirt. "Honestly? The medication has been helping. It's like a fog has lifted a bit. I can think more clearly, but..." I paused, my thoughts shifting to Ruiz. "I've been sketching whenever I feel overwhelmed, just like you suggested. It really does help take my mind off the dark thoughts, but there's something else."

"What's that?" she encouraged gently.

"This girl, Ruiz," I said, trying to keep my voice steady. "I'm developing feelings for her, feelings I can't ignore, no matter how hard I try. It's frustrating, and I keep telling myself it's a bad idea."

Dr. Evans leaned forward slightly. "Why do you feel that way?"

I let out a heavy sigh. "I just don't think I'm deserving of that kind of connection. My past relationships have shown me that I mess things up. I can't help but think that this will end the same way."

"Callum," she said softly, "you need to envision yourself accepting love. You are deserving of it, regardless of your past. It doesn't determine your fate with future relationships."

I looked down, grappling with her words. It felt foreign to imagine myself worthy of something like that. "It's just hard to shake the feeling that I'll only end up hurting her."

"Recognize that feeling, but don't let it dictate your actions. You're in a different place now. You have the tools to navigate your emotions and build something healthy."

I nodded slowly, her encouragement a flicker of light in the midst of my uncertainty. But the weight of my fears still lingered, casting a shadow over the possibility of happiness.

Chapter Twenty

ALMA

Post-New Year's, the office felt like someone had hit the mute button on chaos. Gone was the end-of-year frenzy, the frantic emails, the "circle back" energy, the general sense that everything was on fire. In its place? A weird, almost suspicious calm. The kind where everyone's still showing up, still clicking away at their keyboards, but you just know another storm is brewing.

I didn't hate it. In fact, I kind of needed it, because my brain? Not calm. Not even a little. Every time I tried to focus on work, my thoughts would drift straight to Jamaica. The trip. The rooming situation. The whole fake boyfriend thing that somehow felt less fake by the day, which was concerning.

So I did what any emotionally stable woman would do. I buried myself in work. Emails? Answered. Spreadsheets? Spreadsheeted. Random tasks no one asked me to do? Done with enthusiasm. Anything to avoid thinking about the fact that I hadn't talked to Owen since New Year's. Or Callum. Which, honestly? Felt illegal. Those two had somehow become the main characters in my personal chaos, and now, radio silence.

I wasn't sure if they were giving me space or if they were just over my shenanigans. Both seemed equally plausible. But either way, I accepted the reprieve, because for the first time in a while, things were quiet and maybe I could figure out what the hell I actually wanted before everything picked back up again.

One afternoon during our weekly catch-up, Chris casually slid a folder across the table like he wasn't about to alter the trajectory of my entire life. My heart immediately started doing the cha-cha.

"So," he said, leaning back in his chair, completely nonchalantly, "that PR opportunity I mentioned what feels like a lifetime ago? Apologies for the whole mention it once and then vanish into thin air thing. The client wanted to wait until after the holidays." He tapped the folder. "Here's the brief."

I looked down and blinked. And then blinked again. Because this wasn't a folder. This was a textbook. This was freshman year, *'Intro to Ruining Your GPA'* level material.

"Wow," I said, flipping it open like I knew what I was doing. "Chris, this is extensive." I glanced up at him. "I didn't even think I'd get this far in the selection process. Be honest, what are my chances here? Are we talking romcom third act miracle or background character energy?"

He smiled, like he already knew I was spiraling. "Honestly? I think you've got a great shot. Your work ethic stands out, and this client is looking for fresh perspective."

My stomach flipped.

"Okay, but 'great shot' in a Hunger Games kind of way? Because you also said spots are limited."

He nodded. "They are. So yeah, there's pressure. But that's not a bad thing."

I flipped another page, trying to look calm, collected, like I wasn't internally screaming. "What's the timeline? When do I have to present this masterpiece that will determine my future?"

"A few weeks after the Jamaica trip," he said. "So don't rush it before then, but don't ignore it either."

"Ah," I nodded. "So, mentally relax on a beach while also quietly panicking in the background. I can do that."

Chris chuckled. "Exactly."

I tapped the folder lightly. "Okay. Any insider tips? What are the managers looking for? Besides my sanity slowly unraveling?"

"Creativity," he said. "But grounded in strategy. They want to see you. What makes your perspective different."

I nodded slowly, letting that sink in. This was my opportunity to shine. No pressure or anything. Because it wasn't just about me, it was never just about me. I thought about Mami. Papi. The calls. The money. The quiet "we're okay" that never really meant okay.

I straightened a little in my seat, closing the folder with more confidence than I felt.

"I won't let this slip away," I said.

And I meant it.

Landing this PR position would feel like stepping into a dream, one I'd been chasing so long that it almost felt unreal. A steady paycheck doing the kind of work I'd always wanted, without scrambling for side gigs or worrying about bills getting paid late. I wouldn't just be writing press materials; I'd be creating strategies, managing campaigns, working with clients who trusted me to elevate their brands.

This job could change everything. It could mean no more worrying about whether I'd saved enough to book a flight to the Dominican Republic. It could mean finally feeling like I wasn't just keeping my head above water but moving forward. All I had to do was prove I deserved it.

CALLUM

I stared at my phone, Opened the thread. Closed it. Opened it again and began to type.

Me: *We should talk about Jamaica.*

Deleted. Too vague. Sounded like I was about to dump her, which was impressive considering she was not even my real girlfriend.

I tried again.

Me: *We need to get our story straight for Jamaica. You free tonight?*

I hovered over send. This was strategic. Logistical. Necessary. Not because I wanted to see her, obviously.

I hit send before I could overthink it into oblivion.

Three dots appear almost immediately. Great. Cool. Loved that my heart just did a full sprint.

Ruiz: *wow. no hello? no "how are you"? straight to business. romantic.*

I smirked despite myself.

Me: *Hello, Ruiz. How are you? Now that we've covered pleasantries, be ready in an hour.*

Her typing bubble popped up again.

Ruiz: *you're insufferable*

Ruiz: *...see you in an hour*

I locked my phone, tossing it onto the couch like that didn't go exactly how I wanted it to.

* * *

Later that night, she was sitting on the opposite end of the couch, legs tucked under her, wearing something soft and deceptively innocent, oversized sweatshirt, yet again. It was like she knew it drove me wild. Because it did. It really really did.

I leaned back, arm stretched along the back of the couch like I owned the place. (I didn't. But commitment to the bit mattered.)

"So," I said, glancing over at her. "Jamaica."

She narrowed her eyes slightly. "Wow. You really know how to set the mood."

"I try."

She huffed out a laugh, adjusting her position so she was angled more toward me. "Okay, fine. What about Jamaica?"

I sat forward a little, elbows on my knees. "If we're doing this, really doing this, we need rules."

"Rules?" she echoed, skeptical. "What is this, a contract negotiation?"

"Exactly," I said. "Except the stakes are higher. We're dealing with public perception."

She rolled her eyes. "Oh my God."

"I'm serious," I continued, glancing at her. "We're sharing a room. People are going to assume things. Owen is going to definitely assume things."

Her expression shifted slightly at his name, but she nodded. "Okay, so what are these 'rules?'"

I held up a finger. "One: no breaking character in public. Not even for a second."

She nodded slowly. "Okay, that's fair."

"Two," I went on, "we need to actually act like we like each other."

She snorted. "That might be the hardest one for you."

I glanced at her, unimpressed. "Please. I'm very likable."

She raised an eyebrow. "Debatable."

I ignored that. "Point is, we can't half-ass this. Hand holding. Casual touches. Inside jokes. The whole thing."

"Okay..." she said slowly. "And three?"

I paused for half a second, watching her.

"Three," I said, voice dropping just a notch, "you trust me."

Her eyes flicked up to mine.

"Completely," I added. "No second-guessing in the moment. If I do something, you go with it."

She studied me, searching my face like she was trying to decide if I was about to ruin her life.

"Callum," she said carefully, "that feels like a trap."

I huffed out a quiet laugh. "It's not a trap. It's strategy."

"Your strategies tend to involve chaos."

"Controlled chaos," I corrected.

She shook her head, but there was a hint of a smile there. "And what do you get out of all this?"

I leaned back again, letting the question hang for a second longer than necessary. Because there were a lot of answers to that. Most of which I was not about to say out loud.

Instead, I shrugged lightly. "Entertainment."

She narrowed her eyes. "You're unbelievable."

"Yet here I am," I said, glancing at her, "on your couch. Helping you get your ex back."

Her gaze lingered on mine for a second and she went quiet, which, coming from Ruiz, was my first red flag.

I glanced over and she was staring down at her hands like they had suddenly become the most interesting thing in the room. Fidgeting. Avoiding eye contact. Yeah. Definitely not a good sign.

"Callum…" she started, and I already did't like the tone. "So, I hung out with Owen a few weeks ago."

Cool.

Cool cool cool.

My jaw tightened, but I keep my face neutral, leaning back like this was just another casual Tuesday night conversation and not something that just punched me square in the chest.

"It was innocent," she added quickly. "We went on a picnic. It just happened."

A picnic. Of course it was a picnic. What is he, a Nicholas Sparks character?

She paused, then rushed, "But before you say anything, this is a good thing. We're moving in the right direction. And"—she hesitated, finally looking up at me—"he wanted to kiss me on New Year's."

There it was. She watched me like she was waiting for a reaction, like I was supposed to hand her some kind of approval stamp.

I tilted my head slightly. "And why didn't you?"

"The ruse," she said, holding up her fingers in air quotes. "What's the point if we're still together?"

I let out a quiet breath, nodding once.

"Right."

Ah yes, the plan. The whole point of this.

"Well done, young grasshopper," I said, forcing a smirk, like this was exactly what I wanted to hear. Like my chest didn't just do something weird and inconvenient. Relief flickered through me, sharp, immediate, traitorous. And right behind it? Something else. Something I didn't want to name, because the truth is, a part of me wished she had kissed him. Just so whatever the hell this was, whatever I was feeling, could've been over before it even really started.

But instead? Here we are.

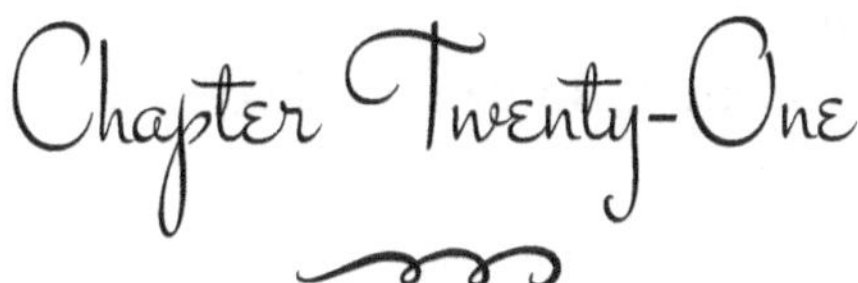

Chapter Twenty-One

ALMA

It was the day before the Jamaica trip, and I could hardly contain my excitement. My bedroom was a whirlwind of clothes, with everything from sun hats to swimsuits scattered across the floor. India was helping me pack, and the air buzzed with anticipation.

"Do you really need to bring five pairs of shoes?" India teased, holding up a pair of strappy sandals.

"You never know what you might need," I said with a grin, tossing another dress into my suitcase.

Holding up a brightly patterned bikini, India said, "Well this is adorable! You're definitely going to need this."

I laughed, taking the bikini from her. "Yeah, definitely."

As we continued to pack, India shot me a sly smile. "So, rooming with Callum, huh? Are you sure you're going to be okay with that?"

I rolled my eyes playfully. "Yes, I'm sure. Nothing's going to happen."

She raised an eyebrow. "You say that now, but I've seen the way you two look at each other."

I hesitated for a moment, then decided it was time to be honest. I took a deep breath. "Actually, there's something I need to tell you."

India stopped what she was doing and looked at me expectantly. "What is it?"

I bit my lip, then blurted out, "Callum and I have this...agreement. A fake boyfriend proposition."

The room fell silent as India absorbed what I'd just said. "Wait, what? Fake boyfriend?"

I nodded. "Yeah. It's a long story, but basically, Callum agreed to pretend to be my boyfriend to make Owen jealous. And in return, if we succeed"—I stopped and hesitated but continued— "he gets...one night with me."

India blinked at me like I'd just confessed to arson. "Hold up. Hold up. A few questions," she said, lifting her hands. "First of all, what exactly does 'succeed' mean? And second, one night with him? That's what he wanted? What does that even mean?"

"I mean, succeed means getting Owen back," I said, like it should've been obvious, even though the words felt shaky coming out. "That's the whole point. If he sees me happy, moving on, i.e., if he thinks someone else wants me, then maybe he'll realize what he lost." I nodded again, feeling a bit self-conscious. "And yes. Just one night. And as far as what it means, I assume he wants to have sex. Right?"

Her mouth dropped open. "And you agreed to this?"

"It seemed like a good idea at the time," I said with a shrug. "I wanted to make Owen realize what he was missing, and I could really use this promotion. And Callum, well, he has his own reasons."

India shook her head in disbelief. "Wow. That's intense. Are you sure you're okay with this?"

I smiled, trying to reassure her. "Yes, I'm okay with it. I'll essentially get what I want. Plus, it's just one night, and it's not like I'm going to fall for him or anything."

She looked skeptical. "You say that now, but things can get compli- cated. Just be careful, okay?"

"I will," I promised. "But honestly, I'm more excited about this trip than anything else. Let's focus on that."

India nodded in agreement. "Okay. Let's get you packed and ready for Jamaica. It's going to be an amazing trip, and I'm so jealous."

With that, we went back to packing. Even with the underlying tension, I felt a wave of relief from having shared everything with my bestie. The excitement for the trip and the adventures ahead easily overshadowed any lingering doubts I had. I couldn't wait to see what Jamaica had in store for me.

CALLUM

As I arrived at the terminal with the rest of the company, the early hour and the collective sleepiness were noticeable. It was only 5:00 a.m., and the terminal was filled with the low murmur of quiet greetings and the clatter of rolling suitcases on the tiled floor. Ruiz was there with Tamara, each of them stifling yawns as they chatted about the trip ahead.

Chris sidled up next to me as we waited in line to check our bags, his voice low and still thick with sleep. "Man, I could use about three more hours of shut eye. Early flights should be illegal."

I chuckled, nodding in agreement. "Tell me about it. I'm barely functioning right now."

He glanced over at Ruiz, who was laughing at something Tamara said, her eyes bright despite the early hour. "You ready for this trip?"

I gave a nonchalant shrug, but my eyes lingered on Ruiz. "Yeah, I'm ready. Just hoping to get through it without too many surprises."

Chris smirked, picking up on my focus. "Sure, no surprises. Let's just see how that works out for you."

I spotted Owen approaching, a smile on his face. He handed Ruiz a steaming cup of coffee. "I figured you'd need it," he said, his eyes twinkling with genuine affection.

I watched as her eyes softened, clearly touched by his thoughtfulness. "Thank you. You always know what I need," she said, her voice carrying a hint of warmth.

A pang of jealousy twisted in my chest as I watched them. I wanted to be the one she looked at like that, with that soft admiration in her eyes. But a voice in the back of my mind told me that I didn't deserve that kind of affection, not from her, not from anyone. The familiar heaviness started to creep in, a reminder of how easily I could spiral. No matter how much I tried to fight it, that darkness always seemed to find a way back in, whispering that I was unworthy of the kind of love she so easily gave to others.

I shook my head to clear my thoughts as we began boarding the plane. Ruiz and Tamara sat themselves in the same row, with Tamara taking the two seats on one side of the aisle while Ruiz settled into the seat directly across from her next to the window. As Ruiz got comfortable, I noticed there was an empty seat beside her. My pulse quickened as I realized that this was my chance.

As I walked down the aisle, my presence seemed to draw attention, even in the tight space. When I reached her row, I slid into the empty seat next to her with a smirk. "Looks like we'll be travel buddies," I said, my voice low and teasing.

"Great," Ruiz replied. I could sense the tension between us, an electrifying mix of excitement and anxiety that was impossible to ignore.

The flight attendants began serving drinks, and the plane's atmosphere shifted from groggy to lively. The buzz of conversation and laughter filled the cabin as everyone started to relax and enjoy the journey. I took a sip of my drink, the alcohol warming me from the inside. Ruiz did the same. I could see her nerves melting away as she joined in on the festivities, her laughter blending with everyone around us.

At takeoff, my chest tightened as the plane began its ascent, like the air had thinned without warning. The cabin lights seemed too bright, then too dim, my pulse loud in my ears. I gripped the armrest beside me, knuckles blanching as the ground fell away beneath us. I'd never been nervous during takeoff before, but something about this trip, about who was on it, had my thoughts spiraling faster than the propellers.

I bent down quickly, dragging my backpack from under the seat. The zipper snagged, which only made my jaw clench harder. I pulled out my sketch pad and pencil and started drawing without thinking, letting the lines form wherever they wanted. It was muscle memory at this point, the pressure in my chest translated into graphite on paper. The tighter I felt, the darker the strokes.

I kept my head down and let the pencil move, not really drawing anything specific, just carving out the noise in my head in sharp, heavy strokes. The vibration of the plane hummed up my legs, but the rhythm of pencil against paper steadied me more than the engines ever could. Each line gave the panic somewhere to go that wasn't my lungs.

I was halfway through shading a dark mess of overlapping angles when I felt it, eyes on me. I glanced up and caught Ruiz looking. Not in a loud, teasing way. Just curious. Soft. Like she'd stumbled onto something she wasn't meant to see.

Heat crept up my neck. I closed the sketch pad a little too quickly and slid it back into my bag, forcing my shoulders to relax like I hadn't just been clinging to it for dear life.

"Thrilling in-flight entertainment, I know," I said lightly, clearing my throat. "Abstract turbulence. Very avant-garde." I nodded toward the window. "You excited for the whole unlimited piña colada situation, or are you pretending to be responsible the next few days?"

She blinked at me, then smiled, slow and a little loose around the edges. "I can be responsible," she said, drawing out the word like even she didn't believe it. "I'm just choosing not to be at this moment."

There was a faint flush in her cheeks, whether from the tiny bottles they'd already passed out or the adrenaline of takeoff, I couldn't tell. She nudged my arm with hers. "But don't worry. I'll pace myself. Wouldn't want to embarrass my fake boyfriend."

Before I could fire back, her phone buzzed. She twisted in her seat, angling toward the aisle, thumbs flying as she grinned at whatever Tamara was sending from across the row. A second later, she was trying, and failing, not to laugh out loud, shoulders shaking while she typed something dramatic back.

And just like that, I was no longer the most interesting thing in her orbit.

* * *

About halfway through the flight, Ruiz must have felt the effects of the alcohol kicking in. She reclined her seat slightly, closed her eyes, and let the plane rock her to sleep. I decided that I should probably do the same before we arrived and made myself comfortable.

When I woke up, I found Ruiz's head resting on my shoulder. Her soft breathing against me indicated she was still asleep. I could feel the weight of her head and the warmth of her body pressed close, surprisingly providing comfort. I'd been half-asleep myself, but now I was fully awake, acutely aware of the situation. Suddenly she had woken up.

Across the aisle, Tamara had her eyes locked on us with a mischievous grin. She subtly gestured for Ruiz to check her phone.

Ruiz stirred and slowly lifted her head from my shoulder. As she unlocked her phone, I caught a glimpse of the screen, a photo from Tamara, showing us both asleep with our heads leaning against each other. Her cheeks turned a bright red as she glanced at Tamara, who was barely containing her laughter.

"Very funny," Ruiz whispered, her attempt to hide her smile failing.

Ruiz shook her head with a small smile, tucking her phone away. After a moment, she shifted uncomfortably in her seat. She must have thought I was asleep because, without hesitation, she began to climb over me. Just as she began to maneuver, the plane hit turbulence, and she lost her balance.

Ruiz gasped, stumbling, her hands landing on either side of me as she awkwardly straddled my lap. I pretend the sudden movement woke me and I blinked groggily, meeting her flushed cheeks with a lazy smile.

"Well, isn't this an interesting way to wake up," I said softly, the playful smirk on my lips. "How did you know my favorite position?"

Embarrassed, she mumbled an apology. Before she could fully recover, I gently took her by the hips and lifted her, guiding her to stand in the aisle.

"No harm done," I said, a hint of amusement in my voice.

Flustered, Ruiz hurried to the restroom. I watched her go, a smile playing on my lips. A moment later, when she emerged, I was waiting just outside of the restroom. She seemed startled to see me and tried to sidestep, but another jolt of turbulence made me lose my balance.

We ended up pressed against the bathroom door, my breath catching at our proximity. The turbulence quickly subsided, and I instinctively reached out to steady her. Our eyes met, and for a brief moment, the charged tension between us was strong.

"Seems like turbulence has a knack for bringing us together," I murmured, my voice low and laced with something I couldn't quite define.

She nodded.

I stayed by the bathroom door, letting my gaze linger on Ruiz a moment longer than necessary. "Well, I'll let you get back to your seat," I said, keeping my tone casual.

"Thanks," she replied softly, my awareness of where my hand had briefly touched hers evident. She hurried back to her seat, visibly shaken by the encounter.

The rest of the flight continued without further drama, but the tension between us was undeniable. I had a feeling this trip to Jamaica was going to be more interesting than either of us had anticipated.

Chapter Twenty-Two

CALLUM

As the group filtered into the hotel lobby, you could feel the buzz of excitement. People checked in and grabbed their room keys, eagerly discussing their plans for the afternoon. Chris gathered everyone's attention and announced that we had a few hours of free time before meeting back in the lobby for a company dinner at 7:00 p.m.

The elevator ride up to the eleventh floor was filled with chatter and anticipation. Ruiz and I rode up together with a few others. As we talked about our plans for the afternoon, her hand brushed against mine, our pinkies almost interlocking for a quick second. The brief contact sent a jolt through me, but I kept my expression neutral.

When we reached our floor and walked down the corridor to our room, her excitement turned to disbelief as she opened the door. "Are you serious?" she exclaimed, staring at the single bed dominating the room.

I stepped in beside her, unfazed. "I assure you, I spoke to Chris myself to make sure there were two beds," I said calmly, though a hint of amusement slipped into my voice.

"Sure you did," her skepticism was evident as she surveyed the room. "Fine, but you're sleeping on the pull-out couch," she said firmly.

"No, I'm not," I said, shaking my head. "We're adults; we can share a bed without anything happening."

She hesitated, clearly unsure.

"Unless you can't," I added with a teasing grin.

"Of course I can," she replied, her cheeks flushing pink as she began unpacking. She quickly tried to change the subject. "So, what are you going to do with your time before dinner?"

I leaned against the doorframe, casually watching her with my hands in my pockets. "I'll probably hang out with Chris and the supervisors," I said. "What about you?"

"I'm going to the pool with Tamara and Owen," Ruiz replied.

My body tensed and my jaw ticked. "Why are you hanging out with Owen again?" I asked, unable to hide the hint of irritation in my voice.

"Why not?" Ruiz replied, shrugging. "I gotta keep him on the hook, don't I?"

"What?" My voice came out sharper than I intended. I stepped closer, my gaze fixed on her. "A real boyfriend wouldn't want his girlfriend hanging out with her ex."

She straightened, meeting my stare head on. "Good thing you're not my real boyfriend. I told Owen that you and I are just hanging out, not dating," she said firmly.

My jaw tightened. "Then what was the point of the proposition?" I asked, my voice low but insistent.

"The point was to make Owen jealous, to show him that I'm moving on. But it's not real, Callum. You and I, we're not real."

Frustration ran through me. "It might not be real, but it has to look real. Otherwise, this whole thing is pointless."

Ruiz sighed, playing with a stray curl of hair. "I know, I know. I just, I didn't think it would be this complicated. I almost have him, I can feel it."

I stepped back, giving Ruiz some space. "Just remember the plan," I said, my tone softer now. "If you want this to work, you have to commit to it. Why buy the cow when you can get the milk for free? Anyway, I'm heading out," I added, leaving the room and closing the door behind me.

I reached for my phone to text Chris and see where he was, but my pocket was empty, so I turned back around and swiped my key card. When I swung open the door and barged back in, Ruiz was in her swim bottoms and reaching for her top.

"Um, excuse me?" she said, startled, trying to cover her top half with her arms.

I glanced at her, a smirk tugging at my lips. "I didn't know I was missing the show."

"Get out!" she demanded, her cheeks flushed in embarrassment.

"I forgot my phone. Where is it..." I started, then spotted it on the bedside table. "Here it is," I said, strolling past her to retrieve it.

She turned her back to me, clearly trying to cover up as much as she could. "Can you please hurry up?"

I took my time picking up my phone, letting the moment linger a bit longer. "Relax, Ruiz. It's not like I haven't seen a woman's breasts before." As I made my way to the door, I glanced back over my shoulder and said with a hint of mischief, "Nice tattoo," before stepping out.

ALMA

My heart raced as I thought about the tattoo Callum had mentioned. It was an intricate design of intertwined ivy, starting from my left shoulder and winding down my back in an abstract, organic pattern. I got it after losing a bet in college. India had dared me to ask a guy for his number at a bar. I wimped out halfway there, and the next weekend, India and I went to a tattoo shop. I ended up choosing the most elaborate design of the group.

It was something completely out of character for me. Callum had called me sheltered before, and in that moment, I couldn't help but think he might be right. I had never really done anything daring, impulsive, or reckless in my life.

As I finished changing into my swimsuit, my mind drifted back to that kiss at the bar. I could almost feel the nervous excitement and adrenaline rush from then. More than anything, I remembered the fleeting sense of adventure it had brought me.

The ivy tattoo wasn't just a design; it was a symbol of that moment of courage, a reminder of when I nearly stepped out of my comfort zone. Callum's presence stirred something inside me, a yearning for more moments like that, moments where I could break free from the constraints I'd imposed on myself.

I shook my head, trying to push those thoughts aside. This trip was supposed to be about relaxing and having fun with my friends, not about proving anything to myself or anyone else. But as I grabbed my towel and headed for the pool, I wondered if Callum's words had struck a deeper chord. Maybe it was time to embrace a bit more risk, a bit more spontaneity in my life, to be less of a control freak.

Stepping into the warm sunlight, I felt the cool breeze against my skin and resolved to let this trip be a chance for new experiences. The gentle hum of the resort, the distant sound of waves crashing, and the laughter of other guests created a vibrant atmosphere. The soft grass beneath my feet and the scent of tropical flowers. The bright pops of colors of the surrounding gardens and the clear blue sky seemed to mirror my emerging sense of adventure.

I reached the pool where Tamara, Owen, and a few other coworkers were already lounging and chatting animatedly. The water shimmered invitingly under the golden sunlight.

"Finally! It took you forever to get down here," Tamara called out with a playful edge as I approached.

"I had to unpack," I replied, trying to defend myself.

Tamara rolled her eyes dramatically. "Of course you did. You're so type A, even on vacation."

Owen came over and wrapped his arms around me and said, "It's okay. I think it's cute."

Despite being in Owen's arms, Callum's words echoed in my head. *Why buy the cow when you can get the milk for free.* That comment stung more than I wanted to admit. I pulled away from Owen's embrace, forcing a smile as I made my way to a lawn chair to set down my things.

I settled into the chair, arranging my towel and sunscreen, and looked around. Tamara moved to the pool, laughing and splashing.

Owen was busy setting up a game of corn hole with others from the company, his laid-back demeanor a sharp contrast to the tangled emotions inside me.

Watching Tamara swim, her carefree enjoyment was a reminder of why we were here, to relax and have fun. I wanted to let go and embrace the spontaneity that seemed to have eluded me for so long. But Callum's words and our conversation lingered, casting a shadow over my thoughts.

"Hey, you coming in or what?" Tamara's voice cut through my reverie.

"Yeah, I'll be right there," I replied, trying to sound cheerful as I applied sunscreen to my arms and legs.

Taking a deep breath, I walked over to the edge of the pool, the cool tiles beneath my feet a sharp contrast to the warmth of the sun. I dipped my toes into the water, a refreshing feeling washing over me, offering a brief escape from the jumble of thoughts swirling in my head.

I joined Tamara in the pool and we began splashing and playing around. For a few precious moments, the weight of my worries seemed to lift, replaced by the simple joy of being with my friends.

But as I glanced over at Owen, still absorbed in his game, I couldn't shake the nagging thought that maybe, just maybe, Callum had a point.

Chapter Twenty-Three

ALMA

On my way back to the room to get ready for dinner, my mind buzzed from everything that had happened today. I opened the door to the sound of the shower running. Callum was already in the bathroom. I took a deep breath, trying to steady my nerves.

I spread my clothes across the bed to examine my potential outfits for the evening, switching between flowy shirts and flirty skirts, unable to decide on the perfect combination. The water stopped, and I heard the bathroom door open. Before I could react, Callum stepped out, a cloud of steam following him. He was wrapped in nothing but a towel, his muscular body glistening with droplets of water.

My eyes widened as I came face-to-face with him. His body was a masterpiece of biceps, chiseled abs, and that tantalizing V-shape that led down from his hips. My breath caught in my throat, and for a moment, I couldn't tear my gaze away.

But what really grabbed my attention was the intricate dragon tattoo on his left side. It spread from under his chest down to his lower abdomen, fierce and beautiful. And then there was the tiny tattoo I'd seen at the office, which was part of a much larger, detailed piece I'd noticed during basketball. His right arm was adorned with a compass, an old-timey watch with Roman numerals, and a rose, all seamlessly blending into one stunning design.

"Oh, sorry," I stammered, quickly turning my back to give him some privacy. My cheeks burned, and my heart pounded in my chest.

"It's fine," Callum replied nonchalantly, though I could hear the amusement in his voice. "I'm just grabbing some clothes."

I was able to hear him moving behind me, the soft rustling of fabric as he got dressed. My mind raced, the image of his perfect body and intricate tattoos seared into my memory. I tried to focus on the clothes in front of me, but the tension in the room was impossible to ignore.

"Are you almost ready?" Callum's voice startled me, sounding closer than I expected. I turned to see him standing just a few feet away, now dressed in a casual button-down shirt and jeans.

"Uh, yeah," I replied, my voice shaky. "Just need to decide on what to wear."

He glanced at the scattered clothes on the bed and then back at me. "Need any help?"

I laughed nervously, shaking my head. "I think I can manage. Thanks, though."

"All right. If it matters, I like that dress," Callum said, giving me a knowing smile and pointing to the little green number on the bed, a sleek, fitted dress with thin straps and a flutter hem. "I'll see you downstairs."

As he left the room, my hand instinctively pressed against my chest, feeling the rapid thud of my heart. This trip was turning out to be more complicated than I had anticipated. Trying to push thoughts of Callum aside, I focused on getting ready for dinner.

After a few more minutes of indecision, I finally settled on the green dress Callum had absentmindedly chosen, but I was already leaning towards wearing it anyway, I told myself. I quickly changed, applied a touch of makeup, and gave myself a final once-over in the mirror. Satisfied with how I looked, I headed downstairs to join the others, though the encounter with Callum, and the unexpected revelation of his fucking hot body, lingered in the back of my mind.

When I made it to the lobby, I spotted Tamara deep in conversation with Chris and Callum. I took a deep breath to steady my nerves, then walked over and slipped into the ongoing conversation, smiling as I did.

"Hey, Alma!" Tamara greeted me with a wide grin. "Ready for dinner?"

"Absolutely," I replied, trying to sound casual as I glanced at Callum.

Just then, Owen approached, holding a drink in his hand. I was about to greet him when, out of nowhere, Callum casually grabbed my hand and interlaced our fingers. The unexpected contact made my heart skip a beat. I looked up at him, confusion written all over my face.

Callum leaned in, his breath warm against my ear as he whispered, "It's go time. Don't settle for being the cow."

My eyes widened slightly as I grasped what Callum meant. He was right, I needed to dive headfirst into this fake dating charade. With a quick decision, I leaned in closer to him, resting my head against his shoulder, feeling the warmth and strength of his body next to mine.

The atmosphere in the group shifted immediately. Chris, Tamara, and Owen all stared at us, surprise and curiosity written on their faces.

"So, this is really a thing," Chris said, raising his eyebrows in surprise.

"Don't make it a big deal," Callum responded.

"I didn't say anything," Chris chimed in, his tone teasing.

"It's about damn time," Tamara quipped. "The tension between you two, wowee!"

I caught a glimpse of Owen's expression hardening, his jaw ticking in clear annoyance. Without a word, he turned on his heel and headed toward the bar, leaving the group behind.

Watching him go, a pang of guilt mingled with my resolve. I squeezed Callum's hand a little tighter, feeling the weight of our fake relationship and the complications it brought. As I leaned into Callum's side, I could sense his satisfaction with the situation, his arm sliding around to rest possessively on my waist.

"Let's not worry about him," Callum murmured softly, his lips brushing against my hair. "Tonight is about fun."

I nodded, my heart racing as I tried to focus on the present moment. The group continued to chat, the air filled with excitement for the evening ahead. Despite my uncertain feelings, I felt a strange sense of exhilaration. I was all in, and there was no turning back now.

The company dinner was a lively affair, everyone with drinks in hand and spirits high. I was having a great time, the buzz of the alcohol adding to my sense of enjoyment. After the meal, a group of us, including Tamara and myself, gathered around a fire pit on the beach. Shots were being passed around, and I found myself accepting one after another, the firelight dancing in our eyes as we laughed and shared stories.

Owen approached me, his face serious as he gently pulled me aside. "So, you're actually dating that guy now? I thought it wasn't a thing."

I sighed, feeling the alcohol giving me more courage than I usually had. "Owen, you broke up with me, remember? Do I have to point that fact out every time? Why do you care if I'm with Callum or not?"

"We said we'd take it slow. And I care about you, Alma. Haven't I made that clear? I don't want you to get hurt."

"Like the way you already hurt me?" I shot back, my voice tinged with bitterness. The alcohol was hitting me hard now, and I could feel my emotions bubbling to the surface, raw and unfiltered.

Just then, Callum sauntered over, the glow of the fire pit casting shadows on his face. "Ruiz, you ready to head up to bed?"

CALLUM

For a second, everything slowed. I looked between Ruiz and Owen, holding my breath like an idiot, waiting to see which way this would go. Which way she would go. Him or me.

God, that was a dangerous game to even be playing in my head. Then she moved.

"Yes, please!" she said, a little too quickly, a little too eager, and she walked straight to me, sliding in at my side like it was the most natural thing in the world.

Closer than I expected. Closer than I was ready for.

Owen's glare hit me like a physical blow. If looks could kill, I would be a chalk outline on the floor.

I just gave him a lazy shrug, like I didn't just win something I wasn't even supposed to be competing for.

* * *

The elevator doors closed, sealing us into a tight, quiet box. And suddenly, it was just us.

She turned to me, and there was something different in her eyes, bolder, sharper. Like she had made a decision and I was just now catching up.

"So," she said, tilting her head slightly, "we're sleeping in the same bed tonight?"

I raised an eyebrow, glancing at her. "That's usually how sharing a room works, yeah."

She didn't laugh. If anything, she leaned in a fraction closer.

"Good," she said, her voice lower now, like she was testing the line between teasing and something else. "Because I think we should really sell this."

My jaw tightened. Yep, she' was definitely testing me.

I turned fully toward her, stepping closer, backing her up just enough that she hit the wall of the elevator.

"Careful, Ruiz," I murmured. "You start talking like that, people might think you actually enjoy this."

"Maybe I do," she shot back, and that did something to me. Something I didn't entirely have control over.

My hand came up, resting lightly at her waist, not pulling her in, not pushing her away. Just there. A warning. A question. Both.

"You don't get to play this game halfway," I said, eyes locked on hers. "You want this to look real? Then you trust me to lead."

Her lips parted, just barely.

"Then lead," she whispered.

Jesus. For a second, I almost did. I almost forgot every reason I shouldn't.

Instead, I leaned in just enough that my mouth brushed past her ear, my voice low. "Not like this."

She exhaled softly, her hands gripping my shirt for a second like she needed something to steady herself.

The elevator dingged and the doors slid open. We both stepped back, like nothing had happened. As if the air between us wasn't completely charged.

We walked to the room in silence, but it wasn't uncomfortable. It was thick. Heavy. Like something was still hanging there between us, waiting to be acknowledged.

I unlocked the door, stepped inside, and she followed. I didn't give myself time to think. I guided her gently toward the bed.

"Get some sleep, Ruiz," I said, keeping my voice even.

She looked up at me, searching my face like she was trying to figure out what just happened in that elevator.

Yeah. Me too.

"We've got a long day tomorrow."

But the truth was I wanted her. Bad. But not like that. Not rushed. Not blurred. Not in some half-moment where neither of us was thinking straight. If I ever crossed that line with her, I wanted her present. Choosing it. Choosing me. And that thought? Well, that was the real problem.

She nodded, cheeks still a little flushed from the elevator, and grabbed her bag before slipping into the bathroom. The door clicked shut. And I just stood there for a second, exhaling like I had been holding my breath since we stepped into that damn elevator.

I dragged a hand through my hair and stripped down to my boxers, the cool air hitting my skin, grounding me a little. The room was quiet except for the faint shuffle of fabric on the other side of the bathroom door, and my brain, the traitor that it was, tried to fill in the blanks. I shut that down immediately. Not going there.

The bathroom door opened, and I glanced up. Big mistake.

She walked out in pajamas that should not be doing what they were doing to me. They were soft, simple, nothing special, and yet somehow they had my dick twitching.

She climbed into bed like this was normal. Like we didn't just almost combust in an elevator ten minutes ago.

I followed, sliding in beside her, keeping a very intentional, very respectful distance. A whole-person buffer zone. And it felt necessary. But still, I could feel her. We were not touching. Not even close. But I still felt her. Like her presence had weight. Like the space between us wasn't empty at all, just stretched thin with everything we weren't saying.

I stared up at the ceiling, hands folded behind my head, trying to act like I was completely unaffected. Which was hilarious because tonight had been a lot. The flight. Owen. That look she gave me when she chose to walk over to me. The elevator. Jesus, the elevator. And now this. Her. Right here.

Chapter Twenty-Four

ALMA

The morning sun streamed through the curtains, slowly waking me to the gentle touch of Callum's hand resting on my back. When I blinked my eyes open, a steaming cup of coffee and a few aspirin sat on the bedside table.

"Thanks," I mumbled, my voice still thick with sleep.

"You had quite a bit to drink last night. Thought this might help," Callum replied, his tone casual.

I managed a half-smile, still feeling the flush from last night's revelry. "You're sweet when you're not being an ass."

"Don't get used to it," Callum shot back, a smirk tugging at his lips.

To my surprise, I wasn't as hungover as I had anticipated. I swung my legs out of bed, feeling a brief wave of dizziness that quickly subsided. After grabbing my swimsuit and clothes, I headed to the bathroom. I changed quickly, while Callum sat on the bed.

I stretched and yawned, still groggy from the early wake up call. "So, remind me again why management thought a team building activity at 5:00 a.m. was a brilliant idea?"

Callum, already fully awake and alert, shrugged. "Chris said something about the drive to the secluded island we're headed to. It's two hours there and back."

When we got downstairs, the lobby buzzed with colleagues gathering near the entrance. Company-branded drawstring bags were being handed out, each packed with a juice box, a banana, a granola bar, sunscreen, bug spray, and a hat featuring the company logo. Tamara walked up, already sporting her hat with a grin. "Nice touch, right?"

We all piled into two 15-passenger vans parked outside the hotel. Tamara settled into one row, while Owen, looking slightly less annoyed than the night before, took the seat next to me. The ride was mostly quiet, with many people taking the chance to nap. I kept my gaze fixed out the window, watching the urban landscape transition into more scenic views, using the distraction as an excuse to avoid any potentially awkward conversation with Owen.

Two hours later, when the vans finally came to a stop, Chris stood up to address everyone. "Okay, gang, we've arrived at Booby Cay Island. Make sure you team up in teams of two for the first activity."

As everyone began exiting the van, they also started pairing up. Just as I was going to make my way to Tamara, Callum smoothly stepped in, cutting between us. I gave her an apologetic smile.

"Looks like we're teaming up, girlfriend," Callum said with a playful smirk, his eyes locking onto mine. His tone was light, but there was a hint of something more serious beneath it.

Owen hesitated, his expression turning to one of annoyance, but he didn't say anything and moved on to find another partner. I felt a mix of relief and excitement at the prospect of spending the morning with Callum.

As we stepped onto the sandy shores of Booby Cay Island, the morning sun bathed everything in a warm glow. The crystal clear water lapped gently at the beach, and the air was filled with the scent of salt. I took a deep breath, feeling a sense of adventure building inside me. When I looked over at Callum, I was surprised to find him staring at me intently, his gaze unwavering.

"Can I help you with something?" I asked, my voice carrying a teasing note. "You're kinda being a creeper." I laughed, the sound light and carefree against the morning breeze.

Callum shrugged, a small, almost imperceptible smile tugging at the corners of his mouth. He slid his hands into his pockets and looked toward the beach. "Come on, let's go," he said, nodding in the direction of the shoreline.

As everyone paired up, Chris announced to the group, "All right, first game, and it's an easy one: Two Truths and a Lie. Each team member shares two true statements and one lie about themselves, and the other members guess which statement is the lie."

I rolled my eyes. "What are we in college?"

Callum smirked. "Well, you just graduated, so…"

People around us began playing the game, sharing their two truths and one lie with varying degrees of creativity and humor. I turned to Callum, who was standing across from me. "Okay, you go first."

"No, no, ladies first," he insisted, a playful glint in his eye.

"Fine. I graduated Magna Cum Laude. I've been skydiving. And I've never been out of the country."

Callum gave a knowing smile. "Vanilla," he said, his tone teasing. "Obviously, skydiving is the lie. You're outside of the country now. Come on, Ruiz, my sheltered girl, you've got to make it more exciting than that. Here, let me show you how it's done." He contemplated for a moment, his eyes twinkling with mischief, then said, "I'm fluent in Spanish, I've backpacked through Europe, and I did NOT get off to you in the shower this morning."

My eyes widened at his boldness, a flush creeping up my neck. "Callum," I hissed, glancing around to see if anyone else had heard. Luckily, everyone seemed absorbed in their own conversations.

Callum chuckled softly. "Relax, Ruiz. So, which one is the lie?"

I narrowed my eyes at him, trying to ignore the way my heart raced. "There's no way you speak Spanish," I said, my voice dropping to a whisper.

Callum raised an eyebrow, clearly amused. "Oh really? Care to place a bet on that?"

"Sure," I replied, crossing my arms. "I think you're bluffing."

Without missing a beat, Callum leaned in close and whispered in rapid, flawless Spanish, "Este lugar te conviene."

My eyes widened in surprise.

"This place suits you, in case you couldn't translate it," Callum said, his voice low and teasing.

"Claro que si, of course I could translate. Okay, fine," I muttered, feeling my cheeks flush. "So, you do speak Spanish."

Callum chuckled softly. "Told you. So, which one do you think is the real lie?"

I took a moment to regain my composure. "Well, I know the shower thing didn't happen, so, I'm going to say that backpacking through Europe is the lie."

Callum's eyes darkened. "Actually, the shower thing is the lie. I did enjoy imagining you on top of me this morning, your hair fisted in my grip, us panting, sweat slicking off our bodies..."

I was momentarily stunned, my breath catching as the intensity of his words hit me.

"I really did backpack through Europe," he continued casually. "It's an amazing experience. Maybe you'll get to do it someday."

Before I could respond, Chris called out, "All right, everyone! On to the next activity!"

As we moved to the next game, I replayed the interaction in my mind. Despite his teasing, Callum had a knack for keeping me off-balance, making me wonder if he was just saying things to unsettle me.

Chris announced, "Now team up in groups of four."

Everyone murmured and shuffled around, forming new teams. I ended up with Tamara, Owen, and another coworker, Terry. We spent the morning hopping from one activity to the next.

During office trivia, I found myself distracted by the earlier interaction with Callum and missed a few questions I would have otherwise nailed. In the human knot game, I could feel Owen's gaze on me, but I avoided eye contact, focusing instead on untangling the knot. As we counted off in sequence for another game, I found myself hoping to be paired back up with Callum and his teasing smile and challenging presence.

Finally, the sun was directly overhead, signaling it was early afternoon. Chris's voice cut through my reverie. "All right, everyone, it's lunchtime. Let's gather by the picnic area."

My stomach rumbled in response. I hadn't realized how hungry I was. I hadn't been on another team with Callum since the first, but I was still reeling from our earlier exchange. I scanned the area, searching for him, and spotted him laughing with a group of coworkers by the picnic tables.

"Ready for some food?" Tamara asked, nudging me.

"Yeah, definitely," I replied, forcing a smile.

We made our way to the picnic area, where a buffet of sandwiches, salads, fruit, and drinks was laid out. I grabbed a plate and filled it with a little bit of everything. As I was pouring myself a drink, fingers grazed the small of my back. I turned and found Callum standing there, his blue eyes piercing.

"Hey," he said, his tone light. "Enjoying the team building games?"

"Yeah, they're fun," I replied, trying to sound casual. "Though, I have to admit, the office trivia stumped me a bit."

Callum chuckled. "I noticed. You looked a bit lost in thought. Something on your mind?"

I felt my cheeks flush as I recalled our earlier interaction. "Just trying to keep up with all the activities. It's a lot to take in."

Callum's tone was playful. "If you ever need a break, you know where to find me."

Before I could respond, Chris called out, "Find a spot to relax. We have some free time before the afternoon activities."

I watched as Callum walked away to join the managers, my heart still racing from our exchange. I made my way to a shaded spot under a tree, where Tamara, Owen, and Terry were already sitting. I joined them, trying to focus on the conversation, but my mind kept drifting back to Callum.

Chapter Twenty-Five

ALMA

The rest of our time at Booby Cay Island was blissfully relaxing. People scattered across the beach, diving into various activities. Some were out on paddle boards, gliding over the gentle waves, while others played a spirited game of volleyball. A few people chose to lounge on the beach, all while drinks flowed freely, adding to the laid-back atmosphere.

When it was finally time to head back to the resort, I found myself sitting next to Callum on the van ride. Every slight bump in the road made our knees brush together, each touch sparking a jolt of electricity. My heart raced, and my pulse quickened with every accidental contact. I could barely concentrate on the ride; my mind was a whirl of thoughts and emotions.

When we arrived at the resort, I felt a little anxious but also relieved. I needed to escape the van and my feelings. I practically dashed out of the vehicle, my steps quick and purposeful. I heard Tamara calling my name, but I didn't stop. I made a beeline for our room, focused solely on finding a moment of solitude.

Once inside, I closed the door behind me and leaned against it for a moment to catch my breath. The room was quiet, a stark contrast to the noise and activity of the beach. I moved quickly to the bathroom, turning the shower knob to the coldest setting. Stripping off my clothes, I stepped under the icy stream of water, gasping as the chill hit my skin.

The cold shower did little to calm my racing thoughts. Images of Callum filled my mind, his lips on my neck, the way his touch had sent waves of pleasure through my body. I shivered, not from the cold but from the strength of my longing. I could still feel the ghost of his breath against my skin, the press of his body against mine.

I closed my eyes, letting the water wash over me as I tried to push away thoughts of him. I needed to regain some semblance of control over my emotions, but it was futile. The connection between us was too strong, too undeniable. I knew I couldn't avoid him forever, and the thought was both thrilling and terrifying.

As I finished my shower and wrapped myself in a towel, I heard the door to the room open. Callum was back. My heart skipped a beat, and I took a deep breath, steeling myself for the inevitable encounter.

I stepped out of the shower, toweled off, and dressed quickly in the clothes I had brought into the bathroom. I applied a bit of makeup hastily, letting my curls fall wild around my shoulders.

As I emerged from the bathroom, my breath hitched when I saw Callum sprawled on the bed in nothing but his boxers. He looked completely at ease. Despite my attempts to stay composed, my heart raced at the sight of him and the closeness of our shared space.

He looked up as I entered, his gaze lingering on me for a moment before he sat up. I struggled to keep my cool, feeling my cheeks flush while I crossed the room, trying to act casual even though my pulse quickened.

"Hey," Callum said, his voice low and smooth. His eyes traced over my body, and I felt a swirl of conflicting emotions: attraction, uncertainty, and a hint of apprehension.

"Hey," I replied, my voice coming out breathless. I cleared my throat and attempted to steady myself. "So, what's the plan for the rest of the day?" I asked, trying to sound nonchalant despite the charged atmosphere.

Callum met my gaze, a flicker of amusement in his eyes. "Actually, management made an announcement while you rushed off the van," he said, sounding casual. "We're meeting for a company dinner in two hours."

I nodded, feeling a wave of relief. I glanced at my phone and saw a text from Tamara saying she was planning to nap. There was also a message from Owen asking if I wanted to hang out until dinner. I hesitated, thinking about my reply, before turning back to Callum.

"What about you?" I asked, curiosity getting the better of me. "What are you planning to do?"

Callum shrugged, a half-smile tugging at his lips. "I was thinking of just hanging out in the room, maybe having a few drinks," he replied. "I was going to jump in the shower first. Just in case I end up too drunk to manage one before dinner."

I chuckled softly, feeling the tension between us ease a bit. "Sounds like a plan," I said, a playful edge to my voice. "Mind if I join you?"

Callum raised an eyebrow, his expression teasing. "You want to shower with me?" he asked, his voice dropping to a low, suggestive tone.

I rolled my eyes, a flush creeping up my cheeks yet again. "No, not like that," I retorted, trying to cover my embarrassment. "I meant I'd like to hang out with you and maybe have a drink or two."

Callum laughed. "Sure, sounds good. I'll be quick," he said, standing up and heading toward the bathroom.

I nodded as Callum walked into the bathroom. The sound of the water starting was oddly soothing, but my nerves fluttered uncontrollably in my stomach.

I made my way to the makeshift bar he'd set up in the room, my fingers trembling slightly as I poured myself a drink. I took a deep breath, trying to calm the anticipation bubbling inside me. The drink was sour but smooth, although a bit too hot as it slid down my throat. I walked out to the balcony, the cool breeze a refreshing contrast to the warmth spreading through me.

My phone buzzing interrupted my thoughts, a call from my mom. I pressed the phone to my ear and listened to her voice crackle through the speaker.

"Your papi's doing a bit better, mija," she said, and I could hear the faint sound of birds in the background. She was probably sitting on the porch, like she always did. "The doctor suggested we change up our meals, so I've adjusted them, less salt, more greens. He's not thrilled, but he knows it's for the best."

I smiled, but it felt thin, like I had to force it. "That's good, Mami. How are the walks going?"

"Oh, we've been taking them every morning," she said, and I could hear the pride in her voice. "Just around the neighborhood for now. Nothing too hard, but it gets us moving. He even smiled this morning, said he feels a bit lighter. That's something, right?"

"Yeah, Mami, that's great," I replied, trying to sound more upbeat than I felt. A bit lighter. It wasn't much, but it was progress, and I had to hold on to that.

"And Alma," Mami continued, her tone softening in that way that made me brace for her kindness, "thank you again for sending the money. You didn't have to, but you've been such a great daughter. I don't know what we'd do without you."

I swallowed the lump that immediately rose in my throat. "Of course. I just want to help. Tu y Papi have done so much for me."

And it wasn't like they were asking for luxuries. The money was going straight to keeping the bodega afloat while Papi recovered. He was back up on his feet more frequently than he had been without getting dizzy, but they'd had to hire Miguel's nephew from down the block to cover the early mornings and the heavy lifting. Extra hands meant extra payroll. Rent on the storefront, supplier invoices, the kid's wages, well, it all added up faster than pride would allow them to admit.

"Still," she said gently, "we appreciate it. You've got a lot on your plate, and yet you're always thinking about us. We're lucky to have you."

We chatted a little more before saying goodbye. I stared at my phone for a long moment after the call ended. It felt like all the air had been sucked out of the room.

I thought about the chance of landing a spot on the PR team. "If I ace this," I murmured to myself, "things will get better."

That presentation was my ticket to getting a raise. More stability. Fewer nights lying awake worrying about how I was going to keep everything together.

I sighed, playing with a curl absentmindedly. I had to make it work. I had no other choice.

From the balcony I could hear Callum moving around in the room, the sounds of him dressing almost irresistible, tempting me to turn around and look. I forced myself to focus on the view instead, the distant crash of waves against the shore helping to soothe my frazzled nerves.

A few moments later, I heard the clink of glass and the soft sound of footsteps. Callum joined me on the balcony, his presence comforting.

"So, where did you learn to speak Spanish?" I asked, trying to sound casual as I turned to face him.

Callum leaned against the railing, his gaze meeting mine with that familiar, easy confidence of his. "I was born in Spain," he began, a faint smile playing on his lips. "Lived there until I was seven, then my family moved to the States."

My curiosity was immediately piqued. We drifted into Spanish, the language flowing between us with a natural ease. As we spoke, I felt a deeper connection forming, a sense of shared understanding that seemed to transcend words.

Callum tilted his head slightly, his expression thoughtful. "Have you visited the motherland recently?" he asked in Spanish. "República Dominicana?"

I shook my head, switching back to English, my voice quieter than I meant it to be. "No. Not since I was little. We moved here when I was five, and the plan was always to go back after I finished high school." I let out a small breath. "Then I decided I wanted to stay for college. And now..." I gave a half-shrug, trying to make it lighter than it felt. "Now this is home. This is where my life ended up."

Callum tilted his head, studying me. "So if this is home now, why aren't they here with you?"

I exhaled slowly, folding my arms like that might steady something inside me. "They moved back right before I started college. The cost of living was a lot better, they even own their own bodega. Plus, it made more sense for them to be close to our extended family. They've got cousins, tías, everyone within a few blocks over there." I gave him a small shrug.

He raised an eyebrow, sensing there was more to the story. "And you? It must have been hard for you to stay behind."

I shrugged, feeling a pang of anxiety at the thought of revealing too much. "Yeah, it was, but...it's what they wanted. I didn't want to hold them back." I forced a smile, hoping to deflect his curiosity. "I'm just glad they're happy."

His eyes softened with understanding. "It would be good for you to visit sooner rather than later. I'm sure they miss you," he said gently.

The conversation continued seamlessly, but then Callum's tone shifted, becoming more serious, almost intimate. The teasing edge softened, his thumb tracing idle circles against the condensation on his glass like he was working up to something. His eyes lifted to mine, holding there a beat too long.

"Ruiz, be honest with me." A pause. Then, softer, deliberate. "Do you want me?"

I froze, my heart racing in my chest. The question hung between us, heavy with meaning. The weight of his gaze made it hard to breathe.

For a moment, I was at a loss for words. The answer was clear in my mind, but voicing it seemed almost impossible. The anticipation, the tension, the undeniable pull between us, it was all laid bare in that simple, loaded question.

CALLUM

As the silence stretched on, I could feel the weight of her unspoken response hanging between us. Whatever she was about to say would shift everything.

Finally, Ruiz spoke, her voice barely above a whisper. "Yes, but I'm scared."

"Of me?" I asked, searching her eyes for answers.

"Maybe," she replied. "Because, what did you call me? Sheltered? Vanilla? And you're..."

She faltered, but I interjected, "I'm far from those things."

The balcony around us seemed to blur, the world narrowing down to just the two of us. I took a step closer, feeling the heat of her body in the space between us. The pull and tension that had been building all day drew us together.

"Do you really think that matters?" I asked, my voice low and steady. "What matters is how you feel, right here, right now."

I watched as she swallowed hard. "It's not just that," she said, her voice trembling. "It's everything. The way you make me feel, the way you look at me, the way I can't seem to think straight when you're around."

I let my expression soften, letting a hint of a smile play at my lips. "Then stop thinking," I said gently. "Just feel."

I reached out, letting my fingers brush lightly against her cheek. The touch made my dick twitch and ignited the craving I had been struggling to suppress. Ruiz closed her eyes, leaning into my touch, momentarily.

"Callum," she whispered, her voice barely audible. "I'm not like you. I don't know if I can handle losing control."

"You can," I replied softly. "You just have to trust yourself. And trust me."

She opened her eyes and met my gaze with a newfound determination. The fear was still there, but it was tempered by resolve. She took a deep breath and nodded slowly.

I reached out and gently took her hand, leading her inside. She followed. The cool air of the room heightening my senses.

Just as she closed the balcony door behind us, I turned swiftly and pressed her against it. The suddenness of the move took her breath away. I placed my hands on either side of her head, my body close but not quite touching hers.

"Ruiz," I whispered, my voice low and husky. "Tell me to stop, and I will. But if you want this, if you want me, just say the word."

She looked up at me, her breath coming in shallow gasps. The weight of the moment pressed down on us, but there was a clarity in her expression that hadn't been there before. She wanted this. She wanted me. The fear and uncertainty were still there, but they were overshadowed by a stronger, more insistent desire.

"Callum," she murmured, her voice trembling but firm. "I want it."

Slowly, I lowered my head, my lips brushing lightly against hers. Her hands found their way to my shoulders, gripping them tightly.

I deepened the kiss, my mouth moving against hers. The world seemed to fade away, leaving only the two of us, wrapped in a bubble of heat and urgency. My hands slid down to her waist, pulling her closer until our bodies were pressed together.

Ruiz responded instinctively, her fingers tangling in my hair as she kissed me back with equal fervor. The tension that had been building between us for so long was finally finding its release, and it was exhilarating.

I grabbed her hands from my shoulders and pinned them above her head, kissing her deeper and more hungrily. Just then, her phone pinged with a text. The sound instantly jolted me out of my trance, and I pulled away, the spell between us momentarily broken.

Stepping back, I released her hands, my breathing heavy. "We should...see who that is," I said, trying to steady my breath.

She nodded and reached for her phone, her fingers trembling slightly as she unlocked the screen. The mundane reality of the text message felt jarring after the moment we had just shared.

She read the text saying everyone was meeting downstairs in the lobby bar until the company dinner. I noticed I had a message too and before she could speak, I said, "Chris also sent a message about meeting at the bar to grab a drink." I watched as Ruiz started to speak, but I cut her off, saying, "We shouldn't have done that. Nothing should happen between us. Not yet. I was being reckless."

Her eyes showed confusion and hurt. "So, you want me for one night, but that night can't be now? Make that make sense."

"One night means just that, one night. Not multiple nights," I replied, trying to sound reasonable. "And we have a proposition. You still haven't gotten what you want. Why should I get my end of the deal granted to me before the mission is over? Seems counterintuitive, no?" My tone was matter-of-fact, almost clinical, but the muscles in my jaw tensed as I spoke.

She rolled her eyes, her frustration evident. "So, everything is on your terms?" Her voice was edged with anger.

"Actually, the terms we agreed upon together," I said, trying to stay calm, though I felt something deeper stirring deep down.

She shook her head, clearly struggling with her emotions. "Fine. Let's just go meet the others," she said, her tone resigned but firm.

The hurt in her voice was unmistakable, despite her attempt to hide it.

We walked in silence to the elevator, the earlier heat between us now replaced by a cold, frigid distance. Inside the small space, the tension was almost tangible, each of us trapped with our own thoughts. I couldn't shake the gnawing feeling in my gut. I could see her eyes darting towards me in the reflection of the elevator doors, trying to gauge my expression, but I kept my face carefully neutral.

Her presence, so close and yet so distant, only magnified the sense of emptiness that had settled in me. I wanted to reach out, to close the gap between us, but the thought of it felt futile. She deserved more than what I could offer, more than a man who had long ago stopped believing he was worth loving. The walls I'd built around myself were too high, too thick, and I doubted anyone, least of all her, could ever break through.

When the elevator doors opened, the lively sounds of laughter and conversation from the lobby hit us like a wave, a stark contrast from what I was feeling. Tamara waved us over, and Ruiz mustered a strained smile, clearly making an effort to push aside her confusion and frustration.

"Hey, there you two are!" Tamara exclaimed, her gaze shifting between us. "We were starting to wonder if you were going to make it."

"We're here," Ruiz said, her voice surprisingly steady. "Let's grab that drink. I need a big one."

As we joined the group, slipping back into our usual roles, the unspoken weight of what had happened lingered thick between us. The air seemed charged with the unresolved tension, every accidental brush of my arm against hers sending a jolt through me.

I watched as Ruiz tried to focus on the conversation around us. My thoughts drifted back to the intense moment we had shared and the aftermath that followed. The group's laughter and chatter felt distant, a mere backdrop to the silent battle between us.

My heart pounded in my chest. I knew she was putting on a brave face, determined to get through the evening, but the tension between us felt like a storm cloud, ready to burst at any moment.

Owen came over and started chatting with Ruiz, and I saw the relief in her eyes as she welcomed the distraction. "What did you do with your downtime?" he asked, leaning in a bit to be heard over the noise of the bar.

"I just had a drink and decompressed in the room," she replied, her smile forced but trying to appear casual.

As we walked toward the resort restaurant, many of us with drinks in hand, the lively atmosphere was a stark difference to the turmoil inside me. The restaurant buzzed with laughter and the clinking of glasses.

Dinner itself was fine, but my focus kept drifting back to Ruiz. Every time I glanced over, she was looking back at me, her gaze meeting mine, which was both thrilling and unsettling.

After dinner, people began to break off into groups. Ruiz, Owen, Tamara, and I ended up at the beach bar with Chris and some of the management team. The sounds of waves provided a soothing backdrop to our conversations. Chris and a few others were enjoying cigars, the rich, earthy scent blending with the salty sea air.

"Want to try one?" Chris asked Ruiz, offering her a cigar.

Before she responded, I jumped in. "It's not really her scene."

I saw the surge of defiance in her eyes. She was clearly tired of being seen as predictable and sheltered because she replied, "Actually, I would," her gaze meeting mine with determination.

Chris handed her a cigar and helped her light it, giving her instructions on how to smoke. Ruiz listened closely and took her first tentative puff. She coughed a bit but she persisted. She took another puff and exhaled slowly.

The group watched with varying degrees of amusement. My expression remained neutral, but I couldn't tear my eyes away from her. Watching her try something new, shedding the image of predictability, stirred pride within me.

"How is it?" Chris asked, smiling at her.

"Gross, actually," Ruiz said, her voice slightly raspy. She took another puff, feeling more confident.

Tamara cheered Ruiz on, and even Owen gave her an encouraging nod. The conversation flowed around her, but her attention was fixed on the cigar in her hand and the way I was watching her. I enjoyed this shift in her demeanor, this new boldness and sense of freedom emerging.

As the night progressed, Ruiz seemed to relax more. She laughed and joked with the group, looking more at ease than she had since our arrival. Despite the lively atmosphere around me, my gaze remained on her, captivated by the change I was witnessing.

Eventually, the group started to thin out as people headed back to their rooms or to other late-night activities. Ruiz lingered for a moment, savoring the last few puffs of her cigar. The beach bar had grown quiet and serene, the complete opposite to the earlier buzz.

I approached her, intending to speak, but just then, Owen appeared, interrupting the moment. "Hey, Alma, want to take a walk on the beach?" he asked, his tone hopeful.

Ruiz looked surprised but agreed, glancing briefly at me. I gave her a small nod as she left with Owen, watching them disappear into the moonlit night.

Later that night, when I arrived at the room, Ruiz was already fast asleep. The dim light of the bedside lamp cast a warm glow over her as she stirred, groggy and disoriented. Her attempt to speak was mumbled, her words slurred and barely audible.

"Hey," I said softly, noticing her struggle to wake up. "You should go back to sleep."

I walked over to the bed and gently pulled the covers up over her shoulders.

"Callum..." she whispered, her voice barely a breath.

"Shh," I soothed, brushing a curl from her face. "We'll talk tomorrow."

In her half-awake state, her frustration was obvious, but my presence seemed to offer her some comfort. As she drifted back into sleep, I let my fingers linger on her shoulder for a moment longer before pulling away. I knew tomorrow would bring some sort of confrontation.

Chapter Twenty-Six

ALMA

I woke up to the smell of freshly brewed coffee filling the room. A steaming cup was waiting for me on the bedside table, which made me smile. When I grabbed my phone, I saw a text from Owen.

Owen: *Good morning, pretty girl.*

Another message from Tamara said she was heading to the breakfast buffet and then to the pool if I wanted to join. It was already 10 minutes old.

Still groggy, I got out of bed, brushed my teeth, and slipped into a bikini. With my coffee in hand, I headed out, wondering when Callum had started his day since it was still pretty early and he hadn't even been back when I went to bed last night.

As the elevator doors opened, I almost collided with Callum. He looked incredibly sexy in just gym shorts and running shoes, his body glistening with sweat and tattoos on full display. I had to force myself not to gawk.

"I'm going to grab breakfast. Want me to wait for you?" I asked, trying to sound casual.

"No," he replied curtly, dismissing me.

I was taken aback by his attitude, watching him walk away in confusion. Disappointed, I stepped into the elevator.

At the breakfast buffet, I met up with Tamara. As we chatted, she asked about Callum. I tried to brush off the morning's awkward encounter, claiming we were just having a good time.

"So, have you guys hooked up yet?" Tamara asked, a mischievous glint in her eye.

I felt my cheeks flush. "No."

"Why not? He's hot. An ass, but hot," she said, raising an eyebrow.

"I don't know," I admitted, feeling a bit embarrassed. "But that might change tonight."

Tamara laughed and I couldn't help join, even though I felt a knot of anxiety in my stomach. As we finished breakfast and headed to the pool, I couldn't shake the image of Callum from my mind. I was determined to figure out his attitude and finally take the plunge with him. Tonight, I decided, things would change.

The day passed in a slow blur. Tamara and I spent most of it alternating between the pool and the beach, with frequent stops at the pool bar. By the afternoon, I was exhausted from sitting in the sun all day, so I told her I was heading up to my room for a nap before the company dinner.

When I got to the room, Callum was just getting out of the shower, a towel draped around his waist. The small space was filled with his presence, and the scent of his body wash mixed with the lingering steam. It seemed like the perfect moment to confront him.

"What's been up with you? You seem like you're in a bad mood," I said, trying to keep my tone light.

"I'm fine," Callum replied.

"You don't seem fine," I pressed.

"Ruiz, I told you I was fine."

Frustrated, I grabbed his arm and spun him around to face me. We stood there, just inches apart, the tension crackling in the air between us. I leaned in to kiss him, but he stepped back.

"I think that's a bad idea," Callum said.

"Why?" I asked, my voice both hurt and angry.

"Because we aren't hooking up. You can't handle losing control."

"Why's that?"

Callum's gaze was intense as he looked at me. Then he asked, "What's your body count, Ruiz?"

I blushed, caught off guard by his question. "That's none of your business."

"So, it's low," he said, his tone surprisingly gentle. "Which is perfectly fine. But what I want to do with you might be too much. I want you to surrender all of you."

"Show me," I whispered, my voice trembling.

His eyes darkened, and for a moment, I thought he might actually give in. He moved closer, his breath warm against my skin. The room felt charged, every second stretching into eternity.

He traced a finger along my jawline, sending shivers down my spine. "You don't know what you're asking for, Ruiz."

"Maybe I don't," I admitted, "but I want to find out."

CALLUM

My resolve wavered as I let my finger linger on her skin. The silence between us was heavy, charged with unspoken desires and underlying fears. I felt like my heartbeat was palpable, each beat echoing the uncertainty of what was to come.

Leaning in, I whispered in her ear, my voice low and husky. "How often do you touch yourself?"

Ruiz's breath hitched, my pulse quickening as she processed my question.

"Come on, don't be shy. You've at least touched yourself once since we've been here, right? In the shower?" I asked, my tone teasing.

She blushed deeply, shaking her head, the heat rising in her cheeks.

I kept my gaze locked on hers, intense and unyielding. "Okay, while I won't fuck you tonight, I will help you come for me," I said firmly, leaving no room for argument.

I closed the distance between us. Every nerve in my body tingled with anticipation. My fingers brushed her cheek, then trailed down her neck, sending shivers through my entire being. I leaned in closer, my breath warm against her ear.

"Show me," I murmured, my voice a soft command.

Ruiz looked confused. "Show you what?"

"How you touch yourself," I said with a dark grin.

Her eyes widened, but she nodded. Taking a step back, her hands trembled as she began to unbutton her shirt. I watched her every move.

"Lie down," I instructed gently.

She complied, and I sat beside her, my eyes never leaving hers.

"Now touch yourself," I said, my voice a low rumble.

Ruiz hesitated for a moment, then slowly slid her hand down her stomach, her fingers brushing over the waistband of her bikini bottoms. She looked up at me, her eyes filled with apprehension and longing.

"Tell me what you're feeling," I whispered, my voice barely cutting through the charged silence between us.

Her breath quickened, shallow gasps escaping as she slipped her hand beneath the fabric, her fingers finding their way to her most sensitive spot. "I'm...I'm touching myself," she breathed.

I watched her, the power of the moment wrapping around us. "Describe it," I urged, leaning in closer, needing to hear her every word.

She swallowed hard, her fingers moving in slow, deliberate circles. "I'm slipping two fingers inside. It feels good. Warm. Wet," she murmured, her voice laced with vulnerability and raw need.

"Good girl," I murmured, my voice thick with want. "Keep going."

Her breath quickened as she pumped her fingers in and out, her body responding eagerly. "It's...it's getting more intense," she managed, her voice shaky. "I can feel the heat spreading everywhere."

I leaned in closer. "Faster," I urged.

Her fingers moved quicker, the sensations building with each passing moment. "I'm so close," she gasped, her body trembling.

My hand found its way to her thigh, squeezing gently. "Let go, Ruiz. Let yourself come."

With a final, skilled touch, she got herself over the edge. Her body arched, a cry of ecstasy escaping her lips as waves of pleasure crashed over her. I watched her unravel, lost in the moment.

As she came down from her high, she opened her eyes to find me watching her, a satisfied smile playing on my lips. I brushed a stray curl from her forehead, my touch gentle and affectionate.

Her phone buzzed, momentarily pulling our attention away. She glanced at it, but before she could react, I placed my hand on her wrist, my grip firm.

"You're not going anywhere tonight," I said, my voice a low, commanding growl, leaving no room for doub. "Tonight, you're mine. I want to watch you touch yourself over and over again," I continued, my gaze unwavering. "I want to see the face you make just as you hit the peak."

I took hold of her hand. Slowly, deliberately, I brought her fingers to my mouth, my tongue flicking out to taste the remnants of her pleasure. The feeling sent jolts of need coursing through me. Fuck she tasted good.

I kept my eyes locked on hers as I licked each finger, savoring her. I could see her breath catch in her throat and the way her body responded to the raw intimacy of the moment.

"Again," I commanded softly, releasing her hand. "I want to see you do it again."

My pulse quickened as she moved her hand back to her body. I watched as her fingers slipped beneath her bottoms once more, the familiar touch sparking a fresh wave of arousal. Her eyes fluttered shut, lost in it.

"Look at me," I instructed, my voice a husky whisper.

She opened her eyes, meeting my intense gaze. I could see the heat and caving in her eyes, and something possessive that mirrored my own.

"You know the rules, tell me what you're feeling," I demanded.

Her fingers moved in slow, deliberate circles once more. "It feels good. So good. Soft. And so wet. I want to go faster."

"No, slow down. Take your time," I urged, keeping my tone gentle but laced with urgency.

I watched her intently, my own breath growing heavy. The air between us was thick with desire. Moving closer, I untied the towel from my waist and began stroking myself, our eyes locking in a moment of intense connection.

She glanced down at the grip of my hand on my cock, her eyes flickering with hunger. I could see her trying to match my slow, deliberate rhythm, her breath coming in shallow gasps.

"Now," I murmured, voice dropping low. "We're going to come together. Hard, messy, completely undone." A soft, rough edge creeped into my tone. "I want to feel you. I want to make you fall apart with me."

She answered with the faintest whimper, barely there but full of need. "Yes, please."

"That's my good girl. Always so perfect, so obedient."

My hand stilled for a moment before I dragged my thumb through the slick warmth at the head of my cock, spreading the cum slowly, teasingly to coat my dick.

"Open wider for me," I instructed, steady and commanding. "And don't look away." She listened, of course she did.

As we continued, I noticed the way her body tensed. "Callum, I need to go faster. I...I can't hold it," she said, her voice trembling with urgency.

"Easy," I cut in. "We take our time." My voice dipped again, possessively. "Touch what's mine. Because it's mine."

I let the moment stretch before guiding her again.

"Now slide your other hand down slow. Spread your lips open while you pump your fingers in and out of your tight, wet, pussy. I want to see all of you."

I watched, completely focused, as she followed every word, hand gliding, fingers moving exactly how I wanted. The tension building until I matched her rhythm, pushing us both higher.

Her body arched, breaking at the edge as she cried out, "Callum!"

She repeated my name, her voice trembling as she continued to move, lost in the moment.

A deep, guttural sound escaped me as I reached my release, the rush of relief overwhelming. Panting heavily, I grabbed my towel, quickly cleaning myself up, my chest heaving as I tried to catch my breath.

I looked at her, her eyes still hazy with pleasure. "Now it's your turn," I said, my voice steady but commanding. "Put each finger in your mouth, one by one, and lick them clean."

Her eyes locked onto mine, a flicker of something curious passing between us. Slowly, she brought her fingers to her lips, tasting herself with a tentative swipe of her tongue. The moment felt charged, every second stretching out as she explored the lingering sweetness on her fingertips.

I watched her, captivated by the way she held my gaze, my senses seeming to ignite. I leaned in closer, my voice a low rumble against her lips as I whispered, "You're stunning."

My hands found her waist, pulling her up to straddle me until our bodies were pressed together, the heat between us unmistakable. Her breath hitched, her fingers digging into my shoulders as she surrendered to my touch.

Our kiss was hungry, a desperate need that words couldn't capture. Her mouth moved against mine, eager, tasting, and feeding every bit of me. Her scent, her taste, mixed with mine, overwhelmed my senses. I responded just as fervently, my hands exploring her skin, igniting a fire that burned hotter with each second.

Then I felt it, the tightening in my body, and she pulled back, breaking the kiss to glance down. A soft chuckle escaped her, and when she looked back at me, there was that familiar mischievous glint in her eyes.

"Ready for round two?" she teased.

I couldn't help but smirk, though I kept my tone firm. "Remember, we're not hooking up."

"Oh, I know," she replied, that glint in her eyes growing more pronounced. "But there are other things we can do, as you so skillfully showed me earlier."

Before I could respond, she gracefully slid off me and knelt in front of me. She brushed her curls aside, her lips wrapping around my hard-ened length, sending a shock of pleasure through me.

Her eyes locked onto mine, and I was captivated, completely under her spell. The way her tongue moved, exploring, teasing, drove me to the edge. Each gentle stroke along my shaft made me grip the arms of the chair, my breath hitching as I tried to hold on.

She continued, her movements deliberate and careful, drawing out the pleasure, and when I closed my eyes, I let myself fall into what she was evoking.

With unhurried motions, she took me fully into her mouth, driven by a hunger I could feel in every movement. The feeling of her lips and tongue working over me was overwhelming, and I tightened my grip on her hair, guiding her rhythm with a firm hand. A low growl escaped me as her pace quickened, the room filled with the sound of my deep, ragged breaths.

My body tensed and seized, and finally, I found my release.

Ruiz licked her lips, and I couldn't resist a smirk. "And here I thought you were sheltered."

She chuckled softly. "Maybe I'm not as sheltered as you thought. Something about you makes me want to do things that I shouldn't."

I grinned, my demeanor relaxed. "Clearly."

She got up and sat on the bed, sitting close. "So, what now?" she asked, a hint of curiosity in her voice.

I shrugged nonchalantly. "I suppose we carry on as usual. No strings attached, remember?"

She nodded. "Right. No strings."

I leaned back, taking a moment to study her. There was something different about her, something I hadn't fully realized until now. "But you're different, Ruiz. I can see that now."

She raised an eyebrow, intrigued. "Different how?"

I hesitated, choosing my words carefully. "There's more to you than meets the eye. I also think that you're hiding a side of yourself you don't want others to see. I don't know what that is, but it intrigues me."

A flicker of uncertainty crossed her face, mixed with curiosity. "Is that a good thing?"

I offered a soft smile. "I think it might be."

As the words left my mouth, I instantly regretted them. Yes, Ruiz was different, more than just a conquest, but admitting that out loud felt like a mistake. I didn't want to lead her on or give her hope where there shouldn't be any. The truth was, I didn't deserve someone like her, and I knew it. She was too good for the mess I brought into people's lives. Sometimes the depression I experienced was too consuming and I pushed people away. I couldn't let myself have her, not when I knew I'd only end up hurting her in the end.

We sat in silence for a moment, both of us contemplating the tension in the room.

Finally, I spoke with a hint of resolve. "As your fake boyfriend, after this trip, I think we should end things."

She raised an eyebrow, folding her arms. "Why do you think this should end when we get back home?" she asked.

"Because Owen is going to ask you to be his girlfriend any day now," I replied casually, leaning back.

Ruiz frowned slightly, shaking her head. "And you'll get what you want, me." She paused, a touch of bitterness in her tone. "Though it seems like you've already had me."

I shook my head. "This is nothing compared to what I have in store for you," I said cryptically. "We should head down," I finally said, changing the subject and nodding towards the door. "Don't want to keep the others waiting."

"Sure," she replied. "I just need to shower quickly."

I nodded, holding her gaze for a moment longer before turning away. A faint smile played at the corners of my lips. "Take your time. I'll see you there."

Chapter Twenty-Seven

ALMA

The next day was our last full day in Jamaica, and Tamara and I had a jam-packed schedule planned. By the time we gathered in the hotel lobby, the sun was already high in the sky, and the air was warm with a gentle breeze, perfect for our adventures.

Our first stop was a hidden waterfall tucked deep within the island's lush rainforest. At the trailhead, Chris, Callum, and Owen showed up, ready to join us for the hike. Callum's surprise presence added an extra spark to the day, though I was doing my best to push thoughts of yesterday aside.

"Hey, glad you could join us," I said, flashing a smile at the guys.

"Wouldn't miss it," Owen replied, grinning back.

Chris chimed in, "Yeah, when we heard what you girls were getting into, we had to join in on the fun."

The hike to the waterfall was challenging, with narrow trails and steep inclines, but the scenery was breathtaking. Towering trees formed a green canopy overhead, their leaves rustling in the breeze. The air was alive with the sounds of chirping birds and the distant roar of rushing water.

"This is so beautiful," Tamara said, her voice full of awe as we reached a vantage point overlooking the valley below.

I nodded, wiping the sweat from my brow. "I can't believe how untouched it all feels."

As we hiked, I felt nothing but distraction. My mind kept drifting back to the events of the previous night with Callum. I shook my head slightly, trying to push those thoughts out of my head and focus on the present. My bikini bottoms were getting wet just thinking about it.

Tamara led the way with boundless energy, navigating the twisting path effortlessly. When we finally arrived at the waterfall, it was even more stunning than I had imagined. The water cascaded into a crystal clear pool below, sparkling like diamonds in the sunlight. The sight was mesmerizing, and for a moment, it was enough to pull me out of my swirling thoughts.

"Let's go in!" Tamara shouted, already yanking off her hiking shoes.

I followed her lead, and soon we were standing under the powerful spray of the waterfall. The cool water felt amazing, washing away the sweat and fatigue from our hike. I tilted my head back, letting the refreshing cascade drench my face, feeling a profound sense of exhilaration. I caught Callum watching with a smile before eventually joining us under the waterfall, his laughter blending with ours. Owen and Chris joined soon after.

As we made our way back to our belongings, Owen walked beside me. At one point, he reached out and gently took my hand, his touch warm and tentative. I glanced at him, then took a quick peek at Callum. At the act, my heart pulled between his sweet gesture and my unresolved feelings for Callum. I gave Owen a small, appreciative smile but subtly pulled my hand away, hoping he wouldn't take it the wrong way.

Owen's face tightened with frustration, his voice clipped as he announced, "I'm hiking back to the hotel." Callum quickly followed, saying he'd do the same, while Chris chimed in with a shrug, "Since both the guys seem to want to head back, I guess I'll do the same and let you girls have at it."

Tamara raised an eyebrow and called after them, "You guys sure you want to miss out on the rest of the fun?" Her tone was teasing.

Owen barely paused, shaking his head with a tight smile. "Yeah, I'm sure." Callum gave a short nod in agreement, not meeting my eyes as he turned to go. Chris followed their lead with a casual wave, and just like that, they were gone, leaving a strange hollowness in their wake.

I watched them disappear down the trail, feeling the weight of what wasn't being said between my two choices and me, pressing down on me.

After drying off and grabbing a quick snack, we headed to our next stop: a secluded bay known for its vibrant marine life. The turquoise water shimmered invitingly as we boarded the small boat that would take us to the snorkeling site. I felt a mix of excitement and nervousness as I adjusted my snorkel mask and fins.

"You ready for this?" Tamara asked, her eyes sparkling with enthusiasm.

"Absolutely," I replied with a grin.

We slid into the water, its coolness a perfect relief from the heat of the day. As I submerged my face, a vibrant kaleidoscope of colors unfolded before me. Schools of tropical fish darted among the coral reefs, their scales flashing brilliant hues as they caught the sunlight. I marveled at the sight of a sea turtle gliding by before it swam away.

Tamara pointed excitedly to a group of clownfish playfully weaving among the anemones. I followed her gaze and smiled at the charming sight, feeling like I was living inside a real-life nature documentary. We spent nearly an hour exploring the underwater world, each new discovery filling me with a sense of wonder and tranquility.

By late afternoon, we returned to the resort, exhausted. The day's adventures had been exhilarating, offering a welcome break from the tangled thoughts of Callum and Owen. It was nice to deepen my connection with Tamara, and I silently thanked her for helping me momentarily escape the confusing dynamics of the love triangle I was caught in.

As we headed back to our rooms to rest and freshen up before the company dinner later that night, I felt a renewed sense of determination. Despite the lingering tension, I had managed to enjoy the day's adventures.

When I returned to the room, there was no sign of Callum. I was grateful for this moment alone. The quiet solitude was a welcome relief after a day filled with activity and the tangled web of emotions I had been navigating. I dropped my bag by the door and sighed, taking in the calm of the room.

What I needed was a long, hot shower to wash away the sweat and sand from the day. The warm water cascaded over me, soothing my muscles and giving me time to think.

What had started as a simple ruse with Callum now felt anything but simple. My feelings for him had grown stronger, fueled by the last few nights and the undeniable chemistry between us. I replayed the moment on the balcony, the touch of his hands, the heat of his gaze as he watched me touch myself, and felt a shiver run down my spine.

Was the charade coming to an end? The idea filled me with relief, but also disappointment. I had thought Owen was what I wanted, stable, kind, reliable, but those qualities no longer held the same allure. Owen didn't spark the passion I craved, the danger I secretly desired. I wanted Callum, with all his complexities and the raw strength he brought into my life. He offered me the escape that I wanted, the loss of control that I craved.

I stepped out of the shower, wrapped myself in a plush towel, and moved to the mirror. As I wiped away the fog, I stared at my reflection, searching for answers in my own eyes. Did I even want to be with Owen anymore? The safe choice suddenly felt suffocating.

I took my time getting dressed, choosing a simple yet elegant outfit for the evening. I let my hair fall in loose curls around my shoulders and applied a touch of makeup. The ritual of preparing myself calmed me, giving me a sense of control over the whirlwind of emotions inside.

With a deep breath, I stepped out of the bathroom and into the main room, a sense of resolve settling over me. I didn't know what the evening would bring, but I was determined to face it head-on. Tonight, I was going to confront Callum and lay everything on the table. I couldn't continue with the uncertainty gnawing at me, nor could I ignore the feelings that had grown so intensely.

I slipped on my sandals and gave myself one last look in the mirror. I appeared composed, but beneath the calm exterior, my heart raced with anticipation. Taking a deep breath, I grabbed my room key and headed out.

The walk to the dining area felt longer than usual. My mind replayed various scenarios of how the conversation with Callum might go. I knew it wouldn't be easy, but I was ready to face it.

The resort's dining area was buzzing with activity when I arrived. I quickly spotted Tamara already seated, chatting animatedly with Owen. I smiled and waved, making my way to the table. As I sat down and exchanged pleasantries, I couldn't help but keep scanning the room for Callum.

Owen seemed to notice my distraction and reached out to touch my hand. "You okay?" he asked, concern etched in his eyes.

I nodded, forcing a smile. "Yeah, just a lot on my mind."

As the evening progressed, it became increasingly difficult to focus on the conversation at the table. My thoughts kept drifting back to Callum. Where was he? I needed to talk to him, to clear the air and figure out where we stood.

Finally, I spotted him entering the dining area, looking effortlessly handsome in a crisp shirt and jeans. My heart skipped a beat as our eyes met across the room. He gave me a brief nod before heading toward a different table, joining Chris and a few others from the management team.

I tried to focus on my dinner, but my mind was a whirlwind of thoughts about Callum and what I needed to say. The meal felt endless, and I barely tasted the food. Owen tried to engage me in conversation, but I could only manage half-hearted responses. All I could think about was the upcoming confrontation with Callum.

When dinner finally ended, I excused myself from the table. "I need to talk to someone," I said to Tamara. She gave me a knowing look but didn't press for details.

I waited outside the dining area, my pulse quickening with each passing second. When Callum finally emerged, I approached him with a sense of determination.

"We need to talk."

CALLUM

When Ruiz approached me, I was surprised but nodded in agreement. "Sure, let's go somewhere quieter."

We walked to a row of lawn chairs by a secluded, lit up pool on the other side of the resort. The soft glow of the pool lights created a calm atmosphere, starkly contrasting with the storm of emotions I could see in her eyes. She leaned against one of the chairs, visibly trying to steady her nerves as I faced her.

"I need to know where we stand," she said, meeting my gaze with a seriousness that caught me off guard. "This thing between us, it's not just a game to me. It might be stupid to admit, but I have feelings for you, and I need to know if you feel the same or if this was just part of the charade."

Sometimes, the darkness in my mind was all consuming, dragging me down to places I didn't think I could escape from. Getting close to someone, especially someone like Ruiz, terrified me. What if I pulled her into that darkness? I didn't trust myself not to mess it up, not to hurt her. I'd screwed up so much in the past, and the idea of ruining things with her was almost too much to bear. I could already feel the cracks forming inside me, the fear gnawing at the edges, telling me I wasn't good enough. But damn it, I couldn't stay away, even if I knew deep down that I should.

Her words hit me hard. I stepped closer, feeling the weight of her confession. "Ruiz, this was never just a game for me," I confessed. "I've been keeping my distance because I didn't want to complicate things. I don't deserve you."

Her eyes widened. "Why do you think you don't deserve me?"

"Because you're too good," I replied, my voice thick with emotion. "I'd only mess up your life." I sighed, running a hand through my hair. "I've been trying to protect you. I didn't want to drag you into something you might regret. But seeing you with Owen made me realize I can't just stand by and let you slip away."

Ruiz reached out, taking my hand in hers. "I don't want Owen. I want you. All of you. The danger, the passion, everything."

Before I could fully process her words, I found myself leaning in and pressing my lips to hers in a fervent kiss. We moved so quickly that we both tumbled into the pool, laughing as we surfaced. Floating there, we exchanged glances.

I moved closer, pressing her against the pool wall. With my hands braced on either side of her, I kissed her again, more intensely. The cool water, juxtaposed with the heat of our kiss, amplified every sensation. My hands cradled her face, my lips moving hungrily against hers. Her arms wrapped around my neck, pulling me closer, our bodies pressed tightly together in the shallow end of the pool.

When we finally broke the kiss, both breathless, I rested my forehead against hers. "I can't promise you anything, Ruiz. I'm not meant to be anyone's boyfriend. People get hurt when it comes to me. I carry too much baggage."

She gazed into my eyes, searching for any sign of hesitation. "I didn't ask you to be," she said softly. "The proposition is done. It's just you and me now. No games."

I tucked a stray wet curl behind her ear, my fingers lingering on her cheek. I leaned in, my voice a whisper against her skin. "I can do that, but can you? Is that enough for you?"

She met my gaze with unwavering resolve. "Yes, Callum. It's more than enough. I don't need labels or promises. I just need you."

Chapter Twenty-Eight

ALMA

We swam leisurely to the pool entrance, the water gliding over us as we moved. As we emerged, droplets cascaded down our skin, catching the ambient light and leaving a shimmering trail. Callum reached out his hand, his touch both tender and strong as he helped me out of the water.

As we walked toward the elevators, the soft sound of our footsteps echoed in the hallway. I stole glances at Callum, noting the way his damp hair fell slightly and how the droplets accentuated his features. He met my gaze.

Waiting for the elevator, my anticipation grew, the air around us charged with longing. When the doors finally opened to reveal the empty interior bathed in soft light, Callum drew me close without hesitation. His touch was possessive as our lips met in a hard, urgent kiss, reigniting the fire that had been smoldering between us.

One of his hands curled around my throat, firm enough to make my breath hitch, while the other anchored at my waist, pulling me closer like he didn't plan on letting me go anytime soon. My hands pressed against his chest, feeling the steady rise and fall beneath my palms, grounding and completely undoing me all at once.

And God, I hated how much I loved it.

The way he held me like I was his, like he'd already decided that, sent a rush straight through me. It was intoxicating, the kind of thing that made my head spin and my thoughts blur, knowing he wanted me like that, fully, unapologetically. It was dangerous. And I leaned into it anyway.

The elevator ascended smoothly, our soft murmurs and the echo of our breathing filling the enclosed space. I lost myself in the feeling of Callum's lips on mine, his taste lingering on my tongue like a promise of what was to come. His touch, both tender and urgent, spoke volumes about the passion we shared.

When the elevator doors opened again, Callum held my hand firmly, guiding me with purpose toward our room. Along the way, our kisses continued, playful giggles punctuating the moments we pressed against the walls in a teasing dance of desire and laughter.

When we arrived at the room, we burst inside, our sopping clothes discarded in a hurried flurry of movement. The air crackled with anticipation as our kisses grew more urgent and fervent, our bodies pressed tightly together.

The soft light streaming in from outside illuminated my bare skin. Callum's gaze traveled over me, filled with undeniable need. He took a moment to appreciate the sight before speaking softly. "Walk over to the desk and bend over, your back towards me."

My heart raced as I followed his instructions, my breath catching in my throat as I waited for what would come next.

Callum grasped my hair firmly but gently, pulling my head back as he traced his tongue from the nape of my neck up to my earlobe, where he lightly nibbled. The sudden smack of his hand on my ass sent waves of pleasure racing through me, electrifying my senses.

"You drive me crazy, you know that?" he murmured.

With my neck cranked to the side, I met his gaze, my own emotions raw and exposed.

"I've wanted this," Callum admitted quietly, his free hand tracing a path down my arm, leaving a trail of tingling goosebumps in its wake.

He pinched my nipples and pressed himself against me, his craving for me obvious. "Did you want this too?"

I nodded, our eyes locked as his grip tightened around my hair. The air between us was charged with anticipation, on the brink of something we both craved.

"I want you, Alma," Callum finally said, his vulnerability taking center stage.

The moment he said my name, I snapped to attention. He'd never called me by my first name before, and just hearing it sent a jolt through me. My knees felt weak, my thoughts scattered, and my core grew slick. I was overwhelmed with a fierce yearning for him to be inside me.

As he slid on a condom, Callum used his leg to part mine, releasing his grip on my hair and bending me over the desk until my body pressed against the cool surface. He thrust inside me, filling me completely. A cry of pleasure escaped my lips as my hand gripped the edge of the desk for support. Each thrust sent waves of ecstasy coursing through me, igniting sparks of bliss with every motion.

The feeling of Callum's body on top of me built my climax steadily, pushing me higher. His movements were urgent, fueled by the intense passion that had been building between us. My breathy moans grew louder with each thrust, resonating softly in the room as I neared my peak. Callum's pace quickened, his breaths ragged and uneven as he drove us both toward climax.

"Come for me, baby girl," he breathed heavily, his movements becoming more frantic as he got close to exploding. "Allow yourself to lose control." With a final, forceful push, he drove me over the edge. I gasped, my body arching as waves of sensation washed over me. "Good girl," he whispered into my ear.

Soon after, he groaned, reaching his own release as he collapsed on top of me, our bodies slick with sweat.

As we lay there, our breathing gradually returning to normal, the room was filled with an uneasy stillness. I shifted slightly, my mind racing with the whirlwind of emotions I had just experienced.

Callum pulled away first, his movements controlled and deliberate. "You okay?" he asked, his voice low with a dangerous edge.

I nodded, a small smile playing on my lips. "Yeah, I am." I met his gaze. "Are you?"

He chuckled, though the sound was more dark than light. "I'm fine, Alma. More than fine." Leaning in, he pressed a brief, possessive kiss to my forehead. "We need to pack up. Then we should get some rest. We leave tomorrow."

I sighed, the weight of reality settling back in. "Yeah, I guess we do."

We disentangled ourselves, each movement purposeful. Callum dressed with quiet efficiency while I took a moment to smooth out my hair.

"You know," Callum said, breaking the silence, "this was fun. But it is what it is, right?" He sauntered over and gave me a small kiss on the lips.

I looked up at him, my heart pounding with a bit of sadness. "Right. Just a casual thing."

Callum nodded, his expression dark and serious. "Good. Let's keep it that way."

CALLUM

As I packed my things, the weight of our trip ending loomed over us, but the electric tension between us was loud. I tossed a few more items into my suitcase and then glanced over at Alma, a wicked grin spreading across my face.

"You know," I said, my voice taking on that dangerous edge, "I'm not quite done with you yet. How about round two?"

Her eyes sparked with apprehension. "You really think you can handle me again so soon?"

I walked over, locking my gaze onto hers with a predatory intensity. "Oh, I can handle you, Alma. The question is, can you handle me?"

She looked up at me. "Why don't we find out?"

My grin widened as I reached out and pulled her into my arms. Our mouths met in a heated kiss, and all thoughts of packing and reality melted away. My hand slowly drifted down her stomach, stopping between her legs where I tenderly caressed her, sending a shiver through her body.

She barely whispered, "Callum, we need to pack."

I hushed her softly, my breath warm against her ear. "I just want to see your face experience euphoria again. It's my favorite sight."

I captured her lips in a deep, passionate kiss, my hand moving with deliberate care. My fingers played with her as she rocked her body to meet each pump of my fingers.

I held her gaze and whispered, "How does it feel, Alma?"

A shiver ran through her as she replied breathlessly, "It feels incredible. Don't stop, Callum. Please, don't stop."

My touch became more insistent, each movement precise. Her breaths came in ragged gasps as her body arched towards me.

"You're amazing," she managed to say, her voice a mere whisper. "Every touch..." She couldn't finish her sentence as she moaned aloud.

I absorbed every reaction, every tremor of pleasure with my intense gaze. "Good girl," I murmured, my voice low and husky. "That's exactly what I want to hear."

I continued, my lips finding hers again and deepening the kiss as my fingers moved with a rhythm that drove her closer to the edge. My world narrowed to the sensation of her feel on my fingers, the sound of her voice, and the fierce, unrelenting passion that consumed us both.

As the energy built, her breaths grew more ragged, her body tensing as she approached her peak. "Callum, I'm so close," she gasped, her voice trembling with anticipation.

My fingers quickened, pushing her closer and closer. "That's it, baby. Let go," I urged softly, my voice a rough whisper against her ear.

With one final, shuddering breath, her body convulsed in pleasure, her cry of release echoing in the room. I couldn't tear my gaze away from her face, drinking in every moment of her euphoria.

As she slowly came down from her climax, I looked at her with a dark, satisfied grin. Without breaking eye contact, I brought my fingers to my mouth, taking my time to savor the taste, slowly sucking them clean.

I walked to the bathroom to start the shower. The sound of running water filled the room as I turned back to her, extending a hand.

"Come on," I said, my voice deep and inviting. "Let's get cleaned up."

I felt the warmth of her hand as she took mine, undressed, and we stepped into the shower together. The hot water fell over us, washing away the remnants of our passion. My hands roamed over her skin, gentle yet possessive, memorizing every inch of her.

Our lips met with fierce urgency, our wet bodies pressed together, the heat from the shower mingling with the heat between us. Her fingers tangled in my hair, pulling me closer as our kiss deepened.

"Callum," she breathed against my lips.

I responded with a low growl, my hands gripping her hips with a possessive strength. I pulled her even closer, our bodies melding together as the water cascaded over us. "You're mine," I murmured, my voice rough.

She shivered at my words, the primal tone sending a thrill through us both. She hopped up and wrapped her legs around my waist, the solid strength of my body supporting her. My lips trailed down her neck, leaving a path of burning kisses that made her gasp.

I slid into her once more. My pace was unyielding, each motion deep and demanding. Her arms wrapped around my shoulders, her nails digging into my skin as she clung to me. Her body pressing against mine was overwhelming. She gasped and moaned with every movement, her body arching instinctively in response.

"Talk to me, baby girl," I said, my voice a husky whisper.

"I'm coming," she gasped, her head falling back against the glass. "Right there, Callum. Please."

My breaths quickened as her body responded to each thrust, leaving her trembling. The steam from the shower wrapped around us.

"Let go, Alma," I urged, my voice rough with desire. "I want to see you come undone."

With a final, shuddering breath, her body convulsed in pleasure again. I gripped her hips firmly, holding her steady as she rode out the waves.

When she finally came down from her high, I looked at her and kissed her gently, letting my lips linger on hers. "Now we can pack," I said, my voice a low rumble.

She nodded, her breath still coming in uneven gasps. We stepped out of the shower, and the steam began to dissipate as the cool air hit our skin. I handed her a towel, letting my touch linger on her arm.

As we dressed and gathered our things, the reality of our situation began to sink in. I broke the silence first, my voice gruff. "What happens when we get back home is up to you, Alma. I can offer you something casual, something fun. Nothing more," I continued. "And I'm still down to help you with the presentation. I made that promise and I'm going to keep it," I said, reassuring her.

"Thank you, I would appreciate that. And, like I said, I just want you, as you are."

I nodded. "Then that's what you'll get."

We continued to pack, the mood between us shifting back to a semblance of normalcy. She folded her clothes neatly, placing them into her suitcase, while I moved with a certain efficiency, my mind elsewhere.

After a while, I said, "What about Owen?" I tried to keep my tone neutral, though I could feel my brows furrowing with concern.

Alma paused, holding a pair of jeans. "We'll be friends, but I don't want anything more from him," she replied, her voice steady.

I felt my jaw tighten. "Good," I said, my voice low and intense. "Because I don't want him near you. You're mine, Alma."

She looked up at me, with surprise and curiosity in her eyes. "I thought we agreed not to put a label on this."

"We did," I said. "But that doesn't mean I want anyone else trying to take what's mine. I won't share you with anyone, especially not your ex."

Alma nodded slowly, the weight of my words clearly sinking in. "I understand."

We went back to packing in silence, the unspoken understanding between us growing stronger with each passing moment.

* * *

The room had gone quiet in that late-night, soft kind of way, lights low. Alma was curled up next to me, wearing my undershirt like it belonged to her, hair a mess, grinning at her phone like she'd had this plan all along.

"Stop moving," she whispered, shoving the camera in my direction.

"I'm not moving," I muttered, even though I definitely was.

"Callum," she warned, already laughing.

I sighed like this was a massive inconvenience, like I wasn't already leaning in closer than necessary. "This is blackmail material, you realize that."

"Smile," she shot back.

Click. Then another.

And somehow, we ended up in the same frame, her tucked into my side, our faces too close, both of us smiling like this wasn't fake, like this wasn't some plan we cooked up to make another guy jealous.

Like it was real, because in some ways it was now.

I couldn't remember the last time I laughed like that. Easy. Unforced. That was dangerous.

Eventually, the energy faded, the room settling back into quiet. She shifted, laying her head against my chest like it was the most natural thing in the world, her fingers loosely curled into my shirt.

"Don't delete those," she murmured, already half-asleep.

"Wouldn't dream of it," I said, softer than I meant to.

Her breathing evened out not long after that. And I just stayed there staring at the ceiling. One arm around her, like I had any right to hold her like this.

She looked happy. Safe. And for a second it felt like I was the kind of guy who got to have moments like this. But I knew better. Soledad made sure of that.

I swallowed, tightening my arm around her just slightly anyway, even though I knew I shouldn't. I didn't deserve this. Didn't deserve her. Still, I didn't move. Not all night.

Chapter Twenty-Nine

CALLUM

The next morning, everyone gathered in the lobby early, the mood somber as we prepared to leave. I noticed Alma sitting with Tamara on the ride to the airport, laughing and catching up on the adventures they'd had. They were scrolling through photos on their phones.

As I watched them, their heads bent over the phone, I couldn't help but wonder if she was showing her the pictures we took together. In the quiet of our hotel room, with the night wrapped around us. Not gonna lie, I wanted to hold onto those memories. Now, seeing her share them, I felt pride and fear blossom inside me. Would they see what I saw in those photos? A glimpse of something real, something I wasn't sure I deserved.

Once we got to the airport, everything moved fast. We got through security quicker than I expected and made it to the gate just in time to board. Alma ended up with a seat by herself. I watched her out of the corner of my eye, noticing how Owen seemed to be giving her the cold shoulder. But she didn't seem to care. Instead, she was engrossed in her phone, her focus entirely on the pictures she'd taken, pictures of me, of us, I hoped. That alone stirred something deep in my chest.

I stood, making my way down the aisle until I was standing next to her seat. My gaze must've caught her attention because she looked up, and I saw that flicker of something I had grown to recognize, curiosity, maybe even a bit of wanting.

"Meet me in the bathroom at the back of the plane in five minutes," I said, my voice low and commanding. The words left my mouth before I even realized I was going to say them. But the thrill in her eyes told me she felt the same rush I did.

Without waiting for her reply, I walked away, knowing she would follow. The anticipation coiled tight in my chest as I made my way to the back of the plane. I took my time, letting the minutes tick by slowly.

I was leaning against the wall near the bathroom when she finally appeared, moving casually as if she was just stretching her legs. But the look in her eyes as she glanced around and slipped inside the bathroom said everything I needed to know. My dick hardened at the way she looked at me, carnal, wanting.

I followed her in, the door barely clicking shut behind me before I reached for her. My hands found her hips, pulling her close as our lips met in a fierce, urgent kiss. The space was small, almost too tight, but it didn't matter. All that mattered was the feel of her body against mine, the way her breath hitched as my hands roamed over her.

In that moment, nothing else existed but us, the tight space, the heat of her body against mine, and the electric tension sparking between us. The way her breath quickened and her hands tangled in my hair sent a surge of satisfaction through me. It wasn't just about the physical connection; it was the way she responded to me, how I could feel her giving in to the moment, letting go of whatever doubts she might have had.

My kisses grew more demanding, my fingers digging into her hips as I pulled her even closer. The way she fit against me, like nothing else mattered but feeding this hunger between us, was amazing. For those few stolen moments, the world outside that tiny bathroom didn't exist. It was just her and me, consumed by a passion that felt almost reckless, like we were on the edge of something we couldn't fully control.

I slid my hand into her leggings, my fingers slipping inside her panties. Her sharp intake of breath was all the encouragement I needed.

There was something primal about knowing I could elicit that reaction from her, that I had this kind of effect on her.

Her hands gripped the walls, her knuckles white as she fought to stay quiet, and the sight of it fueled something deep within me. I wanted to push her, to see just how far I could take her before she unraveled completely. As my fingers moved rhythmically in and out of her, I could feel her body trembling with the effort to stay composed.

"Open your eyes and look at me," I said, my voice cutting through the haze of her arousal. "Remember? I want to see you enjoy this."

She forced her eyes open, and when our gazes locked, the connection between us felt electric. Her pupils were blown wide with desire and knowing that I had brought her to this point made my own need even more intense. My fingers continued their skilled movements, pushing her closer and closer to the edge. Watching her fight to keep it together while being so completely at my mercy was a heady rush.

"Come for me, baby girl," I whispered, my voice low, needing to see her finally let go.

The moment she came undone was all I needed. Her body tensed, her hands gripping the walls as she tried to stay quiet, but I knew better. That soft moan escaping her lips told me everything. It was a sound I wanted to bottle up, a reminder that I could push her to that edge and make her fall over it. My eyes never left hers, and as I watched the pleasure take over, I felt a rush of satisfaction, knowing I was the one who brought her there.

When the feeling finally ebbed, she collapsed against me, her breath ragged and uneven. I held her close. The hum of the airplane around us felt miles away, irrelevant compared to the moment we were sharing. This was what I wanted: to have her in a way that no one else could, to see her completely vulnerable and know it was because of me.

I pressed a soft kiss to her forehead. "Good girl," I murmured, my voice filled with a satisfaction that went beyond the physical.

She smiled weakly, still catching her breath. "That was...intense," she whispered, barely audible over the noise of the plane.

I chuckled softly, stroking her hair, letting her know we were far from done. "We're not done yet, but we'll save the rest for later," I promised, my eyes gleaming with anticipation. There was more I wanted from her, and I knew she wanted it too.

With a final kiss, I helped her straighten her clothes, making sure she looked as pulled together as possible before we slipped out of the bathroom, one after the other. As she walked back to her seat, I watched her, knowing that the aftershocks of what we shared were still coursing through her. The way she moved, the slight hesitation in her steps, I knew she was craving more, just like I was.

ALMA

When we landed and disembarked, I spotted India waiting for me outside at the airport. The moment she saw me, her face lit up with excitement, clearly eager to hear all about the trip. As soon as we got in the car, I couldn't hold back, I spilled everything. From the heart-pounding excursions to the steamy updates about Callum, I laid it all out. India listened, her jaw dropping with each new revelation, her expressions making the retelling even more satisfying. The drive home flew by, filled with my animated storytelling and her wide-eyed reactions as she soaked in every detail.

As we sped along the familiar streets of Franklin, India glanced over at me, her curiosity getting the better of her. "So," she began, breaking the comfortable silence, "what does all of this mean moving forward? Are you and Callum just...you know, fuck buddies, or is there more to it?"

I sighed, leaning back in my seat, the weight of her question settling over me. "I've been asking myself the same thing," I admitted. "Callum and I have this crazy, intense connection. He's this dark, mysterious guy who somehow taps into these desires I didn't even know I had. But honestly, I don't know if it's something that can last. We've agreed this is casual."

India nodded, absorbing my words. "Can you handle that? Just a casual thing with him?"

I hesitated, my gaze drifting to the passing scenery outside the window. "I think I can. For now, at least. I don't want to ruin it by putting pressure on whatever it is."

India gave me a concerned look. "And what about Owen? It seemed like there was something between you two before the trip. Like, he might be interested in dating again. Did Callum change that?"

I felt my expression grow serious as I thought about it. "Owen, well, he's been distant lately. I thought there might be something there, but he's been avoiding me, especially after the trip. I don't know if it's jealousy or something else, but it feels like he's pulling away. And I think I'm okay with that."

India frowned, her fingers tapping rhythmically on the steering wheel. "Do you think Owen knows about Callum?"

"Most likely." I shrugged. "He knew Callum and I were spending time together, and we shared a room, for goodness sake. Either way, it complicates things. I care about Owen, but I don't know if he's willing to put in the effort to see where things could go. And honestly, I don't think I care."

India nodded, her gaze focused on the road ahead. "Sounds like you have a lot to figure out. Just promise me one thing."

"What's that?" I turned to face her, curious.

"Promise me you'll look out for yourself first. Don't let anyone, Callum or Owen, take advantage of your feelings. You deserve someone who is all in."

I nodded, the weight of her words settling over me. "I promise."

* * *

Later that night, I was unpacking, dreading the thought of going into the office the next day. At the time, the idea of taking a trip during the January holiday had seemed genius, but now, the fact that the company expected us back at work immediately felt like a cruel joke. Every item I tucked away or tossed in the laundry felt heavier, weighed down by my reluctance.

After I finally finished putting everything away, I headed to the bathroom for a long, hot shower. The water washed away the remnants of travel fatigue, but it couldn't cleanse the dread of returning to routine. As I wrapped myself in a towel and stepped out of the bathroom, I noticed my phone light up with a new text message from Owen.

Owen: *Can I come over?*

I frowned, confused. Owen's sudden interest in hanging out puzzled me. He had been distant and aloof during the end of the trip, and now, out of the blue, he wanted to see me? Despite my confusion, a flicker of curiosity sparked within me. As much as I hated to admit it, I still craved his attention, even though I had told Callum I'd stop seeing him.

I took a deep breath, weighing my options. My heart fluttered with apprehension. Finally, I typed a quick response.

Me: *Sure*

Within 30 minutes, there was a knock at my door. My pulse quickened as I opened it to find Owen standing there, looking uncertain but determined.

"Hey," he greeted me, stepping inside as I motioned for him to enter.

"Hey," I replied, closing the door behind him. "Let's go to my room," I suggested, trying to keep my tone casual. "So, what's up?"

Owen ran a hand through his hair, glancing around my apartment before finally meeting my eyes. "I know I've been distant," he began, his voice low and earnest. "I've had a lot on my mind, and I didn't handle it well. But seeing you with Callum, it made me realize that I don't want to lose you."

My heart skipped a beat, a rush of conflicting emotions washing over me, relief, confusion, and a flicker of guilt. "Owen, I...I don't know what to say," I admitted, my voice barely above a whisper.

He stepped closer, his expression softening in a way that made my defenses waver. "I know I've been an idiot, Alma. But I care about you. I want to make things right between us, if you'll let me."

I searched his eyes, looking for sincerity. It was there, but I also saw a vulnerability I hadn't noticed before. "I care about you too," I confessed, my thoughts tangling in knots. "But things have gotten complicated. Callum..."

Owen nodded, his understanding evident. "I get it. I just wanted you to know how I feel. I'm willing to fight for us."

I was being pulled in opposite directions by the two men who had captured my heart in such different ways. "I appreciate you telling me,"

I said finally, trying to keep my voice steady. "But I need time to figure things out."

Before I could gather my thoughts, Owen leaned in and kissed me. At first, I was surprised, instinctively taking a step back. He paused, giving me space. But then he moved forward again, his lips finding mine once more. This time, I didn't pull away. Instead, I kissed him back, our emotions reigniting a spark that had been buried for too long.

Owen's lips were still on mine when it hit me. Not softly. Not gently. Like a full-body jolt of no. Because all I could hear, over the sound of my own heartbeat, over the way Owen's hand is still cupping my face, was Callum's voice in my head.

She's mine.

And the worst part? I didn't recoil from it. I didn't get annoyed or roll my eyes or push it away like I should. Something in me settled, like a lock clicking into place.

Oh. Oh.

My hands, which had been gripping Owen's shirt, loosened because this, this wasn't it. Not anymore. And for the first time since he walked back into my life, I let myself admit it. Owen wasn't the goal. He hadn't been for a while.

I pulled back, just slightly at first, then fully, my breath uneven as I created space between us.

"Alma," Owen said, his voice rough, searching. "I—"

My phone buzzed. Of course it did. Because apparently my life was a poorly written romcom where timing was a literal villain.

"I should get that," I said, already stepping back, already knowing.

I didn't even have to look to know who it is, but I did anyway. It was Callum. My heart didn't sink. It kicked.

Owen saw it. I knew he did. The way my expression shifted, the way something inside me sharpened instead of softened.

"You should go," I said, quieter now, but steady.

His jaw tightened. "You're going to go see him, aren't you."

There was something in his tone, accusing, almost disbelieving, that made something in me snap into place even further.

"Did you read my text?" I deflected, because I didn't feel like unpacking all of this with him. Not right now. Maybe not ever.

"It doesn't matter," he said, and now there was heat there. "You just kissed me, Alma. And now you're running back to him?"

I exhaled, shaking my head. "It's not like that."

But even as I said it, I knew it was not entirely true because it was exactly like that.

"I have to go," I added, grabbing my keys, my bag, anything to give my hands something to do. "Callum and I need to talk."

"But I want you back."

That stopped me for a second. I looked at him, really looked at him, and I felt it. The history. The almost. The version of me that used to revolve around him. But it didn't pull me in the way it used to.

"I don't think that's a good idea," I said. "You ended things for a reason."

I hesitated, then added the part that surprised even me.

"And...I've moved on."

His expression flickered, hurt, frustration, disbelief, all tangled together.

"Fine," he grumbled, already turning away. "I'll go."

The door opened and closed. And just like that, he was gone.

I stood there for a second, the silence settling in around me, heavier than it should be.

Guilt pricked at me, sharp and uncomfortable. He didn't deserve that. Not entirely.

But underneath it? He was right about one thing. I was going to Callum. And not because of the plan and not because of the ruse. But because when I closed my eyes just now, it wasn't Owen I saw. It was piercing blue eyes and a cocky smirk and a voice in my head that shouldn't feel like home...

She's mine.

Chapter Thirty

ALMA

After getting Callum's address and driving over to his downtown apartment, I sat in my car, nerves on edge with every passing second. The city lights reflected off my windshield, casting a kaleidoscope of colors across the dashboard. My mind raced with questions. Should I tell Callum about Owen? No, I decided. This wasn't about Owen. Should I brace myself for a simple booty call? That thought twisted my stomach. Glancing at my phone, the screen still displaying Callum's address, I took a deep breath. Whatever happened next, I needed to face it head on.

I took another steadying breath, trying to calm my nerves before stepping out of the car. The night air was crisp, contrary to the heat flooding my cheeks. I walked up to Callum's building, the faint buzz of the city life adding to my anxious thoughts. I found his name on the intercom and pressed the button, my heart pounding in my chest.

"Come on up," Callum's voice crackled through the speaker.

I pushed open the door and made my way to the elevator, my thoughts racing with every floor it ascended. When the elevator doors opened on Callum's floor, I stepped out and found his apartment easily. Before I could second guess myself, I knocked.

It swung open, and there he was, casually leaning against the doorframe, his blue eyes scanning my face. "Hey," he said, his voice low and inviting.

"Hey," I replied, trying to keep my own voice steady. "Thanks for inviting me over."

"We have some unfinished business to attend to," Callum said, stepping aside to let me in. His apartment was modern and stylish but cozy, a perfect reflection of him. "Can I get you something to drink?"

"A glass of water would be great," I replied, needing a moment to collect myself.

As Callum disappeared into the kitchen, I took a moment to absorb my surroundings. His apartment was an eclectic mix, giving off both comfort and creativity, a space that felt lived in and undeniably personal. The first thing that caught my eye was the easel in the corner with an unfinished painting perched on top, surrounded by brushes and tubes of paint. Art was everywhere, sprawled across the apartment, hanging on the walls, some pieces even leaning casually against them, as if waiting for their turn to be admired.

The walls were a gallery of his mind, showcasing a range of styles from vibrant abstracts to more somber, intricate sketches. A stack of canvases rested against one wall, and I could see glimpses of different mediums, charcoal, watercolor, and even clay sculptures that sat atop a wooden shelf. Beneath the art, a collection of books was neatly arranged, their spines a mix of well-worn classics and modern titles. Framed photos were scattered among them, offering glimpses of moments and faces I didn't recognize, but that seemed important to him.

In one corner, a guitar rested against the wall. The overall vibe was cozy but charged with creative energy, a space that felt like a true reflection of Callum. It was a glimpse into his world, a world where art and life intertwined seamlessly, each piece telling its own story.

As Callum returned from the kitchen with two glasses of water, I glanced around the room again, my eyes lingering on the art that filled the space. "You never mentioned you were an artist," I said, curiosity lacing my voice as I took a cup from him.

He shrugged, a modest smile playing on his lips. "I wouldn't say I'm an artist. I dabble. It's something I do when I need to clear my head, you know? It brings me a kind of peace."

I nodded, feeling a connection to his words. "I get that. I love art too. I often find myself wandering through galleries for hours, just getting lost in the pieces. There's something about the way art can make you feel so many things at once, how it can tell a story without saying a word."

He looked at me, his expression softening. "Yeah, that's exactly it. It's like a different language, one that's all about feeling."

I smiled, appreciating this unexpected side of him. "You're really good, Callum. Your apartment feels like a gallery itself. I could spend hours just looking at everything you've made."

He chuckled, a bit of color rising to his cheeks. "I don't know about that, but thanks. It's nice to hear you say that," he said, taking a sip of water. "Sit down, make yourself comfortable."

I took a seat, feeling the tension between us crackling in the air. Sipping my water, I tried to calm my racing heart. Callum sat next to me, his gaze intense and unwavering.

"Remember the airplane bathroom?" Callum's voice was low and provocative as he leaned closer, his eyes darkening with want.

My breath caught in my throat. "Yeah," I whispered, my voice barely audible. "How could I forget?"

Callum put his cup on the coffee table and did the same with mine. His hand slid closer, his touch sending a shiver through me. "I can't stop thinking about it," he murmured, his lips brushing against my ear. "The way you felt, how wet you were for me..."

My resolve wavered, my body instinctively reacting to his words. But then a sharp pang of guilt surged through me, and I pulled back slightly, meeting his eyes.

"Callum, wait," I said, my voice trembling with uncertainty. "There's something I need to tell you."

His brow furrowed, confusion and concern flickering across his face. "What is it?"

I took a deep breath, my heart pounding in my chest. "I kissed Owen. I thought you should know."

The air between us grew thick with tension. For a moment, there was silence, and I watched as his expression shifted, from confusion to shock, and then to anger. He stood up abruptly, his jaw clenched tightly.

"Are you serious?" he demanded, his voice low and tight with restrained emotion. "You came here, knowing that, and didn't think to mention it until now?"

Tears welled up in my eyes as I looked at Callum. "I'm sorry. I didn't know how to tell you. It just happened, and I felt so confused."

Callum ran a hand through his dark hair, pacing the room with frustration. "I can't believe this," he muttered. "Why did you even come here tonight, Ruiz? To mess with my head?"

He dropped my first name, my stomach lurched. "No, it wasn't like that," I pleaded, standing up to face him. "I needed to be honest with you. I didn't want to keep it a secret."

"Well, great timing," Callum snapped, his blue eyes blazing with annoyance. "Do you not remember my one request? You're mine. I'm not willing to share you with anyone, least of all him."

"I just...I made a mistake. Please, Callum, don't let this ruin everything," I said, my voice trembling.

He stopped pacing, his expression softening slightly but still guarded. "Ruin everything? You mean our arrangement, which we ended, might I remind you. I don't know if I can just overlook this, Ruiz. You were with him. How am I supposed to trust you now?"

My heart ached at the pain in his eyes. "I understand if you can't forgive me right away," I said, my voice breaking. "But I swear, it meant nothing. I am yours if you still want me."

For a long moment, Callum just stared at me. The anger in his eyes slowly faded. He took a step closer, his gaze never leaving mine.

"Ruiz," he whispered, his voice raw with emotion, "I can't deny that I still want you, but you won't get away with this that easily."

His admission hung in the air, a fragile truce between us. My breath hitched as I reached out, my hand trembling, to touch his cheek. The moment our skin made contact, something broke within him, and before I could even process it, Callum's arms were around me, pulling me close.

Our lips met in a fierce, almost painful, desperate kiss, all the pent-up emotion and tension pouring out like a flood. My fingers tangled in his hair as his hands roamed over my back, pulling me even closer. The kiss left me breathless, my heart pounding wildly in my chest.

"Callum," I gasped between kisses, my voice filled with plea and promise.

He didn't respond with words. Instead, he lifted me effortlessly, carrying me toward the bedroom. The world outside faded into nothing as we crossed the threshold, completely consumed by the need to be together.

Callum threw me onto the bed, his eyes dark with desire as he leaned over me. My hands moved to his shirt, unbuttoning it with urgent fingers, revealing the strong lines of his chest. He responded in kind, nearly ripping off my T-shirt as he yanked it over my head, his touch sending shivers down my body.

As our clothes fell away, we explored each other's bodies with a renewed hunger, every touch and caress urgent. Then, in a swift, unexpected move, Callum flipped me onto my stomach. The suddenness caught me off guard, and I gasped, surprise and anticipation surging through me.

Before I could fully process what was happening, his hand came down with a firm, stinging smack on my ass. The sharp sound echoed in the room, and a shiver of sensation spread through me, intensifying the heat between us.

CALLUM

"Callum," she breathed, her voice a mix of shock and need.

"You think you can play with me like that?" I whispered. "You have no idea what you do to me." My hand smoothed over the spot I'd just struck, a gentle touch different to the earlier sting.

Without hesitation, I moved my hand between her legs, my fingers finding the sensitive bundle of nerves at her core. The moment I began making circular patterns, her body reacted, arching in response to the pleasure. I felt the tension coiling tighter within her, each movement pushing her closer to the edge.

But just as she was about to tip over into release, I stilled my hand, pulling back abruptly. I watched as the frustration and confusion washed over her, her eyes snapping open in desperation.

"Callum," she breathed, her voice edged with need. "Why did you stop?"

I leaned in close, my expression dark and intense. "Do you think you deserve to finish?" I asked, my voice a low, dangerous growl. "After kissing Owen?"

I could hear the raw emotion in her voice cutting through the haze of arousal. "I thought we were moving past that," she stammered, her body still aching for the release I had denied her.

I felt a brief flicker of softness but held firm. "We are," I said, keeping my tone steady, though not unkind. "But you need to understand something, Ruiz. If you ever do that again, if you betray me like that again...my fingers, my cock, will never touch you again. Do you understand?"

She nodded. "I understand," she whispered, her voice trembling. "I promise, Callum. It won't happen again."

I searched her eyes for a long moment, measuring her sincerity. Then, slowly, I cupped her face in my hands, letting my touch soften despite the weight of my words. "Good," I said softly, the tension in my voice easing just slightly. "Because I won't be made a fool of."

She swallowed hard, the gravity of my words sinking in. "It won't happen again," she vowed. "I swear."

I met her gaze, letting my thumb brush across her cheek. "I believe you," I said quietly. "But you should probably go now."

Ruiz blinked, confusion washing over her. "Go? But..." Her words trailed off as she searched my face for an explanation. We hadn't even hooked up yet, and I could see she was struggling to understand why I was asking her to leave.

I softened my expression but refused to back down. "I think you need some time to think about your actions," I said gently. "Don't you?"

I watched her nod slowly, still processing what I was saying. She began dressing, her movements mechanical and distant, while I stood by the door, keeping my gaze steady but unreadable.

Once she was dressed, I walked her to the door, opening it and gesturing for her to step out into the hallway. "Take care, Ruiz," I said softly.

She turned to face me one last time, eyes filled with confusion. "Callum, I..."

"I'll see you at the office," I cut her off. Before she could say anything more, I closed the door, leaving her standing there alone, bewildered.

The door clicked shut and I stood there for a moment, trying to make sense of what had just happened. The weight of the evening's events pressed down on me, a knot of frustration and sadness tightening in my chest. It was a foreign feeling. One I wasn't accustomed to.

The quiet of the room seemed to amplify the doubts swirling in my mind. The familiar, unwelcome emotion of my depression started to creep in, like a shadow inching its way closer. The nagging thought that maybe what happened between Ruiz and Owen was a result of something inherently wrong with me, that I didn't deserve her, or anyone else, for that matter, kept resurfacing. It felt like the weight of my own insecurities was pressing down harder, making it difficult to breathe. The more I thought about it, the more I began to believe that I was destined to be on the outside looking in, never truly worthy of the things I longed for.

I sat down on the couch, with my sketch pad in hand and a pang of regret tugging at me for the way I'd spoken to her. But I knew I wasn't willing to give her what she wanted, a relationship. I wanted her, but only on my terms. And for now, that was enough for me, even if it meant pushing her away tonight.

Chapter Thirty-One

ALMA

By the time I got home, my thoughts were a mess, tangled up in everything that had gone wrong. I kept replaying it, every second of it, like if I looked at it from a different angle it might make more sense. How did things end up so jumbled. If I was brutally honest with myself, Owen wasn't even the one I wanted. He had never been the one I wanted in the end. Not really.

All I could see when I closed my eyes was Callum. Callum, who had driven me away. Callum, who had looked at me like I had hurt him. Because I did. I'd told myself I was fine. That I didn't care. But I did.

Instead of letting myself drown in it, I opened my laptop and dove into some freelance work. Writing press releases for someone else's vision wasn't exactly soothing, but it was a distraction, a way to keep my mind occupied until exhaustion finally pulled me under.

The next morning, I dragged myself into the office. My feet felt heavy, my mind foggy, but I told myself I'd get through the day. I had to.

In the kitchen, I reached for a mug, the smooth ceramic cool against my fingers. Coffee first. If nothing else, maybe a strong cup of caffeine would kick start my brain and push back the emotional weight threatening to drag me under. I took a deep breath, trying to gather the strength I wasn't sure I had.

Suddenly I heard footsteps. And then I turned to find Owen standing there. Why wouldn't he walk in right now, looking unfairly put together like he didn't storm out of my place last night after I basically chose someone else.

There was a split second where something flickered across his face, surprise? But it was gone just as quickly, replaced with something closed off. Cool. Distant.

My stomach dropped.

"Hey," I said, trying for normal, for casual, for not the girl who just emotionally wrecked you less than a day ago.

"Morning," he mumbled, heading straight for the coffee machine like I was just another coworker he barely tolerated.

Okay. That stung.

I sat my mug down, turning to face him fully. "Owen, can we—"

"I'm kind of in a rush, Alma," he cut in, not even looking at me as he poured his coffee.

I pressed my lips together, trying to keep my voice steady. "It'll take two seconds."

He exhaled sharply, finally glancing over at me, and yeah, he was not hiding it. The frustration. The hurt.

"Two seconds?" he repeated, a humorless laugh slipping out. "That about how long it took you to decide to go running after him last night?"

Ouch.

I flinched, just slightly. "That's not..."

"Save it," he said, shaking his head, grabbing his cup a little harder than necessary. "I don't really need an explanation."

My chest tightened. "You don't get to do that."

His eyes snapped back to mine. "Do what?"

"Act like I owe you something," I said. "You broke up with me, Owen. You don't get to be mad that I—"

"That you what?" he cut in, stepping closer now, his voice low. "That you kissed me and then immediately went to him?"

There was no yelling. No scene. Which somehow made it worse.

"I didn't," I started, then stopped, because what was I even going to say? That I didn't mean it like that?

He shook his head again. "I just didn't expect it, okay?"

And there it was. Not anger. Not really. Just disappointment, or maybe even rejection.

"I'm sorry," I said, and I meant it. "I didn't handle that the best way."

"See you around, Alma," he finally said, already turning toward the door.

And just like that, he was gone. Again.

I stared down at my coffee, the surface barely rippling, and let out a slow breath. It hurt, regardless of the circumstances.

All day, a lingering unease gnawed at me. To make matters worse, Callum barely acknowledged my presence. His cold demeanor only added to my irritation. I found myself glancing through the slots of the cubicle wall, searching for any sign of the man who had shown me such fierce protectiveness, despite the night before, but he remained distant, his indifference a painful contrast to what had transpired.

By the afternoon, I needed another coffee to get through the day. I returned to the kitchen, the quiet hum of the office buzzing in the background. As I poured myself a cup, I sensed someone behind me. Turning my head slightly, I found Callum standing close, his body heat radiating against my back.

Before I could react, Callum leaned in, reaching over me to grab a mug from the cabinet above. The sudden intimacy of his proximity made my breath catch in my throat, and I felt the unmistakable press of his hard shaft against my ass. My heart raced as he lingered there, his breath warm against my ear.

"Miss me?" he whispered, sending shivers down my spine.

My body tensed, anger and desire flooding my senses. "What are you doing, Callum?" I asked, my voice barely above a whisper.

He smirked, his eyes glinting with mischief. "Just grabbing a mug," he replied casually. But the way he looked at me, the way his body pressed against mine, told a different story.

As he pulled back, taking the mug with him, I felt the undeniable spark of attraction. I watched him walk away, my mind racing with questions. What game was he playing? And why did I find myself wanting to be a part of it?

The rest of the day passed in a blur, my thoughts consumed by the encounter in the kitchen. I couldn't shake the feeling that Callum was testing me, pushing my boundaries, and I was both infuriated and intrigued by his actions.

* * *

The remainder of the week flew by in a whirlwind of work and basketball. I found solace in the steady rhythm of my job, diving into tasks with a renewed focus. The routine kept my mind occupied, leaving little room for the emotional turmoil that had recently upended my life.

Basketball practice was a welcome distraction. I relished the physical exertion and the exhilaration of the game. The team had come together well, our skills improving with each practice. I found myself laughing and joking with my colleagues, the shared goal of winning bringing us closer. Callum was there, too, his intense presence on the court impossible to ignore. He played with a fierce determination that matched my own, our competitive spirits clashing in a way that was frustrating. Yet, outside of practice, Callum remained distant, his earlier protectiveness replaced by an infuriating aloofness.

Owen was equally distant. Aside from the awkward incident in the kitchen, he made no effort to reach out. I told myself it was for the best, but the silence stung more than I cared to admit. The emotional rollercoaster of our breakup, and everything that happened after, had left me raw and confused.

The highlight of the week was the game. I played my heart out, channeling all my pent-up emotions into every shot and pass. The thrill of competition, the rush of adrenaline, it was exactly what I needed. We beat the other team by a narrow margin, and the postgame celebrations were filled with high fives and a sense of achievement. For a few precious hours, everything felt normal.

The weekend arrived, and I felt relief. I was looking forward to spending time with India. We had planned a fun day out, something to take my mind off everything.

Saturday morning dawned bright and clear. The two of us headed to downtown Franklin, the bustling city alive with activity. Our first stop was a quirky little café known for its eccentric decor and delicious pastries. We settled into a cozy corner, chatting animatedly over steaming cups of coffee and indulgent treats.

After breakfast, we wandered through a nearby farmer's market. The air was filled with the scent of fresh produce, flowers, and street food. My spirits lifted as we meandered through the stalls, sampling homemade jams, trying on handmade jewelry, and laughing at India's enthusiastic bargaining with the vendors.

Next, we headed to my favorite art gallery that was hosting a new exhibit. The gallery was filled with vibrant, thought-provoking pieces.

As I wandered for hours through the exhibits, each piece seemed to resonate with me on a personal level. The gallery's vibrant colors and textures reminded me of the paintings and sketches Callum had shared with me at his apartment. The way he had surrounded himself with his own art, the canvases leaning against the walls, the quiet, intimate space that spoke volumes about his creative soul, those memories flooded back with each new exhibit we explored. I could almost feel the calm, introspective atmosphere of his apartment, where every piece of art was a reflection of his inner world. One I barely got to see.

"This one is my favorite," India said, pointing to a large abstract painting. "It's chaotic, but there's a beauty in the chaos."

"Kind of like life," I mused, my eyes tracing the colorful swirls.

For dinner, we chose a rooftop restaurant with a stunning view of the city. We shared a variety of dishes, from gourmet pizzas to exotic salads with edible flowers, our conversation hopping from one topic to the next.

"So, any updates on the Callum front?" India asked with a mischievous grin.

I laughed, shaking my head. "Nothing to report. He's been distant, actually. It's weird. But I get it."

"Maybe he's just giving you space," she suggested. "Or maybe he's scared of his feelings."

"Yeah, that's definitely not it," I said, rolling my eyes. "The commitment thing is not for him."

"Then why are you putting up with him? Isn't that what you want?"

I made a face, my brows furrowing as I spoke. "I don't know what I want," I admitted, my tone laced with frustration. "But I feel like there's something there, and honestly, I think he feels it too but is not willing to give into it. And the sex!"

India rolled her eyes, exasperation in her expression. "Alma," she said, her voice firm but gentle, "you can't just let physical attraction dictate your decisions. You need to think about what you really want and deserve, not just what's momentarily satisfying. Sex is great, but it's not everything."

I let out a heavy sigh, pulling on a stray curl. "I know, you're right. It's just, I think I'm holding on to the hope that there's something deeper there that he wants to act on. But maybe I'm just fooling myself. With him, I allow myself to let go and I don't do that very often." I looked down at my hands. "I guess I need to figure out if what I'm feeling is real or just the result of how intense things have been."

By late evening, we made our way to a riverside park. We spread out a blanket, opened a bottle of wine, and watched the boats drift by as the sky turned shades of pink and orange. The conversation shifted to something more reflective, and I found myself opening up about everything, my feelings, the confusion, the hurt.

We ended the day lying on the blanket, staring up at the stars. I'd felt a sense of peace, the weight of the week lifting as I realized that no matter what happened, I had my best friend by my side.

CALLUM

On Sunday morning, I sent Ruiz a text.

Me: *You want to hang out later this afternoon?*

As soon as I hit send, I felt a twinge of something, regret, maybe? The last time we saw each other, things got messy, emotions flaring in ways I hadn't anticipated. But for some reason, I couldn't shake the thought of spending more time with her. When her reply came back with a simple yes, it brought with it relief and a bit of nervous anticipation.

A few hours later, I pulled up to her place on my motorcycle, the sunlight glinting off its frame. Ruiz climbed on behind me and tightened her grip around my waist as we sped through the city. The wind whipped around us, and for a moment, it felt like we were the only two people in the world.

I took her to a quaint pottery studio in a quiet neighborhood, a place I'd stumbled upon a while back. As we stepped inside, the smell of clay and the soft hum of a spinning wheel filled the air. I guided her to one of the wheels, unable to resist teasing her a bit. "Ever tried pottery before?"

She looked at the wheel with hesitation. "Not since high school art class," she admitted. "And that didn't go so well."

I chuckled, amused by the uncertainty in her voice. "Well, let's see if we can change that," I said, trying to keep the tone light even though I was more invested in this moment than I wanted to admit. "Here, let me show you the basics."

As I sat behind her, guiding her hands on the wheel, I was struck by how natural it felt to be this close to her again. But there was something different now, something softer, more uncertain. I wasn't just playing around anymore; this was about more than just the physical attraction between us. And that realization scared the hell out of me. But instead of pulling back, I found myself wanting to lean in, to see where this could go, even if I wasn't entirely sure of the outcome.

As I demonstrated how to shape the clay, my fingers brushed against hers occasionally. "Like this," I instructed, trying to stay encouraging. "The key is to be gentle but firm."

Ruiz laughed softly, and I felt a warmth from her proximity. "You make it look so easy. I'm just trying not to make a mess."

"You're doing great," I reassured her. "Besides, making a mess is half the fun."

As we continued working, she managed to create a lopsided but endearing bowl. My laughter came out genuine and unrestrained.

"That's actually pretty good for a first try," I said, admiring her creation.

"You think so?" Ruiz asked, her cheeks flushing.

"Definitely," I replied. "And I think you've got a natural talent for this."

She looked at me with a smile, her expression softening. "Thanks for today. I didn't expect this, but it was really nice."

Her words left a lingering warmth in me. It felt good to be close to her again, and despite the complications between us, this moment was uncomplicated. It was a reminder of how much I enjoyed her company, even if I was still figuring out what this all meant for us.

As I looked at her, something inside me softened. I reached out, gently touching her arm. "I'm glad you enjoyed it. I wanted to do something different, something that wasn't just about..."

"Sex?" she finished for me, her voice hesitant.

I nodded, holding her gaze with a sincerity that I didn't often show. "Yeah. I guess I just wanted to see if we could have a moment like this, something normal."

Her reaction caught me off guard. My heart fluttered with hope. "I think we did," she said quietly. "And maybe we can have more moments like this."

It was a simple statement, but it meant more than she probably realized. There was something about the way she said it that made me want to explore this side of us further, to see what else was possible outside of the physical. But I wasn't sure how to articulate that, so instead, I opted for something that felt natural to me.

"How about we go to my place?" I suggested, trying to keep my tone casual. "I thought we could hang out a bit more, just relax and enjoy each other's company."

I could see the excitement flash in her eyes as she agreed. "That sounds great," she said, her eagerness clear.

As I started the motorcycle, the familiar hum of the engine beneath me, she wrapped her arms around my waist. The sensation of her closeness, the way she held onto me, sent a thrill through my veins.

When we arrived at my apartment, I guided her inside. The soft lighting in the apartment set the mood, the scent of vanilla and musk hanging in the air, a comforting, familiar atmosphere.

I turned to face her, my fingers gently cupping her face. I could see the anticipation in her eyes, mirroring the desire that was building inside me. But I wanted to be clear, to set the tone.

"I don't want to rush anything," I said, though my voice had a teasing edge to it, and I let a smirk play on my lips. "But I'm going to fuck you right now."

The words hung in the air between us, bold and raw, as I waited for her reaction. I didn't just want her to understand my intentions; I wanted her to feel the intensity of what I was offering, without any pretense or games.

"Did we not just have a conversation about taking it slow and keeping the physical to a minimum?" Ruiz asked, breath a little uneven, but her eyes were steady on mine.

I smirked, brushing a stray curl back from her face like I had all the time in the world. "We absolutely agreed to take it slow," I said. "But I never said anything about keeping the physical to a minimum." I leaned in closer, lowering my voice. "Slow is relative. For us? This is slow."

She opened her mouth to argue, but I just chuckled and tugged her gently against me, one hand settling at her waist like it belonged there.

As our lips met, it wasn't just a kiss, it was a collision. Fast, rough, and desperate, like we were both trying to communicate something we couldn't put into words. The urgency between us was palpable, each touch and caress fueled by a need that had been simmering just below the surface for too long.

I guided us to the bedroom, the anticipation thickening the air around us. The soft light from the bedside lamps barely penetrated the charged atmosphere, but it was enough to highlight the raw craving in her eyes, mirroring the hunger inside me.

We didn't waste time; we were on a mission. Clothes were tugged free in a blur of impatient hands and half laughed breaths, fabric hitting the floor as neither of us cared where anything landed. But even in the rush, there were pauses, my fingers tracing the curve of her waist, her hands braced against my shoulders, nails grazing my skin just enough to make me inhale sharply.

I turned Ruiz toward the bed, slower this time, giving her the chance to look at me, to change her mind if she wanted to. She didn't. Her eyes were dark, steady, daring. I kissed her again, deeper, my hand sliding between her legs, feeling how wet she was for me and the way she leaned back into me instead of away. That quiet, mutual surrender only wound me up even more.

When I finally guided her down against the pillows, it wasn't frantic anymore, it was focused. I glided two fingers inside her, pumping in and out of her slowly, deliberately, and my thumb rubbed circular patterns on the nerve endings of her clit. Ruiz's back arched instinctively. The space between us felt like the air before a storm breaks, and every slow breath, every lingering touch, made it harder to keep my control.

Just as she was going to come all over my fingers, I slid them out and offered them to her. "Open your mouth," I instructed. Ruiz looked at me, underneath hooded eyes, and did as she was told. I slowly stuck them into her mouth. "Now suck and enjoy just how addicting you taste." I smirked down at her as she closed her lips around my fingers, swirling her tongue around and between, licking them clean. "Good girl," I praised her.

I pulled my fingers back then whipped her around, pressing her face down into the pillow. My hand found her hip, gripping firmly as I positioned myself behind her, feeling the tension in her body as she arched her back once more, silently urging me on. The thing between us was like a live wire, and it didn't take much more for me to take that final step.

With a slow, deliberate motion, I pushed into her, the sensation hitting us both like a wave. The way she took me in, completely, was overwhelming, like we fit perfectly, pleasure pooling inside of me, making every nerve in my body light up.

She moaned into the pillow, the sound vibrating through me as I set the pace. My hands guided her hips, controlling the rhythm, making sure each thrust hit just right. The power of it was mind-blowing.

I leaned in, my voice rough with the desire I could barely keep in check. "Is this what you want? Is this what you need? What you crave?"

Her response came in a breathless gasp, her fingers clutching at the sheets as she pushed back against me. "Yes, please don't stop."

Hearing her like that, knowing I was giving her exactly what she needed, sent a surge of satisfaction through me. I didn't plan on stopping anytime soon. Every movement, every sound she made, drove me to push harder, to give her more, until the only thing that mattered in the world was this, us, together, in this moment.

My response was a low growl, a sound that came from deep within, almost as if I couldn't contain my control any longer. I thrust into her with renewed vigor, driven by something I couldn't fully explain, a primal need that had been building between us for what felt like an eternity. The room filled with the raw sounds of our bodies moving together, the rhythmic slap of skin against skin, mingling with Alma's gasps and moans.

She tightened around me, her body responding to every movement I made. With practiced precision, I leaned over slightly and traced circles on her clit, knowing exactly how to push her to the edge.

She cried out as she came, her body shuddering. The sight, the sound, the feel of her losing control like that, it was more than enough to push me over the edge. My grip on her hips tightened as I found my own release, our movements perfectly in sync, driven by that same primal force that had brought us together in the first place.

When the feeling finally subsided, we collapsed onto the bed, still tangled together. I could feel the rapid beat of my heart, the warmth of her body against mine, grounding me in a way that was strangely comforting.

She turned to me, curiosity in her eyes. "How did you get into pottery and art?" she asked, breaking the silence.

"Okay random." I chuckled, a bit surprised by the question. "You'd be surprised," I replied, a hint of nostalgia bubbling up inside me. Those hobbies weren't something most people expected from me, but it was one of those things that just stuck, even if it didn't quite fit with the image most had of me.

As I lay there beside her, I couldn't help but wonder what had led us to this point. The physical connection was undeniable, but beneath it, there was something more, something that made me want to know more about her and let her in on the parts of me I didn't usually share. It was new territory for me, and that both intrigued and unsettled me.

"Long story short," I said, grinning at the memory. "After college, I went backpacking through Europe. I ended up in this small town in Andalusia and stayed there for a few weeks. There was this old potter,

Enrique. His studio was tiny, tucked away on a narrow street, but I passed it every day. One day, he invited me in and showed me how to throw a pot. From that moment, I was hooked."

"Wow, that's so cool," she replied, her smile genuine and warm. I could see the interest in her eyes as she absorbed the story. "So, Enrique taught you everything?"

"Pretty much," I nodded. "He was patient, always encouraging me even when I messed things up. But it was more than just pottery. He taught me how to slow down, appreciate the process, and find beauty in the imperfections. It was a lesson I needed."

As I spoke, I could feel the shift inside me.

"The art has become my anchor, a way to steady myself when everything else feels like it is slipping through my fingers. It's where I find solace," I said. "It's a space where I could breathe and regain control." I glanced at Ruiz, her open expression making me feel more vulnerable than I intended. "I didn't expect to talk about this," I said, my voice softer than usual. "But, sometimes, it feels like the weight of everything just...creeps in. The art helps. It gives me a way to manage, to cope."

Her gaze was steady, encouraging. "You don't have to share if you're not comfortable, Callum."

"No, I want to," I said, taking a deep breath. "I've struggled with depression for a while now. It's not something I talk about often. But with you, I feel different. Like I can actually share this part of myself."

She nodded, her eyes soft. "I'm glad you trust me enough to tell me. It's important to have someone you can talk to."

I managed a small, grateful smile. "Thanks. It means a lot."

As I finished speaking, I felt an unexpected lightness, as if a heavy weight had been lifted from my shoulders. Opening up to her, despite my usual reservations, had a freeing effect I hadn't anticipated. Her understanding gaze and the quiet, supportive way she listened made me feel a little more unburdened, like maybe, just maybe, I wasn't as alone in this as I'd always thought. For the first time in a while, I allowed myself to feel a glimmer of relief.

I propped my head casually on my hand trying to read Alma's expression. I could tell something was bothering her.

"What's going on?" I said, keeping my tone soft, hoping to coax her into opening up.

She hesitated, her gaze dropping to her hands. "Honestly, it's just everything. Work, family stuff. You know."

"Family stuff?" I pressed, tilting my head slightly to show I was listening.

"Yeah." She fiddled with the edge of the sheet, and I could see the tension in her posture. "My dad's been sick. It's been hard, especially for my mom, so I've been helping them out, financially."

I felt a pang of concern for her. "You've been helping with money? Since when?"

"A while now." She shrugged, but her voice carried a weight that made my chest tighten. "They've always been there for me, you know? And with everything going on, it just feels like my responsibility. Like, I have to do it."

I nodded, giving her the space to continue. I knew how much family meant to her, but this sounded like it was taking a toll.

"I guess it's not just the money," she went on, her frustration spilling out. "There's this constant pressure to be the perfect daughter. I'm always worrying about how they're doing, if they're okay. And I can't mess up. I can't." She paused. "That's why I want to land the spot on the PR team so badly. It's not just about gaining experience, though that's part of it. I need it because I need to support them, you know? I don't want to be barely scraping by while they struggle."

I watched her for a second, really watching her. Whatever she was carrying? It was heavy.

"Yeah, Chris mentioned the position, and I think you'd kill it," I said with a small shrug, like it was obvious. Because it was.

Then I tilted my head, studying her a little closer. "But, Alma" I let out a quiet breath, my tone shifting just enough to matter—"that's a lot to carry. More than anyone should have to, honestly."

"I know." She pressed her lips together, and I saw the tightness in her expression. "But I don't have a choice. They're my parents. I owe them."

I shook my head slightly. "You don't owe them your whole life, though. Supporting them is one thing, but you can't be perfect. No one can."

She looked away. "I'm not trying to be perfect. I just, I need to be enough."

"You are enough," I said, firm but gentle. "Landing the PR spot is great, and yeah, it'll help, but Alma, you're already doing so much. Don't kill yourself trying to live up to some impossible standard."

Her voice cracked. "I just don't want to let them down."

"I get that," I replied, trying to reach her. "But don't let yourself down in the process."

We fell into silence for a moment, the weight of the conversation hanging between us. I could see her struggling with it all.

"Thanks," she finally said, offering a small, tired smile that didn't quite reach her eyes. "I needed that. To hear how much I don't have to bear this burden alone."

I smiled back, letting my usual playful smirk return, even if just for a second. "Anytime. Just don't forget you've got people here who've got your back, too."

She nodded, and for a moment, I felt a flicker of hope that I had helped lighten her load, if only a little. It wasn't much, but it was a start.

She was quiet for a moment, just taking it all in, and then she looked at me with those eyes that always seemed to search for something deeper. "Callum, I have to ask, what are we doing? What are we? And I know I've been asking this question a lot, but I'm so confused when it comes to us."

Her question hit me harder than I expected. My grin faded as I held her gaze, trying to keep my voice steady. I hesitated and said my usual spiel. "I've been clear from the start. I'm not boyfriend material. We're just having fun."

"Why?" she asked, like she actually wanted an answer and not one of my usual deflections.

I held her gaze for a second, then looked away, dragging a hand along the back of my neck, buying time. I could joke. I could dodge. But instead, I shrugged, but there was no real humor in behind it.

"Because I don't do the whole feelings, expectations, happily-ever-after thing," I said, keeping it short, like if I didn't elaborate, it won't mean as much. "Not built for it."

I glanced back at her, forcing a half-smirk that didn't quite reach my eyes.

"Trust me," I added, "you don't want me in that role."

I saw her expression falter slightly, a small flicker of something like disappointment, but she nodded. "As we've established over and over again, we're just casual."

"Yeah," I said firmly, even though a part of me didn't want to admit it. "I like what we have. I want to keep you mine for as long as you'll allow it. But I can't give you more than that. It wouldn't be fair to you."

The words felt heavy as I spoke them, but they were true. I had too much baggage. Baggage which I'd just revealed to her. I didn't want to lead her on or pretend I could be something I wasn't. Even if there was a part of me that wondered, just for a second, if I was making a mistake by keeping things so defined. But I shoved that thought away. I didn't deserve her.

I reached out and gently cupped her face, my thumb brushing against her cheek. "Thank you for understanding."

She leaned into my touch, and I could feel the weight of her emotions. "All right, Callum. I'm trying to understand, I really am. We'll just enjoy what we have."

I smiled, leaning in to kiss her softly, trying to reassure her, and maybe even myself. "Good. Now, let's not overthink it."

She returned the kiss, and for a moment, everything else faded away. Despite the uncertainty of where we were headed, I decided to focus on the here and now, appreciating the connection we had, even if it was complicated. It wasn't perfect, but it was real, and that was enough for now.

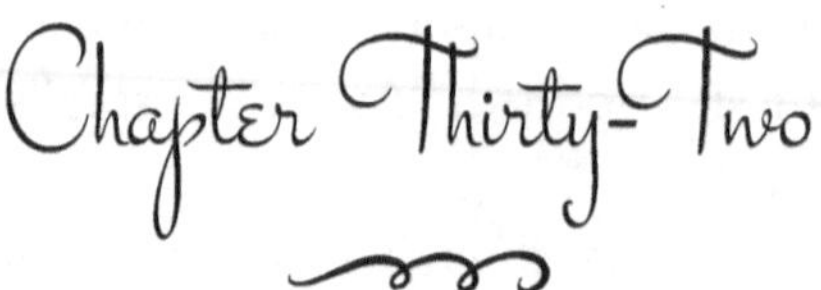

Chapter Thirty-Two

ALMA

Monday morning, and my brain was still very much stuck somewhere between what the hell just happened this weekend and what did any of that mean.

I was halfway up the steps to J&P, coffee in hand, mentally rehearsing how to act like a normal person when I saw Callum again, when...

"Alma."

I turned, and there he was, jogging up behind me like that was the most normal thing in the world.

"Morning," he said, slightly out of breath but still somehow managing that effortless, crooked smile.

"Morning," I echoed, and I hated how my stomach flipped a little.

He fell into step beside me. "Good weekend, wouldn't you agree?"

I let out a small laugh. "Yeah. I mean, eventful for sure."

"That's one way to put it," he said, glancing at me.

There was something lighter about him. Or maybe it was just the way he was looking at me.

We reached the doors, and he grabbed one, holding it open for me like an actual gentleman, which felt illegal, considering who we were talking about.

I stepped inside, turning to say something else when I caught sight of Chris a few feet away, mid-conversation with a woman I didn't recognize.

"It was really nice meeting you," Chris said.. "I'll be in touch."

She smiled and started to turn. Callum stopped. Like, completely stopped.

I glanced back at him. "Hey, you okay?"

He didn't answer. I followed his gaze and the woman was looking right at us. And then she started walking over.

There was something about the way Callum went still beside me, like all the easy, cocky energy just drained out of him. Gone and replaced with something tight. Closed off. Unsettled.

She reached us, and before I could even process what was happening, she leaned in and pressed a kiss to his cheek like it was second nature. Like it was familiar.

"Hi," she said warmly. "It's been ages."

I blinked.

"How are you?" she asked him, studying his face.

Callum didn't look like Callum. He was quiet. A little stiff. Like he was been caught off guard in a way I'd never seen before.

"I, uh, yeah," he stumbled, and Callum does not stumble. "I've been okay." He cleared his throat, glancing anywhere but directly at her. "It's, yeah. It's been a while."

And suddenly, I felt like I shouldn't be here. Like I accidentally walked into something personal. Intimate in a way that had nothing to do with proximity and everything to do with history.

I shifted my weight awkwardly, unsure what to do with myself as they stood there in this weird, quiet tension.

Callum felt distant. Not physically, he was right next to me, but mentally? Emotionally? He was miles away.

The woman's gaze finally shifted to me, her expression curious but polite.

"Hi," she said, offering a small smile. "I'm Soledad."

CALLUM

She was here. Soledad. My brain short-circuited for a second, because no way. Not here. Not now. And then my traitorous mind went, *my Soledad*. Yeah. No. I shut that down immediately. She was never mine.

She studied me for a second, familiar in a way that hit way too hard, way too fast.

"Anyway, it's really good to see you, Callum."

"Yeah," I nodded, clearing my throat yet again. "You too."

She shifted her bag on her shoulder. "I won't keep you, you two look like you're heading into work. But, I'll text you? We should catch up."

Text me.

"Yeah," I said again, because apparently that was all I had today. "Yeah, that'd be good."

She smiled, small, knowing, and then she was gone. Just like that. Again.

I didn't realize I had been staring after her until Alma's voice cut in.

"What was that about?"

I blinked, dragging myself back to reality. To her.

"Nothing," I said too quickly, already turning toward the cubicles. "I've got a meeting, I'm running late."

Smooth. Real smooth.

"Callum..." she started, but I was already walking. Coward.

We made it to our desks, and I didn't even sit down. Just grabbed my notebook and kept moving.

"Catch you later," I tossed over my shoulder, not looking back.

And then I was in the bathroom, gripping the edge of the sink like I just ran a marathon instead of, you know, had a two-minute conversation.

I stared at my reflection.

"Get it together," I told myself.

Because here was the problem. She always knew. She always knew exactly what she could do to me. How easy it was to knock me off balance. How little it took. Just her being there, too close, too familiar, and suddenly I wasn't as steady as I thought I was.

If she wanted to wreck me again? It wouldn't even take that much effort. That's the part that fucking gets me. How much power I handed her without even realizing it. She left. No big speech. No drawn-out goodbye. No clean break. Just...gone.

And it hollowed me out in a way I never really talked about. In a way I covered up with work, with women, with noise, with anything loud enough to drown it out.

But I rebuilt. Slow. Careful. Piece by piece.

And now? Now she was just back? Like she didn't burn the whole thing down the first time?

I was fucked.

Chapter Thirty-Three

ALMA

As the day dragged on, I couldn't stop replaying this morning. Her. What was her name again, Soledad? Yeah. That one.

I mean, I didn't want to admit it, but homegirl was stunning. Like, annoyingly so. Auburn hair, green eyes, tall in that effortless, model-off-duty kind of way. Cool. Loved that for her. Hated that for me.

And the way Callum reacted? The whole deer in headlights but trying to play it off like he wasn't just emotionally clotheslined thing? That lived rent-free in my brain all day.

Before that whole encounter, I'd actually planned on asking him for help with my PR presentation. You know, normal, professional, career-driven Alma things. But now? Now I wasn't so sure.

Still, I spotted him through the glass of one of the smaller conference rooms, already inside, setting up his laptop like the productive, annoyingly competent man that he was, and because I clearly made excellent life choices, I grabbed my laptop, Chris's giant, intimidating briefing book, and whatever was left of my dignity and walked in.

He was hunched slightly over his keyboard, sleeves pushed up, focused, and for a second I just paused because of course he looked like that. Of course he was that guy. And before I could overthink it, I cleared my throat.

"Hey," I said, stepping inside. "So, I was hoping I could tap into your sage insight for this PR presentation."

Yes. Butter him up. Great strategy, Alma. No notes.

He looked up, and just like that, his expression softened into something easy and familiar.

"Of course," he said, a small, genuine smile pulling at his lips. "I'm happy to help." He straightened up and gestured toward the chairs around the table. "So, what's the plan?"

I took a seat, a flutter of anxiety in my stomach. "I want to focus on the PR strategy for the presentation, like proposed campaigns, key objectives, and how we'll manage key performance indicators."

"Good call. You'll need to make it clear and compelling." He pulled out a notepad and clicked his pen, his expression shifting to one of focus. "Let's start with the bullet points. What ideas do you have so far?"

I drew in a deep breath and opened my laptop, the screen lighting up as I pulled up my notes. "I thought we could propose a social media campaign aimed at increasing engagement. Maybe a series of interactive posts and stories that highlight our brand values?"

Callum nodded, jotting down notes. "I like it. You could also incorporate user-generated content, encouraging clients to share their experiences. That'll make it feel more authentic."

"Exactly!" I said, feeling more confident as I saw him getting into it. "And for key objectives, we should emphasize brand awareness and building a community between their target audience and their product."

"Right," he agreed, his pen flying across the page. "You can also include metrics for tracking engagement, such as likes, shares, and comments. If we can show how we plan to measure success, that'll definitely impress them."

I felt the excitement build as we brainstormed together. "I could even include a section on how we plan to analyze KPIs, like conversion rates and customer feedback. It'll show we're serious about delivering results."

"Definitely. Let's create a slide deck that outlines everything clearly," Callum said, already pulling up a new document. "I'll design the slides while you finish outlining the points. All you'll have to do is fill out the slides with your ideas. We'll make it visually appealing and to the point."

As we worked side by side, the atmosphere shifted from anxious to collaborative. I could feel the tension easing as ideas flowed freely between us. We spent the next hour bouncing concepts off each other, Callum's insights sharpening my thoughts, and my ideas sparking his creativity.

"Okay, looks like you have your main campaigns down," Callum said, glancing at the clock. "Now let's add visuals and make it pop. A few images can really enhance our message."

I grinned, feeling more like a team than just two coworkers. "What if we used infographics to represent the data on KPIs? It'll make it easier for them to digest."

"Great idea. Let's also incorporate some of the brand colors in the design to keep it consistent," he suggested, already pulling images from our shared resources.

We dove into the design process, and before I knew it, we had crafted a cohesive slide deck that felt professional and polished. As we wrapped up, I felt accomplished.

"Wow, I can't believe how much we got done in one afternoon," I said, looking over the slides with a sense of pride. "Thanks for your help, Callum. I really couldn't have done this without you."

He leaned back in his chair, a satisfied smile on his face. "Anytime. You've got some solid ideas, and I think the management team will be impressed."

Warmth spread through me at his words. "I hope so. I really want this."

"You'll crush it. Just remember to breathe and own it," he said, his tone encouraging.

As we packed up, I couldn't shake the feeling that this collaboration had brought us closer. And because I was feeling so confident and didn't want to lose my nerve, I went for it.

"Callum, can we talk for a minute?" I asked, my voice barely above a whisper.

He glanced up from his laptop, raising an eyebrow. "Sure, what's on your mind?"

I hesitated, trying to find the right words. "Who's Soledad and what does she mean to you?"

There, I said it. It was out in the open. No take backs.

Callum didn't answer right away. His jaw tightened, and he glanced past me. When he finally spoke, his voice was quieter than I'd ever heard it.

"Sol and I dated in college," he said. Sol? Dated? His mouth curved into something that wasn't quite a smile. "It didn't end the way either of us expected." He rubbed the back of his neck, eyes dropping to the floor. "Things stopped pretty abruptly." There was a beat there, heavy and unfinished. "I thought we were on the same page. Turns out, I was wrong."

My eyes widened in surprise. "Oh."

"It was brief, and it was years ago," Callum added, his tone sincere.

"And what does that mean for you and me?" I asked, trying to sound normal, like my heart wasn't doing that annoying please don't hurt me thing.

He didn't hesitate. "Exactly what we said before," he replied, easy, like this was simple. Like it didn't feel anything but simple. "No labels."

Oh. Okay. Cool.

I nodded like I was totally fine, like that answer didn't just land a little heavier than I expected. "Okay," I said, because apparently that was my go-to word when I was internally spiraling.

He pushed his chair back and stood, already shifting gears. "I've got a meeting with Chris," he added, grabbing his laptop. "Talk to you later?"

"Yeah," I said quickly. "Yeah, of course."

And just like that, he was gone.

The door clicked shut behind him, and I was left standing there in the middle of the conference room, clutching my laptop like it was going to offer me emotional support.

No labels. Right.

I stared down at the presentation slides and let out a slow breath because somehow, despite everything, I thought I was more confused now than I was before.

CALLUM

Later that afternoon as I was sitting at my desk, my thoughts immediately turned to Soledad. I had plans with her tonight, and I knew how she was. She wasn't one to just hang out casually, not when there was an underlying expectation of something more. I'd been trying to keep things simple, to maintain a professional distance, both with her and Alma, but now that line had been crossed, and Sol would expect more than just a friendly evening.

College with Soledad felt like motion, constant and uncontained. She was a free spirit in the truest sense, never still, never anchored, drifting from thrill to thrill with a kind of reckless grace. I followed her happily at first. Late nights bled into early mornings, shared beds, weekends stolen from real life like we were borrowing time we didn't intend to return. Being with her felt electric, like standing too close to something that might burn you.

And then, just like that, she was gone. No long unraveling, no drawn-out ending. One moment we were us, the next she'd dropped me like I was something she'd grown tired of carrying. The speed of it was what wrecked me. I didn't even have time to brace for impact. I just hit bottom.

After she left, everything went dark. Not dramatically, not in a way anyone else seemed to notice, just a slow, sinking heaviness that settled into my chest and stayed there. I stopped reaching out. Stopped wanting much of anything. I replayed it over and over, wondering how someone could leave so easily, and what that said about me. Eventually, the thought lodged itself deep: if she could walk away without looking back, maybe I hadn't been worth staying for at all. And that belief had followed me long after she was gone.

And here I was, like a puppy crawling back for seconds.

I ran a hand through my hair, pacing the room as I tried to process everything. I'd wanted to keep things clear between Alma and I, to avoid any confusion or messy entanglements, especially with Soledad in the picture. But now, the line between what I wanted and what I had had blurred.

I grabbed my phone and texted Sol, asking if we could meet for a quick chat before our plans tonight. As I hit send, I felt a heavy weight on my shoulders. I was about to dive into an uncomfortable conversation with her, one that could complicate things even further.

I watched as the text notification popped up on my phone. Soledad's reply was quick and enthusiastic.

Soledad: *Can't wait for tonight! I'm really looking forward to it. See you soon!*

I stared at the message for a moment, feeling guilt and uncertainty. I had hoped for a chance to explain how this was strictly a friendship hang, to somehow soften the blow, but her excitement only made me hesitate further. I knew the right thing to do was to be upfront with her, but in that moment, I couldn't bring myself to disrupt the evening's plans. It was easier to pretend everything was fine, to go along with the routine, even if it meant lying to both her and myself.

I took a deep breath and typed back:

Me: *Looking forward to it too.*

I was a fucking puppy.

Chapter Thirty-Four

CALLUM

As I prepared to meet Soledad later that evening, the weight of the situation pressed down on me. I could only hope that by the end of the night, I'd have some clarity, or at least a clearer sense of how to move forward.

I rode my motorcycle to the restaurant and my thoughts were tangled in a mess of confusion. The night ahead promised an evening of casual company, that was it, but my mind kept drifting back to Alma.

Soledad had been my everything for so long, but she crushed me without remorse. But couldn't we be what we once were? Then there was Alma. The way I'd felt with her was something different. The time we'd spent together, both under the sheets and outside of them, and the way she looked at me had stirred up emotions I'd been trying to keep at bay. I couldn't shake the feeling that I wanted more, something real, something genuine with her.

Soledad was already there when I walked in, like she always was, easy smile, bright green eyes, looking like she'd stepped straight out of a memory I hadn't asked for. I slid into the seat across from her and went through the motions. Polite conversation. Familiar jokes. The kind of laughter that came automatically, like muscle memory.

But the whole time, I felt like I was playing a version of myself I'd already outgrown. Nodding when I was supposed to. Smiling when it made sense. Careful not to give too much away. My past with Sol sat between us, unspoken but heavy, and it made me hesitant in ways I couldn't shake. I'd learned what it felt like to want more than someone was willing to give, and I wasn't eager to repeat it.

And then there was Alma. Slipping into my thoughts when she had no right to be there, pulling my attention away, no matter how hard I tried to stay present. Every time I caught myself drifting, I realized I wasn't fully here. I was pretending. Again.

As we finished dinner, I excused myself for a moment, stepping outside to get some fresh air. I stared out into the night, the cool breeze doing little to calm the storm inside me. The realization was sinking in: I wanted to be with Alma. I wanted to take that leap into the unknown, to explore whatever this connection between us could become. I wasn't just interested in a casual arrangement anymore; I was ready to pursue something more meaningful.

The more I thought about it, the more certain I became. Alma had shown me a side of myself I hadn't fully acknowledged before. I wanted to be open to that, to see where it could lead. The night with Soledad would end, and then I would make my way to Alma's place. I needed to tell her how I felt, to be honest about my intentions and see if we could build something more together.

My fingers hesitated for a moment before I started typing.

Me: *Hey, I know it's late, but I really want to see you tonight. Are you up for a visit?*

I hit send, my heart racing with the uncertainty of her response. A few moments later, my phone buzzed with her reply.

Alma: *I'm out with India and Tamara, but I should be home in about 45min?*

Me: *That works. See you then*

I felt a surge of relief, knowing that I had a chance to talk to her, to be honest about what I wanted. I took a deep breath as I headed back inside to rejoin Soledad.

I sat back down with a forced smile. As the evening progressed, I did my best to stay engaged, but my mind was focused on the conversation I hoped to have with Alma.

When it was time to say goodbye, I thought we were just ending it. Normal. Civil.

And then Sol stepped in, and before I could even process it, her hand brushed my arm, she leaned up and pressed a kiss to my lips like no time had passed. Like it was us. And for a split second?

I forget how to breathe.

ALMA

India was quite literally shoving me through the entrance of a question-able-looking dive bar in downtown Franklin, neon beer signs flickering like they were on their last leg and the floor already suspiciously sticky under my heels.

"Come on," she insisted, laughing as I dragged my feet. "You said you wanted a distraction. This is a distraction."

"This looks like where distractions go to die," I whined, wrinkling my nose as the smell of cheap tequila and regret hit me.

Tamara snorted behind us. "Relax, Alma. Two drinks in and you'll be thriving."

"Bold of you to assume I'll make it past one," I shot back, already scanning for the nearest exit.

And then I stopped. Dead. So abruptly that Tamara walked straight into my back.

"Hey, why the abrupt halt, weirdo?" she said, steadying herself, then followed my line of sight.

And everything inside me just dropped.

Callum.

Because why wouldn't he be here? And why wouldn't he be...kissing her.

Not just a quick kiss. Not just a friendly, hi-nice-to-see-you-again kiss. No. A kiss. The kind that says history. Familiarity. Something that made my stomach twist in a way I didn't want to examine too closely.

"Oh fuck this shit," India snapped beside me, already rolling up imaginary sleeves.

Tamara, on the other hand, was moving. Fast.

"Oh absolutely not," she said, already marching in their direction. "I'm about to whoop his ass."

I grabbed her arm. "Tamara, no."

She looked at me like I was the one overreacting. "Alma—"

"No," I repeated, firmer this time, even though my voice felt distant, like it was coming from somewhere outside my body.

I forced a shrug, like this didn't bother me, as if I didn't just feel something crack a little in my chest.

"If he wants to get back with his ex," I said, keeping my tone as even as I could, "he can."

The words tasted bitter.

"We never had a label on whatever that was."

And there it was. The loophole. The technicality. The thing that made this okay when it absolutely didn't feel okay.

I didn't wait for them to respond. I turned on my heel and pushed back out the door, the cool night air hitting me like a slap. I paced the sidewalk, arms wrapped around myself, trying to shake the image out of my head. I was failing...spectacularly.

"Are you kidding me?" India said, storming out behind me. "That man has audacity."

Tamara followed, equally fired up. "No, because the way I almost dragged him by that stupid leather jacket."

"Guys," I cut in, a little sharper than I meant to.

They both stopped.

I took a breath, staring out at the street, headlights passing, people laughing like the world didn't just tilt slightly off its axis.

"I just want to go home." My voice came out quieter this time.

And the night was officially over.

Chapter Thirty-Five

CALLUM

It took my brain a second to catch up. One second I was standing there, the noise of the bar buzzing around us, and the next Soledad's lips were on mine. And for a split second, it was like muscle memory. Like my body recognized her before my brain could step in and shut it down. Then it hit me. What the actual fuck.

I pulled back fast, hand coming up between us, putting space where there shouldn't have been contact in the first place.

"What the hell are you doing?" I asked.

She looked at me like it made sense. Like it was normal.

"Callum," she said, stepping closer, "I miss you. I miss us."

"No."

The word came out quick. No room for interpretation.

I shook my head, backing up a step. "No, you don't get to do this. Not again."

Her expression shifted, that familiar edge of defensiveness creeping in. And there was the version of her that rewrote things when they didn't go her way.

"You broke me," I said. It landed between us, solid. "You walked away like what we had didn't matter. Like I didn't matter."

I didn't wait for her response. I just turned and pushed through the crowd, out the door, needing air, space, anything that wasn't her standing too close.

I barely mde it to the sidewalk before I heard her heels behind me.

"Callum, that's not fair," she said, following me out. "It was intense. Too much, too fast. You know that."

I let out a short, humorless laugh, dragging a hand down my face. "Funny how it was only 'too much' when it stopped working for you."

She crossed her arms. "We're different now. We've grown up. That doesn't mean we can't try again."

I looked at her then. Really looked at her. And for the first time, I didn't feel pulled in. I just felt tired.

"Being older doesn't magically fix what you broke," I said, my voice steady now. "It just means we should know better than to repeat it."

She opened her mouth, but I shook my head, already done.

"I'm not that guy anymore," I added. "The one you can walk away from and then come back to when it's convenient."

There was a beat and silence stretched between us. This was final. And weirdly? It didn't scare me the way it used to because for the first time, I was not wondering if she was going to leave again. I was the one choosing to walk away.

I glanced back toward the bar for half a second, and that was when it hit me.

Alma.

Shit. A flicker of guilt hit, sharp and immediate. I was supposed to see her tonight. Talk to her. Fix whatever this thing was between us, and instead...

I exhaled, running a hand through my hair, already stepping toward my bike.

"Take care, Sol," I threw over my shoulder, not stopping.

I didn't wait for her response. I didn't need to because there was only one place I wanted to be and for once, I wasn't overthinking it.

I swung my leg over my motorcycle, engine roaring to life beneath me.

I needed to see Alma.

I got to Alma's place and barely had time to knock before the door swung open.

"Callum. Uh, you should leave," India said, arms crossed, eyes blazing.

I raised my hands, taking a cautious step forward. "India, wait, please. I need to talk to Alma."

She shook her head, stepping closer, like she was daring me to argue. "Talk to Alma? You mean like the way you were talking to that girl at the bar downtown? Or shall I say, kissing her?"

My stomach dropped. "It—it wasn't what it looked like. It was a misunderstanding, I swear."

"Sure it was," she said, smirking, and my stomach dropped lower. "That's what they all say when they slip and their dick lands in another girl's pussy."

I blinked. Then blinked again. "I didn't sleep with her. Please, I just need to talk to Alma. Explain everything. She deserves that."

India folded her arms tighter. "Callum, that's not happening tonight."

Before I could even open my mouth, she slammed the door shut in my face.

I was left standing there, hand frozen mid-knock, and the street suddenly felt a lot colder than usual.

Chapter Thirty-Six

ALMA

I had somehow managed not to see Callum all day, which honestly felt like a personal win. A small, beautiful gift from the universe.

According to Tamara, he'd been out on client visits with Chris, which explained his blessed absence from the office, and for once, I wasn't mad about it. The gods had looked down at me and said, you know what? She's been through enough. Truly. A miracle.

So imagine my delight, my absolute joy, when I pulled into my driveway, stepped out of my car, and saw him leaning against his stupid motorcycle like some kind of brooding, leather-jacket-wearing omen of emotional distress.

I slammed my car door a little harder than necessary. "What are you, a fucking stalker now?"

He pushed off the bike immediately, running a hand through his hair like he'd been waiting for this moment. "Alma, you have to listen to me."

I laughed, short and humorless, already heading toward the door. "Oh, do I?"

"I didn't kiss Soledad," he said quickly, stepping in front of me. "She kissed me. I promise, that's what happened."

I stopped, looking at him. Really looking at him. And God, I hated that a part of me wants to believe him.

"I saw all I needed to see, Callum," I said. "Your lips were on hers."

"That's not how it went down."

I shook my head, crossing my arms like that would somehow hold me together. "Okay, fine. Let's pretend I believe you. What were you doing there with her in the first place? On a not-date date?"

"It wasn't a date," he insisted. "We were just out. Catching up like old friends." He exhaled, frustration creeping in. "And yeah, maybe I shouldn't have gone. I know that now. But I don't want her."

The words hit something in me, but not in the way he probably hoped because it was not about her. It was about me.

"I thought we had something real," I said, and I hated that my voice wavered just a little. "But now it just feels like everything we had was a game to you. Something to pick up when it's convenient."

The space between us stretched, thick and uncomfortable.

"I don't have time for games, Callum."

For once, he didn't have a quick comeback. No smirk. No clever line. Just silence.

And when he finally opened his mouth to say something, anything, I shook my head. "No."

I turned before he could get the words out, walked up the steps, unlocked the door with hands that were only slightly shaking, and stepped inside. Then I closed it behind me and this time, I didn't look back.

CALLUM

Well that went spectacularly wrong. Like, if there were an award for fumbling the moment, I'd have a trophy in each hand and a speech prepared.

I stood there on the sidewalk staring at her closed door, half-expecting it to swing back open so I could try again. Say something better. Say anything at all. But it didn't.

And was stuck replaying it, her voice, the way it cracked just a little, the look in her eyes, and my brain just blanking. Like I got hit with a one-two punch and dropped straight to the mat, no count needed. Knockout. Game over.

I dragged a hand down my face, exhaling slow, because what the hell was that? Why didn't I fight for it? For her?

And then there it was. That voice. The one that's always hung out in the background, waiting for its moment.

See? it said. *This is your out.*

I shifted my weight like maybe I could shake it loose.

You don't have to do this, it continued, calm and convincing in a way that made it worse. *You don't have to fall. You don't have to risk it.*

Because that was the thing about not trying, you couldn't fail at something you never really had. If it was never real, if it never meant anything, then there's nothing to lose. No damage. No fallout. No waking up one day wondering how the hell you let someone matter that much.

I glanced back at her door. The spark. The way she looked at me like I was more than just whatever I'd decided I was.

That wasn't real, the voice pushed. *It couldn't have been. Not for someone like you.*

And yeah, it had a point, didn't it?

* * *

To distract myself from thoughts of Alma, I started going out more than I had before I'd met her. One particularly slow night, I found myself at a bar, nursing a drink that I barely tasted, as I stared out the window. The city lights blurred together, and I couldn't shake the sense of loneliness that had settled over me. I reached for my phone, scrolling through old messages and pictures, trying to remember what made things with Alma so special.

As I leaned against the bar, a blond, her hair shimmering under the dim lights, slid onto the stool next to me. Her blue eyes caught mine as she introduced herself.

"Hi, I'm Jenna. Are you okay? You seem a bit distracted with sad, puppy eyes," she said, her voice light and playful.

I forced a smile. "Just a lot on my mind. It's been one of those weeks."

Jenna tilted her head, a curious smile on her lips. "Well, if you need a distraction, I'm here. What's been bugging you?"

I tried to focus on the conversation, but my thoughts kept drifting back to Alma. "Just work stuff. Nothing major."

A few weeks later, I found myself chatting with Sarah, whose red hair and sharp brown eyes made her stand out. Her confidence was infectious, and she spoke with a sophisticated edge that was initially intriguing.

"So, what's your story?" Sarah asked, her gaze steady as she took a sip of her drink.

I shrugged, feeling the familiar pang of disconnection. "Just trying to figure things out. Been a bit of a rough patch lately."

Sarah raised an eyebrow, her eyes narrowing slightly. "Rough patch? Sounds like there's more to it. You seem like you're somewhere else entirely."

Her perceptiveness only reminded me of how much I missed Alma's presence, and I couldn't muster the enthusiasm I knew Sarah wanted.

Later that week, Emily, with her dark curls and hazel eyes, joined me at the bar. Her soothing demeanor and kind smile were a welcome change.

"Hi there," Emily said softly, her voice calm. "You seem like you could use some company. Mind if I join you?"

"Not at all," I replied, trying to push away the thoughts of Alma. We talked about the places we'd traveled, and though the conversation was engaging, it felt like a temporary fix.

"You seem miles away," Emily said gently as we spoke. "Is everything all right?'

I sighed, unable to shake the feeling that none of these connections could fill the void Alma had left. "Just dealing with some personal stuff. Nothing to worry about."

As the weeks passed, each of these encounters served only to highlight how empty things felt without Alma. No matter how pleasant the company was, nothing compared to the spark I had with her.

* * *

The office was unusually quiet one afternoon, the kind of quiet that amplified every small sound, the click of a keyboard, the hum of the AC, the distant murmur of conversations. I hadn't seen Alma all day, and it was getting to me more than I wanted to admit. It was like she had found a way to blend into the background, and the more I tried to focus on work, the more I felt her absence.

As I finished up an email, I caught a glimpse of her through the glass walls of the conference room. She was heading towards the kitchen, her expression focused, maybe even a little tense. I pushed back from my desk, the chair rolling smoothly across the floor, and decided to follow her.

I found her in the kitchen, pouring herself a cup of coffee. Her back was to me, and for a moment, I just watched her. She had her hair up in a messy bun, a few loose curls framing her face. Even in the sterile office lighting, she looked beautiful, and it took everything in me not to just walk over and tell her that.

Instead, I cleared my throat softly as I walked in. "Hey," I said, trying to keep my tone casual, as if I hadn't been replaying this moment in my head all day. "How's it going?"

She glanced over her shoulder at me, her expression guarded. "It's fine," she replied, not meeting my eyes as she continued to stir her coffee.

I leaned against the counter, searching for something to say that might get her to open up, or at least to smile. "How's prepping for the presentation going? It's later this week, right?"

Alma's lips twitched, like she wanted to smile but was holding back. "Good so far," she said, her tone polite but distant. It wasn't much, but it was something. "I'm going to head back to my desk."

She walked past me, her shoulder brushing against mine as she left the kitchen. I stood there for a moment, trying to collect my thoughts, but all I could think about was the look in her eyes when she told me I wasn't her boyfriend. It hurt, and I couldn't shake the feeling that I was losing her, that maybe I already had.

Chapter Thirty-Seven

ALMA

I stood outside the conference room, my heart racing as I adjusted my blazer and took a deep breath. Today was the day of the presentation, and everything I had prepared for was about to unfold in front of the management team. I heard a low murmur of voices inside, and nerves bubbled in my stomach.

As I pushed the door open, I was greeted by the sight of the managers seated around the table, their eyes fixed on me. Callum sat quietly, a smile on his face that told me I had this. Chris nodded in encouragement from the head of the table, and I stepped forward, ready to share my vision.

"Thanks for considering me for this position," I began, trying to keep my voice steady. "I'm excited to present my ideas for the PR strategy."

I set up my laptop and began clicking through my slides, highlighting our proposed social media campaigns and the importance of building community engagement. The managers nodded along, and my confidence surged.

"Alma," one of the senior managers, Karen, interjected, "can you explain how you plan to measure the success of these campaigns?"

"Absolutely," I replied, smiling at her. "We'll focus on key performance indicators such as engagement rates, conversion rates, and customer feedback. By analyzing these metrics, we can adapt our strategies in real time and ensure we're meeting our objectives."

"Great," another manager, Tom, chimed in. "What specific platforms are you considering for these campaigns?"

"I recommend focusing on specific social media platforms depending on audience," I explained, feeling the energy in the room shift. "These platforms have shown higher engagement rates with our target audience."

"Interesting approach," Chris noted, leaning forward. "How do you plan to incorporate user generated content?"

"That's a key component of our strategy," I said, my passion for the topic bubbling up. "By encouraging the clients' audience to share their experiences with the products, we can create authentic connections and enhance brand loyalty. This also opens the door for us to engage directly with their target audience."

The questions continued, and I felt myself hitting all my talking points with clarity and confidence. With each answer my nerves began to dissipate. I was in my element, and it felt exhilarating.

Finally, as I wrapped up my presentation, Chris smiled at me. "Thank you, Alma. This has been an insightful presentation. The team will make a selection on who will join the PR team in a couple of weeks."

I nodded, feeling a wave of relief wash over me. "Thank you for the opportunity. I'm looking forward to your feedback."

I gave one last look at Callum as I gathered my things.

As I stepped out of the conference room, I felt lighter than I had in weeks. I had done it. I had presented my ideas and answered their questions confidently. I couldn't help but smile to myself as I walked back to my desk. Whatever the outcome, I knew I had given it my all, and that was something I could be proud of.

As I settled back into my chair, a wave of gratitude washed over me when I thought of Callum. He had been instrumental in helping me put together the slides and brainstorming ideas that brought my presentation to life. His encouragement and insights had made all the difference, and I couldn't shake the warmth that spread through me at the memory of our afternoon spent working together. But along with that came a pang of longing for what we had shared, a connection that felt electric but was so complicated. I drove those thoughts aside, reminding myself to stay focused. I had my own goals to pursue, and I needed to channel this energy into securing my place on the PR team. Still, a small part of me wondered where our dynamic might lead if things were different.

* * *

The living room was dim, lit only by the glow of the TV and the faint light from the kitchen. India and I were sprawled across the couch, both too drained to muster much energy. She flipped idly through streaming options, her sock-clad feet propped up on the armrest. I had a throw pillow hugged to my chest, staring blankly at the screen as she scrolled.

"Anything catching your eye?" she asked, her voice soft and a little teasing.

"Not really," I murmured. The adrenaline from my PR presentation had long since faded, leaving behind an odd exhaustion. "Pick whatever. I'm fine with anything."

India glanced over, her sharp brown eyes narrowing as she studied me. "You're not still stressing about your presentation, are you? I'm sure you killed it, Alma. Seriously, I'm pretty sure they're going to put you in charge of a whole PR department soon."

I let out a dry laugh, shaking my head. "I wish. But no, I'm not stressing about it, just thinking."

She snorted, tossing the remote onto the coffee table. "You're always thinking. Work, life, whatever guy you're keeping at arm's length. When's the last time you let yourself just relax?"

I shrugged, trying to brush her off. "I'm relaxing right now."

India sat up, turning to face me fully, her expression softening. "Okay, so what's on your mind, then? Work? Romance? Rent?"

At the mention of rent, my cheeks flushed. I sat up too, fiddling

239

with the corner of the pillow in my lap. "Actually, about rent," I started hesitantly. "I might need a little extra time to pay my share this month."

India's face didn't betray even a flicker of annoyance, only concern. "Is everything okay?"

I hesitated, but her steady gaze made it impossible to lie. I sighed, leaning back against the couch. "It's just my family. Things are tight for them back home, and I've been sending what I can to help out. But with everything else, bills, groceries, and trying to keep up with my own life here, it's been hard."

India nodded slowly, her expression thoughtful. "That's why you've been taking all those side gigs, isn't it? Writing press releases and whatnot late at night?"

"Yeah," I admitted, my voice barely above a whisper. "I didn't want to say anything because I didn't want to seem I don't know, irresponsible, or like I'm struggling. But I am a little. And I just feel this constant pressure to help them. They sacrificed so much for me, and I can't just not help."

India reached over, placing a comforting hand on my knee. "Alma, first of all, you're not irresponsible. You're doing everything you can for your family, and that's more than most people would even attempt. But you've got to cut yourself some slack. You're just one person, and you can't fix everything on your own. It's okay to prioritize yourself sometimes, too."

I looked at her, my throat tight with emotion. "But what if I can't balance it all? What if I let someone down?"

"Then you let them down," she said firmly. "It's not the end of the world. The people who love you, and that includes your family, will understand. And you've got me, okay? You're not doing this alone."

Her words hit me like a lifeline, and for the first time in weeks, I felt the weight on my chest lighten just a little. I managed a small smile, reaching over to squeeze her hand. "Thanks, India. You're a good friend."

"Don't mention it," she said, settling back against the couch. "Now, how about I pick a movie so we can actually relax for real?"

I nodded, the knot in my stomach easing as she grabbed the remote. For tonight, at least, I'd let myself breathe.

Chapter Thirty-Eight

ALMA

I walked into the pottery studio, the familiar smell of wet clay and faint traces of glaze filling the air. The hum of spinning wheels and soft chatter from other patrons created a comforting rhythm, one that almost drowned out the noise in my head. Almost.

Callum had brought me here once, months ago, before everything fell apart. I remembered how his hands had looked, strong and steady as he shaped the clay, the teasing look in his eye when he told me I'd ruin my nails if I wasn't careful. I shook the memory off, refusing to let it take hold. I was here for myself, to escape the ache I couldn't quite shake, and to forget, if only for a little while.

Time kept slipping by, the days blurring together as I threw myself into work and anything else that might keep my mind occupied. But no matter how busy I stayed, his betrayal lingered beneath the surface, like a dull throb that refused to fade completely. And now, with the announcement for the PR position looming, the tension was unbearable. I needed something to ground me, to remind me that I could still find peace in the chaos.

I picked a seat by the window, the light filtering in soft and warm against my skin. The instructor handed me a lump of clay, and I pressed my fingers into it, feeling its cool resistance. It was messy, imperfect, and exactly what I needed. As I worked the clay between my hands, the knot in my chest loosened slightly.

But even here, in this space that should've felt like an escape, the memories crept in. I could see him in my mind, leaning over the wheel, his voice low as he explained the process. The weight of his apology played on repeat, mingling with the moments we'd shared. And now, at work, all that remained were polite nods and brief, stilted exchanges.

The clay started to take shape beneath my hands, a shallow bowl forming slowly but surely. It wasn't much, but it was something. I focused on the smoothness of the surface, the way it spun beneath my palms, and tried to let the rhythm quiet my thoughts.

The pain wasn't as sharp as it once was, but it lingered like a bruise that refused to heal completely. Mornings were the worst, staring into cold coffee, replaying everything that had gone wrong. Even now, as I sat molding the clay, I couldn't help but wonder if the numbness would ever go away. If I'd ever stop feeling the weight of what could've been.

But for now, at least, I had this. My hands, the clay, and the promise of something new taking shape, however small or fragile it might be.

Later that evening, I found myself lying on my couch, flipping through channels aimlessly, when my phone buzzed with a notification. I glanced at it, hoping for a distraction. I picked it up, seeing Tamara's name flash on the screen.

Tamara: *Hey Alma! I'm heading to a speed dating event downtown tonight. It's supposed to be a lot of fun and a great way to meet new people. Want to join? I can cover your entry charge, it's not much, and I'm already on the site. Could be a nice change of pace!*

I hesitated for a moment, my mind racing with thoughts of Callum and the lingering ache of everything that had happened between us. It wasn't easy to shake off, but Tamara's enthusiasm and the chance to break out of my routine were tempting. Plus, it helped that she'd insisted on covering my entry fee tonight, which meant I wouldn't have to dip further into my account than necessary. I took a deep breath, reminded myself that it was time to move on, and began typing my response.

Me: *That sounds like a great idea. I could use a change of scenery and a bit of excitement. Count me in! What time are you heading out?*

Tamara replied almost immediately:

Tamara: *Awesome! Let's meet up around 7. The event starts at 7:30, so we'll have some time to grab a drink beforehand. See you soon!*

I put my phone down, feeling both nervous and excited. It had been a while since I'd been out on the dating scene, and the thought of meeting new people was exhilarating, but still a bit intimidating. I stood up, stretching out the stiffness in my body, and began to prepare for the evening.

I decided that a sleek black dress that flattered my figure, paired with a light, airy cardigan, was just the right choice for a speed dating event. I applied makeup, aiming for a natural look that would still make me feel confident. As I styled my hair, letting a few curls frame my face, I caught a glimpse of myself in the mirror. I looked different, more alive, like my old self again.

I grabbed my purse and slipped on a pair of comfortable yet chic heels. The evening felt like a chance to reset, a small step towards rediscovering parts of myself that had been overshadowed by the recent past.

With one last glance in the mirror, I took a deep breath and headed out the door. The downtown bar where the speed dating event was being held wasn't too far from my house, so I decided to walk. The crisp evening air was refreshing, and I welcomed the chance to clear my mind as I made my way.

The place was buzzing with activity, a lively mix of laughter, clinking glasses, and upbeat music. The warm, dim lighting gave the room a cozy, inviting feel, contrasting with the energetic chatter that filled the air. The bar was stylish, with modern decor, sleek wooden tables, high stools, and walls adorned with eclectic art. The scent of mixed cocktails and the faint aroma of bar snacks wafted through the air, adding to the ambiance.

Tamara and our friends had already claimed a table near the back, which offered a good vantage point of the entire space. I joined them, grabbing a seat and settling in with a cocktail Tamara handed me. The noise around us seemed to blend into a pleasant hum as I took a deep breath, mentally preparing myself for the speed dating event.

"Alma!" Tamara greeted with a warm hug. "I'm so glad you made it!"

I smiled, feeling the tension in my shoulders begin to ease. "Thanks for inviting me. This should be fun."

We settled into our seats and sipped on our drinks, and I let myself relax, focusing on the chatter and laughter around me. The nerves were still there, but they were beginning to be overshadowed by a sense of anticipation. Tonight was about new beginnings, and for the first time in a long while, I felt ready to embrace them.

As the event kicked off, a host began explaining the rules and the format. He had the women sit at the high-top tables while the men would be making the rounds from table to table. I looked at Tamara, who was perched up and looking confident, as always, as we waited for the fun to begin.

The first guy who approached me was Josh. He looked friendly enough with an easy smile. We started talking, and he seemed genuinely interested in getting to know me.

"So, Alma, what do you like to do for fun?" Josh asked, leaning in slightly as he spoke, his blue eyes piercing through me.

I smiled, feeling more at ease with his engaging approach. "I love playing basketball, and I'm really into exploring new places around Franklin. I also love art and like to hit up galleries whenever there's a new exhibit. What about you?"

Josh's face lit up with enthusiasm. "That's cool! I'm really into hiking and outdoorsy stuff. I've got a few trails I've been dying to try. Maybe you can take me to an exhibit sometime? And I'll take you hiking."

Our conversation flowed naturally. We talked about our favorite spots in the city, his recent adventures, and shared a few laughs. It was refreshing to have a pleasant, engaging chat with someone who seemed genuinely interested in connecting.

When the timer signaled the end of our conversation, Josh gave me a friendly nod. "It was great talking to you. I'll see you around!"

The next guy to sit down was Toby, and from the moment he settled into the seat across from me, I couldn't help but notice his eyes kept drifting to my chest. His gaze was persistent and distracting, making me uncomfortable despite his friendly tone.

"So, what's your favorite video game?" Toby asked, his eyes still not meeting mine.

I tried to stay upbeat, focusing on making the best of the situation. "I'm not really into video games, but I've heard a lot about them. What's your favorite game?"

"Oh, man, I'm obsessed with this new RPG that just came out. It's got this epic storyline, and you can customize your character in so many ways. I've been spending every free minute I have on it. You should totally try it out!"

As he talked about his video games, his gaze continued to wander, and it became increasingly hard to focus on the conversation. It felt like he was more interested in talking about his hobby than getting to know me, and his lack of eye contact made me feel like an afterthought.

The conversation felt one sided and shallow, and when the timer ended, I was relieved. Toby flashed a quick, distracted smile and moved on to the next table. I sighed, taking a sip of my drink, and looked around the bar. The lively atmosphere was still buzzing, and I was determined to make the most of the evening despite the awkward encounters.

As the night wore on, the conversations started to blur together. There was Mark, cute, with a charming smile, but he seemed obsessed with his work. He spent most of our time talking about his latest project, barely pausing to ask anything about me. I tried to engage, but it was clear that his mind was elsewhere, lost in deadlines and meetings.

Then there was Justin. I could barely focus on what he was saying because his breath was, to put it kindly, overpowering. Every time he leaned in, I had to fight the urge to lean back. It didn't help that our conversation was stilted, with long pauses that made the minutes stretch on painfully.

And then there were countless other men, each with their quirks. Some were too eager, others too aloof. A few seemed nice enough, but there just wasn't that spark. With each new face, my mind kept drifting back to Callum.

No matter how hard I tried to focus on the men in front of me, I couldn't shake the feeling that something was missing. They just weren't him. I hated myself a little for it, knowing how things had ended, but the truth was undeniable. None of them made me feel the way Callum did, even now, after everything. The connection, the banter, the way he could make me laugh even when I didn't want to, it was all still there, lingering in the back of my mind like a shadow I couldn't escape.

I sipped my drink and forced a smile for the next guy who sat across from me. It wasn't just that these men weren't a match, it was that they weren't Callum. And I wasn't sure what to do with that.

The night at the speed dating event ended with me getting Josh's number. He was the only one who seemed genuinely interested in getting to know me, and there was something easy about our conversation.

Over the last week, we texted each other often, and I couldn't help but feel a little flutter of excitement every time my phone buzzed with a message from him.

At work, I couldn't wait to tell Tamara about it. We were huddled in the break room, and I was mid sip of my coffee when Tamara leaned in with a knowing grin.

"So, how's it going with Josh?" she asked, her eyes sparkling with curiosity.

I smiled, feeling something spread in my chest. "Actually, he asked me out on an official date. Finally!"

Her eyebrows shot up. "Seriously? That's great! You've been needing this. Are you excited?"

"Yeah, I am," I admitted, trying to keep my voice casual but failing miserably. "It feels different, you know? He's sweet, and we've been talking a lot. I'm actually looking forward to seeing where this goes."

Tamara nudged me playfully. "That's what I like to hear. A fresh start with someone new could be exactly what you need. You deserve to have fun again. Enjoy the date, and don't overthink it."

I knew she was right. After everything that happened with Callum, I had to let go of the past and focus on moving forward. And maybe, just maybe, Josh could be the beginning of that new chapter.

Chapter Thirty-Nine

CALLUM

On my way to the kitchen to grab another cup of coffee I caught the tail end of Alma's conversation with Tamara. Their voices carried just enough for me to catch a few words. Alma was talking about a date. My heart clenched in my chest, and I stopped dead in my tracks just outside the kitchen entrance, unable to move.

A date. She was going on a date.

I felt like someone had punched me in the gut. The jealousy hit me hard and fast, paralyzing me as I tried to process what I'd just heard. Alma, my Alma, was moving on. And here I was, standing in the hallway like an idiot, my coffee forgotten, my thoughts a tangled mess.

I should've known this was coming. It had been months since everything between us fell apart, but hearing her talk about someone else, knowing she was interested in someone else, it made it all too real. The thought of her with another guy, laughing at his jokes, smiling at him, her straddling him the way she used to straddle me, it was more than I could bear.

I leaned against the wall, trying to steady myself, but the images kept flashing in my mind. Who was this guy? Was he better for her? Did he make her happy in a way I couldn't?

I wanted to walk in there, say something, anything, to stop her, to tell her how much it killed me to think of her with someone else. But I couldn't. I had no right. Not after what I did.

So I just stood there, feeling the bitter sting of jealousy and regret, knowing I had no one to blame but myself.

After what felt like an eternity, I forced myself to move, pushing off the wall and walking into the kitchen. My heart pounded in my chest, and my mind raced, but I couldn't stand out here forever. As I stepped inside, Tamara was on her way out, laughing about something I couldn't bring myself to care about.

Alma was still in the kitchen, standing by the counter, seemingly lost in thought. She hadn't seen me come in yet, and for a moment, I just watched her. She looked different somehow, maybe it was the way she was carrying herself, or the distant look in her eyes. She was somewhere else, maybe thinking about that guy, and the jealousy flared up again, sharp and painful.

I cleared my throat, trying to shake off the unease. "Hey."

She looked up, startled, her eyes meeting mine. For a second, something flickered there, surprise, maybe, or something else I couldn't quite place, but it was gone as quickly as it had come. "Oh, hey, Callum."

I forced a casual smile, though it felt like it was tearing me apart. "You all right? You seemed deep in thought."

She shrugged, looking away, her fingers tracing the edge of the countertop. "Yeah, just...you know, things on my mind."

I wanted to ask her what things, to know if it was him she was thinking about, but I couldn't bring myself to do it. Instead, I grabbed a mug from the cabinet, trying to keep my hands steady as I poured myself some coffee. "Anything you want to talk about?"

Alma hesitated, biting her lip. She looked like she was considering it for a moment, but then she shook her head. "No, it's nothing. Just the usual."

Before I could think of something else to say, Alma pushed off from the counter, grabbing her mug.

"I should get back to work," she said, her voice quiet, almost as if she didn't want to leave, but couldn't stay either.

"Yeah, sure," I replied, my voice sounding hollow even to me. "I'll, uh, see you around."

She gave me a small, tight smile, one that didn't reach her eyes, and walked past me, heading out of the kitchen. I watched her go, every step she took feeling like she was walking further out of my reach.

As I made my way back to my desk, the dull roar of office noise filled my ears, but it was all muted, like I was underwater. My mind was stuck on Alma, on how distant she felt even when she was standing right in front of me. I could barely focus on anything else, and when I reached my desk, I realized I hadn't even brought my coffee with me.

I slumped into my chair, staring blankly at my computer screen, trying to gather my thoughts. But then, I heard voices, familiar ones, drifting over from the cubicles in front of me, separated by slats. Alma and Tamara. They were talking, and my hearing immediately tuned in, the rest of the office noise fading into the background.

"So, where are you and Josh going?" Tamara asked, her tone playful and teasing.

Every muscle in my body tensed as I strained to hear Alma's response.

Her voice was soft, almost hesitant. "We're going to that Cuban fusion place downtown. You know, the one everyone's been talking about."

Tamara let out a low whistle. "Nice. Sounds like he's really trying to impress you."

"Maybe," Alma replied, and I could practically hear the smile in her voice.

"It's been a while since you've gone on a real date."

"Yeah," Alma admitted, and there was something in her tone that made my chest tighten. "It's nice to just have something to look forward to again, you know?"

Tamara laughed. "Well, you deserve it, girl. This Josh guy better know how lucky he is."

I couldn't listen anymore. Every word felt like a knife, cutting deeper and deeper. Alma was excited about this guy, and I, I was just sitting here, watching it all slip away.

But as much as it hurt, I couldn't tear myself away from their conversation. It was like I needed to hear it, to understand just how much I'd lost, even if it killed me.

ALMA

Friday finally arrived, and I could hardly contain my excitement as I walked into the office, ready to tackle the day. I was looking forward to my date with Josh to end the day, but first, it was time to work. The sun streamed through the windows, casting a warm glow on everything, but my focus was solely on the upcoming meeting with Chris. As I approached his office, I took a deep breath, hoping for good news.

"Hey, Alma! Come on in!" Chris called, waving me inside.

I stepped into his office, and he looked up from his notes, a broad smile spreading across his face.

"I have some fantastic news for you."

"Really? What is it?" My heart raced.

"You've landed the spot on the PR team for the new client!" Chris announced, his voice full of enthusiasm. "And you'll play an integral role in managing the account alongside the VP."

I blinked in disbelief, my stomach flipping with excitement. "Are you serious? I can't believe it!"

Chris nodded, still beaming. "Absolutely! Your ideas during the presentation were impressive. All the managers were really taken with the campaigns you proposed. They see great potential in you."

"Thank you so much, Chris! This means everything to me," I said, unable to hide my grin.

He leaned back in his chair, clearly pleased. "You earned it. Just keep that creative energy flowing. I'm looking forward to seeing what you'll do with this account. With the new role, you'll slowly transition off the renewals team." He continued. "This position does come with a hefty pay bump.".

As I left his office, a rush of exhilaration washed over me. I had worked hard for this, and now I was stepping into a role that could shape my career. I couldn't wait to get started and prove that I was more than capable of handling this opportunity.

I picked up my phone and typed a message to my mami, my excitement bubbling over.

Me: *Mami! You won't believe it, I got the PR position for the new client I told you about!*

Mami: *Mija! That's amazing! I'm so proud of you! Felicidades*

Me: *Gracias! I'll be managing the account with the VP too! It feels like a dream*

Mami: *You've worked so hard for this. I knew you could do it!*

Me: *Thank you, Mami. Love you!*

I smiled, feeling a surge of pride and love for my mom, knowing I would always have her support.

And of course, because the universe loves a good plot twist, Callum spotted me. He started making his way over, all easy confidence.

"Wow," he said as he reached me, shoving his hands into his pockets, a small smile tugging at his lips. "So I heard congratulations are in order."

I mirrored the smile, because apparently I'd decided to be mature now. Growth. Loved that for me.

"Thank you," I said. "And, for the record, thanks for your help. I don't think I could've pulled it off without you."

He shook his head immediately, like I'd just insulted him. "Yeah, no. That's definitely not true. Those were all your ideas. I just sat there and agreed like a very supportive, very handsome accessory."

I let out a soft laugh, and then...

He looked at me. Not casually. Not jokingly. Just looked. And it did something stupid to my chest. That warm, swell-y, inconvenient kind of feeling I absolutely did not have time for right now. Nope. Abort mission. *Shut it down, Alma.*

* * *

Later that night, I buzzed with excitement as I waited for Josh to pick me up. When he arrived, he came to my door, greeting me with a smile that made my nerves flutter. "You look beautiful," he said, his voice warm and sincere.

As we drove to the restaurant, Josh's hand hesitantly found its way to my leg, his fingers tracing light circles that sent shivers up my spine. Goosebumps rose on my skin, and my core immediately ached, the sensation startling me. I hadn't felt that way since Callum. I forced the thought out of my mind, determined to focus on tonight, on Josh. This evening was about him, not about the memories I was trying to leave behind.

When we arrived at the restaurant, the ambiance was vibrant, with salsa playing in the background. The air smelled like grilled pineapple, charred jerk spices, and something citrusy and sweet. It had a vintage Caribbean charm, with dark wood paneling and plush red booths. Framed black and white photos of island streets and vintage Havana cars lined the paneling, and somewhere near the bar, bottles of bright, jewel-toned liquor caught the light like stained glass.

As we were seated, Josh slid into the booth beside me instead of across, which struck me as a bit odd. I was used to sitting face-to-face on dates, but I shrugged it off, trying to adapt to the unfamiliar setup. Maybe this was just how he felt comfortable.

As Josh and I settled into the booth, the conversation started light, mostly about work and mutual interests. Then, out of nowhere, he asked, "So, when was your last relationship?"

I froze for a moment, not wanting to dive into that mess tonight. I had been so determined to keep my mind on Josh and away from Callum. But the question lingered in the air, and I felt compelled to answer. "It ended about three months ago," I finally admitted, my voice low. I paused, hesitating before adding, "If you can even call it a relationship. It was more of a situationship."

Josh nodded, seemingly understanding. "Those can be the hardest to get over. It's like you're stuck in this gray area."

"Yeah," I agreed, though I didn't really want to dwell on it. The last thing I needed was Callum creeping into my thoughts again tonight. "What about you? When was your last relationship?" I asked, though the truth was, I didn't really care to know. I just needed to shift the focus away from me.

As Josh started talking about his ex and how things ended, I tried to listen, but my mind kept drifting. The air around us felt thick, like the atmosphere had shifted, a familiar tension prickling at the edges of my consciousness. I glanced around the restaurant, and that was when I saw him.

Callum.

He strolled into the restaurant with that easy confidence of his, as if he belonged there. My heart skipped a beat as I realized he wasn't just here by coincidence, he was walking directly toward us. Panic surged through me, mingled with a strange sense of anticipation. What was he doing here? And why was he coming to our table?

My breath caught in my throat as Callum closed the distance, his striking blue eyes locking onto mine, leaving me with no escape.

The air between us felt charged as Callum approached our table. My heart thudded in my chest, and I could barely process what was happening.

"Callum," I started, my voice sharp as I tried to keep my composure. "What are you doing here?"

He didn't answer right away, his gaze flicking to Josh for the briefest moment before returning to me. "I need to talk to you, Alma. It's important."

I shook my head, refusing to let him derail my night. "No, Callum. Whatever it is, it can wait. I'm on a date."

Josh, who had been watching the exchange with a frown, finally chimed in. "Yeah, man, we're on a date. You should get lost."

Callum's expression darkened, his usual confident demeanor replaced by something more raw, more desperate. "This has nothing to do with you," he snapped, his voice low and edged with frustration.

Josh stood up, his posture rigid as he puffed out his chest, trying to assert himself. "It has everything to do with me. She doesn't want you here. So why don't you just leave?"

The tension was palpable, the restaurant's ambient noise fading into the background as I felt the weight of both their gazes on me. I knew I had to step in before things escalated any further.

"Callum, just go," I said, trying to sound firm, but my voice wavered slightly. "You've lost your chance to talk to me."

His eyes softened, pleading with me in a way I hadn't seen before. "Please, Alma. Just give me a few minutes. That's all I'm asking."

Something in his tone made me hesitate. Despite everything, despite the hurt and the betrayal, a part of me still wanted to hear what he had to say. I sighed, feeling a pang of guilt as I turned to Josh.

"I'm sorry, Josh. I'll be right back, I promise," I said quietly, sliding out of the booth. Maybe I just needed to placate him so he'd leave us alone.

Josh's jaw tightened, but he nodded, though I could see the frustration in his eyes. "Fine. But don't take too long, okay?"

"I won't," I assured him, even as I felt the uncertainty gnawing at my resolve. I didn't know why I was doing this, why I couldn't just send Callum away. Maybe it was curiosity, or maybe it was that small, stubborn part of me that still cared about him.

But as I stepped away from the booth and followed Callum outside, I wondered if this was a mistake.

As soon as we were outside, the cool evening air wrapped around me, totally different than the heat simmering under my skin. I crossed my arms, trying to maintain my composure, even as my heart raced with conflicting emotions.

"What the hell are you doing here?" I snapped, my voice clipped and full of frustration. "Why would you come here just to ruin my date?"

He looked at me, his expression pure regret. "I'm sorry. I'm sorry for all of it." His voice was low, almost tender, and it took everything in me not to let it break through the wall I'd built around my heart. "I couldn't stand it anymore. Not being with you, not hearing your laugh, not seeing your smile. Not being completely open," he confessed.

I opened my mouth to respond, but the words caught in my throat as his eyes darkened, taking on a look that sent a shiver down my spine.

"And I missed not seeing you come undone for me," he added, his voice a husky whisper that I felt deep in my center.

My breath hitched, and a familiar warmth pooled low in my belly, betraying me. Damn him. Damn him for still having this effect on me. I took a step back, desperate to put some distance between us, but I felt the rough texture of the brick wall behind me, trapping me.

He followed, closing the gap between us in one smooth motion. My pulse quickened as he leaned in, his mouth brushing against my ear, his minty smelling breath warm and intoxicating, filling my senses with memories of every moment we'd shared.

"Apparently I'd been starving until I tasted you," he murmured, his words sending a jolt through me, straight to the core. My resolve was crumbling, and I hated myself for it, but the way his body hovered so close to mine, the heat radiating off him, the familiar scent of him, everything was drawing me in, pulling me under.

I pressed my palms against his chest, meaning to push him away, but instead, I found myself lingering, feeling the strong, steady beat of his heart beneath my hands. The connection between us had never truly severed, no matter how much I tried to convince myself otherwise. It was still there, simmering, threatening to consume us both.

"Callum," I breathed out, my voice betraying the turmoil inside me.

But he didn't back off. Instead, he cupped my face with his hand, forcing me to meet his gaze. His eyes searched mine, as if looking for the answer to a question neither of us could fully articulate.

"I miss you," he whispered, his thumb brushing softly over my cheek. "I've been a wreck without you. I can't keep pretending that I'm okay because I'm not. I need you."

His words were like a match to dry kindling, igniting everything I'd been trying so hard to keep buried. But despite the fire, the heat, and the undeniable pull I felt towards him, the pain he'd caused still lingered, raw and unhealed.

I closed my eyes, trying to steel myself against the tide of emotions. "Why now?" I asked, my voice cracking. "Why did you wait until I tried to move on?"

He hesitated. "Because I'm an idiot," he finally admitted, his voice thick with regret. "I was scared of screwing things up even more, but seeing you with someone else, I couldn't handle it. I couldn't stand the thought of you being with someone who isn't me."

His confession hung in the air, heavy and charged with everything we hadn't said. I opened my eyes, meeting his gaze, and for the first time in months, I saw the vulnerability he usually kept hidden behind his confident facade.

I wanted to stay strong, to resist him, but the intensity in his eyes, the sincerity in his words, it was all too much. The dam I'd built around my heart was cracking, and I didn't know how much longer I could keep holding it all back.

I stood there, the cool night air swirling around me, my thoughts racing as Callum's confession weighed heavily on my mind. I knew I needed to confront everything that had happened, to get some closure, but the reality of it all was overwhelming. I took a deep breath, trying to steady myself.

"All right," I said, my voice steady but firm. "I'll come by your place after my date. We can talk things through."

His face lit up with relief. "Thank you," he said softly. He gave me one last, intense gaze before turning and walking toward his motorcycle. The sight of him straddling it, the way he revved the engine, only added to the complexity of the emotions swirling inside me.

As he rode off into the night, I stood there for a moment longer, contemplating my next steps. It was clear that seeing Callum again, even just for a conversation, wasn't going to be the end of it. I had to face the reality of our past and determine if there was any future for us, or if I was just clinging to a ghost.

Thirty-five minutes later, Josh and I stood outside my door, the porch light casting that slightly-too-flattering glow, and Josh was looking at me like the night was very much not over in his mind.

"So..." he said, rocking back on his heels, flashing a hopeful grin. "You gonna invite me in?"

I blinked. Ah. I shifted my weight, forcing a polite smile. "I don't know if that's a good idea."

His smile faltered just a little. "Was it that guy?"

"Callum?" I asked before I could stop myself, then quickly shook my head. "No, no, not at all. This has nothing to do with him."

"Then why can't I come in?" he pressed, stepping a little closer.

And just like that, the vibe was off.

I crossed my arms, putting a little space between us. "Because I think this is where the date should end," I said, keeping my tone light but firm. "We had a good time, right?"

"Yeah," he said, smiling again, but there was something off about it now. "And I think we could have even more fun."

Oh no, sir. Annoyance flared, sharp and immediate, because of course, of course the nice guy with decent conversation turned out to be a little douche bag.

I opened my door, already done. "Goodnight, Josh."

And before he could try again, I slipped inside the townhouse and shut the door behind me.

Chapter Forty

CALLUM

I paced the small area of my apartment, glancing repeatedly at the clock. I kept my phone close, waiting for that reassuring ping that never came. Every minute felt like an eternity as the night stretched on. Alma had said she'd come over after her date, but as the hours ticked by, my hope was dwindling.

I pulled out my phone and sent another text, a simple, "Are you still coming?" I hit send and then watched the tiny blue bubbles indicating delivery, but there was no reply. I tried to convince myself that she might be running late or maybe her phone had died. But deep down, I knew better.

I sank onto the edge of the sofa, feeling the weight of the day pressing down on me. The silence of the apartment was suffocating. I picked up my phone again, staring at the screen, hoping for some miraculous change. But as another hour passed with no response, the harsh reality set in.

Frustration and a deep sense of defeat built up inside me. I threw my phone across the room, watching as it clattered onto the floor, the screen flashing briefly before it lay still. My heart pounded, each beat echoing the hollow feeling in my chest. I was angry, not just at Alma but at myself for hoping too much, for thinking she'd come back to me so easily.

I ran a hand through my hair and rubbed my face, trying to shake off the anxiety and frustration. The apartment felt emptier than ever, the reality of my own loneliness settling in. I slumped back on the couch, staring blankly at the wall, my mind a jumble of regret. I had made mistakes, and I was paying for them now. All I could do was wait, but the waiting was unbearable.

I flipped open my sketch pad, the familiar weight of the pencil feeling like a lifeline in my hand. I sketched a figure, perhaps a reflection of my own restless spirit, caught in a moment of contemplation, a slight smile playing on its lips. Each stroke provided a momentary distraction, but my thoughts kept drifting back to Alma. She was sure to come. I just needed to wait a bit longer. The anticipation gnawed at me, though. I could almost feel her energy filling the empty spaces in my apartment, brightening the shadows that lingered in the corners. But for now, I buried myself in the art, trying to ignore the anxiety curling in my stomach like a coiled snake.

* * *

I jolted awake on the couch, the harsh light of morning streaming through the windows and hitting me square in the face. I squinted against the brightness, realizing I was still in the same clothes from the night before. I sat up, my body aching and my mind heavy with the weight of the previous evening.

The memories hit me like a freight train. Alma's promise that she'd come over, the hope I had clung to, and the crushing disappointment when she didn't. The way I'd laid everything bare, only for it to be met with silence. I'd poured my heart out, confessed my feelings, and for what? To be left waiting, alone, with nothing but my own mistakes echoing in the empty apartment.

I rubbed my face, trying to chase away the fog of sleep and regret. I had hoped she'd come back, that we could sort things out, but now, all I had was a lingering sense of loss and a gnawing ache in my chest.

I pushed myself up from the couch and stumbled into the kitchen, grabbing a quick bite before heading out. I was determined to put the night behind me, to find some way to forget about Alma and the mess I'd made.

Later that evening, I met up with Chris at a bar, hoping the distraction would help clear my mind. The place was buzzing with activity, a typical Saturday night crowd. As I scanned the room, I noticed a brunette across the bar giving me the kind of look that was hard to ignore. I felt a flicker of interest, my dick hardening, a distraction from the swirling thoughts of Alma that had been eating at me all day.

Chris nudged me, following my gaze. "She's cute," he said with a smirk. "But you don't seem like your head's in the game tonight."

I shrugged, trying to brush it off, but Chris wasn't letting it go.

"This about Alma?" he asked, his tone more serious now. I didn't answer right away, just took a long sip of my drink.

"Man, I don't know what's going on with her," I finally admitted. "I thought we were getting somewhere, but now it feels like I've just messed everything up. Again."

Chris leaned back, considering. "Office relationships, Callum. They never really work out, do they? Too many complications, too much baggage. You gotta decide if she's worth it."

I sighed, knowing he had a point. "Yeah, but it's different with her. She's...I don't know how to explain it. It just feels like she's worth the risk."

Chris looked at me for a moment, then nodded slowly. "Maybe you need to do something about it then. If she's worth it, prove it. You ever thought about making a big gesture? Show her you're serious?"

I scoffed, half joking. "Like what, some grand romantic move? That shit only works in movies."

"Maybe," Chris replied, grinning, "but it wouldn't hurt to try. Women like Alma, they want to know you're willing to put yourself out there. Could be what it takes to get her back."

I mulled over his words, the idea of some grand gesture feeling both ridiculous and oddly tempting. But then, reality set back in. "But what if I mess it up even more?" I asked, doubt in my voice.

Chris shrugged, giving me a level look. "You've already messed up plenty, right? What's one more shot? If it works, it works. If not, at least you know you tried."

I nodded, anxiety settling in. Maybe Chris was right. Maybe this was the time to stop overthinking and just go for it. "All right," I said, more to myself than to him. "I'll think about it."

Chris grinned, raising his glass. "That's the spirit. Just don't do anything too crazy. You've got to keep some dignity, man."

I chuckled, clinking my glass with his. "Yeah," I muttered, taking a slow sip. "Dignity. I'll try to remember that."

He laughed, already moving on to something else, but I stayed quiet.

As my wheels began to turn, I could feel it, the shift. The part of me that had been pacing back and forth for weeks, weighing every possible outcome, finally starting to lean in one direction. I was tired of replaying the same moments in my head. Tired of pretending I didn't care as much as I did. Maybe Chris was right. Maybe thinking it to death wasn't going to change anything.

I set my glass down, jaw tightening just slightly.

I wasn't going to do anything reckless. But I wasn't going to sit still anymore either.

Chapter Forty-One

CALLUM

The day I decided to talk to India and Tamara was a day I could honestly say scared me. The weight of it sat heavy on my shoulders all day, pressing in, reminding me at every inconvenient moment that I'd officially run out of options. Alma remained front and center, like my brain didn't get the memo to move on.

So here I was. Swallowing what little pride I had left and doing the one thing I swore I wouldn't do, asking for help.

I was standing outside this cozy little café as the sun dipped below the horizon, the warm glow from inside spilling out onto the sidewalk like an invitation I wasn't entirely sure I deserved. My hands were shoved in my jacket pockets, nerves buzzing under my skin in a way that felt ridiculous considering I'd handled million-dollar clients with less anxiety than this.

Tamara was not exactly thrilled when I reached out. Actually, "reluctant" felt generous. And I was about ninety percent sure it took some serious convincing on her end to get India to even consider showing up today instead of, I don't know, keying my bike. Which, honestly? Fair.

I exhaled, glancing at the door, then back down the street. This was either a really good idea or the exact moment my life turned into a public execution.

The door to the café chimed softly as I pushed it open, the warm smell of coffee and baked goods enveloping me. I spotted India and Tamara at a corner table, their expressions wary as they noticed me. It wasn't hard to see the protective instincts in their eyes, and I couldn't blame them. I'd be the same way if someone had hurt a friend of mine the way I had hurt Alma.

I approached the table slowly, and tried to keep my nerves in check. "Hey," I greeted them, attempting to sound more confident than I felt. "Thanks for meeting me."

Tamara, with her arms crossed and a skeptical look on her face, was the first to speak. "So, what's this about?"

I took a deep breath, pulling out a chair and sitting down across from them. "Look, I know I'm probably the last person you want to hear from right now. And I get it. I messed up with Alma, badly. But I'm here because I need your help."

India raised an eyebrow, exchanging a glance with Tamara. "Help with what, exactly? Alma's not exactly feeling well right now, and if you're here to mess with her head again, we're not interested."

"No, it's not like that," I said quickly, leaning forward. "I've spent the last few months trying to move on, trying to forget about her, but I can't. She's everywhere, in my thoughts, in the way nothing feels right without her. I haven't been able to shake this emptiness since we've been apart. I know I've hurt her and I'm willing to do anything to prove that to her."

India's expression softened slightly, but there was still hesitation in her eyes. "You really expect us to believe that after everything?"

"I know words aren't enough," I admitted. "I'm not here to play games."

India and Tamara exchanged another look, this time a more serious one. I could see the gears turning in their minds, the silent conversation happening between them. My heart pounded in my chest as I waited for their response, hoping that they'd see the sincerity in my words.

Finally, India spoke up, her tone more measured. "If we help you, and you mess this up again, it won't just be Alma you'll have to answer to. It'll be us too."

"I understand," I said, nodding. "And I wouldn't expect anything less. But I promise you, I'm not going to mess this up. I just need a chance to show her that I'm serious."

Tamara sighed, her arms uncrossing as she leaned back in her chair. "All right, Callum. We'll help you. But you better be ready to put in the work, because Alma deserves the best, and if you're not going to give her that, we're out."

Relief flooded through me, and I couldn't help the small smile that tugged at my lips. "Thank you. I won't let you, or her, down."

As we began to discuss the plan, I felt a renewed sense of purpose. This was my shot to make things right, to show Alma that I was ready to fight for her.

ALMA

After three long days cooped up in bed, battling the flu with a steady diet of rest, medicine, and soup, I finally felt like myself again. The morning light filtering through my blinds was almost too bright, but it was a welcome change after the fog of sickness. I got dressed, feeling a bit lighter in my step, and made my way to the office, eager to dive back into work and catch up on what I'd missed.

When I walked into the office, everything seemed normal at first, papers shuffling, phones ringing, the hum of conversation.

"Hey, Alma! Feeling better?" Tamara asked, her voice a little too chipper.

"Yeah, much better," I replied, studying her closely. "Thanks for checking in on me these last few days. What's been going on here?"

"Not much. Just the usual madness," she replied.

I nodded, but something in her demeanor kept nagging at me. She was being weirdly evasive, which wasn't like her at all. We chatted for a few minutes, but the conversation felt stilted, like she was holding back. My suspicion grew as the morning wore on. I tried to focus on my work, but I couldn't shake the feeling that something was up.

Then, just before lunch, I saw them. Tamara laughing softly with

Callum in the entryway of the office. And to my surprise, they walked outside together.

I blinked, caught off guard. Callum? Tamara? Together?

I watched the doors close, my mind racing. What on earth was that about? Tamara had always been civil to Callum, but they weren't exactly close. In fact, she loathed him. And since when did she start grabbing lunch with him?

Feeling both curiosity and unease, I headed back to my desk, my thoughts swirling. I tried to shake it off, telling myself it was nothing, just a coincidence, maybe. But a nagging voice in the back of my mind kept asking, what were they up to? I couldn't help but wonder if it had anything to do with me.

The afternoon dragged, but despite my best efforts to dive into work, my mind kept drifting back to Callum and the curious lunch meeting with Tamara. I tried to stay focused, but the mystery gnawed at me.

When the clock finally struck five, signaling the end of the workday, I packed up my things, eager to head out and hopefully clear my head. As I was heading towards the door, I caught sight of Tamara.

"Hey," I said, trying to sound casual. "I feel like I haven't seen much of you this afternoon. How was lunch?"

Tamara's eyes widened slightly, and she forced a grin. "Oh, hey! It was nice."

I could tell she was being evasive, but I decided not to push it. I didn't want to come across as too nosy, especially after being out for a couple of days. Instead, I made small talk and said my goodbyes, and all while the nagging feeling lingered.

As I walked out of the office, my phone buzzed with a new text message. It was from India.

India: *Hey, just wanted to let you know we're planning something for this weekend since you've been sick for days. It's going to be a lot of fun.*

I frowned at the message, trying to decipher its meaning. Planning something? What could it be?

I decided to call India to get more details. She answered on the first ring, her tone bright but somewhat guarded.

"Hey! What's up?"

"I got your text. What's this about 'planning something?' Is it something I need to know about?"

She hesitated for a moment, and then said, "Oh, it's just a little get together. We thought it would be nice to have everyone unwind and catch up. It's nothing big, just a chance to hang out."

"Sounds good," I said. "You know I'll be there."

I hung up and wondered what was really going on? And why was Callum suddenly in the mix with Tamara? I tried to push the worries aside as I drove home.

The rest of the week flew by in a blur of work and home life, leaving me feeling more disoriented than ever. At the office, Tamara's behavior grew increasingly peculiar. When she interacted with me, there was a noticeable shift, a forced cheerfulness.

My interactions with Callum were limited to the occasional encounter in the hallway or brief exchanges in team meetings. There was a certain tension whenever we crossed paths, a reminder of that unresolved mess between us. He never mentioned me standing him up and I wasn't going to bring it up. If things were through, then they were through. Despite the awkwardness, there was an unspoken understanding that neither of us wanted to confront directly.

At home, India's demeanor was just as off kilter. She seemed distant, lost in her own world. Our usual easygoing conversations were replaced with vague responses. I noticed her glancing at her phone more frequently, as if she were waiting for something. I tried to broach the subject a few times, but she'd brush it off with a quick change of topic or an excuse to leave the room.

The mounting curiosity and the strange behavior of those around me left me feeling uneasy. It was as if I was standing on the edge of something, and the anticipation was beginning to wear on me. All I could do was wait and hope that Sunday's girls' hang would shed some light on the strange and unsettling behavior of those around me.

Chapter Forty-Two

CALLUM

On Saturday morning, I slid into the booth at the diner, the familiar scent of coffee and sizzling bacon wrapping around me like a warm blanket. Dan, the leader of my support group, arrived shortly after, a reassuring smile on his face as he settled across from me.

"Hey, Callum. Good to see you," he said, gesturing for the waitress. "Coffee?"

"Yeah, that'd be great," I replied, my fingers tapping nervously on the table. I needed to unload, and I could already feel the weight of my thoughts pressing against my chest.

Dan nodded to the waitress before turning his full attention back to me. "What's on your mind?"

I took a deep breath, trying to organize my thoughts. "It's about Alma. We've been complicated lately." I hesitated, not wanting to reveal too much too fast, but the words tumbled out. "I messed things up. I drove her away when I should have been there for her, and now she's moving on. And I want her back."

Dan leaned in, his gaze steady. "What do you think she needs from you?"

"I don't know. I just want to show her that I'm deserving of her love, that I can be the person she needs," I admitted, my voice thick with emotion. "I want to be better, for her but especially for myself."

"Sounds like you're already on the right path," Dan said, his tone encouraging. "Recognizing your mistakes is the first step. But you need to show yourself that you're committed to changing. Actions speak louder than words."

"Yeah, but how do I do that?" I asked, my frustration bubbling up. "What if it's too late to fix myself?"

"It's never too late to become a more grounded version of yourself," Dan replied firmly. "Take small steps. And most importantly, work on yourself. You can't expect to rebuild something strong if you're not strong yourself. With this girl, show up for her. Listen to her."

I nodded, absorbing his words. "You're right. I need to focus on being better, not just for her, but for me too."

"Exactly. And remember, it's a process. Be patient with yourself and with her," Dan said, giving me a reassuring smile. "You've got this, Callum."

As the waitress set down our coffee, I felt a flicker of hope ignite within me.

The rest of the day passed in a blur, each hour blending into the next as I worked relentlessly to finish the art pieces. My apartment was a mess, clay scraps on the floor, charcoal smudges on my hands, and half-empty paint tubes scattered around. I was held up, finalizing each piece, pouring everything into them.

The clay piece was the most challenging. I'd shaped it carefully, smoothing out imperfections, trying to capture the essence of what I wanted to convey. The curves, the details, they all had to be perfect. It was something that needed to be felt, not just seen.

The watercolor piece was more fluid, the colors blending and bleeding into one another in a way that felt almost alive. It was vibrant yet soft, like a memory captured on canvas. I let the colors flow freely, allowing them to take on a life of their own.

The chalk piece was raw, bold strokes creating sharp contrasts. There was something visceral about working with chalk, the way it crumbled slightly under pressure, leaving behind a trail of emotion on the paper. It was a piece that spoke of passion and something more primal. It reminded me of us.

And then there was the coal. Dark, rough, yet capable of creating something beautiful if handled just right. The coal piece was different from the others, edgier, more intense. It had depth, layers of darkness with hints of light peeking through, like a struggle caught in time.

I'd spent days working on these, pushing myself to the edge, each piece carrying a part of me, a message I hoped she'd understand. But there was still more to do. This was just the beginning, the foundation of something much bigger.

I stepped back, taking in the pieces, feeling exhaustion and satisfaction at the same time. Each one was a piece of the puzzle, a step towards something greater. I just hoped she'd see it, understand what I was trying to say.

* * *

I woke up the next morning in a daze, barely registering the sunlight creeping through the blinds. Sleep had been elusive. The few hours I had managed were more a restless drift than any real rest. My mind was too busy, too wired, and the adrenaline pumping through my veins kept me from finding any peace. I'd spent most of the night adding the finishing touches to the last few art pieces, tweaking details that, to anyone else, might have seemed insignificant. But for Alma, I needed them to be perfect.

Bags under my eyes and the shadow of exhaustion etched on my face stared back at me in the bathroom mirror. I'd never felt this way about anyone before. Not even Soledad. The nerves, the anticipation, they were foreign to me. But there was also a strange sort of clarity in it, a certainty that she was worth every sleepless night, every ounce of effort. I was willing to put in the work, to do whatever it took to be with her.

I reached for my trimmer, focusing on my beard. Alma had mentioned once, in passing, that she liked my scruff. Not clean-shaven, but just enough to add that rugged edge. So, I carefully trimmed it, making sure it was neat but not too polished. A small smile tugged at the corners of my mouth as I thought of her fingers brushing against my jawline, a memory that fueled my determination.

I stood under the hot water, letting it cascade over me, hoping it would wash away some of the anxiety. But even as I scrubbed and rinsed, my thoughts stayed with her, replaying every moment we'd shared, every smile, every touch.

After drying off, I picked out my clothes, something sharp but not too formal. I went with a crisp white shirt, the sleeves rolled up to the elbows, paired with dark jeans and my favorite boots. The simplicity felt right, like me, but a little more put together. I ran a hand through my dark hair, giving it a quick tousle, and then grabbed my watch from the dresser, strapping it on as if it were armor.

Chris had been cool enough to lend me his Jeep for the day. My motorcycle wasn't going to cut it, not with the art pieces I needed to transport. I needed to get everything there in one trip, no room for mistakes. The thought of trying to balance everything on my bike was almost laughable, and not in a good way.

I loaded the pieces carefully, one by one, into the back of the Jeep. Each piece represented a part of me, a part of us.

As I shut the Jeep's trunk and took one last look at the loaded art, my chest tightened. This was it. I was putting it all out there, no safety net, no backup plan. And for the first time in a long time, I felt something other than nerves, a glimmer of possibility.

I climbed into the driver's seat, gripping the wheel tightly for a moment before starting the engine. The Jeep rumbled to life, and I took a deep breath, steadying myself. And as I pulled out onto the road, the weight of what I was about to do hit me like a tidal wave. But instead of pulling me under, it propelled me forward. This wasn't just another day; it was the beginning of something I hoped would change everything between us. The hum of the engine under me, the clear midmorning air, the light streaming through the trees, it all felt like a sign, like the universe was aligning in my favor, even though my nerves told me otherwise.

Driving through the familiar streets of downtown Franklin, I replayed everything I had planned in my mind, double checking every detail.

The minutes ticked by as I navigated the turns, each one bringing me closer to the destination, closer to the moment I'd been working toward for weeks, hell, even months if I were being honest with myself. I knew Alma, knew her moods, her likes and dislikes, the little quirks that made her who she was. And I also knew that if I messed this up, there might not be another chance.

But I was all in. I wasn't going to hold back, not this time. I'd let my guard down, let her see the real me, the guy who was crazy enough to spend nights on end making art pieces just to tell her how much she meant to him. The guy who wasn't going to let fear or pride get in the way of something that felt too damn important to lose.

I pulled up to the studio, the Jeep's tires crunching on the gravel as I came to a stop. It was perfect, everything we'd planned was coming together, the place was set, and in just a few short hours, Alma would be here. My heart pounded in my chest as I turned off the engine and stepped out, taking in the scene before me. Tamara would arrive soon, and I could already picture the hustle and bustle of setting everything up.

But right now, in this quiet moment, it was just me and my thoughts, and I felt ready. Ready to face whatever was coming, ready to put it all out there, and ready to see where this road with Alma would lead. Today, I was going to show her that she wasn't just someone I wanted in my life, she was the one I couldn't live without.

Chapter Forty-Three

ALMA

India and I were lounging on the couch, a lazy Sunday afternoon stretching out before us. I felt much better after the flu, but my energy was still low, making it easy to sink into the cushions. India was scrolling through her phone, occasionally glancing up at me with a look that made me suspicious.

"You should wear that green dress tonight," India said, her tone casual but her eyes focused on me.

I stiffened, immediately remembering the way Callum had once looked at me in that dress, the way his eyes had darkened as he told me how much he'd love to see me in it. A pang of sadness washed over me, and I tried to push the memory away, but it clung to me like a shadow.

India noticed the change in my expression and quickly added, "It's just you look amazing in it. We're going out, having fun, and that dress, well it's perfect for tonight."

I forced a smile, not wanting to dampen her enthusiasm. "Yeah, okay," I said, though my heart wasn't really in it.

"Great!" India hopped off the couch, practically dragging me to my room. "Let's get you ready."

I went through the motions, picking up the green dress from the back of my closet. The fabric felt smooth under my fingers, and as I slipped it on, I caught a glimpse of myself in the mirror. The dress clung to my curves, the deep shade vibrant against my caramel-colored skin.

India, sensing my hesitation, gave me a reassuring smile. "You look stunning. Seriously. Tonight is about you, having a good time, and forgetting everything else."

I nodded, trying to shake off the melancholy. I applied a bit of makeup, just enough to bring some color back into my cheeks, and fluffed my curls. India helped me with the final touches, adjusting the straps of the dress and giving me a once over.

"Perfect," she said, stepping back with a satisfied grin. "You're going to turn heads tonight."

I smiled back at her, a real smile this time, though my thoughts were still tangled up in memories. I tried to focus on the present, on the girls' night ahead, and on leaving the past where it belonged.

I stood at the kitchen island, swirling the espresso martini India had made for me, as my mind drifted. The rich coffee flavor, mixed with the smooth kick of vodka, provided a comforting distraction. But it wasn't enough to fully shake the unease I felt. India's laughter echoed down the hall as she got ready, leaving me alone with my thoughts.

As I scrolled through my phone, the idea struck me like a bolt of lightning. Why wait? I had been putting it off for months, but now, with the new position in my grasp, I could finally afford to make it happen without stretching myself thin. I opened the airline app, my fingers moving quickly as I searched for flights to the Dominican Republic.

I found a round-trip ticket for a long weekend a month from now. It would be short, just three days, but enough to hug my parents, catch up, and remind myself why all this hard work was worth it. The price was reasonable, and for once, I didn't hesitate. My thumb hovered over the "Confirm Purchase" button for only a second before I pressed it.

A wave of relief and excitement swept over me as the confirmation email landed in my inbox. I grinned, setting my phone aside for a moment to take a breath. After months of excuses, I was finally going home.

But there were still some logistics to take care of. I opened my email and quickly typed a message to Chris.

Subject: PTO Request for Family Visit

Hi Chris,

I'd like to request PTO for Thursday and Friday, May 21 and 22, to visit my family in the Dominican Republic. I'll make sure all my tasks are squared away before I leave. Let me know if there's any issue with this.

Thanks,
Alma

I hit send, confident that he'd approve it without any hassle. Chris had always been understanding about things like this.

Feeling a rush of excitement, I immediately dialed my parents on a video call. It took a moment for their faces to appear, but when they did, I couldn't stop the wide smile spreading across my face.

"Mami, Papi! Guess what?" I said, the anticipation bubbling in my chest.

"Qué pasó, mija?" Mami asked, her face lighting up in curiosity.

"I'm coming to visit! I just booked my flight. I'll be there in a month!"

Their joy was immediate and contagious. Papi clapped his hands together, and Mami gasped, her hand flying to her chest.

"Alma, eso es maravilloso. We can't wait to see you," Papi said, his voice brimming with excitement.

We chatted for a few minutes, talking about what we'd do during my visit. Mami was already planning what meals she'd cook, and Papi joked about saving me a seat in his domino games.

Before we could dive deeper, India poked her head into the room, her makeup flawless and her outfit on point. "You ready for girls' night, or are you planning to stay on that call forever?" she teased, her tone light but impatient.

"Coming!" I called, laughing as I turned back to the phone. "Mami, Papi, I have to go, but I'll call you soon, okay? I love you both."

"We love you, too," Mami said, blowing me a kiss.

"See you soon, mija," Papi added, grinning.

I ended the call, the glow of their happiness still warming me. India raised an eyebrow as I grabbed my purse and jacket.

"You're glowing," she said as we headed out.

"Yeah," I admitted, smiling to myself. "I think I needed that."

* * *

As we drove downtown, the lights of the city flickering past us, I couldn't help but ask, "India, where exactly are we meeting Tamara? I thought we were heading to our usual spot." I leaned back in my seat, feeling the hum of the car beneath me as we passed the exit I was sure would lead us to our favorite bar.

India glanced at me briefly, her lips curving into a mysterious smile. "Oh, you'll see. It's a surprise," she said, her tone light and teasing.

I raised an eyebrow, glancing out the window as the scenery grew less familiar. "A surprise? You know I'm not the biggest fan of surprises," I said with a playful edge, trying to mask the growing curiosity and slight unease creeping in.

"Oh, trust me, you'll love this one," India reassured, turning onto a street I didn't recognize.

I stayed quiet, watching as we navigated through unfamiliar streets. My mind wandered, trying to piece together where we could possibly be heading. Finally, we turned into a small parking lot, and I blinked in surprise as the car came to a stop.

"Wait, isn't that the art gallery we visited a few months ago?" I asked, excitement bubbling up inside me. I loved that gallery, the way it celebrated art in all its forms, each piece telling a different story. But it was definitely not what I had in mind for tonight. I had been ready to drink my sorrows away with my best friends, not admire sculptures and paintings.

India turned off the engine and grinned at me, her eyes sparkling with mischief. "Surprise," she said again, this time with more emphasis.

I looked at her, trying to read between the lines. "Okay, but why here? I mean, I loved this place that one time we came, but I was kind of expecting a night of cocktails and maybe some bad decisions."

India chuckled, stepping out of the car. "Trust me, this is better than any night of cocktails. Just go with it, okay?"

I sighed, still puzzled but willing to play along. As I got out of the car, something caught my eye, was that Chris's Jeep? I frowned, now thoroughly perplexed. "India, why is my boss's Jeep here? What's going on?"

India only shrugged, but her expression was too innocent to be believable. "That's a pretty common Jeep. Likely someone else. Come on, let's go inside."

I followed her, my heart starting to race a little as we approached the entrance. The gallery doors loomed ahead, and with each step, my curiosity grew. What was India up to? And why did it feel like something big was about to happen?

I stepped into the gallery, my breath catching as I took in the scene before me. The entire space was bathed in a soft, warm glow from dim lighting, with silk drapes cascading down the walls, creating an intimate atmosphere. White roses and blue hydrangeas were everywhere, their sweet fragrance mingling with the air, adding to the ethereal beauty of the room.

But it was the art that truly captivated me.

To my left, expressive charcoal pieces seemed to tell stories of their own, each stroke filled with raw emotion. Watercolor paintings hung nearby, their colors blending and bleeding together in a way that felt almost magical. My eyes wandered from piece to piece, admiring the care and skill that went into creating each one.

And then I saw the pottery.

A particular piece caught my eye, a small, intricately carved bowl with delicate patterns that wound around its surface like ivy. The texture of the clay was rough in some places, smooth in others, and the design felt familiar, comforting even. It reminded me of Callum, of us, of how our relationship had always been a mix of rough edges and smooth moments, intricate and layered.

As I absorbed everything, I became aware of Tamara and India in the room, each of them watching me with anticipation. They exchanged knowing glances, and without a word, they quietly exited the main room, leaving me alone.

The sound of footsteps drew my attention back to the entrance, and when I turned, there he was.

Callum stood in the doorway, looking more incredible than I'd ever seen him. His scruffy beard added a rugged charm that sent a thrill through me, and his eyes, intense and focused, locked onto mine. For a moment, I couldn't breathe, couldn't move, as the realization of what this was all about hit me.

It was him. All of this was him.

Chapter Forty-Four

CALLUM

As Alma took in the gallery around her, her gaze lingering on the art pieces that seemed to echo every emotion I'd poured into them, I felt a rush of vulnerability. The weight of my feelings for her, the yearning, the hope, it all came crashing down as I stepped closer to her.

I watched her eyes soften as she took in the pottery, the delicate carving on the bowl making her pause. It was almost like she was piecing together the story I'd tried so hard to tell through these works. I took a deep breath, summoning the courage to lay it all out.

Then she turned around and it knocked the air clean out of me.

She was wearing that green dress from Jamaica. The one that has been burned into my memory since the second I saw it. It fit her like it was made with her in mind. Against her skin, the color made her glow. Not in some exaggerated way. Just...warm. Radiant. Alive.

"Alma," I began, my voice trembling slightly as I approached her. I could feel the weight of every moment we'd shared, every high and low, pushing at the edge of my emotions. "I've never felt this way before, about anyone. This"—I gestured around at the gallery—"isn't just a grand gesture. It's everything I've ever felt for you, laid out for you to see."

But as I stood there, I realized something.

"This project was more than just a declaration of my love for you. It's a declaration to myself. Each piece, each stroke of charcoal and splash of paint, was a reminder that I'm deserving of love, real love. For so long, I'd doubted that, convinced myself I didn't deserve someone like you. But this, this gallery, this moment, it is proof that I'm bettering myself. I'm not the same guy who made all those mistakes. I'm working to be someone worthy of the kind of love I feel for you. And that's why this isn't just for you, Alma. It's for me, too."

I walked closer, my eyes never leaving hers. "I'll take our good days with our bad days," I said, my voice steadying. "I'll walk through storms. I'll do it all because I love you."

There was a brief, piercing silence between us. The gallery seemed to fade into the background, leaving just the two of us in this intimate space I'd created. I watched as her eyes glistened with what I hoped were happy tears and not signaling the end.

"I've spent every waking moment these past few days thinking about how to show you just how much you mean to me," I continued, feeling a knot form in my throat. "The way everything seems duller without you around, what used to satisfy me now falls flat, the sunlight feels muted, and the nights stretch on in silence. It all leads back to you. Everything I've done here is for us, for what we could become together."

I reached out, my hand brushing hers, and I saw a flicker of something, hope, perhaps, cross her face.

"I know I've made mistakes," I said softly. "And I know I was a dick. Hell, I'm still a dick. But I'm here, and I'm willing to do whatever it takes to make things right."

She scanned the room, then her eyes met mine, and for a moment, the world outside ceased to exist. I held my breath, waiting for her response, hoping that the words I'd chosen, the emotions I'd poured into every piece of art, would bridge the gap between us.

I watched Alma's mouth opening and closing as if she was trying to find the right words. Her lips moved as if to say my name, but no sound came out, her voice caught in her throat. My heart raced, and I couldn't let this moment slip away.

"Alma, please," I urged softly, unable to keep the desperation out of my voice. Afraid she'd reject me, I pressed on.

"Every day that's come and gone has been brutal with you not actively in it. Your laugh, your smile, the way your curls fall around your beautiful face. I don't want to lose what we have...what we had."

Her eyes widened, and she raised a hand to stop me. "Markum," she said, her voice firm and unexpected.

The use of my last name caught me off guard. It stirred memories of when I used to call her Ruiz, back before my feelings for her had become so intense. Hearing it now, I felt a pang of nostalgia.

Her eyes held a mixture of emotions, and for a moment, the air between us was charged with an electric tension.

ALMA

As I looked at Callum, my heart pounded so fiercely it felt as if it might burst through my chest. I was caught between the surge of emotions and the sheer need to make him understand what had been simmering inside me. I took a deep breath, trying to steady my voice, and began to speak.

"I need you to know something."

I could see the way he was hanging on every word, his eyes fixed on me.

"You had me," I said softly, "at the part in your grand speech where you said all of this"—I gestured around the venue—"wasn't just about showing me how you feel. It was about realizing you're deserving of love."

I stepped a little closer, holding his gaze.

"What you don't understand, is that you've always been deserving. You just never let yourself believe it."

He dropped his head, staring at the floor, like my words needed somewhere solid to land. For a second, he just stood there, quiet, actually letting them sink in. Then he looked back up at me.

"You thought that was my grand speech?" he said.

There it was, that familiar smirk, slow and deliberate, tugging at the corner of his mouth.

"Please. You haven't heard anything yet."

He took a step towards me.

"I'm addicted to you," he said, tilting his head to one side, letting me feel the weight of his words. "Addicted to the way you feel, the way you make me laugh. I'm captivated by the way you taste." A mischievous glint flickered in his eye as he added, "It's not just the taste, it's everything about you."

"I'm going to interrupt you with a little Oscar-worthy acceptance speech of my own," I said as we stood there, just a few steps between us.

I took a breath before speaking again, this time more vulnerable.

"With you, I don't feel like I have to carry everything by myself. You make it easier for me to let go of some of the weight I've been holding onto. I don't have to be so independent all the time, so perfect. I can just be me, and you're still here. It's like, with you, I don't have to face everything alone."

He took another step closer, his voice dropping to a whisper. "As I was saying, I'm addicted to how you feel on my skin, to the way your touch sends shivers through me. You've become a part of me, and I can't imagine my life without you in it."

My eyes misted over, and I tried to blink back the tears threatening to escape. I interrupted again. "I want to be yours and only yours," I confessed, my voice breaking slightly. "I want to give you everything I am, all that I have. I want to be with you, not just today or tomorrow, but for always."

I could see the effect of my words on him, the way they seemed to sink in, reaching deep. The raw honesty in my confession was a mirror of my deepest feelings. I reached out and took his hand, hoping he could feel the sincerity of my emotions through that simple touch. The room felt smaller, the air thicker, as we stood there, our hearts laid bare.

Callum's eyes locked onto mine, a blend of disbelief and profound relief swirling in their depths. His breath hitched, and I could see the struggle to contain his feelings.

He took yet another step closer, his fingers gently squeezing mine. "Alma," he whispered, his voice rough with unspoken emotions, "you have no idea how long I've wanted to hear that, how much I needed to hear that. I've been waiting for this, waiting for you to feel the same way I do."

My heart swelled with joy at his words. The intensity in his gaze made my knees go weak, but I stood firm, needing to be close to him.

Callum's hand slid to my cheek, his thumb brushing away a tear I hadn't realized had escaped. His touch was tender, electrifying. "You've changed everything for me," he continued, his voice growing steadier. "I thought I knew what I wanted until I met you. Now, I know I just want you."

His words wrapped around me like a warm embrace, and for a moment, everything else faded away. It was just us, standing in the middle of this beautifully transformed gallery, surrounded by art and memories, with the promise of a future that was finally within reach.

He leaned in, his forehead resting gently against mine. "Let's make it right. Let's be together, fully, without any more doubts or fears. No fake relationships. No making someone else jealous. Just you and me."

I closed my eyes, savoring the closeness, and nodded, my voice barely more than a whisper. "Yes. Let's do that."

He smiled, a tender, radiant smile that spoke volumes. As Callum's lips met mine, the kiss was anything but gentle. It was urgent, passionate, like he needed to fuse our very beings into one. His hand found its way to my neck, his touch firm and possessive, just the way I craved. His grip pulled me closer, and our bodies pressed together, the heat between us intensifying with every second.

The kiss deepened. My head spun, lost in the feeling of his lips moving against mine, his tongue finding mine, his touch setting every nerve in my body alight. For that moment, nothing else existed, just the two of us, consumed by the raw, unfiltered connection we shared.

But then, amidst the fervor, a light cough interrupted us. I pulled back, my heart racing, only to find India and Tamara standing there, their faces lit up with broad smiles. They were clearly thrilled, barely containing their excitement.

Tamara, ever the sassy one, crossed her arms and raised an eyebrow. "So, I'm guessing it worked. Y'all are a thing now? For real this time?"

I laughed, feeling both embarrassment and relief. Callum grinned, looking as happy and relieved as I felt. The tension that had once weighed so heavily on us seemed to melt away, replaced by a sense of joy.

India, with her usual enthusiasm, clapped her hands. "It's about time! We were starting to think you two were going to make us wait forever."

"Come on, let's celebrate!" Tamara exclaimed, pulling us towards the center of the gallery where the decorations and art provided a perfect backdrop for our newfound happiness.

The gallery, with its soft lighting and elegant decorations, became the stage for our celebration. India pulled out her phone and started playing music. Tamara disappeared from the room and returned with champagne and little clear plastic cups. We proceeded to pour ourselves drinks, danced and laughed, the weight of past doubts and fears lifting as we embraced this new chapter together.

Callum's arm wrapped around me, his touch reassuring and affectionate. We stood together, and I couldn't help but think that this was exactly where I was meant to be.

And then, because clearly my life was a full-blown romcom and not a place where things happened in a calm, rational manner, Callum leaned in close. His breath brushed my ear, warm, sending a very inconvenient shiver down my spine.

And in a voice so quiet it felt like it was just for me, because it was...

"I love you."

My heart? Oh, it absolutely forgot how to function.

Chapter Forty-Five

ALMA

We stumbled into Callum's apartment, our laughter echoing off the walls. Clothes were being ripped off in a frantic frenzy. I yanked at his shirt, my fingers fumbling as I tried to tear it from his body. The buttons flew everywhere, scattering like little metal confetti across the room. We both laughed, the sound a mix of exhilaration and sheer, unrestrained joy.

It was then, amidst the chaos of our disheveled clothes, that I took a moment to really look around. The apartment was a complete mess, with paint tubes, brushes, and sketchbooks strewn haphazardly across every available surface. There were smudges of paint on the walls, and the floor was littered with crumpled pieces of paper and spilled coffee cups. It looked like a whirlwind had hit the place.

"What happened here?" I asked, my eyes wide as I took in the disarray. The apartment was the perfect reflection of the creative storm that had clearly been brewing here.

Callum grinned sheepishly, catching his breath. "I've been working on these art pieces for the past two weeks. I didn't have time to clean up before heading to the gallery." His voice was full of embarrassment, clearly more focused on the art than the mess.

I couldn't help but smile at his dedication, but my attention was quickly diverted back to him. As I watched him, my gaze softened. There was something incredibly endearing about the chaos of his creative process, and it only heightened my feelings for him.

Before I could say anything else, the urge to be closer to him over-whelmed me as I crossed the room, the mess barely registering now. I ran to him with a sudden burst of energy, and he caught me easily, his strong arms wrapping around me as I leaped into his embrace. My legs wrapped around his waist instinctively, pulling him closer as our bodies pressed together.

The heat between us was palpable, and his touch sent shivers down my spine. I buried my face in his neck, breathing in the familiar scent of him. The chaotic surroundings seemed to fade away as our world narrowed down to just the two of us.

His hands roamed over my back, his touch both tender and urgent, and I felt the pounding of his heart against my chest. In that tangled, fervent embrace, with the world outside forgotten, we were simply us, lost in the electric thrill of finally being together.

As Callum carried me to his bedroom, the urgency of our earlier moments was replaced by a tenderness that sent a shiver to my toes. He laid me gently on the bed, his hands lingering on my skin, his touch as soft as a whisper. Each touch felt like a promise, each caress a declaration.

He started at my lips, his kisses gentle, as if he wanted to savor every second. His lips trailed down to my collarbone, planting kisses that made me tremble with pleasure. I saw him looking at me, his gaze filled with admiration and something deeper, something that made my heart race.

"You're stunning," he said, his voice filled with awe. The way he looked at me made me feel like the most beautiful woman in the world, and his words only made me wetter.

He leaned in again, his kiss more tender this time, a soft exploration that sent warmth through me. His hands moved to unclasp my bra, his fingers deftly freeing me from its confines. The sensation of his touch against my bare skin was electrifying, each brush of his fingers leaving a trail of fire.

As he left my lips, his hands slowly moved to my panties. I lifted my hips instinctively, and he slid them down my legs with a care that made my breath hitch. His touch was gentle but filled with a purpose that spoke of his love for me.

In that moment, as he removed the last of my clothing, I felt a sense of vulnerability and trust that was both exhilarating and comforting. The power of his gaze and the way he moved with such reverence made me feel cherished in a way I'd never experienced before. Our connection, deep and passionate, was all-consuming, and I knew that this was what we both wanted. Not just me this time.

As Callum removed the remnants of his torn shirt, his tattoos became fully visible, showcasing the intricate designs that adorned his arms and chest. His muscular physique, defined abs, and the way his body moved as he unbuttoned his jeans captivated me. It had been months since I had seen him like this, and the sight of him, his strong form, every inch of him, stirred a deep want within me.

He looked at me and made my heart race. The way he stood there, his presence commanding and undeniably magnetic, was a beautiful contrast to the chaos of his apartment. I took in every detail of him. There was a raw honesty in the moment that seemed to bridge the gap of time and distance between us.

Callum's gaze softened as he approached me. His hands were gentle now, a softness that didn't match the fire he'd shown just moments before. As he leaned in, I couldn't help but surrender to the moment, my emotions and senses overwhelmed by how much I wanted, no, needed, him inside me.

He moved onto the bed with a purposeful grace. He lifted one of my legs, cradling it with a tenderness that sent a shiver through me. As his lips began to explore from my ankle, the sensation of his kisses traveled up my leg, each touch igniting a trail of goosebumps across my skin. The intimacy of his touch made me feel vulnerable yet cherished.

When he reached my thigh, he paused and looked up at me with a darkened, serious expression. "Do you love me?" he asked, his voice barely above a whisper, filled with need.

I nodded, my heart pounding in my chest, but he wasn't satisfied with just a nod.

"Use your words, baby girl. I want to hear you say it. I need to hear you say it," he urged, his eyes locked on mine.

The magnitude of the moment enveloped me. "Yes, I love you, Callum," I replied, my voice trembling with the weight of my emotions.

Callum remained on his knees, and as he leaned in close and buried his head between my legs, my center was about ready to exploded. Every nerve ending seemed to respond to each and every one of his licks, his nibbles, his sucking, making the moment exhilarating.

Just as I was about to come undone, he lifted his head, his lips glistening as he licked my taste from them, and said, "You are mine. And I am yours."

CALLUM

The room was shrouded in darkness, but even so, Alma's beauty glowed, almost as if it radiated through the dim. I was captivated by her, the way she looked in the low light, her features softened and serene.

I tugged her by the leg, pulling her closer to the edge of the bed. Her surprised yelp quickly turned into a bubbling giggle that was music to my ears. It was a sound I was becoming addicted to, a sound that made everything feel right.

Leaning down, I pressed my lips close to her ear, my breath mingling with hers, feeling the warmth of her skin. My voice was a low whisper. "Every time I fuck you," I murmured, "it's like we're setting the whole world on fire. I'm seriously thinking about keeping a fire extinguisher by my bed just in case."

"There's the cocky man I know and love," she giggled to me.

I could feel her breath hitch against my neck as I slipped two fingers to her center, reveling at how wet she was for me. I grinned, savoring the moment. Alma's breath came in soft, uneven gasps as I gently explored her, pumping my fingers in and out of her. She arched her back, her body instinctively responding to every caress. The way she moved was captivating, each shift and sigh a testament to how she felt about me. Her eyes fluttered closed, lost in what I was evoking.

As she neared the edge, a peak that seemed so close, I slowly withdrew my fingers out of her. The look in her eyes, the way her breath hitched, was all I needed to know about the effect I was having. With deliberate slowness, I brought my fingers to my lips, savoring the taste of her, my gaze unwavering from hers. The act an unspoken conversation between us.

Her voice, a soft, pleading whisper, cut through the haze of our shared anticipation. "Callum, that's enough teasing. I need you, please." The sincerity in her plea struck a chord deep within me, making my heart race and my mind focus solely on her. Her request, filled with urgency and desire, was a clear invitation.

I guided Alma gently to the edge of the bed and spread her legs apart so that they were on either side of me while I stood. Resting my hands firmly on her hips, I thrust into her with one swift movement that had her yelling out my name.

As I repeatedly slammed into her, our breaths mingled and quickened, and she gripped the edge of the bed, her fingers crumpling the sheets as if trying to anchor herself. Her sounds of pleasure were soft, almost muffled as she brought the sheets to her mouth. Each movement between us was charged, and I could see the emotion etched on her face. She loved me.

With a final, deep thrust, I felt Alma reach her climax, her cries of pleasure echoing my name as her body trembled with the strength of her release. I soon followed, a wave of euphoria washing over me, leaving us both breathless and spent.

I collapsed next to her, our bodies entangled and glistening with sweat, and our breaths coming in soft, uneven bursts. Her warmth was comforting, and as I rolled to the side, I pulled her closer, enveloping her in my arms. Her head rested gently against my chest, our hearts beating in a synchronized rhythm.

As we lay there, wrapped in each other, I looked down at her, feeling an overwhelming sense of love. "Alma," I murmured softly into her hair, "you've managed to turn my world upside down. Who knew that your clumsy coffee spill on your first day would lead to this?" She giggled and swatted at my arm. I continued, "I'm damn glad you did, though. You've made me laugh, challenged me, and kept me on my toes, all while making me fall head over heels. With you, every moment feels like a new beginning. I promise to cherish every second we have together and make each one count."

Her eyes met mine, and in that quiet, tender moment, I knew that our journey together was only just beginning.

"I love you."

Epilogue

ALMA

One year later, and somehow my life looked nothing like it did back then, and everything like something I used to daydream about when I was supposed to be paying attention in meetings.

The Dominican Republic greeted me like it always did, warm, loud, and oh so alive. The air was thick with salt and sunshine, the breeze carrying the faint scent of fried platanos and ocean water. It wrapped around me the second we stepped out of the car, like home saying, *there you are.*

"Dios mío, mira mi hija!" Mami called from the doorway of the casita, already rushing toward me with open arms.

"Mami!" I laughed, dropping my bag just in time to catch her hug, her hands cupping my face like she needed to make sure I was real. "I was just here, you act like it's been years."

"Too long," she said dramatically, then immediately turned her attention past me. "Callum!"

Standing a few steps behind me, sunglasses pushed up into his hair, holding his bag in one hand like he was unsure if he should step forward or wait for permission. He didn't need it.

Mami pulled him into a hug next, already obsessed. "Mi hijo," she said, patting his cheek.

He grinned, a little sheepish but completely charmed. "Hola, señora. Es bueno verla."

From inside the casita, Papi's voice carried out. "Finally! Déjame ver a mi niña."

"Papi!" I called, stepping inside, and there he was, stronger than the last time, standing behind the small wooden counter that separated the kitchen from the living space.

"Ven acá," he said, pulling me into a tight hug. And it's different this time. Steadier. Stronger.

I pulled back, studying him. "You look good," I said, a little emotional. "Like really good."

He waved me off but he was smiling. "Estoy mejor. The doctor says I behave now," he added, glancing at Mami like she was the real enforcer.

"She makes sure of it," I teased.

"Of course I do," Mami chimed in. "Now he only works a few days at the bodega. Not every day like before."

Papi nodded. "And I have help now. Carlos comes in the mornings. I just go to supervise." He said it like he didn't love it, but I could tell he did. It gave him purpose without running him into the ground.

I glanced over at Callum, who was listening. "Eso es bueno," Callum says, stepping closer. "You have to take care of yourself."

We settled into the rhythm of it all so easily, Mami bustling around the kitchen, insisting we sit, eat, relax. Papi talking about the bodega, about the neighbors, about how "todo está tranquilo ahora."

At one point, I stepped back, leaning against the doorway, just watching.

Callum was sitting at the small table with my parents, sleeves rolled up, fully engaged in conversation.

"And el trabajo?" my dad asked him.

Callum nodded. "Bien. Busy pero me gusta."

"And Alma?" Mami cut in, smirking. "Does she behave?"

Callum glanced over at me, a slow grin spreading across his face. "Depende del día."

"Hey!" I protested, but I was laughing.

"Es buena," he added quickly, softer this time. "Muy buena."

My chest tightened in the best way.

Because it wasn't just what he said, it was how he said it. Like he meant it. Like he knew it. And as I stood there, watching him with my family, my world, it hit me. Hard and certain and undeniable. I loved him, but not in the chaotic, confusing, what-the-hell-is-happening kind of way we started. But in the steady, grounded, this is my person kind of way. The kind that felt like home.

Callum looked over at me again, like he could feel me staring, and raised an eyebrow. "You gonna come sit with us, or just admire me from afar all night?"

I rolled my eyes, pushing off the doorway. "Don't flatter yourself."

But I walked straight to him anyway. And when I sat down beside him, his hand found mine under the table like it was second nature, like it always belonged there.

CALLUM

The thing about the Dominican Republic was, it slowed everything down. Time moved different here. The air was warmer, heavier. The ocean didn't rush. The night stretched out like it had nowhere else to be. Which was exactly how I ended up here, standing barefoot in the sand, heart beating like I was about to jump out of a plane without a parachute.

I tugged at the collar of my shirt, exhaling. "This is insane," I whispered to myself.

"Talking to yourself now?" Alma's voice called from behind me.

I turned, and, yeah. There she was.

Alma. My Alma. My soul.

Curls loose from the humidity, that soft sundress she wore earlier now catching the breeze, her skin glowing under the fading sunset like the universe was personally trying to make my life harder.

"You said you wanted to walk on the beach," she said, stepping up beside me, bumping her shoulder into mine. "What's with the brooding? You look like you're about to confess to a crime."

I huffed out a laugh. "Maybe I am."

She squinted at me. "Callum…"

God. There was no smooth way to do this, was there?

"Walk with me?" I said, nodding toward the water.

She studied me for half a second, like she knew something was up, but she nodded anyway. "Okay."

We started down the shoreline, waves brushing up against our feet, the sky shifting into that ridiculous pink-orange color that felt way too cinematic for what I was about to do.

"You're being weird," she said after a minute.

"Yeah," I admitted. "I am."

She stopped walking.

I took two more steps before I realize she wasn't next to me anymore. I turned back, and she was just standing there. Watching me.

"Callum," she said softly, "what's going on?"

And that was the moment. No more overthinking. No more running. I walked back toward her, my chest tight, heart loud enough I was pretty sure she could hear it.

"You remember the first time I told you I wasn't boyfriend material?" I asked.

She raised an eyebrow. "Vividly. You were very annoying about it."

I huffed a quiet laugh, shaking my head. "Yeah, I was, wasn't I?"

I took a breath, running a hand through my hair.

"I said that because it was easier," I admitted. "Easier to pretend I couldn't be that guy than risk being not enough. Easier to keep things light than actually show up for someone."

Her expression softened, but she didn't interrupt. Good. Because if she did, I might lose my nerve.

"But then you happened," I continued. "And suddenly, nothing about that made sense anymore. Because I wanted to show up for you. I wanted the hard stuff. The real stuff."

I stepped closer.

"I want all of it. The chaos, the good days, the bad ones, the stupid arguments about nothing, the making up after all of it. And I don't want to do any of it without you."

Okay, no turning back now.

I dropped to one knee.

Her eyes went wide immediately. "Callum—"

"Yeah, I know," I cut in, a small, nervous smile pulling at my mouth. "Shocking character development."

She let out a breathy laugh, one hand flying to her mouth.

I pulled the ring out, holding it up between us, my hand steadier than I felt.

"I'm not perfect," I said. "I've messed up. I probably will again. But I swear to you, I will spend the rest of my life choosing you. Fighting for you. Being better, for you."

Her eyes were glossy now. And mine probably weren't much better.

"Alma," I said, softer this time, "will you marry me?"

There was a pause. A long one. And for half a second, I think my heart might actually give out.

"Yes."

I blinked. "Yeah?"

She nodded quickly, laughing through it now. "Yes, you idiot, of course yes!"

Relief hit me so hard I actually laughed, pushing up to my feet as she threw her arms around my neck.

I caught her easily, spinning her once as she laughed against me. I pulled back just enough to slide the ring onto her finger, my thumb brushing over it like I needed to make sure it's real.

She looked down at it, then back up at me.

"You're really not boyfriend material," she teases softly.

I grinned, leaning in until our foreheads touch. "Good thing I'm aiming a little higher."

Acknowledgments

The biggest thank you to my editor, Rosie Potter, for not changing my voice but helping amplify it. You guided me through the editing process with care, honesty, and the exact level of sharpness this story needed. You were the shark I didn't know I needed to help take Alma and Callum's story to the next level.

I'd also like to thank Rachel Fitzjames for her eyes like a hawk, her sharp attention to detail, and the kind of thoughtfulness every writer hopes for in a proofreader. Truly, you've been the absolute best I could have asked for, your care, precision, and unwavering dedication made this book so much stronger.

A heartfelt thank you to my incredibly talented big brother, Juan Rafael Almonte, for bringing this cover to life. In a moment when I truly needed it, he showed up without hesitation and translated my vision for In Good Company into something even more beautiful than I imagined. Seeing this story reflected so thoughtfully through his work has been deeply meaningful made all the more special because it came from someone I love so much.

To my writer bestie and beta reader, Meghan Dahnert, thank you for being one of my biggest champions. You've encouraged me through every stage of this journey and have been something of a sensei as I've navigated the indie publishing world. Your support, guidance, and ability to keep this Type B personality somewhat organized means more than you know.

To my other beta readers, Terri Corle and Taylor Olsen, your feedback was invaluable and helped elevate the story in ways I'm deeply grateful for.

To my husband, Kevin, thank you for always playing into my delusion. When we weren't exactly in the best place financially for me to self-publish this book, you didn't hesitate when I said I was going to do it anyway. You listened to my deadline spirals, my plotting rambles, and every complaint along the way. More importantly, you were simply there whenever I needed someone to talk things through with.

And lastly, I want to acknowledge something deeply personal. Living with mental illness is not always easy, but in its own complicated way it gave me the courage, or perhaps the delusion, to believe I could write this story and share it with the world. My hope is that stories like this help create more space for conversations about mental health and remind readers that vulnerability is not something to hide from, but something that connects us.

Thank you to everyone who helped bring In Good Company to life.

With immense gratitude, Joanne

About the Author

Joanne Almonte Mason is a Dominican-American writer based out of Northern Virginia, just outside of our Nation's capital. She writes contemporary romance for readers who like their love stories a little messy, deeply felt, and grounded in emotional truth. Her characters fall hard, say the wrong thing, and learn how to choose themselves (and each other) along the way.

Her debut novel, In Good Company, earned her a place in the Smooch Pit mentorship program, recognized for its emotional vulnerability, sharp character work, and unflinching honesty about modern love.

When she's not writing about love, vulnerability, and the mess in-between, you can find Joanne at OrangeTheory breaking a sweat, cheering on her kids at any of the countless extra-curricular activities they're a part of, or rewatching any one of her early-2000s comfort movies.

Connect with Joanne on the web at www.joanneamason.com

www.ingramcontent.com/pod-product-compliance
Lightning Source LLC
Chambersburg PA
CBHW051307130726
47987CB00004B/1694